Maxwell's Point

Maxwell's Point

M.J. TROW

Allison & Busby Limited
13 Charlotte Mews
London W1T 4EJ
www.allisonandbusby.com

Hardcover published in Great Britain in 2007.
This paperback edition published in 2008.

A CIP catalogue record for this book is available from
the British Library.

10 9 8 7 6 5 4 3 2 1

ISBN 978-0-7490-8039-6

Typeset in Sabon by
Terry Shannon

Printed and bound by
JH Haynes & Co. Ltd, Sparkford

M.J. TROW is a full-time teacher of history who has been doubling as a crime writer for twenty years. Originally from Rhondda in South Wales, he claims to be the only Welshman who cannot sing or play rugby. He currently lives on the Isle of Wight with his wife and son. His interests include collecting militaria, film, the supernatural and true crime. The author of the Inspector Sholto Lestrade series and nine non-fiction books, *Maxwell's Point* is the twelfth novel featuring Peter 'Mad Max' Maxwell.

To Tali, the original Nolan.
Zicker, zicker.

CHAPTER ONE

The nonsense stopped as soon as he entered the room. He let the door crash back and stood there, watching Tasha Whatserface smear lipstick all over her cheek. A look of panic came over Tall Chloe's face as he caught her in mid-text on her mobile; that wasn't going to help win any spelling bees, was it? Jade quickly unwrapped herself from Dale's clutches, stuffing what passed for a breast back into her blouse. Dale himself looked suitably blank, so there was no change there. Even Laura looked sheepish, aware as she was that she had a black, non-regulation top on under her white Leighford High blouse; the mark of the beast. Martin, he of the weasel-eyes and uncertain temperament who hovered on the fringes of autism and glue-sniffing, reached surreptitiously down to replace his outlawed trainers with his black school shoes, lace-up, for the use of. Why, oh why, did those kids go to the unholy lengths of carrying them all day in carrier bags? Could it possibly have made their lives easier?

The hubbub died down as he crossed to the desk. He flipped open the laptop carelessly, with a nonchalance born of years at the chalkface. His fingers hammered on the keys and a PowerPoint presentation, beloved of Ofsted inspectors the length and breadth of the UK, burst onto the screen in glorious Technicolor. Words spun and rotated, interspersed with wild images of the world we have lost: Winston Churchill ordering the troops *out* of Tonypandy; Joe McCarthy hugging Joe Stalin; history like it really was. He felt rather than heard someone stick a piece of chewing gum on the underside of a desk. He twirled slowly, still writing the lesson's objectives clearly on the whiteboard – Aim: to knock some sense into a band of misfits before it was too late – handling the board-marker as smoothly as Napoleon used to handle his cannon.

There was a new boy in the corner, a face he didn't recognise, but he knew the signs; could read the attitude. The lad wore a pale-blue hoodie and a white baseball cap at a rakish angle – he who had never heard of Babe Ruth in his life. His jaw seemed to be working around a piece of half-day old gum. And why not? He'd watched telly for hours as countless football managers with an IQ the size of a pinhead chewed frantically on the side-line between roaring some timely expletive to the even bigger morons on the pitch. They were all his heroes. Why was it, the teacher wondered – and not for the first time – that kids who joined the school late in the year always seemed to be delinquents with ASBOs? Then he answered his own question – they were probably the children of a parent (never two, of course) on the run from the ever-shortening arm of the law. At least wherever they came from would be a safer place.

He noticed the kid at the back, the Chav With No Name, slide his right arm sideways. That settled it, he thought – it was the paper-flicking season again and he was reaching for his elastic band. He'd wait before he struck, biding his time, letting the Chav hang himself. There'd be no warning shot, no barked defence, 'Stop. Armed educator'. But he was to be disappointed. Dom Creddle, the lad next to the Chav, caught the boy's arm and hissed, 'No, mate. That's Mad Max's kid. He'll have yer.'

The Chav frowned, unimpressed. 'But he's a baby. Still wearing bloody nappies.'

'Even so,' Creddle warned solemnly. 'Don't mess. It runs in the family, madness. Don't mess. Don't...'

But it was too late. The elastic band had barely cleared the desktop when Mad Max's kid sent the board-marker hissing through the air. It scythed past Dale's ear with the speed of an Exocet, whistling past the waist of Tall Chloe – I said she was tall, didn't I? – and took the head of the Chav off his shoulders, as well as the smirk off his face. There was blood everywhere, spattering over the desk and down the wall. And the screaming started...

Mad Max woke up with a start. God, he hadn't done that before. Fallen asleep in his own office. For the briefest of seconds he expected to see little Nolan saunter in through his door, tossing a bloody board-marker in his hand and grinning, his nappy dangling between his legs.

'Got another one for you, Daddy!'

Maxwell chuckled. How unlikely was all that? Little Nolan was only ten months old; he still found walking a tad of a challenge, still less sorting out shitheads in a History lesson. Maxwell checked his watch. Half past four. Time to go home – the radio jingle of his childhood echoed faintly through the cavernous recesses of his brain. He downed the last of his coffee, toyed with taking home a pile of books to mark, thought better of it and made for the door.

An apparition in green stopped him.

'You'll never guess what they've bleedin' well gone an' done now.'

Maxwell hesitated. Was that it? Was that all he was going to get? This was Mrs B, the Lady Who Cleaned for him, both here, at the chalkface that was Leighford High, and at his *chez lui* along leafy Columbine, to the south west. Usually, Mrs B spoke in a torrent, spitting out statements like a Gatling gun, if that wasn't lobbing too many metaphors into the suet-pudding of conversation.

'Er...what?' was his rather lame response.

'Only appointed a new Head Caretaker, haven't they? I mean, what's the point? And she's a real bastard, so they say. What's all that about? Sending a woman to do a man's job? I don't know what was wrong with old Doc Martin, meself. But then, what do I know?'

That was more like it. Maxwell swilled his cup under the tap in the corner and gave as good as he got. 'Yes, I heard. Well, new brooms and all that. Yes, I'd heard that too. Something to do with equal opportunities, I suppose. Neither do I. Quite a lot, Mrs B, if I'm any judge.'

Yes, Peter 'Mad Max' Maxwell was a judge all right. He'd been judging kids' essays, their behaviour and the great mysteries of life now for more years than even Mrs B had bristles in her brush. He used to be jury and executioner, too, before the world had gone mad and they'd created some EU regulations against such things. He'd been at Leighford, man and boy, for nearly four centuries and nothing ever fazed him. Even so, he was sorry to see old 'Betty' Martin go, especially as no one knew the bloke's first name. And his replacement wasn't quite a Head Caretaker; she was a Premises Manager. *Plus ça change.*

'You goin' out tonight?' Mrs B was rummaging in the corner, rustling her black bag in time-honoured tradition and longing for a fag on this no-smoking site.

'No, no,' Maxwell told her, hauling up his battered Gladstone. 'Lesson preparation, Mrs B. Mr Diamond checks, you know. He wouldn't be happy if I didn't prepare my lessons for the next day.'

Mrs B paused in mid-rummage. She was gagging for that fag now and her sciatica was giving her gyp, but she wouldn't show any weakness in front of Maxwell – he was mad, after all, and that was a proven fact. *And* he was her employer – wouldn't do to let him think she couldn't cope. For a moment she looked at him oddly, then her grey old face broadened into a toothless grin. 'Yer, right,' she croaked.

He winked at her and was gone.

He left the office bright with the trappings of his obsession, the film legends of yesteryear. Nikolai Cherkassov stared down at him under the rim of his steel helmet, like a poor man's Charlton Heston, in *Alexander Nevsky*. Tyrone Power, Alice Faye and Don Ameche grinned like three toothpaste ads in *In Old Chicago*. Whoever painted the United Artists' posters, he really wasn't very good. And Jimmy Stewart and Doris Day looked suitably frantic over the kidnap of their son in *The Man Who Knew Too Much* – nobody on Leighford High's staff, that was for sure. Then, he left reality behind and strutted his stuff down the corridors of make-believe, past that ghastly…thing…Year 8 had painted last Activities Week, on beyond Healthy Schools posters and exam notices without end, their reminders that mobile phones were not allowed or the Exam Board would personally come and cut your bum off, four thousand free hours or not.

Maxwell was glad of the fresh air as he strode across the car park. Ben Holton, the Head of Science, was still on the premises, his crumpled Volvo straddling two spaces. With a bit of luck he'd be in a lab somewhere feeding some hapless Year Seven kid to his locusts. Maxwell recognised the gleaming Audi of James 'Legs' Diamond, the Worst Headmaster in History. He'd be pinching some pointless initiative from a website somewhere to try and con parents that he knew what he was doing. For a brief, ignoble moment, Peter Maxwell toyed with keying the silver metal as he walked past. Then uprightness got the better of him, he remembered he used to be a public schoolboy and he just kicked some broken glass under the wheel. Well, it was a health hazard. Surely the Premises Manageress would approve.

He lashed his briefcase behind the saddle of White Surrey, his faithful charger-turned-bike, one of those coursers that changed the course of history. The original Surrey had been Richard III's horse at Bosworth – and just *look* what happened to him. Out of his pocket came the cycle-clips, officer's undress, and in a flash he'd hooked them round his trousers and was pedalling like a thing possessed out of the school gates and into legend.

All right, so the South Coast wasn't what it had been. There was a time when mad old George III had swum off Brighthelmstone while the band, up to their waists in water, played 'God Save the King'. A time when 'Prinnie' had doffed his hat to the swells along the Steyne; when Kaiser Bill raced his gleaming yacht through the glittering waters of the Solent; and a much older time when William the Bastard had come ashore at Pevensey, looking for road signs to Hastings and just reading 'Normans, go home' everywhere. But somehow, all that was so...elsewhere. 'Here in Leighford,' read the Tourist Board signs of Maxwell's imagination, 'Nothing Happened At All.'

It was approaching the height of the season, the sun flashing on car roofs and bonnets, the breeze fluttering the little flags that bedecked the Esplanade. Even as he braced himself for the Flyover, he could hear the mechanical music of the fairground wafting in waves on the sea-salt air. He chuckled to himself as he realised he was slowly turning into Dylan Thomas – slow, black, quick, quick slow. Well, perhaps it needed work. Porkpie hat firmly on his barbed-wire hair, he waved gaily at the motorist who roared past him, bouncing on his car horn and waving a finger that had an altogether different message for him. It was a sad fact that at the dawning of the twenty-first century, nobody except Peter Maxwell thought bike anymore. And he was mad.

And then, Surrey's tyres were purring down Columbine and all was right with the world. He noticed as he turned onto the pavement, carefully negotiating the doggie-poo as he did so, that Juanita's car was not in the drive. 'Drive' was actually rather a grand term for the space in front of Number 38, but it was what it had said in the Estate Agent's brief when Maxwell had moved in, so it had to suffice. He wheeled Surrey round the back, through the side gate and hauled off his briefcase, sweeping the hat off in an extravagant gesture.

Shit! Look at that lawn. It was like the Serengeti; yellow and knee high. He could almost smell the wandering herds of wildebeest. He'd have to break off from all that lesson preparation later to become Lawnmower Man. If his hayfever didn't get him first.

Odd. The back door was open. If Juanita had slipped out with Nolan, surely she'd have locked it? John Cleese, of course, would explain it all by saying she was from Barcelona and would have clipped her around the head, but that wouldn't do very much for Anglo-Spanish relations, and ever since the Armada, we did have some bridges to build.

'Hello?' Maxwell called. 'Halloooo!' No reply. The girl must have taken the Wee Lad – so called for his habits – down to the beach. Now, Peter Maxwell didn't miss a trick. He could have Observed for England. And he noticed, as he reached the kitchen, that the sunblock was still there, along with little Nolan's towels, sunhat and spade. All right, Maxwell pinged off his cycle clips and reached for the mail, piled on the surface by the kettle; Juanita had taken the boy to the shops. She wouldn't get much for him, Maxwell mused, remembering the difficulties Mr Bumble had once had with Oliver Twist. Even so, the hat and the sunblock, in weather like this, wouldn't have come amiss.

Maxwell turned a livid shade of pale at the sight of the Saga holiday offer in the post. With unerring skill, he lobbed it into the bin. 'Have you been hurt in an accident at work?' the next missive wanted to know. 'None of your Goddamn business,' he growled and the second lob followed the first. 'Holy Mother of God.' The third envelope offered the most ghastly knick-knack Peter Maxwell had ever seen – a seven inch porcelain depiction of Princess Diana to take pride of place on Maxwell's mantelpiece. Actually, it took pride of place in Maxwell's rubbish.

He checked the clock. Nearly five. Jacquie would be home in just over an hour. Did he have time? He caught sight of his reflection in the mirror. 'Go on, Maxwell,' he snarled in his finest Clint Eastwood impression, the .44 Magnum of his imagination gleaming in his fist. 'You owe it to yourself to live a little.' So, he began to make his day. He threw his jacket and bow tie somewhere on the furniture in the lounge as he passed through, then on up the second flight of stairs, past little Nolan's nursery and into the master bedroom. 'What a dump!' he pouted, being Elizabeth Taylor in *Who's Afraid of Virginia Woolf?* being Bette Davis in another film nobody could now remember. His wife's fol de rols were lying on the floor next to her shoes which stood at an impossible angle to each other, like Charlie Chaplin on speed. Then he was up the third flight of stairs to his Inner Sanctum, the War Office, that holy of holies from where only Peter Maxwell returned.

Only Maxwell? Not exactly. 'Afternoon, Count,' Maxwell bowed slightly as he caught sight of the cat on the linen basket's lid. The great black and white stirred himself, but not unduly, looking like a couch potato's Guinness ad. He and the Master went back a long way, since Count Metternich was a little black and white nothing of feet and fur, endlessly astonished, in the three-second memory span of cats, to find he had a tail somewhere behind him. Maxwell hadn't quite celebrated his own Millennium then, so some of his hair was still brown and Surrey's crossbar presented no challenge at all. That, of course, was then – the historian's mantra. This was now.

'What's new, pussycat?' Maxwell ventured. It was a passable Tom Jones.

Metternich wasn't going to respond to a cliché like that. They just served to show his man's age. He merely flicked his tail to give it the contempt it deserved and watched as the Great Man sank into his modelling chair, flicked on the lamp and picked up those stupid bits of plastic again.

The stupid bits of plastic in question were the legs and torso of Lieutenant Landriani of the Sardinian Army. And Peter Maxwell had been putting this one off for years. Laid out before him, under the skylight and stretching into the increasingly gloomy distance of the loft at Number 38 Columbine, sat Lord Cardigan's Light Brigade, 54 millimetre and correct – thanks to another of Mad Max's obsessions – to the last detail; every buckle, every strap. 'At the last count – oh, no pun intended,' he mused to the cat, 'Lieutenant Landriani makes the five hundred and sixteenth figure that I have assembled over the last quarter century. That only leaves...' Metternich saw the man's spare fingers and his eyelids flutter as he wrestled with the maths of it all, '...one hundred and sixty-two to go. Think I'll make it, Count, before that great day dawns and I'll go quietly into that netherworld called retirement? 'Cos they stop your pay and all this,' he swept an arm over the brigade, 'will be a thing of the past. Then there are Nolan's school fees and what with university top-up.' He tutted and threw Lieutenant Landriani's legs in the air. 'Problems, problems. Nothing but problems. Right,' he caught the legs expertly. 'Now I know more or less where the good lieutenant was sitting – with Cardigan and a little, I suspect, to his left. That puts him in front of Captain White's squadron of the 17th. No, the problem, Count, is what the hell was he wearing? Sardinian, so lots of cocks' feathers in his hat, I bet.' Maxwell glanced up at Metternich. 'You're drooling, Count,' he smiled. 'Not even you would take on a full-grown cockerel, would you? So, the uniform, then. What…powder blue? I don't mean to cast aspersions on our Sardinian allies, but they didn't join until the damn war was virtually over.'

He suddenly stopped in mid-ponder. Over the intercom, the one Jacquie had insisted be set up in every room, Maxwell heard the gurgling sound and the sibilant lip-smacking of a little boy waking up. Jesus! Landriani – both bits of him – hit the deck, Maxwell's chair overturning as he sprang. Metternich, not known for his sudden movements in daylight, launched himself off his perch and Master and cat hurtled down the stairs, Maxwell making contact with the treads only marginally more often than Metternich.

For one ghastly moment, Peter Maxwell expected to see a scene from that tragic story of the dog Gelert he had read as a boy; to find the nursery ripped and bloody and with, at first, no sign of his darling son. But there was no blood, no torn sheets, no bloodied but unbowed faithful hound and sure as hell no dead wolf. Just little Nolan Maxwell, rediscovering his toes with all the joy of an Archimedes or an Einstein and smiling up into his daddy's anxious face.

Maxwell swept him up out of the cot in a deft movement and winced as the little tyke carried out his favourite parlour trick. It was called 'Swinging from Daddy's Sideburns.' And it hurt like hell.

'Where's Juanita, fella? Hmm?'

Nolan gurgled his nearly toothless grin, not being terribly helpful.

'Phew!' Maxwell's nose wrinkled. 'Not been here for a while by the look of it.' He gingerly removed his hand from Nolan's nappy area. 'What a squelcher. Come on, old son.' He laid the baby down. 'Assume the position.'

In moments like these, it all came flooding back. The memories of long, long ago, when his first child had been gurgling in her daddy's arms. Maxwell had been a young teacher then, just starting out. And the smell of his little girl's neck was just like Nolan's today. He found himself smiling. Then the other memories started, the ones he couldn't control, couldn't separate from the sunshine and the laughter. The wet roads, the screaming tyres, the crystal hardness of broken glass that had shattered his heart and had seen his first family swept away. He shook himself free of it and pressed the boy's new nappy into place.

'Ah, Velcro.' He rubbed his nose against Nolan's. 'Where would we be without it, eh? Come on, let's you and me look for dragons.'

He knew exactly where to find one and he didn't have to cross a river either. He swept up Nolan's white hat from the kitchen and plonked it on his soft, fair curls. The little hands came up as he carried him through the house.

'Oh, no,' Maxwell chuckled. 'That stays on. We're going out into the sun now, dear boy. It's still quite scorching out there and your mother would have a fit if I took you out without it.' Their eyes met. 'Women, eh? Cha!' and Maxwell swept the lad downstairs. 'And I'm not even going to mention mad dogs and Englishmen.'

The dragon was coiled in her scaly steelness on a special offer steamer-chair from B&Q, a large sun-stopping hat on her tousled old head and a little drinkie in her hand.

'Mrs Troubridge.' Maxwell announced himself these days, ever since he'd crept up on the old next-door neighbour with unintentional stealth and she'd nearly decapitated him with her garden rake in her surprise.

'Oooh, hello.' The dragon uncoiled, laying her drink down on the patio table, and began poking baby Nolan with her talons, smiling inanely and cooing baby-babble, as incomprehensible to Maxwell as it must have been to his son.

'Have you seen Juanita?' Maxwell asked.

'Who, dear?' the old girl's attention span wasn't what it was and she was currently in baby-mode. Alternatively, she had been out in the sun for a while.

'Juanita,' Maxwell repeated with what patience he could. 'Spanish girl. Looks after Nolan here. Lives with you.'

Mrs Troubridge blinked at him under the raffia of her chapeau like a startled iguana. 'Isn't she with you?'

'No.' Maxwell was still just about smiling, though he'd never got beyond NVQ level in Tolerance.

'Well, that *is* odd.' The old girl was still wrestling with Nolan's fingers, grinning inanely. 'What time is it?'

'Sun's over the yard arm,' Maxwell told her, peering up into the great orb briefly. 'Fiveish.'

'Only, they do have their siestas, don't they, these foreign people? Perhaps she's snoozing.'

'Perhaps,' Maxwell nodded. 'But I'd have thought while she was in charge of my child she'd have the courtesy to snooze reasonably close to him. At least in the same house.'

'Shall I check her room?' Mrs Troubridge offered.

'Shall we both check?' Maxwell countered.

'Well, I...oh, of course, Mr Maxwell. As it's you. Ever the perfect gentleman. Could you manage the stairs by yourself? My hip's playing up a little today, I'm afraid. It's the sun, you know. Leave the little one with me. I'll look after him.'

'Thank you, Mrs Troubridge,' Maxwell smiled, wrinkling his nose at her in what he hoped wasn't *too* patronising a way, 'but he's a little fractious at the moment. I'll just tuck him under my arm. So. We'll be fine.' And he was gone, striding across the garden of Number 40 Columbine, Nolan bouncing on his hip. Maxwell hissed at him, 'Look fractious, dammit, unless you want to be dribbled on by Black Annis back there.'

Nolan just grinned at him, then shoved an obliging fist in his mouth. Angst, baby-style. Nice to see the Method School still going strong.

Maxwell knew where Juanita Reyes' room was. Mrs Troubridge's house was, of course, a mirror-image of his own. He padded through her chintzy lounge on his Eighties brothel creepers and on up her stairs to the landing. A rather disconcerting photo of the late Mr Troubridge leered at him from a silvered frame on a wall-side whatnot and Maxwell remained glad he had never had the pleasure. He clicked open the door of the Spanish au pair's room. The bed was a tip, like one of those exquisite entries for the Turner Prize (although anything, it had to be said, was better than an original Turner). Clothes were strewn about, including the unmentionables that Mrs Troubridge hadn't mentioned, but were clearly foremost in her mind when she momentarily dithered about letting Maxwell go up there. There was a half-read Wendy Holden beside the bed (which didn't surprise Maxwell at all) and a bra slung over it that looked as though it was designed to hold two pigeon's eggs. A Spanish newspaper, days old, had been tossed into a corner. Franco was dead.

Maxwell checked the wardrobe. The drawers. Difficult to tell if anything was missing. If you don't know how many skimpy tops a girl has to begin with, how can you do the calculations now?

'Hello!' He heard the dulcet tones of his neighbour waft up from two floors below. 'Is everything all right, Mr Maxwell?'

'Yes, indeed,' Maxwell called, muttering to Nolan, 'Except for the fact that the woman employed to look after you, sonny Jim, appears to have gone walkabout. The curious incident of the girl in the daytime, hum? That's an allusion to...' He looked at his little boy, who was reaching out for the girl's bra in a half-hearted way. 'Oh, never mind. We'll talk later.' And he whisked him downstairs again.

'You didn't see Juanita go out, did you, Mrs Troubridge? I mean, her car's not there.'

'Isn't it?' the old girl frowned. 'Well, how terribly queer. No, I've been at the back here for most of the afternoon. Even had my lunch on the patio. It's such a glorious day, isn't it?'

'It certainly is,' Maxwell beamed at her. 'Getting more glorious by the moment. Well, thank you, Mrs Troubridge. Er...when Juanita gets back, could you ask her to pop round? Nothing vital, just a little matter of dereliction of duty, neglecting a minor, abandoning a helpless child, that sort of thing.'

'Oh, Mr Maxwell. Juanita is a lovely girl. I'm sure she meant no harm.'

Maxwell nodded, intrigued by the old biddy's relaxed take on it all. 'Yes, so am I,' he told her. 'But all the same...'

'Yes, of course. It *is* rather short-sighted, I can see that. Shall I hold baby while you conduct a fingertip search?'

Maxwell frowned. The old girl had been watching re-runs of *Frost* again. 'Thank you, no. It's time for his tea. I'll see myself out.'

Peter Maxwell swore he'd never do what he was doing now. He'd placed Nolan in his bouncy thing and let him watch day-time television. True, it was gone six and technically evening television, but that wasn't the point. And to be fair to Maxwell, he did have an urgent call to make. And Nolan seemed quite enthralled by the way Jessica Fletcher was clearing up the unsolved murder rate in Cabot Cove. What a woman! Everybody's favourite granny. Jane Marple without the senility.

'Jacquie Carpenter, please.' He spoke into that weird plastic thing that Metternich had never understood, the one all these humans, except the little one, pressed to the side of their faces.

'Can I ask who's calling?' the disembodied voice asked in the ether and the magic of late nineteenth-century technology.

'Peter Maxwell.'

There was a pause. They all knew who Peter Maxwell was down at Leighford Nick. First, because he was Jacquie's partner and second, because he was an interfering pain in the arse. If he wasn't real, you'd have to make him up.

'Sorry, Mr Maxwell. I'm afraid she's been called away.'

'Away?' Maxwell repeated. 'But it's home time. She should have put her chair up on her desk and said her prayers by now.'

The desk man was Den Morrisey and he'd never really cottoned on to Maxwell and his off-the-wall take on life. He wasn't going to let the chance pass. 'Well, you see, unlike you teachers, we police persons don't keep regular hours. No doubt she'll be in touch when she can.' Click. Brrr.

Bitch.

What Jacquie Carpenter was in touch with that bright, impossibly sunny July day, as afternoon turned to evening and the shadows lengthened over Dead Man's Point, was all the ghastly reality of sudden death. She'd been here before, too many times if truth be told, and each time she wondered how much more she could take. They'd tied a yellow ribbon round the old oak trees that ringed the sandy slopes of the dunes. They were high here, higher than the herring gulls that glided below them on the air currents, shearing the sandstone face of the cliffs. The sea pinks nodded in the stiffening breeze and it felt suddenly chill.

Jacquie watched the surreal scene emerge as she had so often before. The men in white coats might yet come to take her away, but at the moment, they were taking photographs inside the hurriedly erected tent, measuring angles, microscopically checking broken twig-ends and teasing loose fibres into carefully labelled plastic bags. She was an attractive woman, thirty-something, with large grey eyes and a wave of auburn hair. Not far away as the gulls flew, the men in her life were doing their best to cope without her. Priorities. Always priorities. Putting her life on hold.

Silent, upon a peak near Leighford, stood Detective Chief Inspector Henry Hall, gazing, like his favourite sergeant, out to sea. The gulls cried to each other, bickering as they circled, annoyed by the intrusion into their world. Beyond it all was the sibilant, rolling hiss of the surf, booming far below, and the line of wake that trailed behind a cross-channel ferry breaking the haze of the skyline.

'Dead Man's Point, Jacquie,' Hall didn't turn to her. 'How corny is that?'

CHAPTER TWO

There is something about a Scene of Crime. What earlier today was a beauty spot, just part of a coastal path walk that echoed to the thud of ramblers' boots and rang with the patter of tiny tourists was now a no-go area, taped off and guarded, crackling with radio contact and surveilled by the staccato thunder of a helicopter, its searchlight throwing lurid shadows along the line of the cliffs.

Inside the tent, throwing weird Jakartan puppet-shapes onto the canvas, Dr Jim Astley was summing up what he had. What he had was a long and rather undistinguished career. He'd been tipped for the top once, but...well, the breaks just hadn't come his way. So here he was, police-surgeon-cum-pathologist attached to the West Sussex CID. He met more dead people than live ones. And such was the case that night as the last purple bars of the sunlit clouds built from the south-west and put out the summer light.

'Male, Henry,' Astley was peering at the corpse now. 'Age is a bit trickier. Forties, fifties.' He prised open the mouth. 'Still got all his own teeth, which is more than can be said for some of us.'

'How long in the ground, Doctor?' Henry Hall was sitting slightly in front of the body, on a fold-up canvas chair. He needed some answers, sooner rather than later.

Astley carefully forced the black and swollen tongue behind the lips. One of the dead man's eyes stared up at him, dull and blank and still. Henry Hall had never got used to that, even if Jim Astley had – bright eyes no longer bright, blindness where there should have been sight. The other eye had all but gone, lost in a mass of blackish-purple tissue. 'I'll have to check for the blow-fly larvae,' Astley said, 'back in the lab. Text book stuff, but you'll have to wait for it. My guess would be two weeks, perhaps three.'

'Early to mid-June,' Hall was mentally back-tracking.

Jim Astley looked at him, the arc lights shining off the rimless specs, hiding as always, the eyes and the soul of Detective Chief Inspector Henry Hall. 'What were you doing on the night in question?' It was an unusual moment of levity from the Chief Inspector.

Astley smiled. 'I couldn't vouch for yesterday, never mind three weeks ago. I don't know how you blokes do it.'

'Policemen do it on the job,' Hall reminded him.

The men, except the dead one, looked up as the tent flap moved.

'Jacquie,' Hall eased himself upright. He'd been sitting watching Astley at work now with his tweezers and his gloved hands for well over an hour and his bum was as numb as his legs. He was grateful for the opportunity to move. 'Anything?'

Jacquie Carpenter hadn't been home yet. Nobody had. She'd briefly rung Maxwell to let him know she wouldn't be back for a while and he was to go to bed. She'd got the answerphone because Max was up in the attic, (Nolan was asleep on the floor below), trying to make sense out of

Lieutenant Landriani's uniform and waiting for the AWOL Juanita to give him some sort of explanation for her odd behaviour. He'd hurtled downstairs to reach the phone but Jacquie had already left her message and gone.

'Sorry, darlings,' he heard her voice say. 'Something quite nasty's come up at Dead Man's Point. Don't wait up. Love you both.' Goodbye, that's all she said.

Now, she was back on the coastal path, her Ka wedged between the police vehicles in the car park where they'd asked Luigi's Ices to move on hours ago. Two uniforms had to stay with the vehicles at all times to keep away Nosy Joe Public. Nothing like the finding of a body to bring out the morbidly curious.

'Right.' Jacquie's notebook was out of her handbag faster than you could say foul play. 'Couldn't get much out of the couple who found the body, guv.'

'You got something, though?' Hall motioned his sergeant outside. He'd never been at one with cadavers, and rummaging about in them all – Astley's domain – had never really been Henry Hall's thing.

Jacquie nodded, secretly as glad as her boss to be out in the cool, sweet air of the headland. 'A Mr and Mrs Philip Downer from Carshalton. They've got a caravan at Willow Bay. Regulars, apparently.'

'So they know the area?'

'Patches does.'

'Patches?' Hall's eyes narrowed. Not that Jacquie could see that behind the frosted lenses – only the faint reflection of the pale moon rising over the sea; twice.

'Their dog. Border collie.'

Hall knew when Jacquie was trying to lighten the moment. She was the best DS he'd had in years. Anybody else would have smiled. But then, Henry Hall wasn't anybody else. He was the Buster Keaton of Leighford CID and he had a reputation to maintain.

'The Downers were naturally upset,' Jacquie told him.

'Naturally.'

'Mr thought that Patches had found a rabbit or something. The place is riddled with them. By the time he got close, he realised it was an arm.'

'Then what?'

'Mrs Downer had the ab-dabs and had to be calmed down big time. She started screaming apparently to such an extent, volume and duration that Dave Conklin had to intervene to find out what was going on.'

'Conklin?'

'Luigi,' Jacquie told him. 'Has the ice cream franchise in the Dead Man's car park over there.'

'Indeed,' Hall remembered. 'Does a mean Ninety-Nine if memory serves.'

'Well, he left his float to investigate, thinking something was going on.'

'Good of him to get involved,' Hall observed. 'Many people these days wouldn't.'

'Said it was his civic duty. Anyway, trade was a bit slack by then.'

'What time was this?'

'Three, three-thirty. He couldn't be sure.'

'Anybody else around?' Hall asked, wandering back along the path through the canopy of blasted oaks overhead, their stunted branches black against the moon.

'Couple of kids, the Downers remembered. Probably locals. Teenagers, certainly.'

'From Leighford High?' Hall had stopped and looked down at her. In the right light, Henry Hall could blot out the sun. Or by this time, the moon. She knew the reason for the question. She recognised the weight in the voice. Leighford High meant Peter Maxwell, their Head of Sixth Form, Jacquie's partner in crime. Peter Maxwell meant trouble. Not perhaps, but definitely. Not now and again, but always.

'Possibly,' Jacquie was a past mistress at missing the point and she looked at her boss with as much wide-eyed innocence as she could muster. Hall was not impressed. He had, after all, known Jacquie and Maxwell for a while now.

'Skivers, at that time of day?'

'Not necessarily,' Jacquie explained with the inside knowledge of a woman who lives with a teacher. 'And I believe the phrase is 'bunkers' these days, guv. Could be Year Eleven or Year Thirteen after exams. They all finished a couple of days ago.'

'All right.' Henry Hall's kids had grown up and flown the coop. He'd forgotten, as parents do, all the nitty-gritty of things like that. 'Anybody else?'

'Well, the world and his wife eventually. Word got round the car park. People coming from the Littlehampton direction. Apparently Dave Conklin's got a lot of contacts and his mobile phone was red hot by the time he'd finished. I'm just amazed we haven't had the *Advertiser* up here yet.'

'We have,' Hall nodded. 'While you were back at the Shop talking to the Downers, the editor himself no less waddled up, demanding exclusives like they're going out of fashion.'

They both knew the two-edged sword that was the Fourth Estate. Handled well, the paparazzi could be your finest ally in the fight against crime. Handled badly, get them pissed off, and they're about as useful as a sieve in a shipwreck.

Hall carried on walking, careful now that the path was dark and the ground uneven. Men in fluorescent jackets carrying torches walked past him on their way up to the Point, grunting greetings in the quarter light. 'Anything untoward about the Downers?'

'Don't think so, guv.' Jacquie walked with him until they reached the cars. 'She'd calmed down by the time I talked to them. Seemed a very ordinary couple. Been coming to Leighford for the best part of fifteen years now.'

'Hmm,' Hall murmured. 'Haven't we all? What about Conklin?'

'Salt of the earth type,' Jacquie assessed the man. 'Underneath the vest and the tattoos, just a nice fast food retailer trying to get out.'

'And nobody saw anything – anybody – suspicious in the area?'

Jacquie knew what Hall meant. Suspects *do* return to their scenes of crime, not able to leave it alone. They're not all Ted Bundy having sex with rotting corpses; but they just want to reassure themselves that all is well, that no nosy dog with extra scentsory perception hasn't sniffed out their evil deeds. They'd have been seriously worried by this afternoon's events.

'We don't know about the kids,' Jacquie said. 'We need to find them.'

Hall looked into her grey eyes, clear, cool, professional,

with just the merest hint of a stirring bitch in them. 'Get on it tomorrow,' he said. 'In the meantime, Jacquie, go home. You've got a little baby waiting, haven't you?'

'So rumour has it, sir,' she smiled.

'Off you bugger, then.' Hall sighed. He had no such excuse. 'I've got a body to shift.'

The lights burned blue along Columbine and in the kitchen of Number 38, second floor back, a tired couple sat opposite each other on the benches of the dining table, propping up their eyelids with romantic smalltalk about murder.

'What did they look like?' Maxwell asked. He was in his pyjamas by now, but he hadn't obeyed Jacquie's instructions and gone to bed. He'd pottered around, sticking this bit of plastic, painting that. He'd settled on a roan for Lieutenant Landriani's horse. Unfortunately, Messrs Humbrol didn't do a roan colour, so Maxwell had to mix it a bit. Well, he wouldn't have it any other way.

'Now, Max,' Jacquie scolded. She was still in her day clothes, minus the white galoshes she'd worn at the Scene of Crime, of course. 'You know what I'm going to say, don't you?'

'Of course,' he nodded, smiling and flicking the skin off his cocoa. 'You're going to say, "Max, don't get involved. We don't know who the kids are. They're probably not yours anyway. And even if they are, they'll have nothing to do with the murder. I am a detective sergeant in the West Sussex CID. You are a civilian and have absolutely no right of entry into what is entirely a police matter." Something like that?' He arched an eyebrow.

'Astonishing!' She threw up her hands in admiration. 'It's as if you can read my mind.'

'Now, I'm not going to remind you of the criminal history lectures I hope you attended at the Police Academy Three, Woman Policeman. Of that little psychological weirdness called folie à deux, where two otherwise respectable youngsters spark off each other and become the couple from Hell – Burke and Hare, Leopold and Loeb, Jones and Hulton, Bonnie and Clyde...'

There was a pause.

'What did they look like?'

She hit him with a kitchen roll. 'Max, you're such an infuriating old bastard.'

'All right, all right.' He held up his hands in supplication. 'Let's back track. Tell me about the dead man.'

It was her turn to raise an eyebrow. 'Is there *any* point in talking to you?' she asked. 'About integrity, I mean; professionalism.'

'Noooooooo!' He shook his head. 'But two heads are better than one, Woman Policeman, and you know you won't sleep tonight anyway.'

She looked at him. The Old Fart she'd come to love. The father of her baby. No, she wouldn't sleep tonight and yes, how well he knew her. Two heads *were* better than one, especially when one of those heads belonged to Peter Maxwell, Cambridge Historian and all round clever dick. He knew his onions, did Maxwell. They were hanging in the veg rack. He knew his murders too.

'Seemed to be middle-aged.' She didn't like conjuring images of rotting corpses but it brought home the bacon. It solved killings from time to time as well. 'What appeared to be dark hair, but it was a bit difficult to tell. He was wearing a black leather jacket and white shirt. Had a crucifix round his neck. May have been used as a ligature to kill him.'

'Strangulation, eh? Well set-up chap?' Maxwell was pondering the options.

'Hard to say. The gases had blown the body up a bit. Looked like the Michelin Man when I saw him.'

'Chummy's pretty powerful, then?' Maxwell was stirring his cocoa.

'Could be,' Jacquie nodded. 'Or, if the man at the Point was drugged or pissed or just plain asleep, Mrs Troubridge could have done it.'

Maxwell clicked his fingers. 'Of course!' he crowed. 'Got her at last! Do you want me to make some enquiries?'

'Max...' she growled.

'At school, I mean,' he said, all innocence and ingénue. 'About those two kids?'

'No, Max, I don't,' she told him. 'No enquiries at all, thank you. Of any kind. Now, let's change the subject. How was Juanita today?'

'Conspicuous by her absence,' he told her.

'What?' Jacquie frowned.

'Gone.'

Jacquie was sitting upright. She hadn't been in long and ever since she'd stumbled in through the door the talk had turned to murder, as it often did along Columbine. There hadn't been time for other niceties. 'Max, what are you talking about?'

'Well, it was the damnedest thing. I got home about half four after toiling up the sheer side of the chalkface and there was no sign of Juanita. Her car had gone, but sonny Jim hadn't.'

Jacquie was incredulous. 'Are you telling me that Nolan was here on his own?'

'Now, don't get all she-wolfie about it,' he said, patting the air around her with both hands. 'No harm done.'

'No…' She lowered her voice. 'No harm done? Anything could have happened, Max. What did she say about it?'

'Don't know,' Maxwell shrugged. 'Haven't seen her.'

Jacquie stared at him in disbelief. 'Max, why didn't you tell me about this?'

'I tried to,' he told her. 'Rang the nick. They said you were out. What's his name? Got a chip on his shoulder.'

'Oh, Den Morrisey.'

'The same. I guessed your situation was probably more fraught than mine. All the same, it's odd she hasn't called round. Must be back by now.'

Jacquie shook her head. 'No, Max,' she said. 'There was no car outside when I got back. She drives a clapped out Hyundai, right?'

Maxwell nodded, though he had to confess car makes weren't exactly his thing.

'I just assumed she was out for the night, not that she'd been out for the whole bloody day as well.'

'It couldn't have been all that long,' he reasoned.

'Why not? What state was Nolan in when you found him?'

'Happy as larry,' he shrugged. 'Full nappy, but then the little fella can poop for England, as we know, so that didn't tell me much. There was water in his tray and a drop of the hard stuff – oh, wait a minute; that's Metternich.'

Jacquie pulled a face. It wasn't the first time her husband had mixed the two up – son and heir and cat hair. He was a funny age – her mother had warned her, but Jacquie thought she knew better. The woman who was partner, mother and detective sergeant was on her feet. 'I'm going round there,' she said.

'No,' Maxwell held her arm. 'Darling, it's nearly one o'clock and Mrs Troubridge won't hear the bell.'

'We've got a key – remember?' she asked him.

'If you walk in on her, she'll probably have a heart attack. Let it go. There's nothing to be done tonight.'

For a moment, Jacquie dithered. Then she relented. It *had* been a long day. 'All right,' she said. 'But first thing tomorrow, I'm round there.'

First thing in the morning, Jacquie was round there. Like many old people, Mrs Troubridge didn't actually sleep well, for all Maxwell had painted a picture of her dead to the world for the statutory eight hours. When Jacquie Carpenter had originally planned to storm her portals in the wee small hours of the morning, Mrs Troubridge was actually up playing patience in her conservatory. Now, as the sun climbed to the Heavens for another relentless, hosepipe ban day, she was doing what she did best, playing merry Hamlet with the convolvulus in her flower beds. She could have sworn she'd cleared this lot only yesterday.

'Hello, my dear,' she waved a green-gloved hand at her neighbour. 'Would you like some lavender?'

'Thank you, no, Mrs Troubridge. Just some answers.'

The old girl stopped in mid-prune. 'Oh, how wonderful. Am I a suspect? I've always admired what the police do and a distaff policeperson living next door now, well, it's a real bonus, isn't it? I tell all my friends about you, you know.'

Jacquie smiled. 'Thank you,' she said. 'No, it's not an enquiry of that sort,' she told her. 'I was wondering if you'd seen Juanita at all?'

'You're the second person to ask me that,' she said, cryptically, rather foolhardily tapping her nose with her secateurs.

'Oh? Who was the first?'

'Mr Maxwell,' Mrs Troubridge confided. 'Just yesterday.'

'Quite,' Jacquie nodded. 'But did she come back last night? Perhaps after you'd gone to bed?'

'No, dear,' the old neighbour confided. 'I'm sure I would have heard her. I don't think her bed has been slept in, though I have to confess, it's difficult to tell. She does her own laundry and so on. I don't interfere.'

'Did she say she was going anywhere, Mrs Troubridge?' Jacquie asked. 'Been called away suddenly, perhaps?'

'No,' the old girl frowned. 'No, I'm sure I'd have remembered. Oh, can I have your dear little man today? Just until Juanita turns up? I'm sure she won't be long.'

'Thank you, Mrs Troubridge,' Jacquie smiled. 'You're so kind, but I'm going to drop Nolan at a friend's for the day. He'll be fine. She's got a girl about the same age.'

'Well, if you're sure,' Mrs Troubridge trilled, tottering off in search of more plant-life to kill.

Jacquie doubled back home and dashed up the stairs to the

second lounge, which they'd turned into a study. She checked her computer one more time in case an email had arrived from the wayward au pair. Nothing. Just a dazzling hotel offer in sunny Leighford. Jacquie couldn't wait.

'I've got him, Max,' she called, lifting Nolan, plus bags and baggage, out of the nursery on the next floor up. He clung to her, looking loving and confused at the same time, as kids do until they're about fourteen.

'Is Pam all right about this?' Maxwell emerged from the bathroom, his lower face a disturbing white with shaving cream. Nolan couldn't remember his first Christmas. Perhaps Daddy was reinforcing the existence of Santa?

'She's fine,' Jacquie told him. 'We got on like a house on fire in the Maternity Unit. Look, I've no idea how today's going to go. Pear-shaped if I know the first day of a murder enquiry. Can you get him on the way home?'

'Of course,' Maxwell came barrelling down the stairs, whirling the baby away from his mother and throwing him in the air. Nolan laughed hysterically every time. Maxwell rubbed noses with the boy. 'So trusting, aren't they?' he grinned. 'Little does he know I'm going to do that one day and just walk away.'

She hit him with a box of nappy liners. 'He thinks you're joking,' she said. And she took the boy back. 'Come on, little baby boy, don't let that horrid, nasty man hurt you.'

Maxwell kissed Nolan on the head. 'Be good, old man,' he told him. 'Do everything Auntie Pam tells you – persevere with the tinned macaroni cheese and remember, whatever little Zoë does,' he lapsed into his Edward Fox out of *The Go Between*, 'it's never a lady's fault. *Ciao, bambino.*'

Jacquie's eyes rolled skyward. 'Robert de Niro's waiting,' she muttered, 'talking Italian. You have a good day, Peter Maxwell.'

'Likewise, half my soul,' and he kissed her too.

And on the fifth day, God created Friday. Surely, nowhere in His Great Plan, however, was Eight Eff. They had the collective IQ of the spider plant that had somehow snuck into Maxwell's office, the one that Mrs B grudgingly dusted once a term whether it needed it or not. But at least they hadn't yet started to smell. That unique privilege belonged exclusively to Year 9, when hormonal changes brought on a sour odour that was probably acceptable when their ancestors still hunted the cave bear. By Year 10, they'd discovered Lynx with its ability to stop asthmatics in their tracks and a certain equilibrium of pong had settled on their lives.

So, it had to be admitted that Cromwell's Irish policy left Eight Eff a *little* bewildered, but Maxwell's impeccable Richard Harris gave it a bit of a lift and when he threatened to introduce more role play with him as the New Model Army and Eight Eff as the hapless inhabitants of Drogheda and Wexford, they sat up and took notice.

He'd just settled down to put the latest Self Evaluation document to good use by rolling it up as a fly swat when Nursie popped her head round his office door. She closed it quickly. 'Morning, Max.'

Sylvia Matthews was a good looking woman in the mid-morning light. She wasn't bad in any light, in fact, but Maxwell really loved her for her goss. She was that indispensable digger-out of unconsidered trifles that makes the world go round in secondary schools, and quite probably everywhere else. There was a time when she had loved Peter Maxwell too, not in the sense he meant it, but for real. But he'd been blissfully unaware, married to his job, his cat, his model soldiers, his bike and had been oddly distant in a way Sylvia had never quite fathomed. Then there was Jacquie for him, and Guy for her, and the moment had gone forever. Perhaps it was just as well...

'Morning, Matron Mine. Anything untoward?'

Maxwell and Sylvia Matthews went back a long way. He knew her moods as she knew his. She'd seen it all, heard it or occasionally done it herself. There wasn't much she didn't know about teenage kind. But today she looked a little rattled. 'Steph Courtney,' Sylvia said in hushed tones, perching on the arm of Maxwell's indescribably uncomfortable L-shaped sofa, the one he'd half-inched from a Deputy Head, long gone, during a decorating spree some years back.

Maxwell frowned, closing his eyes. 'Verbal Cat Score 114. Non-Verbal 109. Predicted History Grade B with a following wind. Nice kid. I used to teach her dad.'

'I'm sure all that is spot on, Max,' the School Nurse told him. 'But she's outside now. And she's sort of scared.'

He looked across at her. 'I don't do Year Elevens, Nursie, you know that. Head of Sixth, that's me. You know, Years Twelve and Thirteen. In September, I'll be delighted to talk to her.'

'Don't be picky, Max,' Sylvia scolded. 'She'll be Year Twelve as you say a couple of months' time. And anyway, she asked for you. Says she's seen a murder.'

The Head of Sixth Form was suddenly all ears. 'You'd better show her in,' he said.

* * *

Jim Astley had excelled himself. In times gone by, he'd have been taking advantage of the glorious weather to be up at the golf course, teeing-off with the County Set whose company he craved. Today, however, he did his job instead and got his head round how a man had died. Well, if truth be told, his game was a bit off these days. He was better at the old Nip and Tuck.

It may have been brilliant sunshine out there, with children who should have been at school splashing happily in the warm ripples of Willow Bay, and the patrons of the Leighford Bowls Club at the other end of the town and the age spectrum, gliding across matchless turf in their off-whites, dentures rattling in the gentle breeze, but in Jim Astley's morgue, it was business as usual. Donald, a martyr to KFC and indeed any food that was fast, sat in a corner in his slightly snug white coat and noted down, for the record, what the great man was saying.

'Caucasian male,' Astley was peering down on the handiwork created by God, parents unknown, a killer and his own Y-shaped surgery. Bits of the Caucasian male lay in chrome vessels around the room, rather like a sanitised 13 Miller's Court, the home of the luckless Mary Kelly when Jack the Ripper had finished with her back in the Autumn of Terror, 1888. Peter Maxwell was in Nursery School at the time, so at least he had an alibi for that one. 'Age…' Astley checked the teeth again and measured the thigh. Never do these things just once, his old mentor had told them. Do them as often as necessary to be sure. There'll always be some bastard brief for the defence who's paid to rattle you. 'Forty to forty-five. Well-nourished to the point of obesity.'

Donald bridled a little, but Astley was unaware. Donald had long ago realised that the clinical definition of obesity was ludicrously wrong – Victoria Beckham was a borderline case if you believed the stats. 'We've got some old scarring on the forearms and legs. Childhood, most probably. Tree-climbing sort of thing; nothing sinister. Most of this later scarring on the legs is post-mortem. He was dragged over rough ground before being placed in the body bag.' Astley stopped in mid-probe. 'Has that gone to the lab, by the way?'

'This morning,' Donald assured him. 'Usual courier.'

'Good, good. Adenoids the size of walnuts. I don't think he'd have won any public-speaking competitions. Cause of death...' Astley was turning the bloated, blackened head from side to side. 'Strangulation by ligature. Viz and to wit...'

He waited for Donald's response, 'Er...silver crucifix. Also sent to the lab.'

'Excellent. The marks of the chain links are very clear on the right, so something was used as a kind of tourniquet to twist the chain on the left. Hyoid bone,' Astley's scalpel hit something hard, 'broken in two places.' He straightened, much to the relief of his back. 'This was a vicious one, Donald. He wouldn't have gone quietly. Killed indoors, by the way.'

'Oh?' Donald paused. 'How do we know?'

'*We* know nothing, Donald,' Astley told him, pursing his lips afterwards as he always did when Donald got too pushy. '*I* know because there are fibres all over the back of the body and legs. And he was naked when he died.'

'Somebody dressed him?' Donald asked.

'Corpses don't dress themselves,' Astley looked over his

pince-nez at the man. 'Not in my experience.'

'So this is a sex thing, then?'

Astley screwed up his face. 'He may have been sodomising every choir boy between here and Dungeness, Donald,' he said. 'But that's not what we do here in pathology, is it? We don't indulge in idle speculation. We leave that sort of amateurism to Henry Hall.'

Henry Hall sat in his office in Leighford Nick, a range of depositions in front of him. Out there, beyond the glass, his Murder Team had assembled, those hapless human beings who were going to have to put their own lives on hold for a time, while they worked out how the man at the Point lost his. They'd done this before, all of them. And as sure as God made little green men from Mars, they'd be doing it again one day. Hall looked at his SOCO photographs – the car park, empty in its black and white starkness apart from police vehicles. The little steps that led up to the lane that wound its way through the trees, the gnarled oaks blown and stunted by the winter winds. The sudden dips and hollows in the sandy soil where the short, rabbit-chewed grass vied with spurge and sea pinks, all curiously grey in the photography. One wistful vista could have come straight out of *South Coast Visitor*, a moody shot of the sunset over the sea and the eroded sandstone of the cliffs. Then, the serious business began – the close-ups of a dead man, in ghastly colour this time; the arm that Patches had half dug up; the torso with its cheap jewellery and ruptured throat; the legs uncovered by SOCO. All of it so badly done, so shallow and so near to the cliffs. So near to the cliffs and so near to the road.

Why was that?

CHAPTER THREE

There's something about an Incident Room. Oh, they'd upgraded themselves in terms of technology. When Henry Hall was a green, wet-behind-the-ears copper, there were shoe boxes where now there were computers. At least shoe boxes didn't shut down suddenly for no reason. It was almost impossible – unless you were *very* peculiar – to complete an illegal operation on them. And they hardly ever needed defragging. That said, they were kind of slow. Cross-referencing a car number plate could take weeks. As for tyre-tracks, forget it. But it wasn't the technology that Hall noticed every time he set one up; it was the tension, the air of expectancy, of urgency. In the United States of America, a homicide takes place every three minutes; that's how long it takes to boil a very runny egg in Leighford. Now that was a good thing and a bad thing. Good in that murder was rare in this little seaside resort along the South Coast. And bad in that Murder Teams were rusty and had to be brought up to speed quickly – instantly, in fact, before the trail went cold. Forty-eight hours was the allotted time to find a murderer. After that, it wasn't impossible, but the odds lengthened uncomfortably.

Bringing up to speed was the DCI's job and Henry Hall

stepped out of his office to do it. The hubbub died down as he took centre stage.

'Yes, George.'

George Bronson was the new DI on the block. 'New' was a bit of a misnomer actually, because his dad used to be the desk man at Leighford back in the Seventies and George had served his time in the Thames Valley force before too many corny old jokes about Inspector Morse had made him leave. He hadn't got round to changing his name, however, so people still called him Charles behind his back. Some of them meant the Polish-American actor of *Magnificent Seven* and *Death Wish* fame (actually, only Peter Maxwell); others (that was everybody else) the moustachioed thug-turned-celebrity of Her Majesty's detention centres various. There was one thing in common; George was built like a brick shithouse.

'Dr Astley's working on the body as we speak,' the DI told everybody. 'Preliminary reports suggest our boy is middle-aged and was strangled with his own jewellery.'

There were a few camp 'coo-ies' until Hall's expressionless stare silenced them.

'We don't have an ID at the moment, but we don't think he's local.'

'Why not?' Hall wanted to know. A Murder Team had a job to do, but Hall saw them as learning exercises too – keep everybody in the loop.

'No missing persons reported, guv,' Bronson told them all. 'Astley's rough guess at this stage is that the body had been in the ground between two and three weeks. In that time we've had three missing persons across the manor – one of them's turned up and the other two are the wrong sex and the wrong age.'

'Anything wider?' Hall asked. 'Who's on inter-force?'

'That'll be me, guv,' Sheila Kindling was a bright young thing, newly seconded. There was a book going round among the lads on whether she was a natural blonde or not. Benny Palister had drawn the straw to find out, but the date hadn't gone wonderfully and Benny found himself going home alone after the first course. He was still trying to work out, three months on, what he could have said to upset her. Surely there was nothing offensive in 'How do you like it?' this far beyond the Millennium? The woman must have been brought up in a convent.

'We're making the usual enquiries country-wide,' Sheila told them, tucking her biro behind her right ear as she usually did when the spot-light was on her. 'Nothing conclusive so far.'

'Well, it's early days,' Hall acknowledged. 'Jacquie, you've talked to witnesses.'

Jacquie Carpenter sat in the second row. 'Yes, guv. Nothing else known at this time. A middle-aged couple – the Downers – found the body. We're working on crowd elimination, but by the time the scene was sealed off, there were quite a few of them.'

'Yes,' Hall scowled, 'and I'm not a happy bunny about that, people. Rubber-neckers we can do without. First, because following up on them wastes our time. And second, because they're likely to have compromised the crime scene. That was sloppy. George, have a quiet word with the ice-cream man – what's his name? Luigi? Let him know we don't approve. Next time,' he lashed them all with his cold, vacant stare, 'and there will *be* a next time, somewhere, somehow, I want that eliminated. Right, compromised or not – Geoff, what have we got from SOCO?'

Geoff Hare was Jacquie's opposite number on the non-distaff side. He was thirty something, rather good looking in a Peter Lorre sort of way, though, as you'd expect, his eyes were a *little* on the poppy side and he didn't have much of a thatch. 'How scientific do you want this, guv?' he asked.

'Just the basics, Geoff,' Hall told him. 'We don't want to confuse anybody.'

A few chuckles. That was good. Everybody was up. Everybody was alert.

'Right,' Hare crossed to the whiteboard, 'Tom?'

The AV man switched on the gubbins and a beam of light threw a map of Dead Man's Point onto the screen.

'For the benefit of anybody new to the area – that'll be you, Mr Bronson...'

'Oh, ha!' the DI grunted.

'...here we are. Leighford Seafront. The Shingle. Willow Bay. And here,' he tapped it with a finger, 'Dead Man's Point. So called because...'

'Spare us the History lesson,' Hall checked him, looking straight at Jacquie, she who was living with the oldest giver of History lessons in the world.

'OK,' Hare smiled. A second image flicked onto the screen, this time a photograph. 'This is the view from the rocks below,' he said. 'It's a fifty- or sixty-foot drop.'

'Didn't a bloke go over there a few years back?' somebody asked.

'Suicide,' Hall remembered. 'Widower couldn't cope any more.'

'Sad,' somebody else commented.

'Geoff,' Hall wanted them all on the here and now, whatever local reputation the Point had.

Another image hit the whiteboard. 'This is an aerial shot,' Hare said. 'Sorry about the quality. New camera on board the chopper apparently. Leaves something to be desired in the crispness department.' He helped them out with his pointing finger. 'Here's the road, obviously, Ringer's Hill and the Point car park. Then, we've got the trees to the right and that leads to…'

The next photograph was clearer, taken as it was from ground level, '…the steps and the path through said trees. Then…' the slide show went on with a clinical thoroughness, 'we're out onto the coastal path proper. SOCO tell me we've got sandstone cliffs here, falling away and pretty eroded.'

'Lot of work there last year,' George Bronson remembered. 'Couldn't take the mother-in-law because they were having to shore it up.'

'Going to throw her over, were you, Inspector?' somebody chipped in from the back.

Bronson didn't turn as the chuckles spread. 'When I do, Jenkins, you can accompany her on the way down. Just to make sure she's all right.'

Hare waited for the noise to subside. For once, Hall didn't intervene. Let it happen. Unless it breaks concentration, leads in the wrong direction, let it happen. It builds a team, cements relationships, does the job. Let it happen. 'Sandstone cliffs, so the soil is very light. Easy to dig, but conversely, holes fill up quickly with sand.'

'So what are you saying, Geoff?' Jacquie asked. 'A two man job, the burial?'

'It could have been,' Hare conceded. 'Whatever, it wasn't well done.'

'What do you conclude from that, Geoff?' Hall asked, sipping his by-now-lukewarm coffee.

'Done in a hurry, I'd say, guv. Foxes may have dislodged enough earth for the Downers' dog to find the body. Dr Astley will tell us if any fingers are missing.'

'Early June,' Hall mused. 'Height of the season. Who's on this? How busy is the Point at this time of year?'

'Difficult to say, guv,' Benny Palister opened his mouth for the first time that morning. 'Tourist Board don't keep stats like that. It's not your lovers' lane type place.'

'I can confirm that,' Hare chipped in, to a chorus of 'Aye ayes' from the Back Row Element. 'SOCO found nothing of what my old Forensics Tutor at the Shop used to call "the detritus of lovemaking". No knickers, johnnies or even used tissues.'

'No hayfever sufferers, then?' somebody wanted to know.

'No,' Palister went on. 'The path goes to the east for nearly three miles out towards Littlehampton. To the west not much more than a mile before it hits the Shingle and terminates at Willow Bay. And the going gets rough to the east. Serious climbing needs to be done along the Middens. Just before you get to Star Rock. Not for the faint-hearted.'

'You could do most of it, though?' Hall checked. 'Any age? Moderate disabilities?'

By now the ciggies were out. The addicts in any workplace thought more clearly when their nerves weren't frayed. And the Incident Room was the one place where smoking was allowed, by order of the General Officer Commanding, Henry Hall.

'We're still faced with the fact,' Jacquie said, 'that we don't know how busy the place gets. But,' she was looking at the photo still on the screen in the thickening smog of the ciggie smoke, 'it's damn near the road.'

'Exactly,' Hall nodded, pointing at her with an approving finger. 'Let's go with that, people. From the shallow grave of the man with no name to the car park is...what...two hundred yards? Three?'

'I paced it at near four, guv,' Hare said.

'Four hundred yards.' Hall stood corrected. 'All right. Conclusions?'

'Mr Nobody was brought by car,' somebody said.

'When?' Hall pushed them.

'Early June – 4th, 5th? Night.'

'Night,' Hall echoed. 'Who's got an almanac? We can't be certain about the date until Astley's done his stuff, but we can find out what the moon was doing on the likely dates and what time it got dark. And get on to the Met Office; Sheila, that's your job. Sun, rain, hail – I want to know what the weather was like in the first two weeks in June.'

'Bloody hot, guv,' someone intervened. 'Same as now.'

'Let's not get casual on this one,' Hall warned them. 'We're doing it by the book and we're doing it precisely. George,' he swivelled to his DI, 'get over to the lab, will you? It may be Friday afternoon, but I don't want a Friday afternoon job from them. Nor do I want us all to be kicking our heels for two days. When you've chivvied Luigi, chivvy them along too, will you?'

Bronson smiled. 'Chivvy is my middle name, guv,' he said.

* * *

'Murder, she said.'

Peter Maxwell was sprawled on his settee, his son sprawled across his chest. Opposite them, Jacquie Carpenter was grateful to put her feet up on the pouffé.

'Come on, Max.' She shook her head. 'Delusional. Teenage girls from here back to Salem, Massachusetts. You know the score.'

'Indeed I do,' he snorted. 'In fact, heart of darkness, *I* told *you*. You may have attended the half hour lecture on hormonal imbalance in the pubescent female, but I have to work with the little buggers – oh, saving your presence, old man,' and he put his hands belatedly over the baby's ears. 'You thought Salem was a car boot until I took you on that educational canter through the History of Witchcraft for Beginners.'

'How bloody dare you!' she trilled, her eyes big. 'You don't have a monopoly on female delinquency and if you weren't hiding behind the kid, I'd throw something at you.'

'All right,' he laughed. 'I'll concede you know what you're talking about most of the time. So why don't you buy this one?'

She sipped her coffee. 'Why do you?'

'That's it,' he muttered, tutting. 'That's it. Answer a question with a question. All right. The bottom line is that I suppose I trust Steph Courtney. Sure, I've known lots of liars in my time, practitioners of the Big Whoppa theory. It's usually to gain attention or to get them out of trouble. And yes, you're right, it's usually girls.'

'Steph Courtney's not the type to be in trouble, then?' Jacquie checked.

Maxwell shook his head. 'She forgot her exercise book in Year Seven once. Inconsolable.'

'Come on, Max,' Jacquie urged him. 'She's in Year Eleven now. On Study Leave, aren't they? I dare say there are a few distractions out there for her. You know, sex, drugs, rock 'n' roll.'

'Oh, probably,' Maxwell conceded. 'I'm not saying she's Mary Poppins. But the fact that she's temporarily off roll at the moment points in the not guilty direction. Why should she come into school – to see me in particular – when there's no need to?'

'Attention-seeking.' Jacquie was playing devil's advocate, but she couldn't resist a certain smugness. She did it so well.

'Balanced girl,' Maxwell countered. 'Only child, so there are no siblings to put her nose out of joint. Two parent family. I taught the dad. Seem to be loving. At least, they've been together since Steph joined the school.'

'That's sort of superficial,' Jacquie felt bound to say. 'How do you know Daddy isn't playing away? Just 'cos he didn't do it in your History lessons. Mummy hasn't got a cocaine habit? Both of them aren't into Satanic Abuse?'

Maxwell looked at her. 'It's obviously being so positive keeps you cheerful,' he said.

Jacquie laughed. 'I'm sorry, Max, but you do take my point.'

Maxwell did. He'd been at the chalkface now, man and probationer, since old Socrates used to walk about Greece talking to people in some vague belief he was educating them. No, you never knew kids well. You daren't. 'Don't get involved', a wise old Head of Department had once told him when he, Maxwell, was still wet behind the ears. They can only fire you for two things – fingers in the till or in the knickers. Oh, he'd known colleagues who'd dated pupils, even married them in some cases. But that was then. It all seemed like a different world now. No, it wasn't wise to close a door with you and a student on one side of it, for fear of accusations of rape. And that was just from the boys.

'I didn't think you taught her,' Jacquie went on. 'So why you?'

'Father-figure,' Maxwell posited. 'Impossibly handsome, a brain the size of the great outdoors. But that's enough about me.'

It went very quiet.

'I'm sorry,' he guffawed, then settled himself as Nolan stirred, his little fingers twitching in his dream-sleep. 'I'm sorry,' softer now, 'I assumed that was what *you* saw in me, too.'

'What I saw in you,' she twisted up her face and wrinkled her nose, 'was a mad old bastard who needed to be taken into care. So here I am. My role in life, my cross to bear.' And they laughed together.

'It's probably…' he began.

'Yes?' she waited.

'It's probably that from time to time I get caught up in the odd bit of skulduggery. Have you ever noticed?'

Had she ever noticed? For years, ever since Jacquie Carpenter had known Peter Maxwell, he'd been there at her elbow, usually, in fact, in *front* of her elbow, digging, ferreting with that razor mind, teasing murder enquiries, worrying evidence along with the sheep, tramping crime scenes without

number. Ever since the early days, when one of Maxwell's
Own was found strangled in the haunted ruin they called the
Red House. It had never gone away since then. And Jacquie's
life and Jacquie's career had been shared with this man – the
career she'd nearly lost because of him; the life she still had
because of him. It wasn't a bad trade, really.

'Tell me about it,' she purred, chuckling. 'All right, so
you're the Miss Marple of Leighford High School and you
trust Steph Courtney. Tell me again what she said.'

'Murder,' he repeated. He chose the Margaret Rutherford
version of the dotty old biddy from St Mary Mead. 'She said
she'd seen a murder.'

Steph Courtney was a pretty little thing with large blue eyes
and a shock of blonde curls. She'd sung in the choir when she
was younger and her parents had put her through the usual
gamut of girlie things – piano lessons, tap, a little light
gymkhanering. She'd sat in Maxwell's office earlier that day
with her best friend Emma and told Mr Maxwell all she knew.
She'd been out with the improbably named Toto, her
dachshund, on the rolling common land called The Dam, not
far from her home. Unlike the coastal path, this *was* a Lovers'
Lane. Worse, it was dogging country and that had nothing to
do with little Toto. Steph wasn't remotely aware of it, thank
God, but various text numbers on telephones and in the
smuttier newspapers gave sites all over the country where
people of a certain persuasion could watch people, of a
slightly different persuasion, having sex. Steph, of course, had
not mentioned anything of this to Maxwell, but Maxwell had
friends in low places and Merv 'the Perv' O'Brien, in the

Media Department, kept everybody abreast of the places not to be. Everyone – except Merv – was suitably horrified or disappointed or both. Merv felt a certain local pride that there was such a place in his area. He'd probably been Dutch or Swedish in a previous incarnation.

Steph had been walking Toto on the high ground. The sea was far away to her right. In fact, Maxwell realised, she could have seen Dead Man's Point briefly until Toto took her down below the line of trees into the glade. There was a car there, Steph had told him. And a couple in it. Or rather, not in it. They were each side of the vehicle, one by each of the rear doors and they occasionally leaned in. It was a man. And a woman. Steph hadn't seen them before. And it was getting dark by this time. In fact, she was late heading home because Toto had scared up a rabbit earlier and whereas his three-inch legs meant he didn't have a hope in Hell of catching it, ever the optimist, he'd had a damned good try. So, dusk as it was, Steph couldn't get a clear view of what was going on.

It was all very confusing, she'd said. First the woman got into the car. Then the man. But they were never in it together. Both of them seemed to be checking the time and keeping watch too. Instinctively, Steph had crouched down and hauled in Toto's lead, keeping him close by her and stroking him to keep him quiet. Then the most extraordinary thing happened. The man emerged again, this time carrying what appeared to be a body. It was very pale and didn't appear to have any clothes on. Steph couldn't be sure whether it was a man or a woman. The couple were both outside the car now and seemed to be arranging the body, placing the feet side by side and the arms across the chest. One arm kept pointing oddly, as though up in the air.

Steph hadn't had the chance to see any more because that was the moment that Toto had barked and Steph wasn't hanging around to face any repercussions. Bearing in mind she'd run for West Sussex Under Thirteens not too long ago, she snatched up the dog, aware that his little legs wouldn't cope, and crashed away through the waist-high bracken as best she could.

'So, Policewoman mine,' Maxwell eased his little boy to one side to try to get the feeling back into his left arm. 'What do you think?'

'Dogging country,' Jacquie said.

'I know.'

She raised an eyebrow. 'Yes?' She took him up on it, 'How do you know?'

'I teach with Merv "the Perv" O'Brien.'

'And how does he know?'

'I've never asked him,' Maxwell smiled. 'To me, a dogger is a Bank somewhere or other – the scene of an almost-war between us and Japan, if memory serves, in 1904.'

'It scares me when those kids are out there,' Jacquie said. 'From what you say, this Steph seems to be a thorough-going virgin.'

'That would be my take on it. Can't you people close the site down?'

'The Dam? It's open parkland. As to dogging, unless we get a complaint, we can't lift so much as a finger. You know that, Max. You know the law.'

'I know how many beans make five too, Heart Of

Midlothian, but it doesn't help. What do you think Steph saw?'

Jacquie thought for a moment, frowning in the soft lamplight. 'I don't really know,' she said, 'Assuming the girl is telling the truth. It *was* dusk, of course. What's her eyesight like?'

Maxwell shrugged. 'You'd have to ask Sylvia Matthews,' he told her. 'Or the girl's doctor.'

'When did all this happen, Max?' she asked him.

'Three, four weeks ago. She wasn't quite sure whether it was the night before her Maths or Science GCSE. She'd gone out with the dog to get some air, clear her head before whichever cognitive onslaught it was.'

'So she doesn't remember the day?'

'No.'

'What did you tell her?' Jacquie asked. 'What did you advise her to do?'

'To talk to the boys in blue,' he said. 'I may have mentioned your name.'

'Has she told her parents?'

'I don't think so. She's an intelligent girl, Jacks, but you don't know what exactly runs through their heads, do you? I think she was more intrigued at first; you know, not quite sure what she'd seen. Then she got scared. Even so, she confided in her friend Emma, not Mum and Dad. Otherwise, they'd have been in touch with the nick, wouldn't they?'

'Maybe yes, maybe no,' Jacquie shrugged.

Nolan stirred on his daddy's chest, sighing and blowing a little bubble from his mouth.

'So this Emma didn't say anything?'

'No. She just came along to hold Steph's hand. Girlies do that. If one of them's sent to get a bit of paper in school, she takes her friend along. They link arms just crossing the quad.'

'I'm not surprised if one of your colleagues is called the Perv,' Jacquie observed.

'I'm sure stories of his debauchery are grossly exaggerated, Dear Heart,' Maxwell smiled. 'He just happens to have an unfortunately rhyming name, that's all.'

'Do you think she will come to us?' Jacquie asked. 'Steph, I mean?'

Maxwell shrugged, in a one-armed, I've-got-a-baby-on-my-chest sort of way. 'I hope so,' he said.

'Were they clothed?' Jacquie asked. 'The couple with the car, I mean?'

Maxwell shook his head. 'I didn't pursue that one,' he told her. 'Though I had Matron in on this interview, there are limits to what a teacher can ask a student. I thought that might be an interview too far.'

'Hmm,' Jacquie nodded. 'You're probably right. Well,' she sighed, getting up. 'We certainly can't do much tonight. Come on, little man, let's get you to bed. It's way past your bedtime.'

'It certainly is,' Maxwell yawned.

'Not you,' Jacquie said. 'Somebody else.' And she took Nolan up in her arms. 'By the by,' she stopped at the foot of the stairs. 'Any news on our au pair?'

The Incident Room was open for business the next morning, bright and early. Benny Palister had been to a stag night the night before and was off to a wedding later that day, if the DCI and the corpse at the Point could spare him, of course.

His head felt like a kicked bucket and he'd driven in to the Nick very carefully, realising that he was still appreciably over the limit and some of his colleagues were nauseatingly honest in the follow-up-to-breathalyser stakes on the grounds that a copper should know better etcetera, etcetera.

'We've got a make on the dead man's shirt, Benny.' Geoff Hare had not been to a stag night the night before.

'Great, sarge,' Palister muttered, desperately trying to remember how to operate the coffee machine. Black. No sugar.

'Something of a toff, by all accounts,' Hare was reading the lab report. 'Not your run-of-the-mill Top Man. Lord Everard, Brighton. Know it?'

Benny Palister squinted up at the man as he bent to collect his paper cup. 'Lord Everard?' he repeated. 'Sounds like Sixties Carnaby Street meets Larry Grayson – and both those images, by the way, come to me via my granddad.'

'I can't help the unfortunate choice of name,' Hare shrugged. 'Lord Everard is a small chain. Well, more a couple of links, really. One in Brighton. The other in Clitheroe.'

Palister's face said it all, but whether it was the after-effects of the night before, the taste of the coffee or the ghastly concept of Clitheroe, no one could be sure. He thought he'd been on a school trip there once, or maybe his granddad took him; it was all a Northern blur.

'So, unless you want to spend all day on the phone to the Yorkshire people…'

'I'll ring Brighton,' Palister volunteered.

'Great,' Hare smiled. 'Jacquie.'

She looked up from her VDU. She'd left her men in bed

before day or battle broke, promising to be home by lunchtime. Nolan was beginning to wonder who this strange woman was who swept in and out of his life, kissed him on the cheek and vanished until the next time. Working Mums – tell Jacquie Carpenter about them. How the lad felt about the missing au pair was anyone's guess. Jacquie and Maxwell might have to wait several years to find out.

'Morning, Geoff,' Jacquie answered.

'Any headway on the dead man's crucifix?'

'It's silver,' Jacquie was only now getting to grips with the lab report, DI Bronson's late Friday afternoon chivvy having worked wonders. 'Hallmarked Birmingham, 1924. And yes, it's very definitely the murder weapon.'

'Astley came through,' Hare beamed. Things were moving at a cracking pace for a sleepy seaside town as the temperatures climbed again to Mediterranean levels.

'Just got an email from his secretary.' She read aloud. '"Cause of death is asphyxiation consonant with death by ligature strangulation, in this case, the heavy crucifix chain worn around the victim's neck."'

'Does he give us a date?' Hare was looking over her shoulder.

'This is Jim Astley, Geoff,' Jacquie reminded him. 'Mister Circumspection. "I can only hazard some time between the first and second week in June. The state of mild decomposition, the very small amount of adipocere tissue, the early growth rate of blowfly larvae…" It all got a bit technical after that.'

'And we haven't long had breakfast,' Hare nodded. 'Slowly, this is coming together. He hadn't been in the ground long.'

'Is it?' She swivelled in her chair to face him. 'Coming together, I mean? Geoff, we've got no idea who our victim is, why he was killed or how the body got there. We've no clue as to why he should have been buried where he was or precisely how long he'd been there. And that's before I get onto the sixty-four thousand dollar question – who put him in the ground? Now that, in forensic terms and police parlance, adds up to Diddly Squat.'

'Yeah, well,' Hare shrugged. 'It's a start.'

He strapped Nolan into the little gadget Norman Westbury had made for the lad. Norman Westbury was one of the old school of Craft teachers, before the educational establishment had invented the term Design Technology and made keyboard skills an essential ingredient. As Norman Westbury put it so eloquently in a staff meeting one Warts-and-All Development Day a few years back, 'If I'd have wanted to have keyboard skills, I'd have become a concert pianist.' Told it like it was, did Norm. No, Norm was a tenon man, a hinge and bracket, Black and Decker sort of guy. If you couldn't use your spoke-shave on it or groove it with your Granny's Tooth, it wasn't worth doing. So Peter Maxwell, very much of an age and a like mind, went to see Norman Westbury with his proposal and for a modest fee – the cost of materials and a couple of pints at the Vine (mercifully, the live music was off, Afterbirth's lead singer having pulled a g-string) – the Great Engineer had built a contraption. It fitted snugly over the rear wheel-arch of White Surrey and buckled with suitably padded straps around little Nolan's legs, waist and back with an upright support for his head. On top of that, a rather smart pennant with the words, 'My father's a Cambridge graduate and all I got is this lousy flag' emblazoned on it nodded above little Nolan's curls.

'All set, old man?' Maxwell asked as he tucked the boy in.

Nolan gurgled at him, not *quite* sure of the level of response required and gasped as the G force hit him and his dad pedalled away from *chez sont* like the maniac he so clearly was.

'We're going to The Dam, dear boy,' Maxwell called over his shoulder. 'No, I know it's not totally suitable for you, but at this time of the morning, we should be all right. Think of it as your first nature ramble. Well,' he glanced quickly behind him, 'the alternative is an hour or two in the cadaverous clutches of Mrs Troubridge; get my drift? And as for Juanita,' he checked the traffic at the intersection, head whizzing from left to right, 'Well, we just don't know, do we?'

CHAPTER FOUR

No one knew why they called it The Dam. At least, Peter Maxwell didn't and if Peter Maxwell didn't, nobody did. It stood at the end of civilization, where Leighford stopped and the Downs began, a rolling, plunging piece of common land that had clearly once been gouged for quarrying. Tall nettles, higher than a man, nodded with the foxgloves in the sudden dips and the morning sun gilded the topsides of the bracken leaves, a knee-high carpet on The Dam's ridges and slopes.

At one end, where Maxwell's White Surrey cut shallow grooves in the sand, were dunes that told the traveller the sea was not far away. Nearest to Leighford, where Mortimer Road trailed across the heathland, it gave way to oaks and those elms that refused to die back in the Seventies, threatened by the Dutch or not.

'You all right there, little fella?' Maxwell was wheeling Surrey now, checking Nolan under the brim of his large, sun-stopping hat. The little bugger had reached the Irritating Stage, which Maxwell knew would last for the next eighteen years or so, where anything in his hand or on his head would be tossed casually to the ground. It was a good game, keeping parents amused for hours and keeping them fit, too, what with bending on average six times a minute. This morning, however, Nolan had either tired of the game, or he felt sorry for his dad, or he actually welcomed the shade; because the hat stayed on.

'Zicker, zicker,' muttered Nolan. It was his version of grown-up speak.

'You got that right,' Maxwell nodded. 'Now, you watch the pretty valley, while I...'

The World's Oldest Daddy got his eye in. From Steph Courtney's description, he was standing where she had been a month ago, walking little Schickelgruber or whatever the Hell the dog was called. He was gazing down on what had once been a quarry floor, but one that was wide and level-bottomed, with access, he guessed, for half a dozen cars. The grass was flattened by countless tyre tracks and there was the usual evidence of foul play – lager cans, tissues, even a solitary condom swinging from a bush. The very prospect made Maxwell's eyes water. What was that? Some sort of trophy? The old watcher of B-feature Westerns knew that the Comanche hung up similar warning signs at Twin Buttes and Lost Dutchman Mesa to keep the cavalry away. And of course, there was the ubiquitous Asda trolley, sideways and rusting in its nettle bed. One day, Maxwell promised himself, he'd conduct an in-depth survey on the incidence of supermarket trolleys in weird places; the nearest Asda had to be nearly two miles away on the other side of town. But then, somebody had probably already done that and got a PhD in Sociology out of it.

He didn't really know why he'd come, to be honest. He felt particularly daft in the bright light of day, four weeks after the event, with a baby in tow and trying to make sense of the ramblings of a post-pubescent girl. But Maxwell knew his post-pubescent girls; he'd been trying to cram some history into them now for decades and he knew a liar and a fantasist when he saw one – come to think of it, that covered most of the Senior Management team at Leighford High. No, Steph Courtney was straight as a die. She definitely saw something odd, but what?

'Zicker,' commented Nolan, and Maxwell half-turned.

'Good morning, little baby!'

Nolan was lost for words now, frowning up at the apparition standing next to White Surrey.

'Good morning,' Maxwell answered. 'Er…I have to answer for him – his teeth are rather new.'

'Glorious weather!'

It was and the newcomer was dressed for it. He seemed to be Maxwell's age or, astonishingly, a little older. But whereas Maxwell had accepted *anno domini* a long time ago and no longer wore shorts to frighten the horses, this man seemed to have gone in the opposite direction. His tawny skin hung like a dead lion's over his white shorts and a pair of spindly legs protruded below them. Maxwell couldn't see his feet for the ferns, but he just knew the old boy had sandals over white socks; he was not to be disappointed.

'Haven't seen you here before,' he said, hauling a canvas haversack off his shoulder.

'Haven't been here before,' Maxwell explained. 'At least, not for a time.'

'Giving the grandson an outing? Why not?'

All sorts of reasons, thought Maxwell, but he'd already spent all of Nolan's lifetime explaining he'd just experienced a senile pregnancy and he wasn't about to do it again.

'Ramble here regularly, do you?' Maxwell asked.

'Ramble?' the old boy looked a little vacant. 'Er…yes. Oh, yes. Charming spot. Particularly after dark.'

'Really?'

'Well, it all depends what you're looking for, doesn't it?' the non-rambler asked, then he hauled his sack onto his other shoulder and tramped off through the bracken. 'See you!' he called.

Now Peter Maxwell had encountered Naturists before. Odd people who insisted on going skyclad even when the weather would freeze the bollocks off a brass monkey. Had he just met one now? Or perhaps he was a bird watcher? An orchid fancier? Perhaps something altogether darker. There was a light in the old boy's eye that Maxwell didn't altogether like.

But Nolan was grizzly. It was fiendishly hot despite the overspreading boughs of the oak and he certainly hadn't liked the grizzled old man that had just loomed over him from nowhere. He was tired and thirsty and he missed his Mummy and he missed his Juanita. He and Maxwell pedalled home, pausing just long enough for Nolan to smear himself liberally with ice cream and cherry sauce.

'And remember,' Maxwell tapped the side of his nose, 'Not a word to your mother. You know how "healthy living" she gets at moments like these.'

'Where?' Maxwell was sitting like Confucius in his back garden, tinkering with his lawnmower. Why was it, he wondered at moments like these, that the bloody green stuff grew every time you turned your back? Confucius never had this trouble. Confucius probably had people for chores like this.

'Brighton, Max,' Jacquie was arranging the parasol over Nolan's pram. The little boy lay in nothing but a nappy, sunblocked to buggery and with a string of bright plastic things across his line of vision. Maxwell had optimistically placed a copy of von Clausewitz's *On War* in there, but Nolan had thrown it out of the pram – overrated in his opinion. 'You must have heard of it. Along the coast a bit. Pier. Candy floss. Kiss Me Quick hats. Bit like Leighford with knobs on.'

'The AIDS capital of the South,' Maxwell nodded.

She looked at him. 'That dates you,' she said.

He remembered the Black Death too, but he wasn't going to admit to that.

'When?'

'Tomorrow.'

'Day of Rest, Woman Policeman,' he reminded her.

'Tell me about it.' Jacquie bent down to plant a kiss on the curly forehead of her little boy. 'It's only shopping.'

'Shopping?' Maxwell nearly cut his thumb on that plastic orange thing that passes for a spanner in the world of gardeners.

'Well, it's a working shop, if you know what I mean. Of course, I can't tell you anything about it.'

'And I can't prevent myself from throwing this lawnmower at you if you don't,' he smiled in a matter-of-fact way.

She laughed, tucking herself up on the steamer chair. 'All right,' she said. 'Just this once...'

And they laughed together.

There was a single cry from Nolan. One that said, 'for God's sake, you two, stop enjoying yourselves'.

As he waited for her to get ready, he saw in that bewildering place that was his imagination, the Minutemen crouching in their buckskins in the long grass, priming their flintlocks and fowling pieces. He saw the lines of red, heard the flags snapping in the stiffening breeze, the muffled rattle of the drums. An ambush – how typical. One day the Americans would come to know what it was like to be sniped at by people who refused to play by the rules of warfare. But that was another 4th July, long, long ago. And a bunch of self-important and self-interested lawyers had written a document that tried to excuse their treachery and self-interest. Put your John Hancock on that.

This 4th July was altogether more peaceful, but it was all one when you were a historian. And mad.

They kissed under the sycamore that shaded the open-plan patch of lawn at the front of 38 Columbine, yellow now with the lack of rain. 'You take care now, Woman Policeman,' he told her. 'And don't talk to any strange men.'

'It's OK, Benny,' Jacquie leaned into the DC's car, parked at the kerb. 'No need to take it personally.' She turned once more. 'Are you going to be all right,' she asked, 'my boys?' This was the first time Jacquie had gone away from Columbine since they'd brought Nolan home. It was just one of those tiny, sad little milestones in a mother's life; there'd be more, she knew.

'We'll cope,' Maxwell stroked her cheek. 'You ring the girls, Nole,' he called up the stairs. 'I'll get the champers on ice.'

He'd wanted to get the boy downstairs for the fond

farewell, but the little chap had been up since four and was now spark out dreaming of a white Christmas or whatever it was almost one-year-olds dream about. Had they done any research on that?

Benny Palister put the plastic to the metal and they were gone, snarling out of Columbine and making for the Flyover and all points East.

'Bloody peculiar, isn't it, sarge?'

'What's that, Constable?' She did the girlie thing for a moment and checked her make-up in the mirror. This was marginally safer than when she usually did it, driving.

'Songs,' Benny said. 'Some of them, for no reason, you just can't get out of your head.'

'Oh, yes,' she remembered. 'How was the wedding?'

'Oh, that.' The lad's face fell. 'Bloody awful, thanks. Remind me never to go through it myself.'

'Wait 'til you're asked,' she told him.

'No, it wasn't the wedding,' he said, crunching through the gears on his way to the A259. 'It's a track on the radio. I keep hearing it and it sort of sums up this case – the man at the Point.'

'Really?' she asked. 'What is it?'

'It's called *Whale on the Beach* by Danny Goodburn.'

Jacquie shrugged. 'Don't know it.'

'Oh, you will,' Benny said. 'Goodburn's going places. Got a band called The Denvers. No, it's just the lyrics…' He broke into song – '"What would you do if you found a whale, a whale on a beach, gasping for air. What would you do, would you something, something, a whale on the beach, that shouldn't be there. How would it know that it moved you…something. The whale on the beach with nobody there. The look in its eye to the la, la, la, la, la, just out of reach in the dark down there. A whale on a beach, gasping for air. A whale on the beach, gasping for air." What was he doing there? The man at the Point?'

Jacquie resisted the obvious answer – 'quietly rotting'. It wasn't worthy of her and anyway, Benny Palister was a curious mixture of Goldilocks and Don Quixote. And Jacquie Carpenter knew all about Don Quixote – she was living with him and had recently given birth to his son.

'That's the sixty-four thousand dollar question,' she conceded. 'I didn't know you could sing – presumably, Mr Goodburn actually can?' She flicked a coin out of her handbag, tossing it expertly in the air. 'Heads or tails?'

'Er…tails,' he opted.

'Bad luck, it's heads.' The coin was already back in her bag. 'Divide and conquer, Benny, my boy. I'll do the shirts. You do the teeth.'

Jacquie wasn't really shopping. True, Lord Everard was only three doors down from Hell's Kitchen, her favourite shop in the world, but, as she told Benny Palister all the way back along the coast road, she honestly hadn't known that when they set out. As it was, an all-singing, all-dancing Moulinex just happened to land in her shopping basket, which she felt obliged to buy pending her next pay rise or when Hell froze over, whichever was the sooner. As for her enquiries, they hadn't been too helpful, but then, neither she nor Henry Hall thought they would be. The dead man's shirt was beginning to decompose, hanging around the purple-blue of his body, but it had definitely been a bright orange when new. Lord Everard's Assistant Under-Manager (Weekends) thought they'd stopped that particular line about eighteen months before. It was part of the Proud To Be Loud promotion and had never really worked. Yes, they had records at Head Office (Clitheroe), but they would only tell you how many orange Louds had been sold, not to whom. Peter Maxwell would have remembered a time when tailors kept details of their customers, if only so the stingy buggers would pay up. Now it was all plastic and online shopping, nothing left the store/van without being paid for. And no one, the Assistant Under-Manager was sure, had gone for the online option, presumably on the grounds that men who bought orange shirts didn't want anyone to know where they lived.

Benny Palister hit paydirt as the Forty Niners used to say way back in '49; but he hit an awful lot of enamel walls and plain aggro first. There probably isn't a profession in the world more ghastly than that of dentistry. Alone of the torturers employed by the Inquisition, they seemed to have survived in the job that time forgot. *Danish Dentist on the Job* was not, as film buff Peter Maxwell could have told you, a piece of badly dubbed porn; it was a horror film focusing on oral sadism of the most depraved kind. Remember *Marathon Man* and the particularly nasty Laurence Olivier drilling seven kinds of shit out of Dustin Hoffman's molars? So true to life. Benny couldn't believe it – one of the dentists asked to give up his Sunday morning round of golf to make his records available actually trotted out the cliché – 'I pay your wages, sonny'. It was true in an indirect sort of way, but it was negative and unhelpful and Benny made a quiet mental note to pass the guy's car registration on to the next Traffic Warden he saw.

Dentist Number Four, however, was not only polite, but came up with a match. Jim Astley's X-rays of the dead man's gnashers found a *doppelgänger* in downtown Brighton. Bingo.

'David Taylor,' the detective said, sinking back into the driving seat.

'The man at the Point?' Jacquie checked.

Benny beamed.

She patted him on the back. 'You little genius, you,' she said. 'My line of enquiry was always going to be more of a gamble.' It was a defensive remark, designed to cover her back.

Benny shot a glance at the Moulinex filling the back seat and said nothing.

'Details?' Jacquie asked.

Benny consulted his notebook in time-honoured tradition. 'David Taylor, aged forty-two. Lives – sorry – *lived* at Flat B, 219 Marston Road.'

'Know it?'

Benny shook his head. There was no reason why he should.

'Let's reconnoitre,' his sergeant said. 'Perhaps now we can solve your riddle for you – find the reason why there was a whale on the beach.'

'Yes?' a disembodied voice crackled over the intercom.

'Mrs Taylor?' Benny asked, peering instinctively into the tannoy by the front door. They both knew they were on CCTV.

'Who wants to know?'

Sunday. Jehovah's Witness Time. Mormon Moments. You couldn't be too careful.

'Police.' Jacquie held her warrant card up to the camera.

There was a click and a whirr and the pair were inside, climbing a blank staircase in a dank, fish-smelling interior. No mint sauce and lamb of a traditional Sunday here. And certainly no roast beef of Olde England.

The woman at the door of Flat B had hair like straw and was dragging heavily on a fag as Jacquie and Benny arrived. 'What's he done now?' she asked, eying them both suspiciously.

'Who?' Jacquie countered.

'Come on,' she growled, with a voice like a Brillo pad. 'Don't piss me about. Jack. I was only up at the Probation with him last week.'

'May we come in, Mrs Taylor?' Benny asked.

'All right.' She dropped her scrawny arm from the doorframe. 'But it's not Mrs Taylor, all right? That was another bloody lifetime.'

'Who's Jack?' Jacquie asked. The lounge was spartan, an Oxfam coffee table in the centre, all-but-buried under copies of the *Daily Express* and *Heat*. Days old, half-drunk cups of coffee jostled with empty Buddies on most conceivable surfaces.

'Are you winding me up?' the woman wanted to know. She was half a head shorter than Jacquie and far below Benny. A social historian like Peter Maxwell would have assessed she was suffering from rickets. 'Are you from Winchester Road nick or what?'

'Leighford,' Jacquie told her. 'Leighford CID.'

'Leighford?' the straw-haired woman blinked, frowning. 'What the fuck's he been up to there?' She looked at the boyish freckles on Benny Palister. ''Scuse my French, darlin', won'tcher?'

'We're making enquiries about Mr David Taylor,' Jacquie explained, looking out of the window at high-rise Brighton where there had been no sign of the sea since 1958.

'Dave?' she repeated (almost). 'He's nothing to do with me no more.'

'But he was?' Jacquie turned back to her. 'Your husband.'

'Ex,' she spat. 'Wiv a capital X.'

'I take it you and Mr Taylor are divorced?' Benny asked.

She looked him up and down. 'You're quick, ain'tcha? No,' she stubbed out her ciggie before reaching for another. It was as well neither of the coppers smoked, because she wasn't offering any. 'No, technically, we're just separated. Well, there's no point. Dave is such a bastard he wasn't going to support us, no way. I'd had enough. I told him to clear off, fuck off out of it and don't come back. And he hasn't.'

Jacquie looked at Benny. Indeed he hadn't, and now he never would. 'What's your name?'

'Annie,' the woman told her. 'Look, what's this all about? Whatever he's been telling yer about me, it ain't true.'

'He told us nothing, Annie,' Jacquie said. 'That's just the point. Look, um...perhaps you should sit down.'

Chance would be a fine thing, thought Benny. Every chair was a pile of debris, from flung clothes to Indian takeaway cartons. 'Oh, yeah,' Annie muttered, the ciggie wobbling between her lips as she talked. 'Yeah. Sorry. It's the maid's day off.'

She swept the settee contents onto the floor and Jacquie gingerly sat down next to her, vowing to shower and visit the dry cleaner before she clapped eyes on Nolan again. She chose her moment. 'I'm afraid I've got some bad news, Annie,' she said softly. 'I'm afraid David is dead.'

Jacquie Carpenter had done this before. So, once, had Benny Palister. There was no easy way to do it. And no telling what the reaction would be. Some relative strangers had cried and screamed and ranted. Some nearest and dearest had shrugged and thanked them. No rhyme. No reason. Shock. Disbelief. Bewilderment. Denial. Anger. The whole melting pot of emotions that comes with sudden death. Why her? Why him? Why *me*? In the end, it often came down to that. Why *me*?

'How do you know?' Annie, once-Taylor, asked.

'We were able to identify him from dental records,' Benny said.

'Jesus!' Annie hissed, shaking her head. 'Where was this?'

'We found his body on a headland above Leighford,' Jacquie said; giving the name of the place seemed a little tactless in the circumstances.

'How...?'

'We don't have any answers, yet, Annie,' Jacquie forestalled the question. 'That's why we're here. Can you tell us when you saw David last?'

Annie blew smoke across the room, searching the middle distance for an answer. 'Six, seven months. I dunno. About Christmas time, I think.'

'When you separated?' Benny checked.

'Christ, mate, we've been separated bloody dozens of times.

The last time I seen him was Christmas – or it may have been New Year.'

'That was here?' Jacquie was trying to focus on the nitty-gritty, the devil that was in the detail of murder enquiries.

'God, no. I wouldn't have him here. Lowering the tone all over the place. No, this was a party. It must have been New Year, come to think of it.' She put on her posh voice. 'It was up at the golf club, don'tchya know,' it wasn't a very good Joanna Lumley. 'He was pawing some tart, as usual. I threw my drink in his face.'

'One for the ladies, was he?' Benny asked.

'You show me a man who isn't,' Annie scowled, looking Benny up and down. 'Unless they're poofs, of course. Well, that was why we split in the first place. He couldn't keep his hands to hisself. Turns out, he gave my bridesmaid one on our bloody wedding day. Well, the joke's on him now, ain't it?'

Perhaps; but nobody was laughing.

'Tell me, Annie,' Jacquie leaned towards her. 'Did David own a crucifix? A silver necklace thing?'

'Not when we was together, no. But he was always into bling. Like a fucking magpie.'

'So…' Jacquie was choosing her words. 'If we asked you to think of anybody who'd want to see David dead…?'

Annie looked at her. 'You're sure it was murder?' she asked. Jacquie hadn't actually said the word, but she nodded anyway.

'Well,' the ex-wife inhaled sharply, 'me, for starters. I'd have cheerfully strangled the bastard.'

For one of those instants, time stood still. Even Annie's smoke seemed to hang in the air. Jacquie stole a sideways glance at Benny. 'I didn't tell you how he died, Annie,' she said.

The straw-haired woman looked at her, sitting up suddenly. 'Is that it?' she laughed, brittle and with realisation dawning of what was going on. 'Is that how he died? Somebody strangled him?'

Jacquie nodded. 'It looks that way,' she said. 'Annie. We'll need to take a statement from you.'

'I'm not coming to Leighford,' Annie snapped.

'No need,' Jacquie said. 'We can do it here. Now, if you've got a minute. Is there anybody else?' she asked. 'Anybody else who had a grudge against David?'

Annie thought for a moment, fingers twitching around her cigarette. 'Dave was into all sorts. Got a record as long as your bloody arm. There was a few blokes he pissed off now and then, in the line of booty, you might say – and that's not one of mine, by the way, but one of his. Always thought he was a clever bastard, did our David. Any one of them might have given him the smacking he so richly deserved. Your oppos down Winchester Road Nick might have a line on that. And when you find out who,' she looked Jacquie straight in the eye, 'you might give the bugger a medal.'

'What about Jack?' Benny asked.

Jacquie was quietly impressed. The boy was coming on, like a terrier with a bone. In twenty or thirty years he might make sergeant.

Annie smiled; bitter, secret. 'Jack *ought* to be top of the list,' she growled, 'the life he had with Dave. But Jack,' she sat upright, sighing, 'Jack is Dave's son. Oh, he's mine too, but he was always Dave's first. The bastard would come home with some tart or he'd be pissed and give me a going over, but Jack couldn't see it. Oh, no, it must have been my fault. I didn't understand him, didn't know the stress he was under. Well, it was me who wiped the kid's nose and arse and went up to the school when he got into trouble. I was with him in court when he went down. I visited him in prison. And Dave? Well, Dave gave him toys that fell off the back of lorries. And took him down the football and to the boozer. And Jack thinks the sun shines out of his arse. There's gratitude for you. He's going to go ape-shit about this.'

'Does he live with you?' Jacquie asked. She was a mother too.

'On and off,' Annie shrugged. 'As far as probation's concerned, this is his domicile. In practice, fuck knows. I ain't seen him for a couple of weeks. For all I know, somebody's strangled him too.'

'Never!' Bill Tomlinson couldn't believe it. 'Wide Boy Taylor? Would you Adam and Eve it? Long overdue, mind. How long have you got here? Only the file's thicker than President Bush.'

The three of them were in the bowels of the police establishment in Winchester Road. Daylight had never penetrated this far below ground and rows and rows of constabulary shelving snaked away into the darkness. It was more or less an exact replica of Records at Leighford. Bill Tomlinson had been on Records now for three years, ever since his hip had gone in that warehouse collapse. No more chasing young tearaways for him. Instead, a leisurely limp down felony lane, reminiscing over the baddies of yesteryear, filing the young tearaways away for posterity. He didn't know it, but Peter Maxwell had a similar set of files at Leighford

High. And the malfeasance of each and every one of them was burned into his brain.

'It's all there,' Tomlinson slid a large cardboard box across the desk. 'One day I'll get this lot on the system. Until then, welcome to the paperful office.'

Jacquie let Benny get the hernia by hauling out the sheaves of paper. 'Not Harold Shipman by another name, is he?' the lad felt constrained to ask.

'By the way,' Tomlinson was already hobbling back into the pool of light. 'If you take my advice, you'll start with Jimmy the Snail.'

The visitors looked blank.

'James Doolan. Originally Irish riff-raff whose great-great-great-grandaddy built the London-Brighton railway, circa 1840 something. Jimmy himself specialises in GBH, lightly peppered with a bit of armed robbery.'

'You think he's our man?' Jacquie asked.

'Let's put it this way,' Tomlinson said. 'Jimmy and Wide Boy were never exactly close. But there was a major falling out about a year ago. Jimmy said Wide Boy had crowded him on his particular turf, whisked away a couple of his likely lads for a job in Pompey. Apparently, it was all Jimmy's idea and Wide Boy took the credit – and the cash, of course. 'Course, it's all innuendo. We've got nothing concrete on either of them for that particular job. Even so, I'd start there.'

He looked at the slightly built, freckled faced kid and the girl. 'And I'd take some back-up.'

CHAPTER FIVE

Peter Maxwell didn't take back-up anywhere. All he had was his wits, his guts, his heart on his sleeve and a long line in put-downs that would usually faze even the hardest low-life. And that Monday morning, as the temperature rose to an unbearable high, he was away with the lowest life possible – the Modern Languages Department at Leighford High.

In the status-hungry Nineties, when that great educator Mr Blair had decided that specialism was the name of the game, Leighford High had applied for Language College Status. It hadn't got it, partially because its language results were lower than whale shit and partially because the forms were filled in by Bernard Ryan, the Deputy Head, who had a Lower Second degree in Mediocrity from the University of Crapshire. So, to a man, the Modern Languages Department felt betrayed, let down and disappointed, and they were already curmudgeonly enough before all that.

'*Bonjour, bonjiorno, gutentag*, how-the-hell-are-yuh?' Peter Maxwell was wasted on the History floor. A class of Year Tens, already wilting in the heat, looked up from their computer screens, only barely understanding a quarter of what the Head of Sixth Form had just said. 'Mr McConnell about?'

The German assistant in front of him looked as vague as his kids. Resisting the urge to scream *'Schnell! Schnell! Raus! Raus!'* and *'Achtung! Jude!'* at him, Maxwell just said, 'This way? Thank you so much, *mein Herr.'*

Julian McConnell was a Scouser. Obviously realising one day that he had one of the least pleasant accents in the British isles, he'd taken to foreign languages – in his case, French – to improve his diction. It hadn't worked and whole generations of old Leighford Highenas had merrily holidayed their way around Europe sounding like the Beatles-Meet-Thierry Henri.

'Bitch of a day, Julianus,' Maxwell commented. Posters around the walls of McConnell's office assured Maxwell the Algarve was the place to be and that Tuscany was the cradle of civilization. It all seemed very unlikely now that summer was here in Leighford and the sun burned on the white-hot sand of Willow Bay and the gulls drooped in the heat. Come January, Maxwell might feel differently.

'We're honoured, Max,' McConnell said with no hint of sincerity at all. 'Come for some culture?'

'Always,' Maxwell smiled. 'Actually, I was looking for Carolina.'

The Head of Modern Languages consulted a large timetable display on the wall next to him. 'MFL Four,' he said. 'She's in with Janet but I expect she can be spared. Want to know a Spanish swear-word?'

'I was hoping to teach her some,' Maxwell said, leaning over to McConnell and whispering. 'Bit convent, isn't she?'

'Makes a rare treat these days. I confiscated a packet of condoms from a girl in Year Nine the other day.'

Maxwell wagged a finger at him. 'It'll be your fault when the kid gets pregnant now.'

'Yeah,' McConnell scowled. 'I know.'

Janet Ferguson was a nice woman, but she had the classroom control of an axolotl. Had Headteacher James Diamond had any sense, however, he'd have hired Maxwell out to other departments to instil terror where it was needed. Hayley Whatserface froze when he swept into the room; Tom Toogood put down the chair he'd planned to hurl at Shaun Riley; Brendon Philips opened his book for the first time that lesson.

'Good morning, Mrs Ferguson,' Maxwell beamed once the class had simmered down. 'May I borrow *Señorina* Vasquez, *por favor*?'

There was a low hoot from several of Ten Eff Three, impressed by their History teacher's grasp of foreign. He winked at them. 'And you thought I was just a pretty face, didn't you, Tom?'

Tom nodded. Two years of Mad Max had taught him that was the best policy. Señorina Vasquez was a mild, retiring person, lurking in the corner. She was pretty in an Andalusian sort of way, with shining black hair and dark eyes. Her nose let her down, but then, wasn't that always the way? She could have been a model apart from that, but her disappointing nose had led her inexorably into teaching. You didn't need a nose to teach, not any more.

Today, however, she was singularly grateful to *Señor* Maxwell. Ten Eff Three first thing on a Monday morning was not her idea of a good time. She was secretly afraid of *Señor* Maxwell, because he was so clever and knew things about the

88   M.J. TROW

history of her country that she didn't. She recognised, however, that he was a perfect gentleman, even though he knew his hidalgos from his caballeros. Outside in the relative peace of the corridor, he accosted her.

'Carolina, heart of al-Andalus, have you seen Juanita?'

'Juanita?' the girl repeated.

'Juanita Reyes,' Maxwell explained as though to someone in Year Eight. 'My au pair.'

Carolina was shaking her head. 'No, Mr Maxwell. I have not seen her for...perhaps a week. We had a barbecue on the beach. Saturday before last. I have not seen her since then.'

Maxwell looked perplexed. 'This is getting odder by the day,' he said. 'My partner and I haven't seen her either; nor has her landlady – you know, she lodges next door to us?'

Carolina did. 'I don't know, Mr Maxwell. Have you asked Rodrigo?'

'Rodrigo?'

'He is...my opposition number at the Hampton High School.'

'Opposition...?' Realisation dawned. 'Oh, opposite number. He's an assistant?'

'*Si*...er...yes. He and Juanita have been going out. Together.'

'Have they? Well, many thanks, Carolina,' he smiled. 'You have a good day. *Buenos dias. Muchas gracias.*'

'*De nada,*' she grinned and plunged reluctantly back into the mini-maelstrom that was Janet Ferguson's Spanish lesson, hoping to hide in the corner again and that no one would notice.

* * *

Littlehampton. The town that spawned a hundred Music Hall jokes. Little Nolan was still at Pam's and Jacquie got time off for good behaviour. That was the thing about murder enquiries. It could run you ragged for twenty-four hours solid, then there was a curious lull and a waiting game when nothing seemed to happen. If Peter Maxwell was ever involved in a murder enquiry, he would have called it a Phoney War, but then, Peter Maxwell was never involved in a murder enquiry, was he?

So it was the waiting time. And during it, Jacquie was as intrigued as her man by the disappearance of Juanita Reyes.

'So, when is someone who has done a runner a missing person?' Maxwell asked Jacquie as they buggered Bognor and drove east. It was still a glorious afternoon, the sun gilding the heavy greenery of summer as they skirted William Blake's pretty little village of Felpham with its winding streets and flint-faced cottages and its tigers burning brightly in its forests – but only, of course, at night-time.

'When somebody reports them missing,' was Jacquie's obvious answer. 'And since you haven't, as her employer, and as Mrs Troubridge hasn't, as her landlady, that leaves us people in blue a little in limbo, doesn't it?'

'Well, no doubt she got the hump over something,' Maxwell was rationalising as he wound down the window and let the wind frolic in his wanton curls. He was trying to think if he'd ever said anything disparaging in her presence about Pablo Picasso or El Cid.

'Maybe,' Jacquie nodded, overtaking on the A259 and raising a solitary finger to a vehicle too far out on the inside lane. 'But I always found her quite a happy little soul.'

'Seemed content with her lot in life, certainly,' Maxwell nodded.

Jacquie checked the Ka's clock. 'Are we going to make this, Max? It's nearly half three.'

'My dear girl, not every school in this great country of ours has a fatuous half-continental day. It's like imperial measures the further East you go in Sussex. They might have named a resort not too far away after Reichsmarschall Goering, but the buggers didn't actually land here, you know. No, it's nine until four of the clock in Littlehampton and Juanita's young *hombre* should still be at the chalkface for at least an hour after that, if he has any integrity at all. Tell me about Wide Boy Taylor.'

Jacquie screwed up her face as far as her sunglasses permitted. 'Shan't,' she said.

'Oh, you!' He kicked the dashboard with hush-puppied feet. 'I bet you say that to all the boys.'

'I was waiting all last night for you to ask me,' she told him. 'You were unusually reticent, I thought.' She looked arch over her glasses.

'Hmm,' he mused, rummaging in the glove compartment for an Everton mint. 'I haven't been well. Humbug?'

She declined, taking the little road that led to Climping Sands. The great British public strolled there, as they did daily along Leighford Seafront, on their way to and from the beach. Lager louts were just emerging ready for a night on the tiles, stripped to the waist and chav-hatted against the fierceness of the sun. Young mums strolled with toddlers smothered in ice cream or grizzling because it was still too hot. One or two of the more adventurous elder-folk of Littlehampton had thrown caution to the winds by abandoning their ties and were staggering out like the mad dogs they were under Panamas of varying degrees of decomposition.

'We're waiting...' Maxwell persisted.

Jacquie tutted. 'If I had a quid,' she muttered.

'Now, Woman Policeman,' he scolded. 'You know that when it comes to the sharp end of logic, some of your colleagues are a little...shall we say, blunt? If Henry Hall were here now...'

'If Henry Hall were here now,' she finished the sentence for him, 'we certainly wouldn't be having this conversation. And anyway, he'd be sitting in a baby seat.'

They drove in silence for a while as the sails of the yachts slid past them in the stiffening breeze from the west and Littlehampton's Museum threatened to bore everybody rigid with the town's history. They were showing *No! No! Nanette* again at Rustington Theatre, so that was bound to be a sell-out.

'I'll have to draw my own conclusions, then,' Maxwell was threatening.

Jacquie knew when she was beaten. The father of her child, the mad old buffer, wouldn't shut up unless she caved in. 'Let's just say we're making our enquiries among the criminal fraternity.'

'Ah, sort of *su casa, mi casa*.' It was a perfect Marlon Brando, even without the cotton wool. 'The family that slays together sort of thing.'

'Just small time villains smacking each other,' Jacquie told him. 'The thing of it is, why Leighford and why Dead Man's Point?'

'I don't follow.'

'Well...is it up here?'

'Sorry, darling.' He tried to find the relevant page in the Gazetteer. First left. Up to the traffic lights, then I *think* it's a right. I haven't been here for ages.'

Jacquie complied. 'David Taylor was a Londoner by birth – it's all there in his extensive rap sheet in Winchester Road records. But he'd lived in Brighton since he was a boy. Got in with the local low life, bit of drugs, bit of robbery. Never afraid to deliver a smacking where he felt one was due. No known link with Leighford.'

'You don't shit on your own doorstep,' Maxwell managed around the slurp on the Everton mint.

'That's true,' Jacquie said. 'But think of the logistics, Max. OK, so you want a corpse as far away from the killing grounds as you can, to divert suspicion. But then, you've got to get it across nearly fifty miles of open country.'

'Ever heard of car boots, dear heart?' Maxwell cocked an accusatory eyebrow at her. 'Ever since Maria Bonetti, they've done a good line in stuffing bodies into trunks in Brighton.'

'All right,' Jacquie conceded. 'Boots, body bags. We know he died indoors, so this was no moonlight hit at a romantic spot. One way rides, underworld style, usually end by roadsides or in a handy ditch somewhere. Whoever topped Taylor would have had to reclothe him – remember he was naked when he was killed – wrap him up in polythene, trundle him into a car boot – the man weighed the best part of sixteen stone by the way – drive to Dead Man's Point, dig a man-sized hole and drive back, presumably under cover of darkness.'

'Right,' Maxwell was thinking it through with her. 'So does chummy know the Point? Or does he just happen upon it?'

'It's off the beaten track,' Jacquie reminded him. 'The A259 is…what…a couple of miles away. Turn left at Star Rock and head along Ringer's Hill.'

'Even so,' Maxwell reasoned. 'He may have been cruising the area and thought the Point looked promising.'

'Sandy soil,' Jacquie nodded. 'Easy to dig.'

'But infuriating.' Maxwell winced as the mint shattered between his molars. 'You and I were never seaside babies, but I do remember beach moments as a kid. As soon as you dug a hole, the sand just fell in if it was dry. If it was wet, it filled with water. Played merry Hamlet with many of my more earnest attempts at Motte and Bailey, I can tell you.'

Jacquie saw the sign to Hampton School ahead and flicked the indicator. 'So what do you conclude, Sherlock?'

'Well, you're not going to get much water-logging fifty feet above sea level,' he pointed out. 'But you will get sand-fall.'

'So…either…' Jacquie was trying to guess which way Maxwell's mind was going.

'So either chummy wasn't very good at this and just wanted shot of the body – in which case, as you say, just drop him in a ditch. Or…'

The Ka purred onto Hampton's tarmac, edging its way past the usual motley collection of staff vehicles. 'Or?' she was looking for a space.

'Or the Point has some significance for the dead man or his killer that we don't yet understand.'

'I'm sorry, miss. You can't park there.' A voice through the window broke Maxwell's thought process.

Jacquie flashed her warrant card to the jobsworth who stood scowling back at her.

'Excuse me,' Maxwell reached across her. 'Are you the car park attendant?'

'Sort of,' the scowler grunted. 'And crossing patrol attendant.'

'I should have thought Hampton School would have better spent its money on a few books,' he said and Jacquie flicked her window closed.

The car park attendant wandered away, muttering. He had a position of responsibility, he did. Who did they think they were? Coppers! Come to think of it, he was doing their job for them. He didn't have to do this, you know. He had a City and Guilds in pneumatic welding.

'If you hadn't been quite so offensive, Max,' Jacquie scolded, 'he might have told us where the Modern Languages Department was.'

'Me?' he swallowed the Everton mint in disbelief. 'It was you flashing at him like that that scared him off. Anyway,' he eased himself out of the passenger seat, grateful to be stretching his legs at last. 'Trust me, lady, I'm a teacher. Seen one bog-standard comprehensive, seen them all. This way.'

They strode across the building's frontage. Maxwell was right. Seen one, seen 'em all. Hampton was clearly built by the same architect who built Leighford, a sort of idiot savant but without the savant. It was two tower blocks, probably not the sort of thing J R R Tolkein had in mind when he was writing, all glass that sweltered in the July sun. Open a window and the wind whips open the venetian blinds, those useless gadgets for which the Venetians should be ashamed of themselves. Close them, and a class of thirty can suffocate in three minutes.

'It'll be down here,' Maxwell said, sliding with accustomed ease down a once-grassy bank now worn smooth and brown by years of bikes and skateboards, neither of which, of course, was allowed on school premises. He managed to retain his balance and a modicum of dignity before reaching a very large plastic sign that read 'Science'.

'Ah.'

And it was back up the hill again. A paper aeroplane flew on the wings of the afternoon to land at the feet of the Great Man. Maxwell bent to pick it up.

'It's a Spad,' he said, looking at the shapeless bit of paper. 'First class aircraft designed for the Richthofen Circus back in the War to End All Wars. A sure sign it's come from Modern Languages. And look,' he held it aloft in triumph, 'as if to prove it, it's made from a French test paper. This way.'

This time, he was right. Beyond the open double-doors, it seemed as if every lesson in the ghastly open-plan milieu was being taught or not, as the case may be, by Janet Ferguson. Jacquie looked appalled, but then, she reasoned, Maxwell would probably be equally stunned if he could see her and the lads rounding up drunks in the good old days when she was in uniform along Leighford Seafront. Both of them contented themselves that it was the last lesson of the afternoon and the end of a long day, not too far away from the end of a long academic year. Maxwell felt smug too – it was nice to know other peoples' institutions were as chaotic as your own.

'I can't help thinking we ought to have reported to Reception,' Jacquie said. 'Some eagle-eyed site manager is probably ringing the police as we speak.'

'Can I help you?' a big-boned woman blocked the corridor

ahead. She was clearly the school rottweiler, all foam-flecked jaws and attitude, like something out of *The Omen*. For one mad, impish moment, Maxwell toyed with claiming to be an Ofsted inspector, but reason and good sense prevailed; this woman had done nothing to him – it just didn't seem fair. Anyway, before he could react at all, Jacquie's warrant card was in the air.

'We'd like to see Mr Rodrigo Mendoza, please,' she said.

The rottweiler noticed the wire haired bloke with the detective hadn't shown her his card too. Perhaps you didn't have to after a certain age. Perhaps it was just as well; all Maxwell could have flashed was his library card and NUT membership documentation – all in all, nothing very remarkable among the staff of a high school.

'Rodrigo?' the woman repeated. 'Why? I mean, he's not in any trouble, is he?'

'I'm afraid I'm not at liberty to tell you that, Mrs...'

'Appleton,' the rottweiler said quickly. 'And that's Miss.'

No surprises there, thought Maxwell.

'I'm Head of Modern Languages.'

For a moment, Maxwell thought of introducing her to Julian McConnell, two miserable linguists together. But he relented; Mrs Julian McConnell was a pleasant woman, when all was said and done. Let sleeping dogs lie.

'You'd better come this way.'

She led the pair past a battery of computers, which Maxwell noted with a self-satisfied air were older than those at Leighford, and into a marking room, strewn with papers and clapped out old teachers of languages.

'Rodrigo,' Miss Appleton took them to a solid, good-looking lad deep in a book in the corner. 'These people are from the police.'

The good-looking lad got up.

'Rodrigo Mendoza?' Jacquie had the warrant card in her hand again.

'Yes,' the lad frowned. 'What is the trouble?'

'We understand you are a friend of Juanita Reyes?' she asked him.

Mendoza noted that various colleagues seemed to be doubly engrossed in whatever they were doing, timetable finalisation at one desk, exercise book marking at another. 'I am,' he said. 'Is there a problem?'

'We have reason to believe,' Jacquie was in full Force mode by now, 'that she has gone missing.'

Mendoza beckoned the couple into an anteroom, piled high with old coursework and dingy coffee cups. 'You mind if we make this not so public?' he asked.

'Of course,' Jacquie nodded and waited until they all sat down as best they could in the cramped conditions.

'Do I understand you?' Mendoza asked, concern all over his darkly handsome face. 'Juanita is missing?'

'We haven't seen her for some days,' Jacquie said.

'Does Mrs Troubridge know? You have spoken to her landlady?'

'Yes, we have,' Jacquie said. 'Juanita's bed has not been slept in. And Mrs Troubridge believes none of her clothes have gone.'

'But this Mrs Troubridge, she is an old lady, yes?'

'How well do you know Juanita, Mr Mendoza?' Maxwell asked.

'We are friends,' Mendoza told him. 'Two strangers in a strange land.'

'You knew each other back home in Spain?' Jacquie asked.

'No, no,' Mendoza shook his head. 'Juanita, she is from Menorca, uh? I am from Barcelona. I have been in this country two years now. Juanita, she has been here for less.'

'How did you meet?' Jacquie asked.

'At a...what you call...bash? We have email link-up between all us language teachers in the county.'

'So you know Carolina Vasquez at Leighford High?' Maxwell asked.

'Carolina?' Mendoza repeated. 'Yes. She is an assistant and I am a qualified teacher, but yes, I know her.'

'Another friend?' Jacquie checked.

Mendoza smiled. It made him, Jacquie had to admit, drop-dead gorgeous. 'We have to hang together,' he said.

Maxwell smiled too. Living down the Armada must be a bitch. 'Do you have a contact number for Juanita? He asked. 'Her mobile doesn't answer.'

'I have email address for her computer,' he said.

That was the laptop Jacquie had noted in Juanita's room. She hadn't wanted to get into all that until now, but now might be the time. 'When did you see Juanita last?' she asked.

Mendoza pursed his lips in thought. 'It must have been three, four weeks ago. There was a party here at Hampton. I called her and asked if she would like to come. She said yes.'

'The party was here at school?' Jacquie wanted to know.

'No,' Mendoza chuckled. 'You don't know English schools,' he said. 'They are not places that make you want to have parties.'

Maxwell did, of course, and he couldn't agree more.

'No, we have a party at a local golf club. Our Vice Principal is a member.'

'How did she get here?' Jacquie asked. 'Did she drive?'

'She come by train,' Mendoza said. 'But I did not want her out late, so I took her home.'

'You drive?' Maxwell checked.

'Oh, yes,' Mendoza told him. 'I have just about got the hang of the right and the left now. Look, is Juanita in any trouble?'

'We don't know, Mr Mendoza,' Jacquie said. 'We hope not. Do you have her home address?'

'No,' he shook his head. 'I did not know her that well.'

'Past tense, Mr Mendoza?' Maxwell asked.

'I wish the children I teach had your grasp of English, *señor*,' he smiled. 'I am sorry. I mean, I *do* not know her that well.'

'Bloody Hellfire!' Jacquie shouted as a white van snarled out of nowhere, cutting her up along the A259. 'I can't see a bloody thing in this sunset.'

'Don't knock it, dearest,' Maxwell felt his heart slither downwards from his tonsils again. 'In other contexts, it's a gorgeously romantic sight, a ball of fire sinking into the sea, rather as the heat of my love is quenched by the endlessness of your caring…'

He looked across at her and they both burst out laughing.

'You old fart!' she rubbed his knee. 'That's why I love you. Pass the vomit bag.'

'And on a more prosaic note,' he said, 'where would any of

us be if the bloody thing went out; the sun, I mean.'

'Where, indeed?' Quantum Physics and the Meaning of Life weren't exactly Jacquie's thing. She changed the subject. 'What did you make of the Spanish connection?'

'Well set-up chap,' Maxwell shrugged. 'No doubt all the girlies in Year Ten line up to swoon over him. Bet there's been a huge take-up in Spanish GCSE this year.'

'I was thinking more of his relationship with Juanita.'

'I bow to your expertise, darling heart,' he told her. 'Do you smell a rat?'

'Not at all,' she said. 'But I am beginning to think that dear Juanita might not be all we thought she was.'

'Meaning?'

'Meaning, we didn't know about Don Rodrigo. And neither did Mrs Troubridge.'

'Jacquie,' Maxwell sighed. 'Mrs Troubridge was at school with Boudicca. There could have been a whole queue of men standing in Mrs Troubridge's garden to service Juanita and the old besom would never have noticed.'

'I suppose you're right.'

'You don't fancy going the pretty way, do you?' he asked her.

'What?'

'Via the Point?'

'Now, Max,' she frowned. 'Pam has had Nolan now for the best part of twelve hours.'

'And when he's Prime Minister and King all rolled into one, she'll dine out on it for the rest of her life. Come on, it's only ten minutes.'

It was. Jacquie's car roared off the A259, making for the

Shingle. The little lights of evening were beginning to show now, dotted on the headland, whose ridges and furrows had merged to form a mass of dark, like the hump of a huge whale. It would not be totally black for a couple of hours yet, but the shapes of the day had gone. Willow Bay lay like a pale crescent below them, tiny dots of people still scampering on the surf booming along the breakwaters. Tired children still squealed happily as the light died and the odd glow and wisp of smoke marked the places where their parents were equally happily scorching bits of meat on their temporary barbecues.

Then they were on to Ringer's Hill and turning into the car park high over the sea. There was a solitary car parked there and a middle-aged couple were standing by the bonnet, enjoying the view and the comparative solitude, like one of those corny ads for life insurance on the telly. Did they know that yards away, under the overhang of the gnarled oaks, the police cordon ribbons still fluttered, marking the shallow grave of a small time crook? It was all so incongruous somehow.

Jacquie and Maxwell nodded as the couple turned, both a little annoyed to have their tranquillity shattered. Not a courting couple, surely, the tourists thought – he was old enough to be her father. Under the canopy, the ground was uneven, pock-marked with the print of a thousand rubber boots. Dead Man's Point was on the 'Walk the South' route every autumn when the rain turned the path to torrents in places. Out on the headland, the air was chill now that the sun was dying. They had ducked under the tape and stood on the edge of the pit as the SOCO team had excavated it.

Maxwell squatted on his heels, picking up handfuls of soil

and watching it fall. Out to sea, beyond the curve of the Bay, a solitary liner, like a ghost ship in full sail, slid noiselessly, lit like a magic lantern against the purple bars of the clouds. He straightened, looking back to the car park, then to his left to where the sandstone fell away to the cliffs. The edge was near, beckoning. He'd only once felt that before, when he'd gone to visit a friend in Bristol and found himself on the suspension bridge at Clifton. He felt it then, drawing him down. How wonderful it would feel to sense the air rush through your veins, how free. He sensed it again now, with his feet on the shifting sand of Dead Man's Point and the sea unreal and silver in the twilight fifty feet below.

'Max,' Jacquie held his arm. Suddenly, she was afraid. And she didn't know why. 'Max, let's go home.'

CHAPTER SIX

Tuesday. Tuesday. Hate that day. At the dog-end of an academic year, with three weeks to go to 'School's Out for Summer', it had to be said that Leighford High was a strange place. Year 13 had gone into that vast abyss of deck-chair attendancy, ice-cream salery and other part-time jobbery that was the lot of teenagers around the coast of this great country of ours. After that was the Gap Year and the great Tony Blair university scam – walker? gum-chewer? You're in. Year 11 had gone too, albeit temporarily. Most of them would be back come September when the grapes were purple and the season misty and mellow. They would have achieved what they set out to achieve, not a clutch of five A grade GCSEs, but the James Diamond–given right to wear non-uniform clothes. And they would automatically become Maxwell's Own. There was a certain irony in the fact that the member of staff at Leighford most conversant with uniform should be in charge of a bunch of misfits that didn't wear any. The new Year 7 of course had yet to join, wandering goggle-eyed around the scruffy corridors, meeting up again with the very people who had bullied them in junior school. There was a God.

And God, that particular Tuesday, was Peter Maxwell. He sat in his film-postered office with the Fridge beside him. All

right, it was very unkind of someone to have called Helen
Maitland the Fridge, but even Maxwell, in a darker mood,
could see the relevance of it. Helen was positively rectangular,
but with smoothly rounded corners and she habitually wore
white. That said, Helen was the salt of the earth, Maxwell's
Number Two. When the Great Man wasn't there, she was,
sorting EMA contracts, teaching GNVQ courses, handling
PMT problems; that woman could acronym for England.

'You do realise, Anthony,' Maxwell was saying, 'that we
allow you to bring your car onto the school premises on the
assumption you know how to drive it.'

'Yes, sir.'

Anthony Cross knew when he was on the carpet. He'd
learned his body language subconsciously from Maxwell and
stood there, hang-dog and not making eye contact. He'd
screeched out of Leighford High's car park yesterday, doing a
wheelie in his clapped out Peugeot, *and* he'd abandoned half
the carton content of the town's KFC on the tarmac. A
flogging offence at the very least. Maxwell thought that too.

'If this was a real school,' he growled, 'I'd have you paraded
in hollow square, with the whole establishment looking on to
witness your punishment. You'd be tied to the triangle,
stripped to the waist and thrashed soundly by the male PE
staff using the iron-tipped leather thongs of a cat o' nine tails.'

He paused while the image sunk in.

'As it is,' he went on, 'I'll take your keys, please.'

Anthony fumbled in his jeans. Anybody who didn't know
Peter Maxwell would have refused to hand them over,
muttering about human rights. This was theft, this was,
taking a bloke's car. It was only overnight, of course. And

Anthony would have the humiliation of catching the bus home. Or worse, he may have to walk. But Anthony knew better than to argue. Ever since Year 7, he'd been locking horns, on and off, with Mad Max and the crafty old bastard had won every time. Anthony's dad knew better than to mix it too, since the Head of Sixth Form could quote every law since Hammurabi to prove he was in the right. And anyway, Peter Maxwell had once taught him, too.

'It's only because you've been in my Sixth Form for the last twenty years that I'm letting you off this lightly. Now…on yer bike!'

The thumb said it all. It would be a cold day in Hell before Anthony drove at anything faster than minus one again. And he'd take his KFC home with him next time.

The lad all but collided in the doorway with a fraught-looking Carolina Vasquez.

'Mr Maxwell, Mr Maxwell,' she blurted. 'It's Rodrigo Mendoza. He's gone missing.'

'Well, it's really none of my business, Max.' Helen was passing her boss a well-earned coffee. It was the Time of the Wall, the wilting hour at the end of the day when teachers either collapse or drift into oblivion or have to be padlocked into their strait-jackets. It was that window of no opportunity after the kiddie-winkies had gone home and before Mrs B arrived with her mops and brooms and vacuum polishers. And peace shall come to Leighford High.

'No, that's not a problem, Helen,' Maxwell said. 'Thanks. It helps me get my raddled old brain around what's going on. From the top, then…Jacquie and I "inherited" Juanita, so to speak, from a family in Tottingleigh. Their circumstances had changed so the girl wasn't needed. The reference was glowing. Juanita had her green card; everything was hunky-dory. Our neighbour, Mrs Troubridge, had a spare room and welcomed the company, so it couldn't have been better. Nolan took to her straight away – even my old bugger of a cat seemed to tolerate her in his usual grumpy sort of way. Then she buggered off.'

'Just left?' Helen frowned.

'Apparently. We still don't know whether she took any of her clothes or not, but she certainly didn't take them all. They're still hanging in her wardrobe. Jacquie's checking the girl's computer as we speak. But there's nothing helpful on it. Usual emails, in Spanish, of course. I'll have to get Janet or Carolina on to them.'

'Don't you have an address? In Spain, I mean? That's the most likely explanation, surely. She's just gone home.'

Maxwell chuckled. 'I knew you'd have a scientific, down-to-earth approach, Helen. That's why I keep you on. That and your irresistible coffee.' He pulled his usual face. 'This *is* coffee, isn't it?'

Helen hit him with an old exam paper. 'I bet you say that to all the Assistant Year Heads, you patronising old bugger. Don't tell me you hadn't thought of it?'

'I'd thought of it, yes,' he said. 'But I haven't got it. Menorca is all I know. A little island in the Balearic group, evacuated at the time of Lepanto.' He reached forward and patted her hand patronisingly. 'That's 1571, by the way.'

'Bog off,' she growled. She and Maxwell had been doing this for years. She'd be heart broken if he ever stopped talking down to her. And as for Peter Maxwell, having the Fridge as your right-hand woman in the mad circus that was Leighford High wasn't a bad thing at all, appalling coffee or not.

'No, the Hendersons probably have it. I might nip over there when I've downed this.' He took a sip. 'Nectar.'

'So where's that darling boy of yours while you're sitting there enjoying my coffee and my company?'

'Mercifully for all of us, Jacquie met up with this lady called Pam – short for Epaminondas, I shouldn't wonder – in her Maternity clinic. Well, between the heavy breathing and sticking their elbows in bowls of tepid water, they got on like a house on fire. She and her husband live out towards Fyleigh and the babies are quite happy to kick seven kinds of shit out of each other, so we tend to drop him round there at the moment. It's good of Pam, she's one of those people they used to call "a brick" in the 1930s – before brickage became synonymous with stupidity, that is.'

'So how do Carolina and this Mendoza bloke fit into it all?' Helen asked.

'Well, I'm not exactly sure,' Maxwell confessed. 'Juanita was having English lessons with Carolina, and no doubt they'd meet up for a jar or whatever the Spanish equivalent for girlies is.'

'Sangria,' said Helen solemnly, past-mistress as she was of package-deal holidays to Iberia.

'No doubt,' Maxwell nodded. 'Rodrigo Mendoza teaches Spanish at Hampton. He knows Juanita too. Stands to reason, doesn't it? All the continentals hanging together, as he put it.'

'And he's vanished into thin air.'

'Well, there's vanishing and vanishing.' Maxwell could be a

cryptic old fart when the mood was on him. 'Carolina seemed upset.'

'Hmm,' commented Helen, talking of cryptic.

Maxwell caught the nuance and raised an appropriate eyebrow. 'And what does that mean, Assistant Mine?'

'Well, I don't pretend to know the girl very well, but there's something about her. I don't know. A bit *too* simpering, don't you think?'

Maxwell nodded. 'She crawls against walls and prostrates herself in obeisance when I enter the room,' he'd noticed. 'I don't have a problem with that.'

'Perhaps toadying is what young women do in Spain,' Helen suggested.

'Come on, Mrs Maitland, she's a young kid in a hostile land. Living by herself, coping with all the little hellraisers in this place – and the kids. And all of it in a foreign language. If I could reach my hat, after the day I've had, I'd take it off to her.'

'Yes, all right,' sighed Helen. 'And as vicious, unfeeling bastards go, you've got a bloody soft centre, Peter Maxwell.'

'That's why I let you interview the sobbing girls,' he winked at her. 'But it doesn't help me with my Spanish problem.'

'I think you're right,' Helen finished her coffee. 'This family – the Hendersons? They might know something. God, is that the time? I've got a barbecue tonight. Whose bloody idea was that?'

Now Mr Maitland was a quiet, retiring mouse. Very nice as quiet, retiring mice went, but quiet and retiring nonetheless. So Maxwell knew the answer to that one straight away. 'That'll be yours, Helen,' he said.

* * *

The sun was still a demon as Maxwell and Surrey took the Tottingleigh Road. It was along here that the High Flyer from Portsmouth had rattled east in the golden days of coaching, postillions blasting for shepherds to clear the way and toll keepers to haul upright their turnpikes. That, of course, was then and tarmacadam and No Overtaking signs had replaced the smooth-cobbled camber and the well-worn ruts of wheels. Progress. You'd have to argue with Peter Maxwell about that.

Maxwell had met the Hendersons before, but never *chez-ont*. He was genuinely impressed by the sweep of the drive and the rhododendron garden. For a moment, as usually happened in these cases, Maxwell flushed scarlet in the Marxist sense and became a stolid member of the *lumpenproletariat*, but the moment had gone by the time he reached the front door, and he was himself again. The place itself was neo-Georgian, with the accent on the neo in that Mr Henderson was a builder who seemed to own most of Sussex. The ghastly twice-life-size wild boars sejeant on either side of the Doric doorway gave a sort of clue that more was more to Mr Henderson.

He rang the doorbell, half expecting a solemn-looking butler in frock coat and Gladstone wing collar to be standing there, asking him pompously for his card and inquiring whether, as it was after three of the clock, this was a morning call. As it was, it was Mrs Henderson, rather more dowdy than Maxwell remembered her, peering around the leaded panes at him.

'Peter Maxwell.' The Great Man swept off his cap with a flourish. Fiona Henderson looked him up and down, taking in the cycle clips and the wild, barbed-wire hair that had just

been blown to Arthur Scargill proportions by the breeze along
the Flyover. Perhaps they should rename it the Combover?
'We met in May,' he reminded her. 'Took your Spanish au pair
off your hands.'

'Mr Maxwell, of course.' Fiona Henderson was not an
unattractive woman in a builder's wife sort of way. She had a
very well coiffured head of auburn hair, not natural like
Jacquie's, but rather old copper and definitely from a bottle.
Once she'd recognised her visitor, she seemed to relax and
straightened so that she was nearly his height. 'Won't you
come in? Is there a problem?'

Think of every naff piece of interior décor you've ever seen
and you've got the picture that faced Peter Maxwell that lazy,
hazy afternoon. It was as though Laurence Llewellyn-Bowen
had had a nervous breakdown and had been given about three
minutes to redress a house. Not that the stuff was cheap, far
from it, but it simply lacked class.

'I was out by the pool,' she said. 'Can I get you a drink?'

It was Mint Julep weather and Peter Maxwell was a
Southern Comfort man deep down, but he went for the
middle ground. 'I'll just have a glass of water, if I may.'

'Ice and lemon?'

'Kind.'

The pool was about the size of Leighford High School,
rather distressingly in the shape of a kidney. Giant plants that
seemed to be hand-me-downs from Kew loomed at every
angle of the building and the sun beat mercilessly on the
sliding glass roof. It was like a mini Millennium Stadium.
Maxwell found himself reclining on a steamer-chair which
had the word 'Titanic' stencilled boldly on the back. Tasteful.

Mrs Henderson was actually quite a striking figure, figure-wise – or was it the weird light thrown from the pool? The water was impossibly blue, like the eyes of the actor Max von Sydow.

'Cheers, Mr Maxwell,' she clinked her White Russian against his glass of water.

'Lang may your lum reek,' Maxwell toasted, although it was clear that the Henderson house had never seen a chimney in its life.

'Now,' she sat on the steamer-chair opposite, crossing her legs at the ankles like the memorial brass of some crusader. 'Juanita Reyes. Is anything the matter?'

'Well,' Maxwell winced, as he swallowed too much ice and his life flashed before him. 'I wondered if you had her address?'

'Address?' She blinked. 'You mean in Spain?'

'Yes.'

'Mr Maxwell…where *is* Juanita?'

It was time for the man to come clean. 'Well, that is rather the problem, Mrs Henderson; I don't know. She left a few days ago and no one appears to have seen her since.'

'Really?' the woman straightened slightly before burying her nose in her glass again. 'Isn't that rather unusual?'

'I'd say so, yes,' he told her. 'So I'm wondering if I could contact her or at least her family.'

'But if she's not there,' Fiona Henderson reasoned, 'Won't that alarm her people?'

'If she's not there, Mrs Henderson,' Maxwell said, 'I think they have every right to be alarmed. Can you tell me how you came across her?'

'Yes. Like you, we answered an advert in the *Leighford Advertiser*. Gerald – you've met my husband?'

Maxwell had.

'Gerald is away a lot on business and Katie was becoming a bit of a handful. If I remember rightly, Juanita came to us from an agency in London. Gerald and I arranged to meet her there. It was all very formal, all very professional. Gerald did the paperwork.'

'I'm surprised Jacquie and I didn't have to go through all that,' Maxwell said.

'How long has she been with you now? Three months?'

Maxwell nodded. 'Something like that.'

'These people are like the Inland Revenue,' she laughed. 'I'm sure they'll catch up with you sooner or later. Gerald will have passed on your details to them, I'm sure.'

'So, was there a problem?' Maxwell asked. 'With Katie, I mean.'

'Well, I have to admit, Mr Maxwell, my daughter is not the most...shall we say...reasonable of children. Oh, Juanita never complained, but Gerald and I talked it over. Better to send her to boarding school. She needed company of her own. A little discipline. It didn't do me any harm and Gerald...well,' she pursed her lips, 'Gerald was always overfond. Given that situation, Juanita was a tad redundant.'

'So you placed the ad in the paper?'

'Yes,' she said. 'Yes, I did.'

'She lived in with you?' Maxwell asked.

'Yes; as you see, we have plenty of room here.'

'Tell me, Mrs Henderson, were there any men friends?'

Was it the light from the pool or did Fiona Henderson's face darken imperceptibly? 'Not that I'm aware of,' she said.

'No one, for example, by the name of Rodrigo Mendoza?'

'I said,' she repeated, 'There was no one.'

'And Juanita didn't leave anything behind?'

'Of course not,' she told him. 'Why should she?'

'No reason,' he shrugged. 'So, that Spanish address?'

'Right,' she stood up and left her drink on the table. 'I shan't be a moment.'

Maxwell let his head loll back on the soft cushion. If only he'd taken that left turn at Albuquerque as Bugs Bunny used to say, all this could have been his. Oh, not the naff fixtures and fittings. But the size, the scope. Instead of this silly pool, his Light Brigade could be laid out here almost to scale, the half a league stretching beyond the palm trees to the nasty little bar that Gerald Henderson had had plumbed in at the far end. Maxwell could really cope with the Wall lounging here. But then, presumably, if he lived in a house this size, there'd be no need for the Wall, because he wouldn't be working. No Leighford High, no Wall. No nervous breakdown, no chalkface. No...

'Sant Lluis.' Fiona Henderson broke the reverie.

'Sorry?' Maxwell was on his feet; he'd been to a good school.

'Juanita's home town. On Menorca. Sant Lluis. Here,' she passed him a computer printout. 'I can't pronounce the road name, if that's what it is.'

'Thank you, Mrs Henderson.' Maxwell finished his drink. 'You've been very helpful. Tell me,' he paused beyond the pool. 'How long was Juanita with you?'

'About six months,' she told him. 'Why?'

Maxwell shrugged. 'No reason,' he said. 'I just wondered if

she was the sort of girl who did a runner every now and again, just for jolly?'

'She was always here when we employed her, Mr Maxwell.' It sounded like a reproach and perhaps it was. Had Maxwell been over-casual in that he had lost a girl in his employ? He merely smiled and went on his way, thanking Fiona Henderson again and unhooking Surrey from the neck of a wild boar.

'Interview commencing 9.21 a.m. Wednesday 5th July. DI Bronson and DCI Hall in the presence of James Doolan and solicitor.'

'Walter Harriot,' the solicitor added for the record.

The four men were sitting in Interview Room Number Two at Leighford police station, shielded from the morning sun by the venetian blinds. This place had a history of its own; things had been said here that it were better the outside world knew nothing about.

'Mr Doolan,' Henry Hall opened the batting. 'Can you tell us your relationship with David Taylor?'

'Relationship?' Jimmy the Snail had a charming Irish lilt, County Mayo via West Sussex. 'I don't think I follow.'

Hall was more simplistic. The bland bastard could play this game all day. 'Did you know David Taylor?'

'I did,' Doolan conceded.

'In what capacity?'

'We were business partners.'

'What sort of business?' George Bronson was cutting to the chase. He had a shorter fuse than his boss and low-life like Doolan irked him.

'Er... I don't think my client is under any obligation to

answer that.' Harriot was starting to earn his crust.

'It's a harmless question,' Hall corrected him. 'Unless, of course, Mr Doolan's business is of an illegal nature.'

'Is that an accusation, Chief Inspector?' Everything about Walter Harriot irritated George Bronson – his dapper tie and highly polished lace-up brogues, his expensive designer haircut and his smarmy I-know-the-law approach.

'Oh, we'll leave the accusations till later,' Henry Hall said.

Doolan looked at his man. The bloke with the ginger hair he could ignore. Oh, he was stocky enough, but he'd have learned all his strong-arm stuff at Hendon or wherever the fuck they trained coppers these days. Jimmy the Snail had men who could take him out, even if Jimmy himself was getting a bit long in the tooth these days. No, if he had a problem at all, it was going to come from the other fella, hiding behind his blank glasses. He was quiet, careful. Doolan couldn't see the bastard's eyes, but he knew he was watching every move. He'd have to tread warily here.

'You and Mr Taylor were business partners in Brighton?' Bronson went on.

'We were,' Doolan nodded.

'That's past tense?' Hall took him up on it.

For a moment, Walter Harriot leaned across to advise his client, but Jimmy the Snail had been here before. He could handle this.

'It is indeed, Chief Inspector,' he said. 'And I just knew you'd been to a good school.'

'When did you last see your partner?' Bronson asked. Peter Maxwell would have recognised something like it as an old painting.

'Ooh,' Doolan leaned back, running a careless finger round the glass rim of the ashtray on the table in front of him. 'Now you've asked me. Let's see. It would have been the New Year, I believe. We met at a party.'

'Did you part on good terms?' Hall asked.

'I must advise my client...' Harriot began.

'No, no, Walter, it's OK, I'm fine. I *always* part on good terms with people, Chief Inspector. Even you and the boy here.'

'Do you know Leighford, Mr Doolan?' A change of tack here. Not only had Hall asked two in a row, but he was off on the friendly policeman kick. In the good old days, Bronson would have flipped a polythene bag over Doolan's head by now and invited him to kiss his arse goodbye. Ah, God be praised for PACE, the EU and Political Correctness.

'I think I came here as a kid,' Doolan beamed. 'Tell me, was there a Freak Show on the Promenade? This would be about 1970?'

'A little before my time,' Hall said. 'Do you know Dead Man's Point?'

Doolan looked blank. 'What an emotive name,' he said, folding his arms. 'Could you show me on a map? Only, I'm a very visual learner, apparently. Have to see things written down.'

'So,' Bronson saw his opening. 'The plans of the Nat West Bank in Hove 1997. You must have seen that on a regular basis – to get the layout of the building, I mean?'

'Oh, get real, Inspector,' Harriot chuckled. 'What sort of question is that?'

'All right,' it was Bronson's turn to change tack. 'What was your relationship with a Mr Edward Hallop?'

'Don't know him,' Doolan shrugged.

'Ben Tilman?'

Ditto.

'Anastas Doropoulos?'

'Inspector,' Harriot adopted a pained expression. 'Are you just ambling through the phone book or is there some point to these names?

Bronson looked at Hall for the go ahead. The DCI nodded.

'We have reason to believe that whatever your client's business is or has been over the years, it involved lending money to the gentlemen whose names I have mentioned. Edward Hallop has been in a wheelchair since 1993. He says your client put him there.'

'He would, wouldn't he?' the brief said.

'My dad told me there was a Father Christmas, too,' Doolan said. 'It took me years to get over that one. A terrible thing, isn't it, to discover your father's a liar? But then,' he winked at Bronson, 'you see, I knew who my father was.'

Hall felt his oppo tense and raised his hand to the level, just below table height. Doolan saw it and smiled.

'Do go on,' Harriot smarmed.

Hall noticed the ridge in Bronson's jaw jumping as he spoke, reading the rap sheet in front of him. 'Ben Tilman disappeared in the early March of 1998. He was last seen drinking in your client's company, in a pub in Brighton.'

'Tilman!' Doolan clicked his fingers. Suddenly, he was all helpfulness. '*That* was his name. Yes, I must come clean on this one, Walter,' he smiled to the man beside him. 'I was introduced to him by a mutual acquaintance. We played a few hands of poker. That was at the Hanging Oak, right?'

Bronson nodded. This Irish bastard had played this game before.

'Anastas Doropoulos,' the Inspector said levelly.

'I expect he'd be a Greek gentleman,' Doolan smiled.

'A Greek gentleman whose dinghy capsized somewhere off Peacehaven in August 2004.'

Doolan shook his head. 'Well, there you go,' he said. 'Those waters are surprisingly treacherous, aren't they? Bit like the Irish Sea on its day off.'

'Are we done here?' Walter Harriot wanted to know.

'We haven't started yet,' Bronson assured him.

'My client came here of his own volition,' the solicitor reminded everybody, for the sake of the tape, 'and it's a rather tedious drive back.'

'And we're very grateful,' Hall said. 'Inspector.' He glanced at the tape.

Reluctantly, Bronson switched it off.

'We'll see ourselves out,' Harriot said.

Doolan extended his right hand. 'It's been a real pleasure, Chief Inspector,' he said.

'Hasn't it though?' Hall looked at him straight faced (how else?) but he drew the line at shaking the man's hand. He knew all too well where it had been.

The sun had already set that evening over Dead Man's Point. John Mason had borrowed his dad's car and driven out beyond the Shingle as another long July day came to an end. Next to him was Louise Bedford, an absolute little cracker who lived three doors down from the Mason's along

Shillingworth Road. John and Louise had known each other for years and had gone all through Junior School and the abyss that was Leighford High, thumping each other, sitting apart and making 'disgusted of Sussex' noises when they'd had to pass each other in the corridor.

Then, suddenly last summer, the daft pair had realised that they'd actually loved each other all along, in that squabbly way that kids do, and now they were off to different universities. John had gone north to London, where he languished in the flesh pots of Camberwell, learning to be a doctor at King's College Hospital. Louise had gone west, to be crammed into the concrete excrescence at Duryard Halls near Heart Attack Hill on the Exeter Campus.

So the last nine months had been an endless flurry of texting and phone calls, mobile to mobile and heart to heart, while the Masons and the Bedfords kept footing the bill and praying that common sense would prevail. But it hadn't. John and Louise were still very much Love's Young Dream as they wandered hand-in-hand along the coastal path that leads from the Point. They watched the dying embers of the sun much as Jacquie and Maxwell had only twenty-four hours before. They faced each other and kissed, slowly, deeply and held each other as if there'd be no tomorrow.

And, for the man in the gardens some yards behind them, there wasn't.

CHAPTER SEVEN

'I never thought I'd be here in a professional capacity.' Jim Astley was still just about able to kneel despite the passage of the years and his variety of medical problems. He was poised over the body of a man, half-hidden under a gigantic rhododendron that stood huge and black against the purple of the night sky.

Around him SOCO were just setting out their wares, with the usual panoply of cameras, measuring devices and grids. They all knew the score, ever since that smug old bastard Edward Locard had come out with the dazzling 'Every contact leaves a trace'. Leo Henshaw, the Ridley Scott of Leighford CID, was treading warily with his camcorder strapped to his shoulder. Everybody was treading warily, come to think of it, in latex suits and shoes, armed with Magnabrushes, tweezers, see-through plastic bags and gummy labels.

Nobody thought they'd be here in a professional capacity. Least of all DCI Henry Hall. It was way past his bedtime and he was getting too long in the tooth for calls in the wee small hours. There was a time when Margaret had got up with him, put the kettle on, made some toast. A time when he'd gone into the kids' room, to check on them, and remind himself that despite the horror he was likely to see, *this* was the real world, his world. But now the kids had gone and Margaret had been through all this once too often; she just turned over in her sleep and he didn't even pause at the top of the stairs.

So here he was, at another scene of somebody else's horror that would become his own. Less fond of the grape than Jim Astley and several years his junior, Henry Hall could still squat. 'Do the gardens often, do you, Jim?'

'Used to,' Astley muttered. 'When Marjorie could still walk upright and was able to tell one flower from another. I always used to find it quite soporific wandering through the Australian garden and the Jungle Room. Gave me an extra frisson, I suppose, that there was a hospital on the site.'

'Ah, yes. Chest, wasn't it?'

'That's right. Bracing south sea air. The wards all had balconies and they all faced this way. Over there, where the gravel path starts. The South Coast used to be full of 'em. If you were consumptive or asthmatic and couldn't afford Switzerland, you came here. Or they sent you to Ventnor, but that must have been like going to Van Diemen's Land.'

'So what's all this about?'

The SOCO's arc lights were throwing lurid shadows across Leighford Botanical Gardens, the giant cedars echoed in shade in all directions – three trunks where there had been one; a hundred branches where fifty would suffice. The evening wind had dropped and there was a hush here despite the traipsings of the law. Nothing but the rustle of plastic, the click of cameras and the sibilance of the sea.

'This,' Jim Astley had to shift to get some feeling back into his right leg, 'is murder, Henry. But then, you knew that

already.' Astley was probing with his torch, flicking it this way
and that. He'd known more difficult, out-of-the-way murder
sites, but half-crawling under the rhododendrons hadn't done
him much good. 'Middle-aged male. Well nourished. Large
amounts of blood around the chest area. I'd say he's been
stabbed, maybe four or five times. The heart was the target,
but he'd have bled to death quickly. The lungs have been
punctured; at least the left one. Know who he is?'

Hall waited until Astley's torch framed the corpse's face.
The eyes were open. So was the mouth. A look of horror. And
of incomprehension. 'No,' he shook his head. 'You?'

'Never seen him before. This was quite an attack. Frenzied.
There's a lot of anger here, Henry.' Astley looked out across
the gloom where men in white coats moved like ghosts across
the carefully manicured lawns. 'How far are we from Dead
Man's Point?'

'About half a mile as the crow flies.' Hall stood up. 'And,
yes, I had made the connection. Thank you, Jim.'

'I'll send you my bill in the morning,' Astley chuckled and
got back to work.

The DCI crossed the gravel path that led to the foundations
of the old hospital. A metal plaque still marked the spot – *The
Leighford and District Hospital for Pulmonary Diseases,
Opened January 21st 1883 by Sir William Anstruther M D.*
Different days, Henry Hall guessed. Different days, Peter
Maxwell knew.

Three people huddled around a Polo Golf parked beyond
the azalea beds. One was a lad about twenty, dark-haired,
good-looking in an ovine sort of way. He was cuddling a girl
about the same age. She was freckly; even the darkness

couldn't hide that, and she'd been crying, her pretty face streaked with tears and her mascara all over the place. The third was Jacquie Carpenter.

'Sir, this is John Mason and Louise Bedford.'

'You find the body?'

'Er...yes,' Mason told him, numbed as he was, still a little taken aback by the DCI's brusqueness. 'Yes, we did.'

'What time was this?' Hall wanted to know.

'Um...'

'It was half past nine,' Louise sniffed, glad after so much waiting around to be *doing* something, moving it all on. John Mason wondered why police people always asked the same questions over and over again. In the hope you'd suddenly remember something? In the hope they'd catch you out?

'Which way were you going?' Hall asked.

'We were taking the coastal path,' Mason said. 'From the Point.'

'Dead Man's Point?' Hall checked.

'That's right.'

'You didn't notice the police cordon? The tape?'

'Of course. But we'd parked by then. At the Point car park. We didn't cross the cordon, if that's what you think.'

'This is your car?' Hall asked.

'Um...my dad's.'

'How did it get here?'

'I thought it advisable to go with them to get it, guv,' Jacquie said. 'Bring it round here for somewhere to sit and keep warm. I sensed it would be a long night.'

Hall nodded. He'd been a little tough on the lad, on the girl. You don't expect to have your romantic evening walk punctuated by stumbling over a dead man. Or to be asked questions several times over by people who seemed to believe you've done it. 'Does somebody know where you are?' he asked. 'Your dad?'

'Yes,' Mason told him. 'I rang him earlier. Louise rang her mum.'

'Good. Can you give us a minute, please? I shall need you to accompany one of my officers to the station, to make statements. Is that all right?'

The pair nodded.

'Jacquie,' a nod was as good as a wink to DS Carpenter and she followed her guv'nor into the gloom. 'What do you make of them?'

'Straight, guv,' she said. 'Wrong place, wrong time, that's all.'

'Yes,' Hall nodded, watching as the SOCO tent went up over the body and the incongruous sound of sawing began as half the rhododendrons were torn away. 'Yes, we've had rather a lot of that in the last few days. When Jim's finished, we'll need to get that lot to the lab; try and establish an ID.'

'No need, guv,' Jacquie told him. 'I know who it is.'

Hall looked her in the eyes. Grey, clear, even in the short July night. 'Who, for God's sake?'

'He's a builder from Tottingleigh. His name's Gerald Henderson.'

'Gerald Henderson?'

Maxwell had waited up, even though she had told him not to. He wasn't wearing his curlers, tapping his foot and cradling his trusty rolling pin in time-honoured tradition. He knew better. Before they'd become one, Jacquie Carpenter would call him in the wee small hours, her voice tired, her nerves shredded; and he'd known. Or, there'd be a ring at the doorbell at 38 Columbine. And a small, frightened girl would stand there, in the wind, in the snow, in the rain. And she'd thrown her arms around his neck. And he'd known. She'd said nothing. She didn't have to. Murder does that to you. Words? Well, what use are they?

This time it was a little different. The man in the gardens wasn't a stranger, Mr Nobody without a life in every sense of the word. This time they both knew him. He was the man they'd got their au pair from and Peter Maxwell had been talking to his wife not ten hours ago.

'Stabbed, Doc Astley thinks.'

'In the gardens?'

Jacquie shook her head, cradling the cocoa between her hands. Even though it was nearly the shortest, warmest night of the year she felt cold, chilled to the bone as she always was when she walked in on sudden death. 'No, Astley thinks he was dragged there and dumped.'

'When was this?' Maxwell sat opposite her in the kitchen-diner, a fluffy clown perched next to his elbow, grinning at them both.

Jacquie managed a chuckle. 'You've obviously never worked with Jim Astley,' she said. '"Miracles," he is wont to say, "take a little longer."' It wasn't a bad take-off.

'Hmm,' Maxwell muttered. 'Ever the man of cliché was our Jim. Was he prepared to guess? Isn't that, after all, what most forensic science is?'

'Don't get me started on that one,' Jacquie shook her head. 'He wouldn't be drawn, but stands to reason it was after dark.'

'Or the body would have been found earlier?' Maxwell was thinking aloud. 'What time do the gardens close?'

'Well, that's just the point,' she said. 'The glasshouses, shop, café, etcetera close at six in the summer months, but of course the gardens themselves actually never do. They're wide open all along the coastal path. There's a fence of sorts, but it keeps getting broken down and they've stopped replacing it. Uniform are for ever moving on winos, glue-sniffers and fornicating couples.'

'Ah,' Maxwell made light of it. 'What would you boys do for a living without Leighford High School?'

'Which means,' Jacquie ignored him. 'Henderson was dumped, if that's what happened, between six and nine-thirty when the body was found.'

'But it was still pretty light at nine-thirty last night. Astley's being logical, but not accurate. Whoever our boy is, he dumped him in daylight. He's taking a hell of a chance.'

'Perhaps that's it,' Jacquie looked up at him suddenly. 'A thrill killer. He's testing us, taunting us even. He's saying "Look, I can kill where I want, how I want and leave my work in broad daylight. What are you going to do about it?"'

'"Catch me when you can, Mr Lusk,"' Maxwell said, his mind suddenly far away.

'What?'

'The Ripper,' he reminded her. 'One of the crackpot letters purporting to be from the Whitechapel Murderer back in the Autumn of Terror. Serial killers?' he asked her. '"Funny little games"?' He was quoting again.

'There must be a link,' Jacquie said. She was on her feet now, rinsing out the cocoa cup, *doing* stuff. Her brain had got over the initial numbness; she was back on the case. 'David Taylor and Gerald Henderson.'

'Brainstorm?' he asked her.

She checked the kitchen clock. Nolan would be awake in half an hour and he did hate his breakfast goodies to be spoiled by the 'zicker zicker' of criminal conversation. The other problem was that Peter Maxwell's brain was bigger than hers. But she consoled herself that her reflexes were faster.

'Heads or tails?' she whipped a coin from her pocket and tossed it. He caught it and slapped it down between his hands, 'Not *that* coin,' he said. 'I choose tails.' He opened his hands again.

'Tails it is,' she told him in wide-eyed innocence. 'Who do you want to be?' She was practising for when he was finally in the Home for Retired Teachers.

'Henderson.'

'You go first.'

'Haunted house,' he quipped. He and Jacquie had played this game before. 'Gerald Henderson. Rich as Croesus. Money comes from the building trade. Lives in Tottingleigh in a house about five hundred times the size of this one. Has a pool like an inland sea.'

'Wife?' Jacquie had flicked the kettle on. Then was cocoa time. Now it was coffee. Keep awake. Move it all on. Push the boundaries.

'Fiona. Attractive woman.'

'Oh?' She arched an eyebrow, in a jealous housewife sort of way.

'...if you like that sort of thing. Daughter, Katie, at boarding school.'

'No longer has an au pair,' Jacquie added.

'Indeed,' Maxwell nodded. 'But then, who has?'

'Kind of bloke?' she prompted him, sensing Maxwell going off the point.

'Based on half an hour's meeting, Christ knows. Er…full of himself. Self-made man. Decision-maker.'

'Taurus,' Jacquie commented.

'Bollocks!' the great man snorted. 'We're not talking about the Zodiac killer here, Jacqueline. Stay with the plot.'

'All right. My man.'

'David Taylor.'

'Known as Wide Boy. Petty crook.'

'Domicile?' Maxwell checked.

'Wherever he hung his hat, basically, but most recently, Brighton.'

'Not exactly Graham Greene, though, was he?'

Jacquie wasn't quite sure who Graham Greene was, so she let it go. 'He's got more previous than History, an ex who hates his guts and a kid who worships him.'

'Does he have a link with Leighford? With Dead Man's Point?'

'None known at the moment,' she told him. 'But I bet he came here as a kid.'

'Yes, indeed.' Everybody did. Either Leighford or the Isle of Wight. Take your pick. The Island might have dinosaurs and Blackgang Chine, but they couldn't compete with Willow Bay, the Shingle, the Little Folks' Castle. And now, Leighford could add another attraction to the Tourist Board's glossy literature – the murder scenes at Dead Man's Point. 'So our first boy's a bit of a lad, eh?'

'The Brighton boys have had reason to invite him to the station for a good smacking a few times,' she concluded. 'Some of them see the light, eventually write their memoirs, do charitable work in the East End.'

'Yes, but we're not talking about coppers now,' Maxwell said. 'Perhaps that was Taylor's intention,' he reasoned. 'To grass somebody up big time. Perhaps he had seen the light – a born-again type. Perhaps he was just a man who knew too much.'

'We're working on that,' Jacquie said. 'Pursuing, as we persist in saying, our enquiries. Nothing yet.'

There was a sudden cry over the baby alarm, followed by a gurgle as Nolan Carpenter-Maxwell rediscovered his toes all over again and found them fascinating. Maxwell was on his feet.

'No,' she held his arm. 'I'll go.'

He smiled and patted her hand, kissing her on the nose. He understood. She needed to smell his neck again, to nuzzle into that beautiful fairies' knitting hair and to watch his face light up as he saw her for the first time all over again. He understood.

'You know, Donald,' Jim Astley said. 'It only seems the other day we were doing this very same thing.'

Donald grunted. He'd got his NVQ in swabbing down mortuary slabs, but he was, after several years of it, beginning to wonder wistfully what people meant when they talked of job satisfaction. He'd wanted to be an undertaker really, but his Careers Teacher had recoiled in disgust and few people talked to him after that without a sideways glance. Besides, these days they didn't make black suits big enough.

'Tell the nice man what we've found.'

The nice man was DCI Henry Hall, sitting behind Jim Astley in the corner of the morgue, a discreet distance from the mortal remains of Gerald Henderson. He wasn't exactly squeamish, was Henry, but he didn't have the gung-ho, viscera-and-all attitude of some of his colleagues, up to their elbows in somebody else's body cavity.

'We have a middle-aged Caucasian male,' Donald said, consulting the clipboard and its bloodstained contents. 'Certain signs of high blood pressure, cholesterol…'

'Cut to the chase, Donald, dear boy.' Astley switched off the light strapped to his forehead and gratefully pulled the contraption off. He sank down on a stool, going head-to-toe with his sciatica at the moment. Unfortunately, the sciatica was winning. 'Mr Hall will be retiring in forty years or so.'

'Mr Henderson was killed in a knife attack.' The fat man flicked over the page. 'Six cuts to the torso, the deepest of them twelve point five centimetres. Judging from the pattern, our man is right handed, pretty strong.' He looked up at Hall. 'And pretty annoyed.'

'*Crime passionelle*?' Hall asked.

Donald thought you found those in a box of Black Magic, but he didn't want to commit himself.

'It's likely.' Astley prised off his bloodied rubber gloves and consigned them to the pedal bin. 'Is there something you're not telling us, Henry? Was Gerald Henderson not as other south coast builders?'

'I'm not telling you anything, Jim,' Hall said, shrugging.

'Because at this precise moment, I don't know anything. What about the murder weapon?'

'Single-edged blade,' Donald was sure. 'About two point five centimetres, but tapering.'

'Typical cook's knife,' Astley added. 'My money's on Anthony Worrall Thompson.'

Wasn't everybody's?

'The second strike killed him,' Donald told them. 'Severed the aorta. He bled to death.'

'But not in Leighford Botanical Gardens?' Hall checked.

'No.' Astley was certain. 'Not enough blood. No, somebody killed him elsewhere, I'd say indoors, and carried him to the rhododendron bushes.'

Hall nodded. 'The question is why.'

'And the question is how,' Donald blurted, enthused until the cold eyes of his seniors knocked some of the stuffing out of him. 'I mean, he weighed fifteen stone.' That was nothing to Donald, but he secretly knew he didn't envy anyone trying to carry *his* corpse across open country.

'Where's the nearest access point, Henry?' Astley asked. 'For a car, I mean?'

'To where we found him?' Hall was reconstructing the Gardens in his mind. 'The official car park is on the high ground, inland from the coastal path by half a mile. Whoever brought him there would have to have carried him down the steps, across the beds and up the slope. Must be half a mile.'

'And if he kept to the paths, more.' Donald was in keen mode again, showing his superiors how wasted he was swabbing down and making notes for Dr Astley.

'If he hadn't kept to the paths, Donald,' Astley sighed, 'Mr

Hall's eagle-eyed boys in blue would have noticed. Bloody great hoofprints all over the mesembryanthemums, a trail of blood across the chrysanthemums. Am I right, Henry? Or is my gargantuan grasp of all this flora passing you by?'

Hall nodded, conceding to the first question, not the second. 'We're combing the Gardens now. Chester Harris is not best pleased.'

'Harris?'

'Head Botanist.'

'God, yes. The David Bellamy of Leighford. He's mad as a tree, isn't he?'

'Doesn't suffer fools gladly, certainly, but then, when push comes to shove, which of us does?' It was perhaps coincidence that both men chose that moment to look at Donald.

'Well, good luck with that one,' Astley said. 'What if the body was brought the other way, from the Point?'

'Further,' Hall told him. 'But easier going with a weight like that. Except for a hundred yards or so where the ground is uneven. It depends how far it was brought. The Star Rock stretch is tricky, but someone with determination...'

'Both so exposed though, aren't they? Whichever way the body was carried it had to be in virtually broad daylight. What've we got on time of death, Donald?'

Donald was secretly seething. He'd been the butt-end of many a vicious lecture from his boss on this very theme. Whole books had been written about it. And science seemed to be walking backwards. And here was the crafty old bastard tossing it out as if it was the simplest call in the world. And the call was Donald's. 'Um...probably about twenty-four hours, give or take.'

Henry Hall had been giving and taking Jim Astley's times of death now for more years than he cared to remember. He knew as well as the other two that Donald had been stitched up and he wasn't going to rise to the bait. 'Wednesday afternoon,' the DCI took it all at face value, a science becoming more impressive as time itself went on. 'The question then remains,' he said. 'Where was Gerald Henderson on Wednesday afternoon?'

'Can you tell us, Chief Inspector, where the deceased was on Wednesday afternoon, which you've pinpointed as the time of death?'

Henry Hall was used to the popping cameras, the barrage of unanswerable questions, the microphones jabbed under his nose. But the Chief Constable of West Sussex, a man for whom no photo shoot was too little or too large, had insisted, so here they were, in Leighford Town Hall, courtesy of the Mayor.

Mayor Godfrey Ledbetter was there in person, mercifully without his chain of office, far less useful in police terms than a chain of evidence. He was a large figure in the mould of Donald, the Morgue Man, but he had his eye to the main chance and could afford decent suits. And he dithered now between a look of suitably abject shock and horror and wondering how he could cash in on behalf of his town. 'This way to the Murderers' Walk.' 'See the Dead Man at Dead Man's Point.' It was a licence to print money. Forget Ian Huntley, Fred and Rose West. Once the law had got this nutter behind bars, Ledbetter would be able to slap a Grade II listing on his house. My God, how the money would roll in!

'My officers are pursuing every enquiry,' Hall gave the stock, bland response.

'What I want to know, Chief Inspector,' a loud voice came from the far corner, 'is what you're going to do by way of compensation for my Gardens.'

There were howls and cat calls. 'Shut up, Harris,' somebody bellowed.

'Now is not the time, Mr Harris,' the Chief Constable, all brushed tunic and flashing silver braid replied.

'It never is,' Harris shouted back. 'Funny that.'

'Get some perspective,' somebody else shouted. 'Two people are dead here. Who gives a damn about your flowers?'

'Who said that?' Chester Harris wanted to know. He suspected the paparazzo from the *Sun*, and was making a beeline for him when two of Henry Hall's men intercepted him and bundled him out of the room, like an old geranium.

'Two people,' another journalist barked at Hall. 'Do we have a serial killer on our hands, Chief Inspector? Who's at risk?'

Hall resisted the temptation to lean forward to the middle-aged man and say 'Middle-Aged Men'. Besides, his attention was drawn to an altogether younger man who was standing near the far door. He didn't appear to be a journalist, though he had a visitor's pass pinned to his rather incongruous hoodie. He was slim and fair-haired. And his fierce, close-set eyes had been burning into Henry Hall all night.

'We are unable to speculate at this time,' Hall said. And by the time he'd finished the sentence, the young man had gone. The Chief Inspector passed to his boss, the Chief Constable, to wind things up with the usual platitudes. After that, it would be up to Ledbetter to undo all their good calming work and whip up the sort of hysteria that sold hotel rooms and cream teas. He was, after all, a child of the Thatcher years and he had Private Enterprise written all over him. But by then, the Chief Constable would have left to put his expensive uniform back into moth balls and the Chief Inspector would have left to do his best to catch a killer. It was as well that everybody knew their place.

The little boy's head lay soft on the pillow, the stars of his night-light twirling silently across the ceiling of his room. His dad bent down to kiss him and the boy murmured, his lips opening with a little bubble.

He left the boy, he left the cot, he took three paces through the room. Across the landing, the woman he loved was sleeping too. With a bit of luck, it would be years before she'd start snoring, but she'd never lose that look, the one that said, 'I'm safe here with you; and I'm glad I'm here with you,' and she smiled in her sleep. He tip-toed up the stairs to his Inner Sanctum, gently closing the trap door of the War Office before he switched on the modeller's lamp. He hauled the ornate, gold-laced pillbox cap from its peg and popped it on at a jaunty Crimean angle on his head. He couldn't remember, after all these years, where he'd bought it. Probably fetch a few bob at Bosley's when he finally fell on the hard, old times of retirement. He looked down at Lieutenant Landriani under his magnifying glass. Give the man a cigar, surely? He'd be sitting his plastic charger a long way from Colonel Shewell of the 8th, who didn't approve of such things. And anyway, Landriani was in a different army, from a different country.

He was there in the Valley of Death that long-ago October as an observer, for God's sake. The usual rules didn't apply to him.

A great black and white beast stirred in the half-light.

'Sorry, Count,' Maxwell muttered, reaching for his craft scalpel. 'Didn't see you there.'

Like hell you didn't; Metternich stretched out a leg and licked his inner thigh, just because he knew Maxwell couldn't – however much he might long to.

'I talked to a widow yesterday, Count,' Maxwell went on, whittling the plastic as he did so. 'Except she didn't know she was a widow. Or did she?' He placed the plastic against the soldier's lips. Relatively, it was the size of a torpedo. Just a *little* off that. 'What do you think of them apples, Count? Could a woman who had just stabbed her husband to death sit casually by her swimming pool with me and engage in small talk about a Spanish lady?'

Maxwell looked up at the cold, unblinking, smouldering eyes. 'Well, don't rush to judgement just now, will you?' he said. 'Of course,' he offered up the cigar again. Better – it was more like a baguette now. 'It is just possible that the late Gerald Henderson was lying, saturated in his own blood – now don't look at me like that. You positively revel in the stuff – you're the Green River Killer of Leighford. Lying in his own blood in the master bedroom, feet from where I was sitting. But for that to be the scenario, Fiona Henderson would have to have gone berserk, done the heinous deed, stabbing the poor bugger however many times, then hosed herself down, because she would have been pretty well spattered I would think, chatted to me in her polite, slightly Essex-girl sort of way, then tossed the husband formerly known as Gerald into her Lexus Estate or whatever, driven like a bat out of Hell to the Botanical Gardens, hoisted the dead weight for a second time and stuffed it under the rhododendron bushes. Perfect!'

And they both knew that Peter Maxwell was talking about the relative size of the plastic cigar rather than his likely case scenario. That needed more work.

CHAPTER EIGHT

George Bronson had never got used to it; perhaps he never would. He was sitting bolt upright in the palatial lounge built by the late Gerald Henderson, looking into the clear blue eyes of the late Gerald Henderson's wife.

'It must have been Wednesday morning that I saw him last.' She was taking her time to answer the DI's question because she wanted to get it right. Part of her said, 'What was the point? He was dead anyway.' She knew that. She'd been to identify him in the morgue. She'd looked at his face, how curiously pale it was, how still. Somebody had covered the body right up to the neck and placed a lily on the pillow beside his head. She didn't know it was all done to cover up the gruesome stitching of Jim Astley; the Y-shaped incision and big, clumsy stitches vying with the six tell-tale wounds that had punctured his body. Peter Maxwell knew that in Geoffrey Chaucer's day people believed a dead man's wounds bled anew in the presence of his murderer. Fiona Henderson didn't know that. And she wouldn't have believed it anyway.

'Was that here, at home?' Bronson was taking her through it, slowly, methodically. Sheila Kindling was sitting alongside him, noting down both her boss's questions and the answers he was getting.

'Yes. He'd come in late the night before and had slept in the East Wing. He has...had a sort of den there. We had breakfast. He said he had to be at Danton's.'

'Danton's?' Bronson knew the name, but he needed confirmation.

'Suppliers to the trade. In the High Street. Smaller than Jewson's, but Gerald and Will Danton go back a long way.'

'Do you know what time this was, Mrs Henderson?' Sheila asked. 'The meeting with Mr Danton?'

'Er...eleven, eleven-thirty. I can't really remember. Look, Inspector, I need to know – who could do this to Gerald? It's all so unreal.'

Fiona Henderson turned to Bronson because he was a man. It was the way she'd been brought up. Ever a daddy's girl, she simply accepted that men had the answers. That was why she'd never gone to university when she had the chance. What was the point? She'd marry some rich man and he'd take care of her – it was the natural order of things. But the rich man had gone now. Now what would she do?

'That's what we're trying to find out, Mrs Henderson.' Bronson hated this, every sickening twist of it; talking to a woman whose husband had been butchered as if they were discussing the price of tea. 'Tell me, is there anyone who didn't get on with your husband? A disgruntled employee, perhaps? Business rival?'

Fiona Henderson shrugged. She was already staring at the photo of the two of them together. When was that? Five years ago already? Katie was only three. There she was in the silver frame, laughing hysterically as her daddy tickled her, her face a mass of ice cream. Then, darker thoughts prevailed. 'I don't know,' she said. 'I think Gerald could be a hard man. He didn't take prisoners. I don't pretend to understand the business world, but I do know it's dog eat dog. Gerald had enemies, certainly, in a commercial sense. Perhaps one or two of his developments were a little…shall we say, controversial? But to be killed?' She suddenly sat bolt upright, breathing in sharply, 'No,' she said flatly. 'It just doesn't make sense.'

By Friday lunchtime, Henry Hall's team had been given permission to poke their noses into Gerald Henderson's financial affairs. The bank wasn't very forthcoming and the deceased's accounting firm seemed at one time to have worked for Al Capone. Even so, it was a foot in the door, a start. Who knew where it would lead?

Coppers were pounding pavements by two o'clock, drafted in from elsewhere in the county. Any old hands watching them work would have tutted and shaken their heads in disbelief. They were in shirtsleeves, for God's sake and there were *women* with them. All walkie-talkies and political correctness and community policing. Bloody get on with it. Ask your questions. Look them in the face and get some answers. Don't faff about on a computer – write it down in your black book and type up the bloody report later. Jesus! How hard can it be?

'Have you seen this man?' echoed and re-echoed around the scorching streets of Leighford. Fiona Henderson had lent George Bronson a recent photograph of Gerald. It was not the one with the ice cream, but a rather po-faced affair of him getting some award or other from the Chamber of Commerce. She'd never really liked that suit. Or the fact that the nauseating creep Godfrey Ledbetter was hovering in the background.

And so the questions multiplied. The knocks on the doors. The rings on the bells. Here a dog barked. A baby cried. 'Who is it?' the old dear in sheltered accommodation wanted to know. And the coppers weren't sure whether she meant them or the man in the photograph.

'Louise?' She turned at the sound of her name. 'Louise Bedford!'

Ocean's Eleven had been everything in its time – a bank, a trendy wine bar. Kelly's Directory for 1851 had hinted it might be a bordello in that rooms were to be had, usually by the hour; probably hired by foreigners on their way to the Great Exhibition. Now, it was a café, bright and breezy with aluminium furniture, nasty coffee and more varieties of ice cream than the parson preached about.

'Mr Maxwell.' The girl behind the counter beamed broadly. She'd always liked Mad Max, ever since she'd first set eyes on him when she was eleven and he was ninety-four. It was crush at first sight. He was so funny, so clever and looked a bit like her mum's favourite pin-up, Tom Conti. But she'd really fallen for him when he'd saved her from a couple of bullies in Year Eleven that time. She never did find out what he actually did, but both lads vanished behind the Sports Hall one day and when she saw them next they were pale and shaking. They never bothered her again. And they'd never bothered Peter Maxwell in the first place. Was he bothered?

'Don't tell me that university of yours has let you out already? What am I paying my taxes for?'

''Fraid so,' she trilled. 'What can I get you?'

He perused the list above the girl's head. It was longer than Schindler's. 'I could just go a Chocolate Nut Sundae,' he beamed, as about the only item he vaguely recognised. 'Seeing as how it's Friday and I've just done a runner from the Establishment.'

'Are you still there?' she asked, fiddling about with impossible-looking machinery that clicked and whirred and squirted.

Maxwell wondered why all Old Leighford Highenas asked that. The girl had only been gone for less than a year, but in that weird timewarp that is being nineteen/twenty, it might have been decades.

''Fraid so,' he winked at her. And he didn't go on to add that James 'Legs' Diamond was still Mr Ineffectual as the Headmaster; Bernard Ryan was still the Grima Wormtongue of the staffroom; and Dierdre Lessing's hair still coiled like venomous serpents as she floated like a ghoul, hovering in the foul air between the Dining Hall and the Girls' Changing Rooms.

Maxwell looked around. Surprisingly empty for a Friday afternoon in the middle of the season. 'Have you got a minute?' he asked.

'A minute?' She looked surprised.

'Join me in the old Chocolate Nut?'

She leaned towards him, more confident, more of a woman than he remembered. 'It's not allowed,' she said with a bass voice that surprised both of them. 'I'll be drummed out of the Ice Cream Makers' Union.'

'Well,' he smiled. 'Just a coffee, then.'

'OK.' She smiled back and went about her business, chatting briefly to the incurably spotty lad who was her oppo behind the counter.

Maxwell led her to a quiet corner. This was, of course, as much of a chance meeting as Hitler's invasion of Poland. He wanted answers and this was just the Old Girl who might provide them. 'Course going well?' he asked, not for the life of him able to remember what the kid was reading or where.

'Great, thanks.' She sipped her coffee, and as if reading his mind, added, 'Social Sciences, Exeter.'

'Any exams or anything?'

Her face contorted. 'Oh, yes. They were OK, though.'

Peter Maxwell had spent the best part of seven years persuading Louise Bedford not to say 'OK'. After all, it was American. And hadn't that very same Peter Maxwell made it perfectly clear that we had fought a war with the Colonies so that we'd never have to hear – or use – that kind of language again? Was it all for nothing? What kind of education were they getting at university these days?

'I hate to mention the subject,' he said, 'but John…'

'Yes,' her face lit up at the mention of his name. 'We're still together and he's lovely.'

'Good for you.' Maxwell was genuinely pleased. He still remembered his first year of teaching, when Mr Gladstone was Prime Minister and Boy Scouts still helped old ladies across roads – whether they wanted to go or not – he'd raised just the same question with a couple who had been an item for years. 'Going to the same place, are you?' the callow youth had asked. The lad had shaken his head and the girl had run out of the room crying. He hadn't risked it since, but sensed he was on safer ground with John and Louise.

'I understand the pair of you had a rather unpleasant experience last night.'

Louise's face fell. The eyes, shining with happiness, glanced down to her coffee cup. 'Who told you?' she asked.

'A little bird.' He licked the chocolate sauce off his spoon.

Her eyes were on him again. 'We...we found a body,' she said softly. She'd never been able to lie to Mad Max. Not when she hadn't done her homework in Year Ten; not when she and John had been found canoodling in the Textiles Stock Cupboard.

'Louise,' Maxwell reached out and brushed her hand. 'Look, you and I go back a long while, yes?'

She nodded.

'I owe you this much,' he said. 'I didn't just happen to be here this afternoon.'

A flicker passed across her face. She suddenly didn't understand. There was something about her Mr Maxwell now. An intensity she hadn't seen before. And it scared her, just a little.

'My narks in Year 13 told me you worked here. I wanted a chat.'

'About the body?'

He nodded.

Louise looked alarmed, her eyes flicking left and right. When she was an adolescent with a crush on 'sir', she'd have given anything to have him hold her hand as he was now. Now, she wished he'd go away. Leave her alone.

'The Gardens,' Maxwell said. 'Do you go there often? You and John?'

'We used to,' she said. 'It's sort of…our place. Do you know what I mean?'

Maxwell did.

'Do you know who the man was?' he asked. 'The dead man?'

A family came in at that moment, all whining children and buckets and spades.

'I've got to go,' she told him. 'I've got to serve people.'

'"To serve them all my days",' Maxwell quoted. 'Louise, I'm sorry. I don't mean to frighten you. And I don't want to make you feel uncomfortable. But two men have died in Leighford in the last week.'

'I've talked to the police,' she said, half out of her seat.

'I know,' he nodded. 'But sometimes the police aren't the people who listen best. Sometimes, they don't hear things. Do you understand?'

Louise was on her feet now, 'No, Mr Maxwell,' she shook her head. 'No, I don't understand. And I don't know anything. Now, please, I must get back to work.'

And she'd gone, crashing through the swing doors into the kitchen. And Peter Maxwell knew by the heaving of her shoulders that he'd made the girl cry.

'To whom am I talking?'

'Aaron Felton, Deputy Head.'

'Aaron, you old bastard. Peter Maxwell.'

'Max. How's it hanging?'

Maxwell resisted the old Jim Carrey joke from *Liar! Liar!* and offered an alternative. 'Fine, thanks.' Yes, all right – it needed work. 'I've been hearing odd things about your Rodrigo Mendoza.'

Time for Aaron Felton to resist jokes and he did it manfully. 'Oh?'

'I understand he's gone missing.'

'Missing? Who told you that?'

'A little bird.'

'Well...come to think of it,' Hampton's Deputy said, 'he did go walkabout for a couple of days. Went down, appropriately enough, with Montezuma's Revenge. Apparently, he was talking on the big white telephone for several hours at a time.'

'Canteen food?' Maxwell guessed.

'What else? That's the great thing about Healthy Schools. We haven't all got to suffer Jamie Bloody Oliver. Do you know Rodrigo, then?'

'We've met,' Maxwell said. 'In the line of duty.'

'I'm not sure he's on site at the moment. Let's see...' There was a rustling of paper as the man tried to relocate his desk top. 'No, you've missed him. He's gone with a trip to Chessington – a special thank you to Year Nine for their Recycling efforts. Was it always like this, Max? When you were a teacher?'

'You cheeky bugger,' Maxwell chuckled. 'No, it was stand up straight and put your hands down your trousers in my day. Recycling was going home from school. I don't envy you young people with another thirty-odd years to go in the business.'

'Oh, God,' Felton groaned weakly and hung up.

Maxwell was already striding purposefully towards the Modern Languages Block.

* * *

A pall of smoke hung over Henry Hall's Incident Room. At the moment he was merely using the Nick, but many more enquiries and he'd either have to have an extension built or move out, commandeering schools and libraries and cinemas and youth clubs as he had in the past.

This was Day Eight of the Taylor murder and Day Three of the Henderson case. There was that rise in tension, that indefinable *something* that teetered on panic. For now, everybody was calm, in check, going about their business. But the smoking had increased, spilling over into areas strictly beyond the agreed limits of the Incident Room. The black coffee drinking almost doubled. There was less patience with computers – you could tell that by the noise of rattle on the keys; fingers stabbing harder and the greater incidence of sucked-in breath and the immortal words 'For shit's sake!' And people were getting snappier with each other; never a good sign. One murder gave you headaches. Two doubled the chance of finding the killer, if the killer was singular; but it also doubled the stress. The Press were already breathing down the guv'nor's neck. The beady eye of the Chief Constable was fully on the Incident Room at Leighford Nick.

'Links, people,' Henry Hall was lolling against his desk, the coastal map on the PowerPoint behind him.

'Distance.' Sheila Kindling must be bucking for promotion, biro behind her ear.

'Go on.'

The DC smoothed down her skirt before she waddled to the front. In her first week as a detective, she'd got the damn thing caught up in her knickers, with the inevitable result. No wolf whistles this time; no 'get 'em off, darling,' so she assumed all was well. She just remembered to whip the biro off her head.

'If we go by road from Dead Man's Point to the Gardens, that's the best part of two miles. But by the coastal path, *much* shorter. That's how it was done.'

'Why?' George Bronson wasn't convinced.

'How busy is the path?' Hall still wanted to know. 'Anybody followed up on this?'

Benny Palister had. 'The National Parks Authority did a survey in the area two years ago. The average age of a coastal path walker is fifty-three. There were six accidents in 2004 and three examples of litigation costing the taxpayer...'

'Benny,' Hall cut in softly, rather like the Policeman's Excuse Me. 'Is this going anywhere?'

'Sorry, guv. It's all they've got.'

'Right,' Hall sighed. 'So we're back to common sense. Timings. Jacquie?'

'We've nothing conclusive on Taylor, guv,' she said. 'We can only assume he was buried after dark since broad daylight would be a little risky.'

'And Henderson?'

'He must have been dumped in the bushes at dusk.' Geoff Hare was stabbing out his fag. 'Same reason.'

'Why not night?' Jacquie checked him.

'That's the big one, people,' Hall nodded. 'And we're going round in circles on this.'

'Perhaps our boy's got a death wish. Wants to be caught.'

It wouldn't be the first time. Jacquie knew it. Hall knew it. Benny Palister knew it now, although he didn't before. Shrewd lad was Benny; he watched his elders and betters and he *learnt*. Peter Maxwell would have been proud of him.

'He could give himself up,' Hare shrugged. 'Save us all a bloody job.'

'Ah, but then there'd be no fun,' Bronson grinned. 'No sense of challenge. And think of the overtime you'd be losing.'

Sniggers all round. Geoff Hare was the Scrooge of Leighford Nick. The sort of bloke who checks the collection plate in church for signs of stolen goods, then passes it on.

'Links,' Hall was nothing if not persistent.

'Bing-go!' Sheila Kindling had gone back to her seat now, her attempt to trace the trajectory of the killer having been somewhat sidelined. Now her arm was in the air, like a kid desperate for a pee. Bronson and Hare were unimpressed. Women on the Force, sure, but why couldn't they all be like Jacquie Carpenter? But all eyes were on the girl, so presumably she was happy enough, pen behind her ear again. 'Gerald Henderson did a building job last year – in Brighton.'

'And?' Hall was waiting for the other shoe to fall.

'His client was one James Doolan.'

'Jimmy the Snail,' somebody muttered. Somebody else whistled. Everybody was secretly impressed. Sheila tried not to preen too much.

'Well done,' Hall said. 'Did you talk to Mrs Henderson about this...George?'

'Didn't know about it then, guv,' the DI had to admit, a little shamefaced. 'We can go back.'

'Jacquie, you do it. Can you get there this afternoon?'

'Yes, guv.' She didn't even look at her watch. This was the first breakthrough they'd had and everybody knew it.

'Good. What's the lab got for us, Geoff?'

Hare was well into his next ciggie, but he waited for the

smoke to clear from his eyes first. 'The lab says Taylor was killed in a vehicle, guv.'

One or two people in the room hadn't got the goss on that yet, so the murmurs rippled like the sunlight shafts between the venetian blind slats.

'And he was naked?' Hall checked.

'Astley thinks he was naked at the time of death, yes.'

'Naked in a car.' Hall was underlining it for everybody.

'*Cherchez la femme*,' George Bronson crowed. He'd been to a Language College. 'Assuming *femmes* were Taylor's thing.'

'That's exactly what we're doing,' Hall said. 'What's the lab got on the car?'

'His own, guv. Merc. Clapped out,' Hare told him. 'Either that or the fibres came from another vehicle of the same age and make.'

'What are the odds?' somebody muttered.

'All right.' Hall was piecing it together. 'So let's assume Wide Boy was enjoying a little R and R in the back of his car...'

'Front, guv,' Jacquie said.

'Don't tell me there's a difference between the fibres of back and front car seats.' Hare couldn't believe it.

'I'm not telling you anything of the sort, Geoffrey.' Jacquie could bridle for England when the mood took her. 'Astley now thinks Taylor was strangled from behind, not from the side. And with quite a bit of leverage involved. So unless our man was sitting with the nodding dog on the shelf, Wide Boy was sitting in the front.'

Whistles and a ripple of applause. Collapse of stout sergeant.

'Anything similar on Henderson?' Hall brought the moment to a halt.

'Definitely killed in his clothes, guv,' Hare said. 'The blood pattern is very distinct. Shirt, trousers. And he was standing up.'

'Attack from the front?' Hall's mind was focusing, but it was George Bronson who got there first.

'We're talking about two different killers, surely.'

'Go on, George.'

'Taylor is killed, naked, in his car, from behind, using a ligature – some instrument inserted in the loop of his crucifix until life was extinct. Henderson, fully clothed, standing up, so presumably not in a car, by six stabs of a knife. Different MO, different scenario, different direction. Hey presto, two killers.'

'Yet,' Hall reminded them, 'two middle-aged men, bodies found a stone's throw apart. And they knew each other. Jacquie, get your wheels out as *The Sweeney* taught us to say. In the meantime, people, keep probing. I want the last known movements of both men on my system by chucking out time. Clear?'

It was.

'No, it wasn't just that,' Maxwell was sprawled on his settee, getting a Southern Comfort down his neck. 'No, Louise Bedford was definitely rattled.'

'Can you wonder at it?' Jacquie asked him, sipping her more modest red wine. 'Crusty old fart of a teacher she hasn't seen for the best part of a year comes the heavy and starts asking about dead bodies. I'd run a mile.'

'Thanks, heart of darkness,' he grunted. 'And less of the old, if you don't mind. I can still give Mr Burns a run for his money. Doh!' and he slapped his head in a perfect Homer Simpson.

'You were out of line, Max,' she shook her head. 'What did you hope to learn?'

'There you have me,' Maxwell confessed, watching the lamplight glow in the clear amber of the glass. 'You and I, angel face, belong to that exclusive and slightly shell-shocked club called The People Who've Stumbled On Bodies. You in your line of work. And me? Well, just lucky, I guess. Louise has joined that club now. There's no doubt about it – you're never the same again.'

'But she'd already had a grilling, Max,' Jacquie told him. 'Me, the first uniform at the scene, Henry Hall. She'd had a bellyful on the night in question. She didn't need you adding to it all.'

Maxwell looked up at her. 'Do I sense a little bit of needle here, Woman Policeman? What is this? All girls together?'

'It's nothing to do with that, Max.' She finished her drink. 'It's that old problem of yours, not being able to keep your nose out.'

It was her turn to look at him. She put the glass down and coiled herself on the arm of the settee, cradling his neck. 'Darling,' she said. 'I know it's difficult. You and Louise go back a long way. Hell, you and I go back about the same time – though hopefully in a rather different capacity.' She raised an eyebrow at him and they both laughed.

'Body language,' Maxwell hugged her with his non-glass-holding hand. 'That's what it's all about. All right, you're right of course, I shouldn't have gone snooping. But having done it, I somehow opened a can of worms. No doubt she was shaken by the whole thing and no doubt, she didn't want to relive it. But there was something more. I can't explain it.'

'Max,' Jacquie was firm. 'Promise me you'll stay away from the kid. It's none of your business and you'll only get yourself into trouble. It's been touch and go so far, but one day Henry Hall is going to reach that distant end of his tether and you won't know what day it is. I just don't want that to happen, sweetheart. Not to you. 'Cos,' she kissed him on the forehead, 'if it happens to you, it happens to me too.'

'Well, there it is, Count. The official kiss off from my good lady partner. Tears and fears from a former student who used to be Little Miss Cheerful. Two men on a dead man's point. Yo ho ho and a barrel of laughs.'

Maxwell caught the narrowed yellow eyes in the gloom of his Inner Sanctum at the top of the stairs. That and the single sweep of the tail, like a car's rear wiper on intermittent. 'No, you're right,' he said. 'Not exactly a moment of high comedy, is it? And I have done a better Robert Newton in my time.'

He hung the pillbox on its familiar peg, squeezing his tired eyes. It had been a long academic year and Mr Retirement was staring him in the face.

'Do you know the Point at all, Count? Bit far for your nightly range, isn't it? Great field mice out that way, though, I shouldn't wonder. No, it's no good.' He switched off his modeller's lamp. 'I'll just have to research it myself. Oh shit!' and he saw extra stars as he caught his temple a nasty one on the way out.

CHAPTER NINE

In the beginning, God created librarians. It was on the third day, between plants bearing seeds of their kind and trees bearing fruits, all the vegetable kingdom in one place. It gave them all a rather superior air, as if they were the Chosen People. Time was when they'd behaved like Kipling's Silent People, pursing their lips behind upright fingers if somebody so much as sniffed. Maxwell could accept all that – it was, after all, part of the Old England of regular, multiple postal deliveries, little blue sachets of salt in crisps and aircraft going bang when they hurtled through the sound barrier. What Maxwell could not accept, however, was the supine dumbing down, the meek acceptance that nobody read books any more. So now, the Chosen People allowed videos and DVDs on the shelves and the Dewey Decimal Sytem began with Arnie Schwarzenegger. Not that Maxwell objected to *films* – they were his lifelong interest, but you shouldn't be able to borrow them from a book depository. He might as well go to his local undertaker's to watch one, or perhaps his beautiful launderette. Come to think of it, it wasn't *that* beautiful the last time he'd looked.

Edna Roxbury saw it differently. She looked not unlike Elsa Lanchester in the *Bride of Dracula*, with a *retroussée* nose and wild, grey-streaked hair. She definitely saw herself as one of the Elect, that band of custodians of culture that had the key to the secret garden. And she noticed Peter Maxwell sneaking in, appropriately enough, past the gardening section.

'Aren't you Peter Maxwell?' She leaned over the counter like a gargoyle straight out of Notre Dame.

'I might be, I might be,' he chose to reply in his best Homer Simpson.

'You owe the library a maximum fee as a result of losing *Windows for Dummies* four years ago. We've sent you plenty of reminders.'

'Indeed you have,' Maxwell nodded, leaning on the woman's counter, echoing her posturally, 'and I have replied to all of them in like vein. "A window" – and I'm quoting now from my favourite reply – "is an opening, usually made of glass, which allows light into a room." Conversely – and again I quote "a dummy is a rubberoid instrument designed to soothe fractious babies by resembling a nipple." – Oh, dear, I've shocked you. The Americans call them pacifiers – dummies, that is, not nipples. Now, I am a man of the world, Librarian, and I am aware that the book to which you refer is neither about glass apertures in walls nor infant comforts. That may possibly give you some idea of the likelihood of my having borrowed the wretched thing in the first place. I am not now, nor have I ever been, remotely interested in computing.'

'Our records are never wrong.' Ms Roxbury bridled, furious at the man's arrogance.

'Oh, come now, dear lady.' Maxwell threw his arms wide. 'Your records are stored on the very machines we are talking about. A very wise man once told me you only get out of one of those contraptions what you put into it. His name was Bill Gates.'

'Meaning?' Ms Roxbury arched an eyebrow.

Maxwell surveyed the staff at Leighford Library. One was a hundred and sixty-eight years old. Another hadn't yet learned to shave. And the third was a combination of the two – Ms Roxbury.

'I rest my case,' Maxwell said. Then he froze and pulled himself up to his full height. 'Madam,' he said with a gravel that could freeze blood. 'You appear to have moved the Local History section.'

'County policy,' Ms Roxbury spoke with all the weight of local government behind her. 'Due to a lack of interest, alack, in local studies, all such material has been removed to Public Records.'

'Public…?' Maxwell was aghast. He closed to her, remembering to close his mouth, despite the shock of the news he'd just heard, praying that his heart was still beating. 'Are you telling me,' he asked, 'that you have placed priceless artefacts in the hands of Malcolm Desmond? Malcolm "eBay" Desmond? It defies belief. Not, you understand, that I know what "eBay" is.'

'All I wanted, Count,' Peter Maxwell was sprawled on his sofa, his infant son doggo on his chest, 'was to ascertain the local low-down on Dead Man's Point.'

The cat was unmoved. He had no idea where this place was or of its significance. It was just part of his Master's madness; you learned, in the end, to live with it.

'Yes, I know it's remarkable that libraries are open on Sundays, when in our day etcetera etcetera…' (it *was* a good

Yul Brynner in *The King and I*) 'but they do close on Thursdays by way of compensation, so let's not get *too* dewy-eyed about it. Or dewey-decimalled for that matter. The plain fact is, I'm no further forward.'

'Bedtime, young man.' Jacquie hurtled round the corner, a pile of fresh nappies under one arm.

'Young man,' Maxwell gurgled. 'How sweet you are.'

'Not you,' Jacquie scowled at him. 'Come on, little one.' She hauled Nolan up onto her other shoulder. 'Wooden hill to Bedfordshire time. You boys, human and feline, chew the fat for a while. Supper in half an hour, OK?'

'Wonderful, heart,' Maxwell said, reaching for the Southern Comfort he'd all but forgotten about. 'And don't say "OK". It's unbecoming of an officer and a lady.'

Metternich yawned. It had been a long, hot, summer's day, not exactly full of soda and pretzels and beer, because, to be brutally frank, he didn't really like those things. The leftover chicken was scrummy, though, for lunch, and he'd ambushed a vole for High Tea. He'd have liked a bit of a doze, but the sidewhiskered old fart would keep whittering on.

'You see, I can't help thinking,' Maxwell winced anew as the amber nectar hit his tonsils, 'that all this has to do with Steph Courtney and that rather bizarre little scene she witnessed at The Dam. But what *did* she see, Count, eh? Oh, you with your twenty-twenty hindsight vision wouldn't find it a problem, would you? But it was a *naked* body. And the good lady who shares this house with us let slip in an unguarded moment that David Taylor, spinster not of this parish, was killed while naked. Killed by a man and a woman. What's that, then? Some sort of Lonely Hearts re-creation? Oh, it's before your time, Count – two charmers called Beck and Fernandez lured lonely men with promises of nuptial bliss and killed them for their money. Anyhoo,' he heard the bedroom door click and Jacquie's feet on the stairs, 'that's enough about her. She's walking in.'

'That little man is really pooped,' Jacquie said. Maxwell poured her a large one as she reached ground level. 'Must be all that chicken.'

'Yep,' Maxwell agreed. 'Bit of a trencherman is our Nole. Well, heart – decision time.'

Jacquie flopped down in the chair opposite the sprawling mass that was her partner in crime. 'Tomorrow,' she said. '*Mañana*, isn't it?'

'You'll do it?' he asked her.

'I'm the one with the warrant card,' she smiled.

'I'm the one with the colleague who speaka da lingo.'

'Well, that's right,' Jacquie said. 'Do you know, I hadn't thought of that. You can get...thing to ring.'

'No, dearest,' Maxwell was patience itself. 'Thing – or to be accurate, Thing*ee* is the morning receptionist at Leighford High. Not to be confused with Thingee Two, who is on in the afternoons. They're both lovely people, but I'm not sure they're up for long distance calls to Menorca to ask a Spanish couple where the Hell their daughter is.'

'No, no,' Jacquie was getting her head around the Tia Maria, 'I was talking about that Spanish girl – what's her name? Carolina? She could do it. And if that doesn't work, I'll step in with my Interpol hat on.'

'And very nice you'll look, too,' Maxwell nodded sagely.

* * *

Sarah Rossiter didn't much like the look of the pallid young man with the hoodie who was sitting in the front office of the *Advertiser* whizzing through the microfiche on the screen. He had taken his hoodie off, to be fair, but even so, there was something about his stare that she didn't care for. And he'd asked to see anything they had on the Taylor murder. He had one of those annoying i-Pod things stuck in his ears, the bass coming through loud enough to bring on one of her heads. How he could hear anything with that noise going on she couldn't imagine. And not content with all that, he suddenly dashed out of the office, nearly bowling over the two journalists nattering in the doorway.

Bernard Ryan was in full cry that Monday morning as the eager Young Turks that were Leighford High students dragged themselves onto the premises.

'You're late.' He caught the eye of a hooded young man lurching along by the limes that shaded the gates. The Deputy Head wasn't *quite* sure whether he attended Leighford High or not, but dressed like that, he must have been one on Maxwell's Own. It was only nine o'two and the sun was already blazing. The lad under the hood must have been awash with sweat, but Peter Maxwell recognised the syndrome. Earlier forms of life had sacrificed all to be the slaves of fashion – broken ribs, ruptured diaphragms, infertility, blood poisoning – all in the name of looking one's best.

'Sorry, Mr Ryan,' Maxwell swung out of Surrey's saddle with a grace and agility surprising in one so old. 'The traffic's a nightmare on the Flyover this morning.'

'I didn't mean you, Max.' Ryan bridled as soon as the hoodie was out of earshot.

'No, really?' Maxwell was aghast. He toyed for a moment with handing the man Surrey to park, but he sensed that Bernard Ryan had probably reached the nadir of respect in this school as it was, and Peter Maxwell never kicked a man when he was down. Unless it was James Diamond, the Headmaster. 'Seen *Señorita* Vasquez this morning? Pretty creature apart from the nose? Flouncy dress and castanets?'

'Yes, I know who she is, Max. Don't you know the meaning of political correctness?'

Maxwell's look would have killed an older man. Or one more sensitive. As it was, Bernard Ryan was probably mid-to-late thirties, born in that deadly decade when education was already going to the dogs. When he was a young teacher they'd brought in Inclusion – Jack's as good as his master. He was still a young teacher when they'd invented Syndromes and naughty little buggers were found to have all kinds of disorders and deficiencies that not only explained, but excused their behaviour. And Bernard Ryan had swallowed it all, hook, line and sink school.

'Wash your mouth out, Bernard,' Maxwell bridled in hushed tones. 'And think yourself lucky that I'm not a bleeding victim of fucking Tourettes, that's pissing all.' He wheeled Surrey towards the Languages Block, turned and winked. 'You have a nice day, now, y'hear.'

'Smile and Come In' was written in various languages on the double doors. Maxwell parked Surrey at a rakish angle designed to trip up the German Assistant and obligingly pushed up the corners of his mouth. He tipped his hat to the CCTV camera overhead.

'Look at him,' snarled Dierdre Lessing, the Assistant Headteacher, Girls' Welfare, half a mile away in Reception, watching the screen monitors as she usually did at that time of the morning. 'What a reprobate.'

Thingee glanced up from her endlessly ringing phone. She *liked* Mr Maxwell. OK, he didn't know her name and he all but patted her bum given half a chance, but he was that vanishing breed, a gentleman and a scholar. And there had been one, magic day, when Thingee was very new, when Peter Maxwell had intervened when a particularly obstreperous parent had rung the school, complaining as particularly obstreperous parents will. She remembered every word of the dialogue. It was etched on her heart.

'Hello?'

'Hello? Who am I talking to?'

'Do you mean "To whom am I talking?" This is Peter Maxwell, Head of Sixth Form here at Leighford High. I have just taken the phone from the receptionist here to whom you have just been appallingly rude.'

'You what?'

'Whatever your beef is, low-life, take it elsewhere. All policy decisions at this school are taken by the Headteacher, Mr Diamond. Vent your spleen, if you must, on him, but do not, on any account, raise your voice or swear in the telephonic presence of our receptionist. And for the fact that you are able to make this call at all, thank a teacher.'

'You can't talk to me like that,' the disembodied parent had said.

'*Au contraire*, sir,' Maxwell responded. 'I just have. And if you call this number again with the attitude you currently hold, I think I can guarantee you will be charged with making malicious phone calls. We do, after all, know where you live.' And he'd slammed the receiver down, winking at the girl. 'Done and done, Thingee. Telephone manner? I'll say.'

So when Peter Maxwell raised his titfer at the CCTV screen, Thingee couldn't help but smile. And when that old cow Lessing said what she said, it was all Thingee could do to stop herself kicking her in the shins.

'Carolina,' Maxwell hailed his colleague. 'Are you free?' His Mr Humphries was a *little* wasted on the Spanish girl, but he did it anyway.

'I have no lesson at the moment, Mr Maxwell,' she admitted.

'Splendid. Fancy making a call?'

'A call?'

Maxwell deftly removed the baseball cap from Dom Creddle. The hapless lad hadn't expected to see Mad Max this far south in the building and he'd been taken unawares. 'End of the day, Dominic. My office. Three of the clock sharp. Or I put this disgusting piece of sartorial inelegance through the shredder.'

'Yes, sir.' Dom Creddle hadn't really understood the last line, but the time and place were already burned into his brain. It was enough.

'To Menorca,' Maxwell swept the girl into the Modern Languages Office, piled high with text books and tapes, looking vainly for a telephone he knew must be there somewhere.

Carolina looked blanker than usual.

Maxwell handed her the phone number that Fiona Henderson had given him just days ago. He'd held off doing what he was now doing for long enough. 'Juanita's home,' he said. 'She still hasn't come back and we're getting a tad worried now.'

'No, no,' the girl's face had darkened. 'I cannot...'

'But you said you were free,' Maxwell reminded her. 'Your first lesson isn't until nine-fifty. Seven Bee, I believe.' Maxwell could read a timetable with the best of them; there was one on the wall in front of him now.

'No, I mean, it is difficult...'

'Carolina,' Maxwell frowned. 'It is quarter past ten in Menorca. Probably only slightly more scorching than it is here. You speak Spanish. I'd like you to ask Mr and Mrs Reyes, who also speak Spanish, if their daughter is with them. Or if they know where she is.'

'No, no,' Carolina was shaking her head rapidly, gnawing her lip and wishing the ground would swallow her up.

'If you can't do this,' Maxwell said softly, 'if you *won't* do this, I shall have no option than to file a missing persons report. That means that the Menorcan police will be calling on Mr and Mrs Reyes. If they don't know where she is, that might not be a very pleasant experience for them. They are bound to fear the worst; parents are like that. Do you understand?'

Carolina's response was to burst into tears.

'Everything all right?' Julian McConnell suddenly popped his head around the door, looking concerned in a Bootle sort of way.

'Spanish with tears,' Maxwell smiled at him. 'I've just had

to tell Carolina her home has been overrun by Moors. Oh, no, wait a minute – that was thirteen-hundred years ago. Doesn't time fly?'

'Max…' Julian McConnell was in the room now, all fluster and concern. He was about to do the all linguists together thing. What's the horrid man said to you, darling? sort of approach. Maxwell wasn't having any.

'Julian,' he blocked his advance with his bulk. 'This is a personal matter. I'd be very grateful if you'd butt out.' He smiled engagingly and Julian McConnell thought it best to beat a retreat. After all, he was a French teacher and discretion had always been the better part of Valois. He closed the door behind him.

When Carolina Vasquez emerged from her flood of tears, Peter Maxwell was leaning against a wall, offering her a box of tissues in an unimpressed sort of way. She took one and blew, shattering the relative silence of the Modern Languages Block (Janet Ferguson hadn't started teaching yet).

'Now,' Maxwell said, only now pinging off his cycle clips and tossing his shapeless tweed cap onto a dog-eared pile of *Le Medecin Malgré Lui* nobody could be bothered to throw away now that the same nobody taught literature any more. 'Would you like to tell me what this is all about?'

'You *are* joking?' Jacquie stared at him incredulously.

'Scout's Honour.' Maxwell gave the Nazi salute. The evening sun was glowing on the wall of 38 Columbine and Maxwell and his lady were sitting on the patio, finishing their wine, biding their time. 'You've sat there while I cooked this fabulous alfresco meal,' she swept her hand dramatically over the fish supper remnants she'd picked up at the Chip and Fin on her way home, 'sat there while we both ate it and *now* you tell me! You unutterable bastard!'

Maxwell pulled a face. 'It's not a *bad* Marlon Brando in *The Mutiny on the Bounty*, although I think you're slightly misquoting, but I must urge restraint, companion of a mile. Not a hundred yards in that direction,' he jerked his thumb over the privet hedge, 'is a lady of advanced years who would be shocked by such language. And not a million miles up there,' he pointed to the partially open window of Nolan's nursery, 'slumbers our son and heir, of extremely tender years. Time enough for him to pick up language like that when he starts playschool.'

'I just can't believe it.' Jacquie was ignoring him. 'Juanita a tea leaf.'

'That's what Carolina said. Sounded kosher to me.'

'But there's nothing missing,' Jacquie sat back, trying to rationalise it.

'No, not from here, darling. but what about Mrs T?'

'What's to steal?' Jacquie muttered. She wouldn't have offended Mrs Troubridge for all the money in the world, but she did have a point. 'Her priceless collection of Mantovani records?'

'Well, we don't know until we've asked her.'

'No, no,' Jacquie was frowning, putting her glass down on the cool of the cast iron and putting pieces together in her head. 'Juanita steals something, from us, from Mrs Troubridge, from the church plate, whatever and drives away into the night. Or rather, day. Leaving a ten-month-old baby and at least half her clothes behind.'

'Guilt.'

'Do what now?' Homer Simpson was infectious.

'Well, according to Carolina, whatever Juanita stole, it was a one-off, spur of the moment thing. She's not a tea leaf in the accepted sense, still less a regular burglar with a fence in downtown Tottingleigh. She's stolen something. Good, Catholic girl, from a loving home. Can't you just see her fiddling with her rosary and saying 'Hail Marys' without number? It all got to her that day and she panicked. Drove into the wide blue yonder.'

'So where is she now?'

'Lying low, trying to decide what to do.'

'Here in England?'

Maxwell nodded. 'That's what Carolina thinks.'

'Has she heard from her?' Jacquie asked.

'The day after she went, yes. E-mail. Said she was in Barnstaple.'

'Barnstaple?' Jacquie repeated. 'Well, I suppose somebody has to be. Max, what do you know about this Carolina Vasquez?'

He looked at her, clicking his tongue, shaking his head. 'You're a suspicious old besom, Woman Policeman,' he said.

'Years at the PACE Face will do that to you,' Jacquie scowled. 'Well?'

'Well, what's to know? She's Juanita's age. From Barcelona. Sweet enough kid. McConnell seems to rate her.'

'Come on, Max,' Jacquie said. 'You invented body language, remember? You've sussed nearly as many murderers as I have. Was she telling the truth?'

'She was upset...' Maxwell began, knowing at once his mistake.

Jacquie laughed. 'So that's it. Pretty little Spanish teacher comes all little girlie, squeezes out a few tears and you fall for it. Max, you've got a heart like the great outdoors, but you'll never learn, will you?'

'So you don't buy it, then?'

'We need to put out an All Points for Juanita,' Jacquie sniffed, serious now. 'I don't know what's going on here, but I don't like the smell of it. You going to eat that last pickled onion?'

'We've met, surely?' Mrs Henderson sat in her living room. The newly bereaved didn't talk in hushed tones any more, wearing black and sitting in the ghostly silence of a curtained room, trying to converse with the dead. True, it wasn't exactly party time at the Henderson's, but the dead man's relict knew that, somehow, life had to go on.

'We have,' Jacquie nodded. 'The last time we met we were talking about your au pair, who subsequently became ours.'

'Of course.' Fiona Henderson clicked her fingers. 'I'd forgotten you were with the police. Has Juanita turned up?'

'No,' Jacquie told her. 'That's really why I'm here.'

'I thought it would be to do with Gerald,' the widow said. She crossed the lounge, pausing briefly by the photographs on the mantelpiece before standing to gaze out of the window at the summerhouse in a bower of rhododendrons. 'He loved that place,' she said softly. 'Spent hours there. Not about Gerald?' She'd turned suddenly to Jacquie, snapping out of whatever memories held her.

'No, Mrs Henderson – Fiona – we can't possibly know how you feel at the moment. The Incident Team is doing all it can, but the sad reality is there are other problems which are on-going. I take it you haven't seen or heard from Juanita?'

Fiona Henderson shook her head. 'Nothing,' she said. 'Your husband asked me the same thing.'

Jacquie nodded. 'Since then, however, we've had further information. Look, I hate to bring this up at a time like this. You've got plenty on your plate as it is, but...why did you let Juanita go?'

The widow of Tottingleigh crossed to her late husband's drinks cabinet. She poured herself a straight gin and didn't offer one to Jacquie. 'I told your husband,' she said levelly. 'Katie was growing up. We thought boarding school would be best.'

Jacquie chose her moment. 'It wasn't because she was light-fingered, was it, Fiona? Juanita, I mean. I mean, did anything go missing?'

'Missing?' Mrs Henderson had an odd look on her face, as if something had occurred to her for the first time. 'No, nothing was missing. I never had any reason to doubt Juanita's honesty. What makes you think there was?'

'Oh, nothing.' Jacquie shrugged. 'A lot of our time is taken up by gossip-mongering, rumour, innuendo. Nine times out of ten it's malicious or just plain wrong.'

'Has the girl stolen anything from you?' Fiona asked.

'Nothing,' Jacquie had to admit. 'That's what's so odd about it. Some people seem to think she's a thief.'

'If there...if there should be any news of Gerald's murderer,' Fiona was staring at Jacquie, her blue eyes burning into her brain, 'I'd be so grateful to hear.'

Jacquie stood up, reaching out to touch the woman's arm.

Fiona Henderson was rigid, like a broomstick wearing clothes. She didn't smile. Didn't move. Jacquie's hand fell away. 'You will,' she told her. 'I promise you, you will.'

As she made her way alone over the gravel drive, her shoes crunching on the loose stones, she glanced back at the huge house with its stone animals and leaded panes and Lichtenstein-sized conservatory. But Jacquie Carpenter had made promises before; promises she had every intention of keeping, but somehow never had. Mothers waiting for their children to come home; children who had gone forever. Wives waiting for their husbands; only to see them again pale and waxen in the morgue. The police tried to solve them all, all the cases that came their way, but some refused to break and tired men and women hit brick wall after brick wall and in the end, the promises they made were broken. And clear-up rates became depressing statistics in the Sunday papers. 'You will,' she heard the voice re-echo in her head. 'I promise you, you will.'

Only a tiny handful – the select – know what happens in Senior Management Team meetings. An unholy trinity sat in the less-than-palatial office of James Diamond that Monday afternoon. Diamond himself, of course, three-piece suited, rimless specs, with a higher degree in Crisis Management. In front of him, two-piece suited, a graduate of the School of Incompetence, sat Bernard Ryan, who was so often the head's mouthpiece. And across the room, casting no shadow whatsoever in the bright July sun, Dierdre Lessing, Leighford's own Cruella de Ville, sat writhing on the husked corpses of the men whose blood she had sucked.

There was only one topic of conversation on the agenda – the removal of Peter Maxwell.

'Appalling,' Dierdre Lessing was saying. 'Always has been, ever since I've known him. A law unto himself. It doesn't matter what initiative you bring in, James, he ignores it. The man's a dodo.'

'He's a very good Head of Sixth Form, Dierdre,' James Diamond had to concede. 'And he certainly knows his history.'

'Of course he does,' growled Dierdre. 'That's because he was there at the time. You mark my words, James. Get rid of him and Leighford will be a better school overnight.'

'Bernard?' Diamond looked at his deputy. 'You're very quiet.'

'I have to share Dierdre's viewpoint on this one, James,' he said. 'I think we've all basked in this man's shadow for long enough. Surely, he's past retiring age.'

Diamond shrugged. 'Not unless he's sneaked into County Hall and doctored his records. And you both know as well as I do there are very precise rules covering dismissal. Maxwell would have to be a lot madder than the students claim to go down that road.'

'Would he?' Dierdre raised an eyebrow. 'Would he indeed? You know, sometimes, James, there is only one road to take. In Maxwell's case, it's the Via Dolorosa, the road of tears. Perhaps he ought to be ready to shed them now.'

CHAPTER TEN

What was it that drew Peter Maxwell back to Dead Man's Point? The weather was still idyllic, recalling the summer of '76, the little rivulets that ran into the Leigh long ago dried up and not a little smelly as the July days roasted on. He could smell the tar burning on Ringer's Hill as he straightened in Surrey's saddle to take the rise. The horizon shimmered in the heat, even though it was past four o'clock, and Surrey's handlebars were a blur of sizzling chrome.

Perfect time for an ice cream, really, so Maxwell hurtled right, oblivious to on-coming traffic, and swung out of the saddle, Marion Morrison style, before parking the snorting, hissing beast in the shelter of the oaks. It was crowded up here today, the sun dazzling on car windscreens and everybody vying with everybody else with the extensive dead insect collection stuck to their bonnets and bumpers. Children – who should have been at school, by the way – laughed and frolicked in the yellowed grass behind the cars, but Peter Maxwell only had eyes for Luigi.

'A Ninety Nine, my man, if you please.' Maxwell swept off his hat and wiped the sweat from his eyes. Time to loosen the bow tie, perhaps.

The tall figure in the shadow of the ice cream van pressed

buttons and pulled levers. 'Two quid, mate.'

Maxwell resisted the urge to faint or remonstrate or both; he needed this man's cooperation. 'You're Luigi, aren't you?' He slurped the ice cream before it trickled all over his hand.

'That's what it says on the van, mate.'

'You're the one who found the body, then,' Maxwell beamed, breathing in awe in the presence of a famous person.

'Sort of,' Luigi leaned forward on his elbows, a smear of strawberry Goodacre all over his apron.

'That must have been...amazing.' Maxwell shook his head in incomprehension. 'I read about it in the paper.'

'What, the *Advertiser*?' Luigi snorted, reaching over for a flask of tea. 'You don't want to believe anything you read in that load of bollocks, mate.'

'So what they said you said you didn't say, then?'

'What?' Luigi looked perplexed. Sentences like that threw him, as they would most people. 'Well, some of it, yeah. But I notice they didn't print my theory, did they?'

Maxwell tucked the flake in the corner of his mouth. Was it his imagination or were they smaller than they used to be? 'You've got a theory?' He was agog. 'Oh well, of course you have. Having found the body and everything.'

'Well, of course, I don't *know*.'

'No, no,' Maxwell was licking like a thing possessed to beat the effect of the sun's rays on his Ninety Nine. 'Of course not, I realise that.'

'So what's your interest?' Luigi asked.

'I'm just morbidly curious,' Maxwell beamed.

Luigi looked at him. 'Oh, right. You local?'

'Ish,' Maxwell shrugged.

Luigi leaned even further out of his van, checking from left to right. A potential Twister-buyer was making his way from his car, so he had to make this snappy. 'There's this bloke, right. Don't know his name. He's a pervert. Wears a vest and skimpy shorts.'

'I think I've seen him around,' Maxwell nodded.

'He's always up here. Courting couples, see. Of an evening. I mean, I don't care. As long as they buy the odd choc ice, I don't give a flying Magnum what else they're doing. But him, well – he's a watcher.'

'A watcher?'

Luigi looked at the man over his shades. How much more explicit could he be? 'Flasher, I shouldn't wonder.'

'You've seen this?' Maxwell checked. 'Flashing, I mean.'

'Leave it out, mate,' Luigi said. 'I'm happily married. I don't have no time for weirdos like that. Afternoon, sir? Twister?' Luigi prided himself on his retail typology.

'No, I'll have a Solero, please.'

Maxwell was actually grateful for the interruption. It gave him time while the customer was being served to demolish his Ninety Nine with what remained of his dignity, ice cream dribbling down his wrist as it was.

'But he was up here, was he?' Maxwell asked when the Solero-buyer had gone. 'On the day in question?'

'No, mate, look,' Luigi had watched *Silent Witness*; he knew his onions. 'You haven't got the hang of this at all. When they…I…found the body, it had been in the grave for…ooh, about two weeks. Now, this bloke, this weirdo – he wouldn't be up here when I found it, would he? No, he'd have been up here two weeks earlier when he buried him.'

'And he was?'

'Sure,' Luigi sipped his lukewarm tea. 'Off and on all over June.'

'Did he buy an ice cream?' Maxwell asked.

'What?'

'Did he buy from you? Talk to you?'

'From time to time,' Luigi nodded, building up his part. 'He's a bit of a regular of mine, in fact.'

'And you don't know his name?'

'Ah, well, no, not in a manner of speaking.'

'Did you report him to the police?'

Luigi snorted. 'The boys in blue?' he snarled. 'I've had the odd run-in with those bastards meself in my time – licensing issues, you understand. You might as well talk Swahili to those blokes. 'Course,' Luigi became all confidential again. 'They had me in the frame for a while, you know.'

'Never!' Maxwell had been lolling against the van, but now he stood upright with the knocked-on sense of outrage. 'Why?'

'Procedure, apparently.' The ice cream man put his cup down and rested on his hands on the counter. 'The sad, stupid bastards think that because you find a body, you must have put it there. As if I'd be that stupid!'

'As if!' Maxwell guffawed along with the man. 'But I thought it was a couple who found the deceased.'

'A couple?' Luigi straightened. 'Cobblers! Couple of low lifes trying to gain some notoriety, that's who they were.'

'Can you see it from here?' Maxwell asked. 'The murder scene?'

'Nah,' Luigi shook his head. 'It's back there, past them

trees. Where some stupid bastard's left his bike.'

'Hmm,' nodded Maxwell. 'Tell me, Luigi, this flasher of yours...'

'Now, let me stop you there, mate,' the ice cream man said firmly. 'I told you – he's not *my* flasher. I'm a happily married man. Got two kids. I can't *stand* blokes like that. Gives us all a bad name, don't it?'

'All right,' Maxwell smiled. 'Figure of speech. Have you seen him since? Since you found the body, I mean?'

'Nah,' Luigi shook his head. 'Nah, he's done a runner. You mark my words. He'll be long gone by now.'

'What about the second body?' Maxwell asked.

'You what?'

'The one in the Botanical Gardens?'

'I don't know nothing about that one, mate. I don't work that patch.'

'But they must be linked, surely?' Maxwell played the ingénue to perfection. 'I mean, it stands to reason. Two middle-aged blokes found murdered within days and a mile of each other. Did the flasher kill him too?'

'Could of,' Luigi shrugged. A man like him could only really handle one murder at a time.

'So, come on then,' Maxwell egged him on. 'You're the theory man. What's the motive? You've got the bloke – it's the weirdo flasher. Why did he do it?'

'Well,' Luigi was leaning on his elbows again. On the one hand he could do with a bit more trade. On the other, he was giving this matey the benefit of his gigantic brain, so... 'It's like this.'

* * *

'Either,' Maxwell's Luigi was impressive and Jacquie sat giggling at him over their evening drinkie. 'Either, the flasher is a queer who gets his rocks off by killing his victims. Or,' his second index finger had joined the first, 'they were his willing partners in sordid disgusting sex until his depraved, unnatural demands got too much for them. Or...' Maxwell, like Luigi, had run out of hands, 'they'd both caught him flashing at their wives or girlfriends and in trying to give him a smacking, he'd sort of turned the tables and given them one instead.'

Jacquie shook her head laughing. 'And all you wanted was a Ninety Nine,' she said.

'I presume he didn't burden your colleagues with those incisive stabs of logic?'

'I think I seem to remember Benny Palister drawing the short straw on that one. Conspiracy Theories Are Us. Needless to say, the lad didn't actually write much down.'

'Well, we were just about to explore the likelihood of alien abduction, anal probes and animal mutilation when the Undecided Family from Kent arrived and it was clear that darkness was going to fall before they placed an order. I took the opportunity to grab Surrey and do a runner. Or should I say a pedaller?'

'Well, now you know how we feel,' Jacquie was smug, sipping her Southern Comfort. She joined Maxwell in his favourite tipple when there was a 'y' in the day. 'For every villain we get who won't tell you his name, we get a dozen oddballs prepared to shop their granny if it gets their name in the papers.'

'The odd thing is,' Maxwell said, lolling back on the settee and staring at the lampglow on the ceiling, 'I think I know the weirdo in question.'

'What?' Jacquie frowned. 'Do you mean he's real?'

'Nolan and I were out at The Dam the other day – improving the boy's navigational and cycling skills – when a gentleman faintly answering Luigi's description came out of nowhere in the bracken.'

'Max, you don't think there's anything in this, do you?'

'Well,' Maxwell laughed. 'If he *is* one and the same, we can rule out Luigi's final theory. The bloke I saw was nine stone wringing wet. He's not likely to have been able to take out not one, but two heavyweights and cart their bodies to out-of-the-way places.'

'Even so,' Jacquie said. 'I'm going to get young Benny on to that tomorrow. Time we blew some dust off the local sex offenders file.'

Dorset Police found Juanita Reyes' Hyundai that Wednesday morning. It was parked in a farmer's gateway, completely hidden from the road, just off the A35 out of Bournemouth. It contained the usual detritus that people collect in their vehicles – old Tesco receipts, a ticket to see *War of the Worlds*, an empty Shloer bottle. There was some lipstick in the glove compartment along with a log book, maintenance manual and a box of antihistamine tablets.

The coppers who found it phoned it in, stuck the Police Aware sticker on the windows, back and front, and left it where it was until they could get a tow truck. And all the way back to the station, they were arguing over whether or not that car was a scene of crime.

* * *

Henry Hall hated himself at moments like these. Moments plural because he'd done this before. He was sitting in his air-conditioned Lexus on the broad sweep of the Downs overlooking Leighford. His patch. His manor. His town. Up here, the cloudless sky was an impossible blue, like the postcards they sold down the Sea Front. The scene was silent, except for the occasional whine of a speedboat, slicing silver through the sea, and the faint coming and going of the dated Muzak from the fairground.

Next to him sat that most unlikely passenger, Peter Maxwell. And Maxwell, too, had been here before. He knew all the signs. When he, Maxwell, was in the way, treading on toes, making a thorough-going nuisance of himself, then it was 'Hands off' via Hall's underlings; gentle persuasion from Jacquie; the cold shoulder from everyone else. When Hall needed help, it was different. The DCI was too much of a professional – and a gentleman – to send Jacquie Carpenter to do a senior detective's work, so he'd go himself to the mountain that was Peter Maxwell.

'Mr Maxwell?' Hall had been put through to the Head of Sixth Form's office by Thingee on reception. 'Henry Hall. Something's come up. Could we meet for lunch?'

Lunch was on Henry Hall. In Maxwell's case, it was a man-size egg and cress baguette from Mr Indigestion's in the High Street, washed down with an amusing lime-hinted Diet Coke.

'So, Detective Chief Inspector,' Maxwell was wiping a veritable meadow of cress from his lips. 'This bribery is all well and good, but to what do I owe the pleasure?'

Hall looked at the man through those infuriatingly blank glasses. How often had he and Maxwell done this, gone head to head in the arena of sudden death, like two battle-weary old gladiators? He'd actually lost count. 'Two children,' the DCI said, 'who may have been the first to find the body of David Taylor.'

'Children?' Maxwell frowned. 'I thought it was the Downers, a holidaying couple?'

'You shouldn't believe everything you read in the *Advertiser*,' Hall told him. 'Still less the *Daily Mail*.'

Actually, it was what Maxwell's partner Detective Sergeant Carpenter had told him, but Maxwell wasn't about to shop her to the rozzers. 'Say on.'

'Daniel Pearson,' Hall confided, 'and Scott Thomas.'

'Well, well,' Maxwell beamed. 'The Leopold and Loeb of Year Ten.'

'I take it you know them,' Hall said. He never beamed.

'In a manner of speaking. Mr Diamond has given the pair of them a damned good letting off on more than one occasion for crimes ranging from spitting on the sidewalk to high treason. You've spoken to them?'

'Not personally and not in this context,' Hall said. 'But they are known to us, yes.'

'I'm not sure I understand…' Maxwell was at his most arch.

'Oh, I'm sure you do, Mr Maxwell.' The DCI would have smiled at this moment had he been a smiling man. It was Robin Hood and the Sheriff of Nottingham all over again, dear old Errol Flynn clashing swords with even dearer old Basil Rathbone. The point was that both of them thought they were Errol. 'Not to put too fine a point on it,' Hall said, 'I feel sure that you can make headway where we cannot. They might talk to you when they won't talk to us. Get my drift?'

Maxwell nodded, washing down the baguette with the rare vintage. 'In the trust stakes, yes, I suppose I do. What do you want to know?'

Hall weighed up his options, but the truth was he was in blood stepped in so far that to go back now might lose him a murderer. He'd trusted Maxwell before; he'd have to do it again. 'Anything,' he said, as cryptic as the late Peter Sellers' Clouseau, but without the mirth. 'Everything. We know they found the body before the Downers and they ran. They may, inadvertently, have seen something else. How will you do it?'

'I'm sorry?'

'How will you broach the subject?'

'I'm a historian, Chief Inspector,' Maxwell bridled. 'We have a hundred ways. Before Political Correctness, Inclusion and Assessment for Learning, I'd merely have lit matches under the lads' fingernails and stood well back until they screamed their confessions. Now…well, more subtle measures will have to prevail.'

Hall raised his hands. 'You're right,' he said. 'Better I don't know.' He checked his watch. 'Do you have to be some-where?' he asked.

'Always,' Maxwell looked nobly into the middle distance. 'The chalkface.'

The chalkface these days was actually the Interactive Whiteboard. Maxwell had fought a long and bitter campaign for the last three years on this front. The rest of his Department, whose total ages added up to twenty-two, had all clamoured for these revolutionary gadgets which created instant lessons, charting progression, regression, made Realms and expanded

Trade and Industry. Maxwell's reply was always the same. He reached out for a board-marker and, with deadly aim, wrote one word on the glossy surface. 'Bollocks.' Whiteboards he had accepted. It was a wrench but he'd thrown his chalk away one damp, depressing morning in March and had never looked back. No more white powder all over his hush-puppies and in his trouser turn-ups. He'd given up hashish too. But Interactive? Never. He'd die in a ditch first. Paul Moss, the long-suffering mixed infant who was nominally his boss tried to come the professional. Sue Davenant had wept all over him, as she did most weeks and to little effect. Debbie Mitchell toyed with a quick seduction in the stock cupboard; he was actually quite a dish, was Peter Maxwell, if you liked your men older. All to no avail. Whiteboards and markers and whiskers on kittens – they had become a few of Peter Maxwell's favourite things and any further, he point-blank refused to go.

When old Boney was a warrior, facing, as he almost always did, two enemies and a war on two fronts, he adopted the best tactics; take on the nearer or bigger bastard and hit him again and again until he gives in. Then turn on the second one and it's only a matter of time. Piece of cake.

'So, Danny.' The master strategist sat behind his desk, his hand tucked into his waistcoat that Wednesday afternoon, as though the field of Marengo lay before him in the blistering heat. 'How are you doing with Miss Davenant?'

Now, Danny Pearson had the hots for Miss Davenant. And Peter Maxwell knew he did. Danny was only in Year Ten, but he realised the mad old bastard wasn't asking about his love life. 'All right,' he mumbled. An unprepossessing little toerag was Danny Pearson. He had a partially shaved head and an earring, an impending ASBO and upwards of six syndromes, but his heart was in the right place – something of a rarity in these days of genetic modification.

'You see,' Maxwell explained, 'I like to check on my people, when they move on. Remember the fun we had in History lessons in Year Nine?'

Danny did, but he'd die rather than admit it.

'Now, we're nearly at the end of Year Ten – over halfway through your GCSE course. Doesn't time fly, eh?'

It wasn't a question Danny had ever been asked before. He didn't really have an answer for it.

'It's just that, well, Miss Davenant is very pleased with you.'

Danny's cynical young heart missed a beat. Miss was very pleased with him. Maybe she'd go out with him now, ride on the cross bar of his mountain-bike, let him snog her back of the Asda store.

'At least, she was...' Danny's fantasy bubble was burst at once by the party pooper that was Peter Maxwell, '...until about two weeks ago. Then she noticed it all went downhill.'

This was news to Danny. He'd been failing to meet his target grade for some time now. In fact, looking back, he wasn't sure he'd ever met it; much more likely to meet his Maker, in the fullness of time.

'Tell me, did anything happen...anything go wrong about two weeks ago? That would be the end of June.'

'No,' Danny shrugged.

Maxwell frowned and leaned back, locking his hands behind his head. 'You see, Danny, that's not how Scott tells it.'

Danny blinked. 'Scott don't do History,' he said.

'Indeed not,' Maxwell sighed. 'And I think he's already

beginning to regret that. No, it's his Maths that's coming unstuck, isn't it?'

Danny didn't know. The pair of them talked about football. And girls. They still had peeing contests to see whose range was longer. And they'd both discovered that essential teenage accessory – Lynx, or how to clear a classroom in seconds flat. What they never, ever did was talk about school work – it was just too depressing.

'No, Scott thinks it was finding the body like that. It must have been a shock.'

Maxwell counted silently to five before Danny came back with the predictable, 'What body?'

Maxwell laughed. 'What body?' he repeated. 'What dead mouse in Mrs Clitheroe's English lesson in Year Seven, Danny? What graffiti calling into question Mr Ryan's parentage in the boys' loos in Year Eight? What about the fire alarm on Speech Day?'

'That wasn't me,' Danny blurted. 'That was…'

'Tall Chloe,' Maxwell said softly. 'Yes, I know.'

And there he had it; in that one sentence. Mad Max *knew*. He knew everything. Even things that Danny Pearson didn't know he knew, he knew. So Scott had dobbed him in, dobbed in both of them. What a shit. Still, Danny and Scotto went back a long way. He'd have had his reasons. 'All right,' he said. 'Yeah. It shakes you up, Mr Maxwell, finding something like that.'

He checked his son sleeping at the end of another long day. What milestones the lad had passed, what firsts, was impossible to say. As had become the pattern by now, Nolan spent the weekdays with Pam and either Jacquie or Maxwell would fetch him on their way home. Everybody at Leighford High knew which one it was because the contraption would be buckled behind Surrey's saddle and Norman Westbury would pat it admiringly – 'a little thing, but mine own'.

All was well. Maxwell checked his watch. It would be an hour before Jacquie was back from her particular chalkface. Time for a little M and R – modelling and relaxation. Lieutenant Landriani hadn't really progressed in the last few days. He still only had one arm and the cigar in his mouth, though to scale, was an unlikely white. His horse had no reins and no crupper. How the man was supposed to guide him one and a half miles down the Valley of Death was anyone's guess.

'It shook them up, Count,' Maxwell was in his modelling cap, light on, magnifying glass at the ready, pyrogravure heating quietly to his left. 'Funny how these kids are such hard men until something like this happens, isn't it? I saw Danny first. I didn't think he'd crack so easily, but he did. Scott was a piece of cake, as predicted. Poor little bugger was in tears when I'd finished.'

Metternich was unimpressed. He'd seen it all over the years. *His* victims cried too – mice with wives and kids, shrews with so much to live for. You couldn't let it get to you. They all had to go. He was a tom, for God's sake. There were standards. Oh, all right, the ones he'd felt sorry for, he'd let go under a building somewhere, but there was a strict quota of these. And only on Thursdays. Otherwise, animals might talk.

'They'd been larking about on the coastal path on their bikes. And, yes, it was them who'd trashed Mr Harris's flower beds and one of them – Danny said it was Scott; Scott said it was Danny – saw something shining in the grass. At the Point, that is, not the Gardens. They went to investigate. This would have been, ooh, half six, seven, I suppose. Yes, I know – the time when they should have been doing their homework. Danny – or was it Scott – picked it up. Only it was stuck, so whoever it was pulled harder. And a hand came up with it. Chewed, Danny said, like it had been eaten. You and I, of course, denizen of the night, know it as rodent infestation. Now, now, no slavering. But it was Danny who went back for the thing, so I can only assume it was Scott who dropped it.'

He rummaged in his pocket and placed the object under the light and the magnifying glass. 'What do you think that is, Count?'

The cat glanced at it, shining in the brightness. Then, he looked away, suddenly far more interested in chomping on his left armpit.

'Well, thank you for that,' Maxwell said. 'It's jewellery, certainly. But whose? And what? Part of a...what? Brooch? Medallion? Wide Boy Taylor was the king of bling, apparently, so it's not too surprising that the boys found it there. Remind me to check with the Mem when she gets home. The lab report would have *something* on this, surely. A broken piece of jewellery, or place where something has been detached. We shall see.'

He held the little silver thing up to the light again, his eyes dazzled by the reflections of its scales. 'It's a lizard, Count. A little silver lizard. Taylor's? Or his killer's? A calling card? Or a deadly mistake that before 1965 would have placed a noose around somebody's neck?'

Metternich slithered off his linen-basket perch and sauntered past Maxwell. For a moment, he toyed with taking a chunk out of the old man's leg, but it would be probably too sinewy to waste good muscle-power on, so he abandoned the project and headed for the stairs.

'Mind 'ow you go, Count,' Maxwell called, in his best Dixon of Dock Green. It was all, of course, wasted on the cat, who only ever watched Sky.

As artists go, Geraldine Buck wasn't hugely successful. But that didn't really matter in the scheme of things, because Greg, her husband, was something in the City and they could afford to indulge Geraldine's passion for the sea. She had a studio flat out beyond the Shingle, not very far from Dead Man's Point, and in the summer months, she'd taken to strolling along the beach beyond Willow Bay, where the pebbles threatened to turn your ankles and the stench of the bladderwrack washed up on them could turn your stomach. It all helped her particular Muse, she said and she liked it best on windy evenings when the surf was a roaring demon, bellowing along the shore, and the gulls cried in panic, wheeling desperately to find land and a safe haven for the night.

It was calm now, like a millpond, the sea far distant as if it had given up its daily battle with the land and was retreating for ever. The flies were a nuisance on nights like this, maddening around your ears and fluttering in and out of your curls. And they seemed focused on the dark bundle that lay ahead. Geraldine got closer, her sandalled feet slipping as the pebbles gave way beneath her and she muttered as yet another patch of tar held her fast for a second.

What *was* that? She found herself frowning as she neared it.

The smell was appalling. Those bastards who dumped rubbish from ships. How dare they? There ought to be a law. There *was*, presumably, a law.

But this was no ordinary rubbish. This, black and battered by the tide, was a man. Geraldine felt the hairs on her neck crawl as she realised. Then she screamed. Then she vomited. Then she ran.

What would you do if you found a whale; a whale on the beach that shouldn't be there?

CHAPTER ELEVEN

There was still a crowd beyond the fluttering tape by the time the moon came out. They were mostly holiday-makers, grockles the locals called them, who would have something a bit different to write about on their postcards to granny. 'It ain't half hot, Gran, and we all looked at a cadaver today.'

One who stood there, by the cordon where the police had placed them, was watching events more closely than the rest. He spoke to no one and no one spoke to him. He pulled his hood further over his head as the night on the beach gradually became more chill.

For the locals, it was becoming business as usual in a grim sort of way. The SOCO team looked like a bad Sci-Fi Doomsday scenario, from a B-movie in the Fifties, wandering the beach in their white, translucent suits, hooded and masked as if an outbreak of Ebola had just occurred.

'Have you any idea, guv, how much evidence there is on this bloody beach?' It had been welling up inside Geoff Hare for some time. He'd been here nearly three hours, not suited up like the others, but receiving their reports on a minute-by-minute basis. Bottles, cans, nappies, broken bits of this and that were carefully collected, labelled, photographed, stashed in black bags in the back of patrol cars and vans. Cynics might see this as a particularly vicious ploy by some environmentalist group to enforce a carrying out of beach clearance.

Yes, in answer to Hare's question, DCI Hall had a very good idea. He'd seen it all being collected too and this was not his first body on a beach. The irony was, he knew deep down that this was all irrelevant. Jim Astley had got it right, as he usually did. Jim Astley had gone home now, muttering about his bedtime and his sciatica, as though the two were somehow linked.

Hall didn't answer his sergeant but wandered back into the canvas erected over the corpse. The arc lights were still on, throwing the body into sharp relief. He was a slightly built man; Astley reckoned in his late thirties. His head, or what was left of it, had a shock of tumbling blond hair à la the early Hugh Grant and his eyes were grey. There was a mass of blood matted into the hair across the forehead and there was no doubt in the minds of either the policeman or the pathologist that the man had fallen from a great height. The presumption was that that height was the cliffs towering above the beach at Dead Man's Point. It was the fall that killed him, pulverising the left side of his face and driving the jagged stones into his skull.

Henry Hall nodded to the SOCO boys waiting for orders. 'OK,' he sighed. 'Bag this one if you've done. That's tomorrow's little task for Dr Astley.'

The only question was, Hall was thinking as he went outside, grateful for the cool air of the beach, did you fall or were you pushed? He looked up to the black eminence of the

Point against the paler purple of the night sky. There were stars tumbling above him and the ghostly glimmer of the quartered moon. And he didn't know why, but the phrase lover's leap crept into his mind.

The great thing about the dog-end of a school year – now, promise you won't tell – is that the timetable tends to implode. Year 13 have gone; so, at least until September, have Year 11. And Year 7 have yet to arrive. So those lazy bastards at the chalkface, who already, be it noted, have thirteen weeks holiday a year, actually have that untold luxury, time off during the day. A bit like: publishers, policemen, retail workers, post office personnel, doctors, dentists and just about everybody else.

So it was that Thursday morning, as the sun climbed again in the heavens and hose-pipe bans came into force with all the majesty of the law, that Peter Maxwell somersaulted neatly over the barbed wire perimeter fence around Stalagleighford, landed squarely in the saddle of White Surrey and pedalled like an escapee for the Botanical Gardens. Unfortunately, his arrival in the car park coincided with that of a coach-party from Grimsby.

'Aye up, chuck. Look at t'prices 'ere.'

'Ee, it don't bear thinkin' about, does that.'

'Well, I never.'

'Not like this at 'ome.'

''Appen not, our Doris.'

And Maxwell remembered anew why he'd once taken a vow to lock himself securely in Columbine from May to September, just to let this particular breed of locusts past.

'Mr Harris in?' he asked the cow-faced girl on the counter, and silently shared the view of the Blue Rinse from Grimsby about the prices. 'And is there somewhere I can park my bike?'

He was and there wasn't, so Maxwell locked Surrey to an abeliophyllum distichum in case one of the Grimsby trawlers was of the light-fingered persuasion. Then he crunched his way over the forest bark in search of his quarry.

Chester Harris was a bearded man in his late forties. He was a botanist, horticulturalist, conservationist and all round pain in the arse, given to writing long and loud letters to the *Advertiser* on the perils of global warming and how we all ignore the unpredictable movements of plate tectonics at our peril. From time to time, Maxwell had considered writing an abuttal on the dangers of historical inevitability and the dire consequences of misjudging epistemic distance, but something more demanding always came along, like wiping Nolan's bottom or watching paint dry. Now, here was the man himself, all golden tan from the great outdoors, with a bandana round his neck and fringed denim shorts around his thighs.

'Mr Harris?' Maxwell was crouching, looking intelligently at the alchemilla mollis.

'That's me.' Chester Harris was always ready with an article for *Groundsman's Weekly* or *Mr Rotivator Magazine*.

'Peter Manton, West Sussex CID.'

The constant gardener shook his hand, 'Morning.'

'Can we talk?' Maxwell asked.

'What about?' Chester Harris was less than fond of the police.

Maxwell frowned. Was the man so totally caught up in his heliotropes that he'd missed stumbling over two bodies on his doorstep? 'The murders,' he mumbled.

'Look...can I see some ID?' Clearly Harris wasn't quite the idiot savant his PR team had made him out to be. People from Grimsby wandering past were giving them both rather odd looks.

Maxwell looked startled. He gently led the man away into a shady bower. The looks from Grimsby were even odder now. 'You mean, no one's been in touch?' Maxwell asked him.

'How do you mean?'

'Oh, Jesus. Look, Mr Harris, I'm really sorry. There seems to have been some John Prescott-sized cock up on the communications front. Leighford were supposed to have briefed you. I can't do this without your permission.'

'Do what, for God's sake?'

'Go undercover here at the Gardens.'

'Undercover?' Harris frowned. The man was hardly dressed for a day on the flower beds.

'This really is the end. I'm from Hove, you see. Unknown face and all, but Leighford are supposed to have cleared it. Um...a DCI Hall?'

Harris snorted. 'Uh, that idiot!'

'Really?' Maxwell was enjoying this.

'Not wishing to be disrespectful to your profession, Mr...'

'Manton,' Maxwell said. 'DI Manton.'

Harris thought policemen retired at fifty-five, but perhaps there were exceptions. After all, nobody seemed to be telling David Jason to move on. 'No, the whole of the local constabulary is a joke, I'm afraid.' He was wiping his soily hands on a rag. 'I mean, take these murders...'

That was exactly what Maxwell had done and, like the ice cream man earlier who wasn't Luigi, the botanist was opening up nicely. 'Mr Henderson.'

'Was that the name? Chappie found here in the Gardens.'

'That's him. Local builder, I understand.'

'Is that all you understand?' Harris asked, looking his man squarely in the face.

'I'm sorry?'

'Look. Do you want to see the murder scene? I assume, in that you're trying to work with Leighford, but are from outside, you haven't seen it already? That kind of incompetence seems par for the course.'

'Not a sausage.' Maxwell shook his head. God, the rubbish he had to work with.

The horticulturalist emerged from the nook with the undercover policeman in tow, brushing bits out of his hair. The people from Grimsby were rather more down to earth; they were looking for grass stains on his back. Harris passed a trowel to a spotty youth all but passing out in a green boiler suit. Maxwell breathed a sigh of relief – he didn't recognise the lad, so he should be all ri—

''Ello, Mr Maxwell.' The lad's face broke into a broad grin.

'Maxwell?' Harris half-turned as he strode towards the Australian Garden.

The undercover teacher tapped the side of his nose. 'I didn't say I hadn't worked in Leighford before,' he said.

Harris was not convinced. 'But Tommy's only seventeen,' he argued. 'Only been here a few weeks.'

'Look, er... Mr Harris. I can't discuss cases, all right?'

'Oh, no, no, of course not.'

'Let's just say "chasing the dragon". Know what I mean?'

'Chasing...? Oh, drugs.'

Maxwell started, looking furtively around.

'Sorry,' Harris hissed. 'None of my business.'

'That's all right,' Maxwell muttered. 'Maxwell was a long time ago now.'

They'd taken the tape away from the rhododendron bushes at Harris's insistence. He'd spent all the previous day closeted away with the *éminences grises* who ran Leighford Trust, who owned the gardens. Mayor Ledbetter was all for putting up signs saying 'Roll Up! Roll Up! See the 'Orrible Murder Site. Get your choc ices here.' He was even prepared to put on the fishnet stockings himself, but that was a side of his nature that the voters of Leighford had yet to be introduced to, so the matter was dropped.

'You've seen the photographs, I suppose?' Harris checked. He'd caught the milder ones at the Press Conference.

'Yes, of course,' Maxwell bluffed. 'But there's no substitute for the real thing.'

'Here we are.' Harris squatted at the base of a huge rhododendron cluster, whose dark leaves and dying flowers rose to the cloudless south coast blue. 'Head under the bush. Feet out to...' he paced it, '...here.'

'You didn't find him?' Maxwell checked.

'No, a couple of kids did. And that's another thing. Courting bloody couples at it all over the park. What are these bloody parents doing, eh? I tell you, I wouldn't let a daughter of mine go out dressed like that.'

'Like what, Mr Harris?'

'Like these girls do.'

'There are girls in your garden?'

'Look there.' He pointed to a flimsy gate, complete with stile. 'That's all the security we have. A blind cripple in a wheelchair can get over that.'

'Any trouble here before?' Maxwell asked. 'Violence, I mean?'

'Few drunks from time to time,' Harris shrugged. 'Bit of glue-sniffing when it was all the rage a few years back. Needless to say, I've been on to the local nick. Nothing ever gets done. Plants are sensitive creatures, Inspector. They need warmth and light and water, sure, but they need quiet and a safe environment too. Young tearaways from the local sink estate won't give them that. And as for the schools...'

'Bad?' Maxwell checked.

'Appalling!' Harris groaned. 'Leighford, The Hampton; there's not much to choose between them to be honest. Even the junior schools suck.'

'So I've heard,' Maxwell muttered. 'Tell me, did you know the dead man?'

'Henderson? No.' Harris shook his head. 'Oh, I've seen him around, here and there. The odd council bash, you know. And of course, his company's signs are all over the place.'

'He never did any work for you, either at home or here at the Gardens?'

'No. He's a bit small fry, I think, for a project this size. We only deal with the big boys. Henderson specialised in executive homes, I understand.'

'And he wasn't a regular here?'

'Here?' Harris chuckled. 'No, no. I don't think there'd be

much to interest his sort here. I have, of course, already told your Leighford people all this.'

'I knew you would have,' Maxwell sighed. 'Like we used to say when we had a rail service, you're only as good as your station master. And if you're right about this bloke Hall...'

'Oh, trust me,' Harris said. 'I am.'

'So...' Maxwell was looking backwards and forwards, trying to get his bearings. 'If the body was dragged from the car park back there...'

'It would have been too bloody obvious, surely?' Harris had had time, as had Leighford CID, to ponder these things. 'It's nearly half a mile to the car park, down some pretty steep steps or very much in the open down the disabled ramp. No, if he didn't die in situ, he had to be brought that way.'

'From the coastal path?'

Harris nodded.

'Look, Mr Harris. Something's gone horribly wrong this morning. I'm going to have to go back to Leighford CID and sort it all out. You up for me starting work here, say...Monday? Even Leighford clearance can't take longer than that. I promise I won't dig up any allium sphaerocephalon. Not unless you tell me to.'

'I don't understand this.' Harris was frowning. 'I was at the Press Conference the other night. Nobody from the Force approached me at all. All I got was the usual verbals from the paparazzi.'

'Huh,' Maxwell snorted. 'Don't get me started on them. I'm going to take a wander along the path a little way. Where does it come out?'

'The nearest landmark is Dead Man's Point,' Harris told

him. 'There's a car park there and it links up with the road on Ringer's Hill. Beyond that, you've got the Rare Breeds and Willow Bay. It's about three, three and a half miles all told.'

'Fine. Oh, Mr Harris,' Maxwell closed to his man, confidential in the dappled sunlight. 'The lad weeding the flowerbeds.'

'Tommy?'

Maxwell nodded. 'Don't mention me, all right? Could be a bit difficult. Know what I mean? If he raises the subject, he'll probably tell you I'm a teacher. Just play along, all right?'

'Oh, yes, of course,' Harris said. 'Not a word. You take care now, for all it's a lovely day, that path can be murder. You know they've found another body, down on the beach?'

'Henry? Jim Astley.'

The police surgeon-cum-pathologist was the last of his breed. Everywhere else, his job was being done by three people. It was killing him slowly, but like the alcoholic drowning himself in a vat of wine, he still had to get out three times to go to the loo. It was still Thursday, as it tended to be once a week for twenty-four hours or so, and they were open.

Even so, Jim Astley took life at a more leisurely pace these days. He needn't rush to the pub because the pub was open all day. Marjorie was lying gaga in the conservatory having ever deeper conversations with her geraniums and other imaginary friends like the widow Cliquot. And it was many a long year since he'd jumped when a senior policeman snapped his fingers. Come to think of it, he'd never done that. But, Henry Hall had a killer to catch. And, as far as Jim Astley had any friends, Henry Hall was one of them.

'Jim. What news?'

Astley shuffled the papers on the desk in front of him. Sunlight never reached this far and he was using borrowed light like Henry Hall was using borrowed time. Donald had excelled himself in typing this lot up so quickly. 'Your boy is thirty-seven to forty years old, five feet ten inches tall, well built. Break to the left arm a long time ago – childhood, almost certainly. All his own teeth; so good there's no dentistry – so checking his records may not be too helpful.'

'Cause of death?' Hall's voice sounded strained over the phone. You couldn't tell looking the man straight in the spectacles, but it was the little, off-guard moments that told you the whole story. He was tired. And getting nowhere fast.

'As I surmised,' Jim Astley did *love* to be right, 'a fall from a great height. Perhaps fifty or sixty feet.'

'Dead Man's Point,' Hall muttered.

'Now, in the world of science, Chief Inspector,' Astley reminded him, 'nothing is one hundred per cent certain.'

There was a pause. 'But if you were asked to stick your neck out?'

'If I were asked to do that,' Astley smiled, 'I'd have to consider it likely, yes. That woman found the body in question on the beach and that's where he died. Your boys been up to the Point?'

'They're there now. Any other signs of violence?'

'None. Broken shoulder, smashed sternum, skull all but demolished – all consistent with hitting the rocks at x miles an hour. He had had sex shortly prior to death.'

'Oh?'

'Semen stains on the underwear. This wasn't ejaculation on

impact. I've known that in my time, though it's rare.'

'So how "shortly" would you say?'

'How "shortly" is a piece of string,' Astley, rather bizarrely, wanted to know. 'Depends on his relationships, how often he changed his underwear. Even I have to concede that forensic science is not the answer to everything, Henry. Maybe your boys up at the Point will find something.'

The sun dazzled on the water below him and the clouded yellows fluttered in the dry, brittle gold of the corn. Maxwell swept off his porkpie hat and wiped the sweat from his forehead. The bow tie had long since come off and the collar was open. The cycle clips were in his pocket and his trouser-bottoms flapped free to let the air get to his legs. Dear old Robert Owen, the crypto-sociologist of the 1820s, had known how important this was. Men became infertile if their unmentionables were encased in corduroy all day, so he'd tried to insist that his workers wore skirts; they wouldn't. And somehow, that golden opportunity was missed, never to come again. So Peter Maxwell, an Englishman in the midday sun, suffered in silence for the sartorial narrow-mindedness of his ancestors. His trousers clung to his legs like they did whenever he visited the Hothouse at Kew or that time that Jacquie had taken him, kicking and screaming, to the Eden Project.

He could hear the squeal of excited children from the beach below and could see the ripples of white edging the silver-blue where the sea temporarily lost its battle with the land. The smoke of barbecues wafted up this high, but not the cloying thickness of Ambre Solaire nor the gritty burntness of quarter pounders; and Peter Maxwell was secretly glad for that.

He barely noticed the lad coming towards him, sweltering in the incongruous hoodie. When he did catch his eye. Maxwell didn't recognise him. Someone with a stare as concentrated as that would stick in the memory. He heard the lad's footsteps thud away as he passed.

He'd paid careful attention to the path all the way from Chester Harris's Gardens. It was mostly sand, with sudden divots and dips where the rabbits had decided to play house or old Mr Erosion had cracked a joke, leaving a gap just wide enough for the unwary tourist to catch their toes and sue the arse off the local council; there was so much bodily metaphor on that headland. If chummy had killed Gerald Henderson elsewhere and brought him this way, from the Point's car park perhaps, he would have had to negotiate some tricky bits. *And* he'd be carrying a dead weight. Difficult…not impossible. *Two* people carrying Gerald Henderson? It was evening, he knew, when the dastardly deed was done, still light according to Jacquie. They must have looked like Resurrection Men, like good old Burke and Hare in the Netherbow, watching graveyards for a funeral and sneaking back to dig the poor bastard up again. But even Burke and Hare had the decency to wait until after dark. Then again, Burke and Hare eventually cut out the middle man and simply descended to murder; so much less hassle than digging up a corpse. Two hundred years ago, of course, on this very headland, the blokes carrying Gerald Henderson would have been smugglers. And everyone, the parson, the squire, they would have all turned respective blind eyes. Even the Preventive Officers.

'Well, well.' Maxwell smiled at the sight that met him. 'Preventive officers.'

A knot of people stood ahead of him, off to his left and to the left of the path. The path had wound its way out of the fenceless corn field now and back onto the short-cropped grass of the rabbits and the sand holes of the swallows. They were standing behind a yellow, flapping ribbon and one of them was kneeling down, perilously close to the edge, examining the grass. Another was wearing a dress.

'Policewoman Carpenter!' He hailed her.

Jacquie looked alarmed. She'd trodden many a murder scene with her man, but always clandestinely, well after the event and never with her trained-to-be-nosy colleagues looking on. 'Mr Maxwell.' She crossed the picket-line and stood facing him, careful in the timbre of her voice that her colleagues were upwind. 'Max, what the fuck…?'

'My favourite Saxon hero,' Maxwell beamed. 'Along with Dish the Dirt, of course.'

'If it isn't too much of a cliché,' she hissed, 'why are you here?'

'Now,' Maxwell peered over her shoulder. 'I could ask the same of you.'

'I'm working.' She was emphatic.

'Damn!' and he slapped his forehead. 'I'm supposed to be up at the school, aren't I? Now, where did I leave my bike?'

'Bugger off, Max,' she warned. 'That's DI Bronson behind me and he doesn't approve.'

Maxwell smiled at the man and tilted his hat. The DI certainly looked like Martin Bormann. 'I'm not sure there's anything in Magna Carta or the Bill of Rights that says I can't walk a coastal path, Woman Policeman.'

'You know what I mean, Max,' Jacquie insisted quietly. 'There's been another one.'

'So I understand,' he said, looking squarely at her again. 'But I had to hear it from Leighford's own Alan Titchmarsh back there. He said there'd been three. I thought perhaps he was mildly dyscalculic.'

'I didn't know myself until I came on duty this morning,' she told him. 'And I'm sorry I couldn't break off to say "Excuse me, boys, while I fill in my better half on this one."'

'Well,' Maxwell beamed. 'No time like the present.'

'Is there a problem?' DI Bronson thought it was time to intrude and he was standing at Jacquie's elbow.

'Three men dead inside a week in an area the size of a kingsize duvet?' Maxwell asked. 'I'd say so, wouldn't you?'

'You are…?' Bronson looked at him with contempt.

'Wondering what we pay our rates and taxes for.' Maxwell winked at Jacquie.

'I'd like your name…sir,' Bronson stood full square across the path, blocking Maxwell's advance.

'Peter Maxwell,' he said. 'And yours?'

'Oh.' Bronson's eyes flickered across to Jacquie who toyed briefly with jumping off the cliff behind her. 'I'm Detective Inspector Bronson,' he said. 'And I've got a horrible feeling you're impeding a police enquiry.'

There was a muffled buzzing behind them, as of a large gaggle of Grimsby elderfolk, the sun dazzling off their bald heads or blue rinses, approached the yellow tape to a rising chorus of 'Ee's and 'Aye's.

'I think you're about to learn the meaning of impeding, Inspector,' Maxwell beamed. 'And don't threaten them. They've got this thing about being charged over the odds.' He tipped his hat. 'Later, Policewoman Carpenter.'

* * *

The last knots of reluctant Year Tens were creeping across the fields at Leighford High as White Surrey threatened to mow them down. Dale was going to yell, 'You're not supposed to ride your bike on the school site' when he realised who the cyclist was and changed his mind. He valued his nuts too much and had his whole reproductive life ahead of him.

High in her eyrie, Dierdre Lessing saw her bête noire gliding noiselessly over the paper-strewn field, like that mad old bastard Don Quixote tilting at windmills again. 'Today would be good, James,' she said, without turning. The winnowed husk that was James Diamond, Headteacher, got up from the soft chair in her office and followed her steely gaze through the second floor window. Maxwell disappeared behind the Sixth Form Block in a blur of white and chrome and wickerwork.

'I'll do what I can,' he said.

And as the door clicked behind him, Dierdre Lessing uncoiled with a clink of claws and a rattle of dead men's bones. 'Pathetic,' she murmured.

'Max.' Diamond hailed his Head of Sixth Form in the corridor on the ground floor. 'Could I have a word?'

Maxwell checked his watch before unpinging his cycle clips. 'Nearly half one, Headmaster,' he beamed. 'Goering's Economic Policy waits for no one, I fear; least of all Year Twelve.'

'This *is* important, Max,' Diamond persisted.

'Very well.' Maxwell ushered the man into his office. If truth were told, James 'Legs' Diamond didn't go into Mad Max's office much, and that was because he didn't like it. There were movie posters everywhere, as if the man were some sort of buff. Men like Legs Diamond didn't have a life outside Leighford High School and he didn't really see why anyone else should have one either.

Maxwell invited him to sit. Now, the Great Man had invented body language and he'd just played a masterstroke. He sat at his desk, in the Siege Perilous, the seat of power, his arms outstretched, hands flat on the desk like Julius Caesar receiving the surrender of Vercingetorix. Vercingetorix, on the other hand, sat awkwardly on a corner of Maxwell's cheap and nasty L-shaped county furniture, outmanoeuvred and outfought before he even opened his mouth.

'Exit strategies, Max,' Diamond said weakly.

Maxwell blinked. 'Sorry?'

'Exit strategies. How long have you got to go now?'

Maxwell looked at his watch again. 'Two and a half hours, Headmaster,' he said, solemnly. 'I assume you've cancelled the Year Heads Meeting due to lack of interest?'

'Er…no, I haven't. And I didn't mean that. I mean, how long till you retire?'

'Well,' Maxwell leaned back in his chair, watching the worm before him squirm. 'The Prime Minister, God bless him, keeps upping the ante in that respect, doesn't he? First it's sixty-five, then it's sixty-eight. I think pretty soon teachers will be like the Pope and we'll die on the job – if that isn't a too politically incorrect or nauseating a concept.'

'No, no, Max,' Diamond chortled. 'That edict doesn't come into effect until 2008. And anyway, you're over fifty.'

'I certainly am, Headmaster.' He was on his feet. 'And believe me, when that great day comes, when I hang up my chalk – oops, board-marker – for the last time, rest assured, you'll be among the first to know. Especially,' he closed to the man and winked, 'since I expect a sodding great present from you and the Senior Management Team. Now – really must fly,' he said, 'as Reichsmarshall Goering was prone to say. Can you see yourself out?'

Dierdre Lessing wasn't bad at body language either. She happened to be passing as Maxwell skipped to his Year Twelve Class, flinging open the door and yelling, in a very plausible Maximilian Schell, 'Vell, my children, vot is it to be? Guns or butter?'

James Diamond on the other hand, skulked out of Maxwell's office as if he'd just been caned.

She didn't have to seek confirmation of how the meeting had gone. A cruel smile creased her thin lips and she muttered to herself, 'Plan B'.

CHAPTER TWELVE

They lay side by side on their steamer chairs that night, the ones B&Q were selling off cheap. The ones up the road were dearer but that was because they had the legend 'Titanic' stencilled on the back. The Hendersons had bought some of those.

Moths were flitting around the candle flames on the patio like men, allegedly, used to flit around Marlene Dietrich and the flames burnt upright and pure in the absence of wind. All afternoon, Peter Maxwell had been stirring it, suggesting to all and sundry that there *was* an upper limit for working temperatures in schools. The Premises Manager was soon screaming at Legs Diamond about Health and Safety issues – apart from the lack of beard and the Scots accent, she was very like Groundskeeper Willie in the Simpsons. About two-thirty, Sylvia Matthews assumed a very similar position and tried to persuade the Head that common sense ought to prevail and at least let the kids go home half an hour early. Year Ten were all for marching in a body – a very sticky, tetchy, Lynx-infested body – on the Headteacher's office, to drag him out and kill him if he got difficult. They'd been to see their own Year Head who advised against it, but Mad Max had said they had right on their side. It was something called Diffidatio, he'd said, and it was a twelfth century thing where if your liege lord (that's a kind of headmaster, he'd said) was not fulfilling his feudal obligations (like keeping the place cool enough) you had the right to overthrow him. Mad Max knew his onions and if Mad Max said something, you just *knew* it was right. Anyway, they were still psyching themselves up when the bell went and the Great Leighford Rising never took place. Never mind; better luck tomorrow.

It was certainly cooler under the stars; Nolan lying in his cot under the fairy lights; Mrs Troubridge snoring like an elephant seal next door in one of her rare moments of sleep; and a black and white killing machine sitting with smouldering eyes, still guarding Nolan's pram even though Nolan was not in it. The boy's parents still couldn't decide whether Metternich regarded the lad as something to be defended or something for a snack if times got lean.

'But apart from that, Mrs Lincoln,' Maxwell was saying, 'how did you enjoy the show?'

'You really are a bastard, Max.' Jacquie was smiling, her face glowing partly from the reflection of the conservatory lights, partly from the red wine she was sipping softly. 'One more crack about the tax payers and the DI would have had you.'

'He certainly seems to be the unacceptable face of Mr Blair's England.' Maxwell was looking at the candle-flames dancing in the distortion of his cut glass of Southern Comfort. 'So, after I left you, did you manage to sort anything out?'

'Well, of course,' she said, wide eyed. 'We dithered a lot and wrung our hands and tore our clothes crying in despair "What shall we do now, without Peter Maxwell?" Then we got down to some old-fashioned police work.'

'You ingrates,' Maxwell tutted. 'You'll be sorry when I solve this one for you.'

'No one will be sorry if *anyone* solves it, Max. It's all looking a bit grim for the DCI.'

Maxwell sat up and topped up her glass. 'Henry's back is broad,' he shrugged. 'He's been here before.'

'Yes and no,' Jacquie said. 'We've got three bodies in eighteen days and, as you so tactfully reminded the DI, all within an area the size of a duvet – that's not *quite* accurate, by the way. The links between Wide Boy Taylor and Gerald Henderson are minimal and we don't even know who the bloke on the beach is.'

'Just another washed up whale, eh?'

She looked at him. 'Where did you hear that?'

'Hear what?'

'*Whale on a beach*. It's a song by Danny Goodburn. It's never off the radio at the moment. One of Benny Palister's favourites. I like it too. Sort of…sad and sinister, all in one.'

'Well,' he confided in her, 'my cat's whisker – oh, begging your pardon, Count – isn't what it was. All I seem to get on it is Alvar Liddell and the news that Crete's fallen. Bit of a bugger, really. Did the Man With No Name go over the edge where you guys were standing this morning?'

'We're pretty certain,' Jacquie nodded. 'The lab are still checking his footprints. As you can imagine, there are quite a few up there on the path – including yours.'

'And yours!' he bridled in the perfect whine of a four year old. Then, serious, 'And a killer's.'

Jacquie sighed. 'That's exactly right. But it's such a mess up there, forensically. You realise we're actually getting less in terms of clues each time this bastard strikes.'

'So Henry's assuming it *is* the same man?' Maxwell checked.

'You know Henry,' Jacquie threw her hands in the air, careful not to spill her drink.

'Plays his cards close to his chest, that man,' Maxwell nodded. 'What are we talking, then? Copycat?'

Jacquie put down her glass. 'I'd better not have any more of this if you want a sensible conversation. MO?'

'MO.' Maxwell didn't put his drink down, except to top it up.

'David Taylor, strangled by ligature.'

'His own crucifix.' Maxwell narrowed it down.

'Chummy must be relatively strong, strong-stomached and determined.'

'Takes at least four minutes to kill a man that way,' Maxwell remembered. 'Like boiling an egg. Gerald Henderson, stabbed from the front.'

'Conventional household knife. Attack pretty frenzied.' Jacquie finished the sentence for him. 'Yesterday's man, fell – or – pushed from a great height.'

'Yesterday's man,' Maxwell nodded. 'I like that, my dear. Is there some sort of award for being a police person *and* a poetess?'

She ignored him.

'So how did he get up there? On the Point like that?'

'And when?' Jacquie was ahead of him. 'His body was found on the beach by Geraldine Buck, local artist, at eight-fifty according to the log-in time. Give her a chance to pull herself together, stop throwing up and ring the nick...let's say, some time after eight-thirty.'

'Still light,' Maxwell was with her. 'But nobody saw him land; so nobody saw him go over.'

'Not yet,' Jacquie said. 'But it's early days and we've got to be optimistic. We've still got a few clues to check out on Jack the Ripper.'

They laughed together in the candlelight.

'So,' Maxwell brought them back to the here and now. 'The Man With No Name is casually walking along the coastal path, minding his own business at some time before eight-thirty last night. He meets Chummy who gives him the bum's rush over the edge. There were still people on the beach at that time?'

'Very likely, but no one we've found yet.'

'And of course, he's mute.'

'What?'

'The Man With No Name. I pushed you off a log last year...what was that...a foot off the ground? You damn near burst my eardrums with your screaming.'

'I'm a girl,' she said by way of explanation.

'That's very true, Jacqueline,' Maxwell said in his best professional tone. 'But if somebody threw me off Dead Man's Point, I think I'd scream blue murder. So either he's mute or he's just one of those stoical guys who accepts his lot in life. And death. Perhaps he was one of those optimists who thinks all the way down "OK so far".'

'Not likely, is it?' she refused to crack a smile at that one.

He shook his head.

'It's not conclusive, though, Max. I can cite you dozens of cases where eyewitnesses see nothing, hear nothing, feel nothing. They're not covering up, they're just not observant.'

'Even so, Jacquie...'

She held up her hand. 'You see what you expect to see,' she said. 'You don't expect to see a man falling from a cliff, so you don't see it.'

'Come on...'

She was adamant. 'You hear a shout, a scream, perhaps even an altercation on the coastal path. You're down by the sea, so the sound's distorted. It bounces off the rocks, the cliffs. You don't know which direction it's coming from. And then, of course, if you're typical Joe Public, you don't want to know.'

Maxwell knew how that worked. He who never turned his back, never walked away; he'd seen how that worked in others. 'Which leaves us where?' he asked.

She shrugged. 'Up shit creek for now,' she said. 'But in the case of the Man With No Name, as I said, it's early days.'

'Time for the Heavy Cavalry, then.' Maxwell jerked something small and shiny out of his pocket.

'What's that?'

'That, dear heart, is a clue.'

'Max?' Jacquie was frowning at him. 'Where did you get it?'

He placed the little silver lizard in the palm of her hand. 'From a kid at school,' he said. 'I swapped him all my cigarette cards of the 1951 All Blacks Touring Team. I'm not sure I got much of a deal, to be honest.'

'What *are* you talking about?' It was a question she'd often longed to ask him.

'Henry didn't tell you?'

There were times in her life when Jacquie Carpenter had felt the floor open beneath her, when the rules didn't apply any more, when the world turned upside down. Those times usually involved Henry Hall, her boss; and Peter Maxwell, her lover. 'No,' she said, slowly. 'Not a dickie bird.'

'Picture the scenario,' Maxwell said as Jacquie peered at the lizard in her hand. 'Henry Hall has two unidentified kids wandering a crime scene, the one that belonged to David Taylor. People who saw them thought they were teenagers. That makes them likely Leighford Highenas – unless they're grockles, of course.'

'Of course.'

'Some excellent probing by your very own Incident Team throws up two names. Names, and I blush to report it, "known to the authorities", viz and to wit Danny "The Flash" Pearson and Scott "Knob End" Thomas. Henry quite rightly believed he'd get nothing out of those two hardened criminals except their ranks, serial numbers and a lot of aggro from their mums and the Bleeding Hearts Lobby. So he had a word with me.'

'Why didn't you tell me this, Max?' Jacquie was outraged.

'Sworn to secrecy, dear heart,' he shrugged. 'Why didn't Henry?'

'So why are you telling me now?'

'Mummy told me it was wicked to swear,' the little boy who was Peter Maxwell lisped.

'You idiot!' and she hit him with a tea towel.

'You can take it to the Boss Man tomorrow,' he said.

'And betray your confidence?' she asked him. 'Don't involve me in your skulduggery. Honestly, I don't know which of you is the biggest arsehole.'

'Er... Henry,' Maxwell decided after the briefest of minutes. 'And that's bigg*er*, by the way.'

'Bollocks.' She poured the dregs of her wine over his head, getting up and laughing. 'Last one in the bathroom's a cissy!'

Jacquie was right. Better she be kept in the virtual dark about the strange and shifting relationship between her guv'nor and the other man in her life and, on that basis, Peter Maxwell took advantage of his late start that Friday and pedalled across the forecourt of Leighford nick. The early sea mist had vanished to leave another demonic day of heat; Maxwell could hear Year Ten sharpening their scythes in Norman Westbury's department in readiness for Day Two of their Revolution. Simon Schama would be along any minute, making notes and deciding which walk to adopt across Leighford's playing fields for the forthcoming documentary – 'Leighford: the School That Died of Heat'.

Sergeant Den Morrisey didn't like the heat either, but he didn't like Peter Maxwell even more. The nasty rash that assailed his neck and jawline was giving him particular gyp this morning and he wasn't sure whether the culprit was the sun or Maxwell.

'Is DCI Hall available?' Maxwell asked, Surrey securely clamped to a drainpipe (this *was* a police station, by definition full of undesirables; you couldn't be too careful).

'Who wants to know?' Morrisey knew the answer already.

Maxwell leaned on the man's counter and smiled at him. 'Who wants to know, *sir*,' he said.

Morrisey straightened. Would it be worth his pension to

fulfil many a copper's pipe dream and put one on this irritating shit?

'It's Peter Maxwell,' Peter Maxwell said. 'And it *is* quite urgent.'

They made him wait in the spartan outer office for over an hour. He carried no mobile, of course, and he thought he ought to save his one phone call from the landline in case he had need of a solicitor. So, come the time for Lesson Two back at Leighford High, his long-suffering Head of Department, Paul Moss, would just have to mug up like lightning on Elizabethan Vagrancy and teach it his bloody self (as most of Year Seven would have put it). Morrisey would have kept the self-righteous bastard longer, but the guv'nor intervened and Maxwell found himself whisked through corridors measureless to man into the Limited Smoking Area of the Incident Room out back.

'I've kept you waiting,' Hall observed. 'I'm sorry.'

'No harm done,' Maxwell assured him. 'The posters in your waiting room are quite instructive. I know all about Quarantine Regulations now. Handy when I try and smuggle my cat out. You might be interested in this.'

He held up the silver lizard. 'I'm sorry my dabs are all over it. I'll give myself up now if you like.' He briefly held out his wrists for the steel bracelets.

'Where did you get it?'

'From those intellectual giants in Year Ten you asked me to interrogate…er…talk to. Pearson and Thomas.'

Hall looked blanker than ever behind those infuriating glasses. 'And where did they get it?'

'The scene of the crime,' Maxwell told him. 'Dead Man's Point.'

'I owe you one, Mr Maxwell.' Hall took the trinket, letting it dazzle in the sunlight.

'Indeed you do, Inspector Hall,' Maxwell conceded. 'So, I'll collect the debt now, if I may. Was it the dead man's?'

Hall should have laughed at the Head of Sixth Form's brass neck; smiled at least. In fact he did neither. 'I don't know,' he said. 'Until the lab checks it out. But we are grateful.'

'You bet your sweet bippie.' The Sixties satire was wasted on Henry Hall. That *teensie* bit younger than Maxwell, culture had passed him by. 'I'll see myself out, Inspector. Oh,' he turned with an immaculate George Dixon, 'Mind 'ow you go,' and saluted.

Maxwell was in the nick car park wrestling with his combination lock for Surrey – aptly, it was 1485, if you're interested – when he saw a face he thought he knew.

'Mr Mendoza,' he called.

The good-looking Spaniard spun on a sixpence. 'Ah,' he said. 'Good morning.'

'Are you bunking off school too?'

'Bunking…?' the man looked confused. 'Ah, yes,' he smiled as he translated it in his head. 'Yes, I am.' Then he was frowning again. 'Too?'

'Sorry?' Maxwell wrenched the lock free.

'You said "too". That implies…'

'That I am also a teacher,' Maxwell confirmed. 'Spot on.'

'But I thought…'

'I know,' Maxwell chuckled. 'When we last met you must have been under the impression that I was a copper. Actually, my partner is. No, we were there because Juanita is our au pair. Is there any news?'

Mendoza grinned broadly. '*Si*...yes, there is. That is why I have come to your police station. She is home.'

'In Menorca?'

'Sant Lluis, yes. The police, they come to see me again, after your visit. They say they find her car.'

'So I believe,' Maxwell said. 'So what's it all about... Rodrigo? You don't mind if I call you Rodrigo?'

'No, I don't mind. You are...?'

'Peter Maxwell.'

'Ah, Pedro, eh?'

'Er...could we make it Max?'

'Max,' Mendoza shrugged. 'OK. I was going to call on Juanita's landlady and you and your wife. To explain.'

'Well, here I am,' Maxwell said. 'I can save you the trouble. Mrs Troubridge is rather elderly and easily thrown, so it might be better coming from me. As for Jacquie...well, her grasp is getting better all the time.'

'Max,' Mendoza was suddenly serious. 'This is very difficult for me. Juanita's parents, they know nothing of this. It would break their hearts if they knew...'

'...that Juanita is a thief.' Maxwell was serious too.

Mendoza's face said it all. 'She stole from you? What was it? Jewellery? Money?'

'No,' Maxwell said. 'Nothing has gone. But it's the story that Carolina Vasquez is putting about.'

'Carolina,' Mendoza shook his head. 'She is a silly girl, but her motives, they are right. It is a shameful thing, Max. We foreigners have a reputation with you English. People will say "I told you so".'

'I wouldn't worry about it, Rodrigo. The same thing happens in reverse every time an English football team goes abroad. There must be lots of "I told you so"s echoing around various European cities. What I don't understand is why Juanita left my baby without so much as a word. Or why she left her car wherever the police found it.'

'She was very frightened,' Mendoza said. 'I have talked to her on the telephone. She cries a lot. She needed help.'

'You can say that again.'

'I will try to persuade her to write to you,' the Spaniard promised. 'You have email address?'

'Yes,' Maxwell said. 'Juanita has it. We'd like to hear. And if we don't, just tell her can you, Rodrigo, that it's all right. No harm done. Will you do that?'

'Of course I will,' Mendoza smiled, his perfect teeth dazzling in the sun. 'But, tell me, Max, if you are not a…copper…what you are doing here?'

'Ah,' it was Maxwell's turn to smile. 'I'm helping the police with their enquiries – a bit like you, but a different case. Our murders here at Leighford.'

'Ah, yes, I read about them. And they were on the television.'

'Indeed,' Maxwell nodded. 'Dead Man's Point looked quite picturesque, didn't it? Meridian did themselves proud.'

'You know something about those murders?'

'Me?' Maxwell looked aghast. 'No, not really. But when you're all but married to the Force, well, it's sort of difficult to stand by really.'

'I see,' Mendoza chuckled. 'Well, you take care, Max…and have a nice day.'

'*Vaya con Dios.*' Maxwell had been brought up on Westerns. Accordingly, he swung into the saddle and drove home his spurs.

'Could this be a first, then, guv?' Geoff Hare wondered aloud. 'Guinness Book of Records stuff?'

Hall looked at him. Looked at all of them in the thick haze of the Incident Room that Friday afternoon. The only designated smoking area in the entire building, it was already bursting at the seams as the bodies multiplied. Even people who didn't smoke were in there, inhaling desperately as if nicotine aided their deductive reasoning.

'Benjamin Frederick Lemon,' Hall was reading from his notes. 'The Matalan barcode in his pocket provided an identity. Occupation: eBay entrepreneur. What are you saying, Geoff? The country's first eBay victim? That I doubt.'

'So what is he, then?' Benny Palister had to be the one to ask. 'Some sort of electronic rag and bone merchant?'

'A cynical way of putting it,' Hall nodded. 'But not too wide of the mark. George, what have we got?'

'Benji Lemon was thirty-nine. Lived in a nice pad on the Littlehampton Road. Milkman reported no taking in of milk bottles for three days.'

'Does that make him a neighbour of Gerald Henderson?' Jacquie Carpenter asked.

Inside, though never out, of course, Henry Hall was smiling. His people were still thinking, clicking, making connections, worrying the information like terriers after rats. Not a bad analogy, in fact, for detectives.

'Hardly,' Bronson deflated her. 'Must be five, six miles

away and a lot of other houses in between.'

'Family?' Hall wanted to know.

'We haven't got very far with that yet, guv,' Bronson told him, between puffs. 'Neighbours say he moved in with his dad some years back, but the dad died. There are rumours of a wife somewhere.'

'Who's on that?'

Sheila Kindling's hand was in the air.

'eBay were enormously helpful,' Bronson went on. 'The figures are still coming through, but Lemon, using the log-on "Zest1967", was making quite a killing...if you'll excuse the phrase.'

Everybody did. It was way past joke time.

'So,' Hare was in the corner, helping himself to another cup of machine coffee, 'in terms of motivation, we've got a potential few thousand irate customers.'

'Four.' Benny Palister looked like the cat that got the cream.

'Four thousand?' Hare checked.

'No, four customers. I had a look at his feedback. He was a Power-seller with a million and a half – or that's how it seemed to me by the end of this morning – positives. "Brilliant eBayer", "Excellent packaging", usual thing. Then these four. Out of the blue. Weird.'

'So, what are we saying?' Bronson was incredulous. 'That somebody pushed the poor bastard over a cliff because his parcels weren't done up right?'

There were chuckles and cat-calls in equal proportion.

'George,' Hall held up his hand for quiet. 'You and I have known people kill because somebody looked at them funny. Ours not to reason why.'

Peter Maxwell would have approved of the quotation and even though George Bronson didn't, he knew it made sense. The guv'nor was, as usual, right.

'All right, people. We know who the dead man is. Now we want some more answers. Sheila, you're on the family. Geoff, take your blokes and turn this eBay thing inside out. Work on the four unhappy clients in particular. What did he specialise in, by the way?'

'Jewellery, guv,' Hare told him. 'Silver trinkets.'

'I just can't believe it,' Jacquie was saying. She was propped up in bed with Nolan on one arm, a Barbara Vine on the other. One was fast asleep, the other unopened. The little boy had had a bad night. He was hot and teething and although his parents didn't know it, he'd had a falling out with Pam's Zoë earlier in the day and they weren't speaking. It was all part of being nearly a year old and nobody understands you – practice, really, for the Terrible Twos and the Teenage Tantrums and the rest of his life, in fact.

'Juanita?' Maxwell was propped alongside her, getting the best of the fan whizzing the air around and re-reading von Clausewitz since, clearly, his disappointing son had no interest in it. 'It is odd, isn't it? Who did Mendoza see at the nick?'

'Sheila Kindling,' Jacquie said, easing her back by shifting the baby ever so slightly. 'She hasn't stopped talking about him since.'

'So, what happens now?'

'Well, we'll have to establish just what has been taken,' she said. 'Nothing from us. Nothing, allegedly, from Her Next Door, although if little green men from Mars came through her roof in a shaft of light and used her for rectal probings, I doubt she'd notice. Nothing from the Hendersons. After that, we go back to the other links the girl had – Mendoza, of course, the people at that Golf Club in Littlehampton.'

'Golf Club?'

'The party she went to. If she was a compulsive tea-leaf, she might not have been able to stop herself when it came to the bling people wear to parties.'

'Now, it's funny you should use that word.' Maxwell gave up on von Clausewitz – the man had nothing on Post Traumatic Stress Disorder at all; nor rapid response capability; what *was* he thinking?

'One "I just can't believe it" at a time,' Jacquie scolded. 'I know what you're going to say; just wait your turn.'

Maxwell laughed softly, so as not to wake the fruit of his loins. 'Go on, then,' he said.

'And finally, the Agency that introduced her in the first place. If something major has gone, there may well be an insurance claim of pretty whacking proportions. And of course, we'll have to get the Spanish police to interview Juanita. Interpol seems a bit overkill now we know where she is and that she's OK. We've got to find somebody else, though, Max. We can't rely on Pam for ever.'

'No, you're right,' he conceded. 'And we'd better check the references a bit more closely next time.'

'Go on, then,' she said after a suitable pause.

'What?'

'What's your "I can't believe it"?'

'Oh, right, Bling. Danny Pearson and Scott Thomas found a silver item near a body at Dead Man's Point. The body in question belongs to Wide Boy Taylor, low life of Brighton and all points West. Benji "Zest" Lemon deals in such trinkets for a living. Coincidence, dear heart? Or am I just a suspicious old fart?'

'Oh, Jesus.' Jacquie suddenly lifted her son and heir at arm's length, the Barbara Vine flopping to the floor. 'Talking of farts, here's a young one needs dealing with. He's followed through and it's your turn.'

Maxwell took the pink bundle, now grizzly anew, and just about resisted the Homer Simpson remedy of wringing the boy's neck and screaming 'Why you...'

He settled for 'Coochie coo,' instead.

CHAPTER THIRTEEN

It was a spur of the moment thing, really. Alan Cole, the Head of Drama…er…Performing Arts was putting on something indescribable by Chekov next term. He was a new broom at Leighford High was Alan and he intended to sweep the place clean of all its myriad cobwebs. Why he thought a play by the bloke who was occasionally given the column in the original *Star Trek* series would make his name or even a ripple in the cesspit that was Leighford High was beyond Peter Maxwell, but what did he know?

So it was that Cole held his auditions that Saturday morning. There was much tutting and sighing from the Premises Manager and eyebrow raising from Legs Diamond, but a breath of performing arts air might be just what Ofsted ordered. And everyone knew that Ofsted could not be far away now. It was like Armageddon – inevitable and terrifying in a 'we're all going to die' sort of way. And so it was that the rising stars of Year 11, soon to be Year 12, turned up, among them, Steph Courtney.

The girl was a *little* surprised to see Mad Max there. Oh, he'd produced more school shows than she'd had hot dinners, but not recently. He *had* stepped in last year to do *Little Shop of Horrors* at a moment's notice, but Steph hadn't been involved in that, busy as she was with the banality of coursework. She strutted her stuff in front of Mr Cole, the Simon Cowell of Leighford High, trying to read something into his bored, elsewhere sort of expression. She knew she was better than Jenny Jenkins; there'd be no contest there. Her only problem was going to be Sammi Leicester, apart from the acne and the train tracks, of course.

While she was waiting for the great man to make up his mind, an even greater man sidled along the rows of chairs put out for assembly on Monday morning.

'Excellent, darling,' he confided. 'Best Uncle Vanya I've seen in years.'

'I was playing...' and she caught his wink. 'Oh, Mr Maxwell!' She toyed with thwacking him with her handbag, then remembered who he was and stopped short. He was Mad Max, for God's sake; he'd be her Year Head in a couple of months' time. What was she thinking?

'I've been thinking,' he whispered. 'This murder of yours...'

'Oh,' she flustered. 'I've been trying not to think about that.'

'I know it's not very pleasant, Stephanie,' he said. 'But it may be important. You didn't talk to the police about it?'

'No.' Her response was too loud and a rather pained Head of Performing Arts turned and glared at them. Trust Maxwell to be behind the interruption somewhere. 'No,' she whispered softly. 'I told you, not even Mum and Dad know.'

'Will you do me a favour, then?' he asked her. 'Will you show me exactly where it was you saw what you saw...'

'When?'

'Now. When the audition's finished.'

'Only if Emma can come.' For all Mr Maxwell was a gentleman and a scholar, a Knight of the Road, he was still a man. And all her life, Steph's mum had told her to be wary of men. The only one you could really trust was your dad. And you had to look at him twice.

'Certainly,' he hissed. 'I'd offer to give you both a lift on my bike but a) it would be hideously uncomfortable, b) it would contravene every safety rule in the book and c) people would talk. Good luck, Steph. I'll wait for you outside.'

'Mr Andrew Carmichael?' DS Geoff Hare flashed his warrant card for the third time that day. 'Otherwise known as freaking-a?'

'What if I am?'

'No law against it, Mr Carmichael. We're just making routine enquiries.' Technically, Hare was out of his jurisdiction. This was Berkshire. If freaking-a got funny, he'd have to go to annoying lengths to get various permissions etcetera and he'd really rather not.

Andrew Carmichael looked up and down the road. He didn't see anybody else's doorknocker getting a pounding. 'Oh, yeah? What about?'

'May we come in?'

Andrew Carmichael didn't like the look of Geoff Hare. He liked the look of Benny Palister even less. 'S'pose so,' he shrugged.

Swirly carpets, leafy wallpaper, spitfire paintings. Get the picture? Nobody ever said Andrew Carmichael had taste. The living room didn't even reach the dubious standard of the hall – MFI meets Bargain Basement.

'You an eBayer?' Hare smiled.

'Now, look, I paid that £38.87, no matter what that bastard wilysmiley says.'

'We're not interested in wilysmiley, sir. We're interested in zest1967.'

'Zest1967?' Carmichael looked blank.

'eBay item number 43712918.' Benny Palister hadn't exactly got the figures tattooed on his brain, but he had them written down in his book. 'A silver ring with filigree decoration...'

'Oh, him!' Realisation dawned. 'Well, there's another bastard. I got my money back eventually, but only after threatening the shit with the law. 'Ere,' Carmichael's sallow features brightened. 'Is that it, then? Have you got him? Major fraud, eh? Yeah, I'll testify. Too bloody right, I will. Makes my blood run cold does that. You know, there are people out there trying to make an honest buck and watch some bastard try and spoil it.'

'Or two bastards,' Hare smiled.

'You what?'

'Zest 1967 and wilysmiley.'

'Oh, yeah, right.'

'Tell me, Mr Carmichael,' the Sergeant said. 'Did you threaten zest1967 with a little more than the law?'

'How d'you mean?'

'He's dead,' said Palister. It was a well-rehearsed routine.

'Freakin' A,' hissed Carmichael appropriately.

'Do you want to talk us through it, Mr Carmichael, blow by blow, so to speak?'

* * *

All the way back from Reading, Hare and Palister pieced it together. It turned out that Andrew Carmichael didn't like confined spaces, which was odd, bearing in mind the glorified rabbit hutch he lived in. So any mention of jug, chokey, stir, porridge, in short serving any time at Her Majesty's Pleasure, filled him with dread. Turned out he'd had one or two minor brushes with the law – cautions, that sort of thing – so he wasn't anxious to renew old acquaintanceships. So Hare and Palister made sure they mentioned the Ultimate Punishment a lot. And Andrew Carmichael was soon singing like a choirboy. Yes, he'd threatened to do more than have the law on zest in his first Feedback, but Marlene had seen it and made him change it before it was sent. Marlene was what the whole venture was about. She was freaking-a's girl and she had this thing for silver, so he'd sent for the ring. It hadn't come and so he'd got sniffy with the seller, zest1967. The ring never turned up at all.

And that was where they'd had to leave it. A disgruntled on-line auction buyer, that was all. Do people kill for that? Perhaps. But both Hare and Palister would stake their reputations that Andrew Carmichael wouldn't.

The sun was a ball of fire by the time Peter Maxwell reached The Dam. Surrey's handlebars and saddle were like the red hot irons of medieval ordeals and his wickerwork drooped in the heat. The bracken leaves, so fresh and dripping in the autumn wet, were hard and brittle now, curling back from their stems and a pale silver-green under the sun's rays.

You couldn't see the sea from here, nor smell it. And the wide-open spaces of the southern end of the wild area, where the breeze blew and the swallows swooped, were gone, focused into the silent, heavy glade of the once quarry. The shade was a godsend and Maxwell parked Surrey and squatted by the trunk of an ancient oak. It was like that brilliant scene in Kurosawa's *Seven Samurai* where the ace swordsman is sitting cross-legged and is disturbed by three bandits. In the blink of an eye his sword is free, slicing them all down so that by the time the first hits the ground, the third is dead. Maxwell toyed briefly with doing much the same to the two girls who crashed through the bracken towards him now, but people would only talk and misunderstand. And anyway, he'd left his Katana at home and the pair of them had never done him any harm.

Emma Austen (what *were* her parents thinking nearly sixteen years ago when they were trawling the lists for suitable names?) was a pudding of a girl relative to the petite Stephanie, but she was a loyal friend and in the spin-off boy stakes, it helped if your friend was petite and Stephanie. Perhaps the bottle-bottom glasses were a mistake. Steph was wearing shades.

'You made it, then?' Good at the obvious ice breakers, was Peter Maxwell.

'I had to collect Emma first,' Steph explained. 'And text Mum so she didn't worry.'

'Did you get the part?' Maxwell asked.

'Don't know,' Steph shrugged. 'Mr Cole said he'd tell us on Monday.'

Maxwell shook his head. 'He's got no heart, that man. Now, Steph, is this the right place? Where you saw the car, the couple, the body?'

The girl frowned, pulling off the shades and walking from side to side, knee-deep in the ferns at the edge of the glade. Below, the nettles were neck-height, but there were plenty of tyre tracks and ruts worn smooth in the dry-baked mud. 'It's more overgrown now,' she said. 'But I think so. More this way. Toto was chasing something or other in that direction.'

She led the pair to her right, beyond the clump of oaks onto lower ground. Maxwell had got it wrong. When he'd come this way before, he'd stood higher.

'Hello again.' A voice made all three of them turn. Crossing the floor of the glade, swinging a stick as he came and hauling the haversack higher on his shoulder, was the old man Maxwell had met here on his last visit. It was as though, if you walked a certain way and stood on a certain leaf, the old boy would appear, perhaps barring the way to the rickety bridge.

'Hello, my dears.' Was it the sun glinting in the red-rimmed eyes behind the glasses or was it something altogether less of the day?

Steph instinctively put her shades back on, so that the old boy couldn't tell she was staring at him. Emma put on a defiant glare, complete with pout. But he didn't seem to be looking at their faces at all.

'This is a pleasant surprise,' he said. 'I haven't seen you two before. Live locally, do you?'

'My daughters,' Maxwell lied. He didn't like the way this conversation was going. If this was the same old man Luigi the ice cream vendor was talking about, he had every reason to be on his guard. And Steph and Emma didn't like the old man either. His scrawny chest had white, wispy hairs bristling

from a faded blue vest and his legs were like a chicken's, pale
and crusty, criss-crossed with thread veins in the midday sun.

'Charming,' the old boy leered with a wink. 'And so like
you. How old are you, my dear?' He closed to Steph who
instinctively hid behind Emma. She blotted her out fairly well,
but who was Emma going to hide behind? Turned out it was
Peter Maxwell.

'Forgive her,' Maxwell smiled. 'I've always taught my girls
not to talk to strange men.'

'Strange… Oh, I see,' and the old man broke into an odd,
wheezy laugh. 'The get up.' He looked himself up and down.
'I'm an ornithologist, dears,' he said. 'Your…daddy…will tell
you that's a bird watcher. I do like watching, you see. And you
have to do it carefully. And quietly. For instance, I've been
watching you for the last five minutes. Ever since you arrived,
in fact. But you didn't see me, did you?'

Steph shook her head. She didn't want to talk to this man
because he frightened her. There was something about his
tone, the over-familiarity in his voice. It was as though he was
looking through her clothes to the curved, honey-gold body
beneath. And the last thing she wanted to do was to let him
hear her voice. It was as though that would let the old pervert
into her world. And if she did that, her world would never be
the same again.

'Time to go, children.' Maxwell's voice was strong and safe
and good. He shepherded them firmly to one side, away from
the old man and they began marching away from him, from
the dark of the glade, to the cool uplands and the cloudless
blue. Steph almost ran, but she wanted to keep Maxwell with
her. And she didn't want to leave Emma behind. And when

they got to the edge of The Dam and the old man and his stick and his bag and his revolting old body had gone, she wanted to hug her soon-to-be Head of Sixth Form. Just for being Mad Max. But Emma was there and nobody would understand. Not even, quite possibly, Mad Max.

'I'm sorry about that, ladies,' he said. 'Nothing to worry about. Just a harmless old man. Have you seen him before, either of you? Steph, when you walk your dog?'

The girls shook their heads.

'All right,' he said, collecting Surrey from where he'd parked him. 'I'll walk you home.'

'It's OK,' Emma said. 'We'll catch the bus.'

'No,' Maxwell was firm, his eyes level, his voice gravel. 'I'll walk you home.'

And he did.

Henry Hall had been here before. Not in the master bedroom of Ingleneuk along the Littlehampton Road out of Tottingleigh precisely, but in the position of trying to build a dead man's life from his furniture.

Ingleneuk wasn't a very apt name for the Mock Tudor sprawl Hall's team were all over that Sunday morning. Back home, he knew, Margaret would be putting the roasters in about now as the church bells of Leighford called the faithful to prayer. And in about an hour, she'd resign herself to the inevitable and eat her lunch alone, having plated Henry's up for the microwave and for later.

Piles of Benji Lemon's clothes lay strewn more or less at random around the room, filling his kingsize bed, the top of the dressing table and a chest of drawers. The doors of his wardrobe were thrown back, his pillows and mattress lying at odd angles the searchers had left them. Not much point in being tidy with this one. There was no family member to grieve and get shirty in the same breath; no loving wife distraught that her husband's shrine was already being desecrated, even before it had been made holy.

'Guv,' Benny Palister had just won himself a gold star. 'I think you ought to see this.'

Henry Hall looked down. A pair of police handcuffs. And they weren't Benny Palister's.

'Well, well,' murmured the DCI. 'Who'd have thought that zest1967 was a Special.'

'Special?' Beryl Johnson was incredulous. 'You mean Special Constable?'

Jacquie Carpenter did. About now, back home, Peter Maxwell would be putting on the roasters, wagging a warning finger at Metternich, as the cat started his Sunday lunchtime slaver as he paced the kitchen. Maxwell would be hurtling past little Nolan on his bouncy doorway thingy, pretending to steal his nose each time he did. If that kid didn't grow up with a complex bigger than Canary Wharf, she'd eat her sandwiches.

'Not when I knew him.'

And that was exactly what Jacquie Carpenter and Sheila Kindling wanted to know all about. When Beryl Johnson was still Beryl Lemon and a dead man was still alive. They were sitting in the woman's comfortable flat in downtown Bournemouth, within a walk of the sea. She'd been born on the South Coast and seaside people rarely left it if they could help it. Beryl Johnson was an attractive woman with short-cropped blonde hair and good bones. Her ex-husband's bones were less impressive these days and still lying on a slab in a cold drawer in Jim Astley's morgue.

'Oh, we were happy enough at first,' she remembered. She looked at them both, the suited women in front of her. Was either of them married, she wondered? She couldn't see a ring. 'It's about now, if this was a *Frost* or a *Midsomer Murders* I'd get out the wedding photos and go all dewy-eyed, isn't it?'

Neither of the policewomen commented. There weren't any policewomen in *Midsomer Murders* and *Frost* was always so patronising to the ones on his show. Anyway, that was fiction; this was real. 'You don't have any?' Jacquie asked.

'No,' Beryl said coldly, lighting another cigarette, though she'd just put out the first. 'No, I burned them. *And* my wedding dress. My hair was longer then. He used to like me wearing it in bunches – you know, schoolgirl style.'

'Was that his thing?' Jacquie asked. 'Schoolgirls?'

Beryl laughed. 'Who knew what Benji's thing was? Yes, I suppose it was schoolgirls at first, then it gravitated to harder stuff.'

'Bondage?'

Beryl nodded, drawing hard on the cigarette. 'Stupid word,' she said. 'Stupid idea. We used to laugh at it when I was a choirgirl – Christ, that seems a long time ago now. Whenever the text was from the Old Testament, about the people of Israel and Moses freeing themselves from bondage, we used to giggle like buggery. There's nothing funnier, is there, than a situation when you can't laugh out loud?'

She got up and walked to the window, watching the sea

shimmer in the noon-day heat. 'Of course, we had no idea what we were laughing at. Stupid word, stupid idea. And it certainly wasn't funny when it became reality. Oh, it was mild enough at first. Benji would tie my wrists to the bedposts, then my ankles. Then the hitting began.'

The pain showed in the woman's face even now; the pain that would never quite go away.

'So, he used the handcuffs on you?'

'What?' Beryl sniffed, fighting back the tears. 'Um...no. No, he didn't. I didn't know he had any.'

'So, what are we talking here?' Sheila Kindling was quietly writing it all down in her notebook. 'Ligatures of some kind? Rope?'

Beryl nodded. 'I was a choirgirl. Benji was a boy scout. He knew all about knots. Funny, isn't it, how such innocent and good things can go so horribly wrong?'

'You divorced?' Jacquie wanted the record straight.

'Yes. When the beatings became so bad I had to be hospitalised.'

'We couldn't find anything on file,' Jacquie said. 'You were living just outside Tottingleigh at the time. All this ought to be there.'

Beryl turned back from the window. 'It's not, because I didn't make a complaint.'

'You didn't?' Sheila and Jacquie looked at each other.

'Call me a coward if you like. I couldn't go through all that again in a court of law. I even thought he'd contest a divorce, but by that time I'd met Mark and he persuaded me to go through with it. The hardest thing was keeping Mark from wringing the bastard's neck.'

'Or pushing him over a cliff,' Sheila said.

'Is that what happened?' Beryl asked. 'Benji.'

Jacquie nodded. 'It's likely to make the nationals tomorrow,' she said. 'Our third killing in three weeks. You'd better be prepared. If we found you, it's odds on the paparazzi will. When did the divorce go through?'

'Three years ago. Mark and I married last Christmas. I haven't seen Benji from that day to this.'

'He came to your wedding?' Jacquie was incredulous.

'He wasn't invited,' Beryl told them. 'Obviously. How he found out the where and the when I still don't know.'

'What happened?' Sheila asked.

Beryl snorted a laugh. 'Well, that was the peculiar thing. We'd just finished the service – it was at St Blasius, you know, the little church by the river?' Jacquie and Sheila did. 'We were walking down the aisle, my people, Mark's people, all smiling and the organ crashing and he just stood there in the church doorway. I thought Mark was going to fell him. He pushed me gently to one side and squared up to him.'

'A punch-up on your wedding day,' murmured Sheila. 'That must have been a moment to remember.'

'But that's just it,' Beryl said. 'There wasn't one. Benji ignored Mark and just said to me, "I'm sorry. I hope you'll be happy from now on." And he walked away.'

'And have you been?' Jacquie asked her. 'Have you been happy from that moment on?'

Beryl's gaze fell on a photo of her and Mark, laughing together along Bournemouth sea front. 'Yes,' she said. 'Yes, I have.'

* * *

'So you don't buy it, then?' Sheila was fixing her face in the Ka's vanity mirror as Jacquie drove them home. It was still a dazzling day, with windows down and Sheila wrestling with her hair, the sounds of snarling summer all around.

'That Mark Johnson waited six months since the wedding and three years since he took up with Beryl to get his own back on Benji? No, I don't.'

'What if he was waiting for the perfect opportunity?' Sheila reasoned, playing devil's advocate. 'He could hardly deck him in the church. It would look bad, spoil Beryl's day and there were probably a hundred or so witnesses looking on.'

'OK.' Jacquie went along with it. 'So Mark's a brooder. He worried it, teased it, finally decided. Then what?'

'Come again?'

'Does he go round to Benji's pad out of Tottingleigh? Take a crowbar to the rather expensive stained glass at Ingleneuk? No. Does he fix his car one night? No. Does he take him out round the back of a nightclub with a baseball bat? No. He rather wussily pushes him off a cliff.'

'It's easier,' Sheila offered a bit lamely.

'So it is, but is it Mark's style? Did you get a look at his photo?'

'Er...not closely, no.'

'Beryl's what...five eight? Five nine? Mark's got to be six foot five of anybody's measurement with something of the air of a brick wall about him.'

'It's still easier.' Sheila clung to her theory. 'And if you're right and you're pushed by Mark Johnson, you stay pushed.'

'Agreed,' Jacquie said. 'Watch it, you geriatric bastard,' and she blasted the Ka's horn, annoyed as she was every time she used it by its reedy tinniness. 'So what does he do? Follow Benji around until he goes for a stroll up on Dead Man's Point, then pushes him over? Bearing in mind the two men know each other and Mark doesn't exactly blend with the background?'

'What, then?' Sheila was being reminded all over again why she was a DC and Jacquie was a DS.

'Uh-uh,' Jacquie laughed. 'This is your scenario, Constable. You carry on with it.'

'What if...' Sheila Kindling came from a long line of optimistic die-hards. 'What if Mark *invited* Benji to meet him, up at the Point, I mean.'

'What, sort of..."You won't remember me, but I'm the nice bloke who married the woman you used to knock about. Please come to Dead Man's Point on Wednesday 12 July at about half past six so we can talk over old times." Right.'

'No,' Sheila shook her head. 'Obviously, he'd use an alias and he'd have a reason.'

Jacquie had stopped laughing now. 'An alias and a reason,' she repeated. 'Now, that, Sheila honey, is the first sensible thing you've said today.' She caught sight of her Number Two mascaraing her eyelashes. 'Who's the lucky man, by the way?'

Sheila fluttered at her. 'Don't know yet.'

Lieutenant Landriani was all but ready. He sat his roan under Maxwell's spotlight, cigar smoking quietly – all right, imagination *does* play a part in model soldiery – checking his left stirrup. Peter Maxwell lifted him gently and placed him to the left of Cardigan, near Fitzhardinge Maxse and in front of

Captain White's squadron of the 17th. Louis Nolan had just galloped across his front and all Hell was about to break loose in a 54 millimetre sort of way.

'Do you approve, Count?' Maxwell's dark eyes flickered up to the laundry basket where the Cat With No Scruples sat watching him in the half-light. A welcome breeze was wafting into the Inner Sanctum through the open skylight and the starry weekend was drawing to a close.

'Good,' Maxwell pulled off the gold-laced forage cap and sat back in his swivel chair. 'Now the serious work's done, let's get down to that little sideline of ours, the gentle art of murder. We have a third victim, Count, did you know that?'

Metternich *sort* of suspected it, but he'd been out foraging while Maxwell, Jacquie and Nolan had tea and, to be honest, he was as mystified by the adults' zicker zickering as the little pink kid was. Then, of course, it was the Sunday evening hunt and *whatever* the Labour Party said, there were just some traditions it was impossible to destroy, so that had gone ahead as planned. So...third victim? Say on.

'One Benjamin Lemon,' Maxwell was pouring himself an unseemly large Southern Comfort. 'Known to his friends as Benji and the world of online auctioneering as zest1967. What was I doing in that year, I hear you ask?' He caught the cat's smouldering eye. 'Better you don't ask. Friend Lemon was in to kinky sex, Count. Well, you and I are men of the world, so I can talk to you. I'll be in a home before Nolan and I can have this sort of conversation. Bondage they used to call it down Egypt way a long long time ago. Shackles, manacles, training helmets. Apparently, young Benji was into all that, but his ex-wife wasn't, and, much more to the point,

Count, who else wasn't, hmm? Who else did the late Lemon offend by posing a position too far? Because you see,' he took a swig of the amber nectar, 'whoever it was probably pushed the noxious bastard off a cliff. I wonder how he liked them apples.'

CHAPTER FOURTEEN

Monday. A day like any other. Maxwell, along with another seventy-plus staff and not a few kids, was counting down the days. A week to go before the hols were here and they'd all throw their satchels and blazers and caps into the Leigh and go skinny-dipping. Oh, but that was then, the dear, dead days of pooh sticks and candyfloss. The kids knew perfectly well that these days teachers just climbed into cupboards and waited there until September.

But this wasn't a day like any other. It was the day that Peter Maxwell's world fell in. And it fell in further because this was not the first time. A tribunal awaited him in the Head's office shortly after Lesson Three. Maxwell knew tribunals like this; he'd faced them historically all his life. Oliver Cromwell, all warts and piety, asking a little boy on a stool when he'd last seen his father. Sweaty, drunken revolutionaries in striped trousers and cockades spitting at the aristos who had lorded it over them for centuries. Some Commissar in an outsize peaked cap presiding over one of dear old Uncle Joe's show trials. And, once before, he'd faced it for real…

'There's no easy way to say this, Max.' James Diamond had been here before too. Same bloke, same potential reason, but this time, there was a crucial, yawning difference. 'A complaint has been made against you by a member of the public.'

When this happens to teachers, a thousand images flash through their brains. The *Mail on Sunday* and the *News of the World* are full of such stories every week – a dedicated man's/woman's life wrecked by a malicious child who cannot be named for legal reasons; or 'Filthy Pervert Touched My Princess'; you'd think the *Mail* could write more sophisticated headlines by now. So what was this one? Tall Chloe being asked to surrender her mobile phone? Jack 'Sam Peckinpah' Loach being restrained from hurling a bantamweight friend through the window? Ranjit Singh being told that the Nana Sahib who massacred white women and children in the house at Cawnpore wasn't a very nice man? No doubt, the Headmaster would explain, at which point Maxwell would defend himself with the Clarence Darrowesque style for which he was famous and wipe the self-satisfied smirk off Bernard Ryan's face for ever.

'Oh?' It was as good a response as any other.

'Not to put too fine a point on it, Max,' Diamond was clearly having difficulty with this. 'You have been seen behaving in an inappropriate manner with two students in Year 11.'

'I have?' Maxwell was incredulous. All right, he came clean in his own mind, he *had* put a headlock on Jack Loach, but he probably saved a child's life as a result. But when he'd looked last, Jack Loach was *one* Year 11 student, not two. Unless of course, the schizophrenia was getting worse…

'Mr Maxwell.' The Chair of Governors was less of a shit than his predecessor, but pomposity was his middle name. He was a large man, was Martin Inkester, with thick glasses and a blotchy forehead in the nearly midday heat. James Diamond had switched off the fan in his office and, for obvious reasons, his windows were closed. No point in letting half Year Eight know the state of play. 'Mr Maxwell, do you understand the severity of the charges?'

'If you could be a little more precise as to the nature of the charges, Mr Inkester, I may be able to assess their severity.'

Inkester shuffled the papers in front of him. 'I note that you were suspended some years ago.'

'I was,' Maxwell said. 'On trumped-up charges that should never have seen the light of day. If I may make the comment, Headmaster, you were a little premature then and you are, no doubt, equally premature now.' He glowered at Diamond. 'I was going to say do you learn nothing from history? But of course you don't; you're a biologist.'

'However trumped up those charges may have been,' Inkester's line remained firm, 'these seem of a different nature.' He held up a letter. 'With your permission, Head.'

Diamond nodded. Maxwell hadn't seen the man look this drained in months, not since the last Ofsted, in fact; although the unexpected arrival of the Auditor out of the blue pulled him up with something of a jolt.

'"I was walking on the patch of Common known as The Dam yesterday,"' Inkester quoted the letter, '"when I noticed a middle-aged man in conversation with two girls. Call me old-fashioned if you like, but these days you read such stories so I thought I should investigate. As I got closer, I realised that he had his hand up both girls' skirts and had exposed himself. When I attempted to protect the girls by remonstrating with him, he told me not to interfere, claiming they were his daughters and he could do what he liked with them. I happen to know who this man is as I have seen his face in photographs in the local paper. I believe him to be a Mr Maxwell, a teacher at your school. The girls were enormously grateful to me and took the opportunity of my intervention to get away. I am sorry to have to burden you with such a sordid revelation, but felt that you, as a person of responsibility in the local community, should take the necessary action against this sad and possibly highly dangerous man. Yours sincerely…" Is that precise enough for you, Mr Maxwell?'

'No,' the Head of Sixth Form answered. 'I'd like the name, please.' He leaned forward to Inkester. 'You see, I tend to doubt the man's sincerity.'

'Max,' Diamond intervened, 'Where were you on Saturday?'

'At home,' Maxwell said. 'And here…and at The Dam.'

Diamond and Inkester exchanged looks.

'What were you doing here, Mr Maxwell?' the Chair of Governors asked.

'Watching the auditions for the forthcoming production.'

'Why?' Bernard Ryan spoke for the first time.

'Why not, Bernard?' Maxwell smiled sweetly. 'I take an interest in all that goes on at Leighford. If you'd looked closely, you'd have seen me cheering on the soccer team last season; in April, God help me, I even went with Year Seven to Chessington World of Adventures. I don't think I saw you on any of those occasions.'

'Was there any other reason, Max?' Diamond asked.

A rock. And a hard place. That was where Maxwell was

now. That was where he'd been all his working life. 'I wanted to talk to Stephanie Courtney,' he said.

Another exchange of glances.

'Why, Max?' Diamond was at his most obsequious. He was turning, with astonishing speed, into Uriah Heep.

Maxwell straightened in his chair. If he was going to die like Edith Cavell, he could sit upright like her too. 'I can't tell you that, Headmaster.'

'Why not?' Ryan went straight for the jugular.

Maxwell's look was one of utter contempt. 'I'd be betraying a confidence,' he said levelly.

'You went with this girl...this Stephanie Courtney...to The Dam.' Inkester wanted to establish a few facts. After all, it wasn't looking too good for Maxwell at the moment.

'No.'

'No?' The tribunal were confused, heads turning in all directions. 'But you said...'

'I said *I* was at The Dam,' Maxwell corrected the Chair of Governors – not for the first time in the career of either of them. 'I didn't say Stephanie was.'

'You deny it then?' Inkester shook the incriminating letter at Maxwell.

'Absolutely,' he said.

'You were not there with the girl?'

'I was there with the girl.'

'For God's sake, Max,' Diamond exploded. 'Stop playing your bloody silly games. We're not just looking at the end of your career here, we're looking at a custodial sentence. And I'm sure you know better than I do what happens to child molesters in prison.'

'And where swallows go in the winter; yes, Headmaster, I do.'

'So, *please*,' Diamond begged. 'Tell us what happened.'

'I don't think I should say anything more until I see my solicitor.'

'Do you have a solicitor?' Inkester asked. 'Do you need one?'

'Two very different questions, Chair,' Maxwell said. 'Let me answer them with the same answer. Do bears shit in the woods?'

Peter Maxwell saw himself out, not just of James Diamond's office, but of Leighford High School. He only had one more lesson to teach, so Thingee who does the cover was told to sort it out for him. He was on full pay until this wretched business could be resolved. But he was warned it might take days or weeks or even months depending on whether the parents of the girls in question chose to press charges.

'Look after Tarantula for me,' he asked Helen Maitland, spraying his bedraggled spider plant one last time.

'Max...' The woman looked numbed.

'Not now, Helen,' he sighed. 'And don't worry. I'll be back.' It was a perfect Arnie Schwarzenegger.

He toyed, as he walked along the corridor towards the bike sheds, with calling in on Sylvia Matthews at the school's MRSA centre, but he thought better of it. It was Sylvia who had borne the brunt of things the last time he'd handed in his gun and shield; she didn't need that again.

'Bad luck, Max,' he heard as he reached the front steps. He didn't need to turn because he knew the acid tone, even before he heard the hissing of the snakes coiling in her hair. He, who'd just handed in his shield to Legs Diamond. Then, an odd thought occurred to him.

'Tell me,' he said. 'How did the concerned member of the public who wrote that charming letter know that Stephanie Courtney was in Year 11?'

Dierdre Lessing stood tall and angular at the top of the steps, like Boudicca without a cause, like some ghastly remake of *Whatever Happened to Baby Jane*. 'Odd how these things happen, isn't it?' she said. 'It's been a real pleasure working with you.'

'Max, are you all right?' Jacquie's voice came and went on her mobile. 'I'm coming home.'

'No, no.' Maxwell was in his lounge, his feet up, his cycle clips, bow tie and porkpie hat lying across the carpet as though washed up by a tsunami. 'No, darling, I'm fine, really. Bit of a sense of freedom, actually. I can get things done.'

'What things?' Jacquie Carpenter hadn't really known Peter Maxwell the last time he'd been in this situation. But she'd known a teacher in Worthing who'd been accused of grossly inappropriate behaviour. And he'd hanged himself shortly before his hearing was due. Not of course, that Peter Maxwell would even consider anything like that... But even so.

'Oh, this and that,' he told her. 'That bloody lawnmower for a start. And, hey, how about a lick of paint in the kitchen?'

'Wild orchid,' she reminded him. At least with her man up a ladder, she'd know where he was.

'Machiavelli Mauve,' he insisted.

'There's no such colour,' he heard her say, on the edge of her mobile range as she was now.

'That's what I'll do, then,' he chuckled. 'I'll invent it. Make a fortune. I've had enough of teaching, anyway. Ninety-five years – it's enough for anybody.'

'Max,' Jacquie said, serious now after the brittle laughter. 'You could collect Nolan from Pam's.'

Silence.

Then, 'Yes. Yes, I could.'

A new murder throws up new hope. At first, it's 'God, not another one', and cries of ineptitude on the part of the police; what are people paying their taxes for? Then it's the more sobering prospects – and this gives new ammunition, a fresh start; and every time chummy carries out another one, it increases the chances of his being caught.

'Benji Lemon.' Henry Hall was in his shirtsleeves this sticky end of Monday, not in his usual position of out front, his whole team before him, but sitting with them, watching intently as the now familiar faces flashed onto the screen from the PowerPoint. 'Links to the other two victims?'

'None known, guv,' Geoff Hare said. 'We've established that Henderson did a building job for Taylor, but that doesn't tell us why Taylor was found in Leighford.'

'Did either Henderson or Taylor buy anything from Lemon?' Hall asked. 'On eBay?'

'We're still looking into that, guv,' Benji Palister told everybody. 'He's been trading since the thing began so there's a lot of clients to get through. Nothing so far, though.'

'Right,' Hall got up and found his coffee. 'Lights, Tom.'

The flashing neon positively hurt after the darkness of the PowerPoint. Jacquie Carpenter felt like an old yak. Her blouse was clinging to her like rubber and she didn't want to know where her tights top had risen to, inextricably linked with her other bits and pieces as it was. The fans had long ago failed to move the warm air anywhere and Hall was secretly regretting permitting smoking – each fag-end seemed to exude a few thousand joules.

'What do we know about Benji Lemon, apart from his auction habit, I mean?'

'Kinky sex, guv,' Geoff Hare volunteered.

'Is that an offer, Geoffrey?' George Bronson sniggered. 'Shall we leave you boys alone together?' There was tired laughter all round.

'Relationships?' Hall ignored it.

'None that we know of,' Jacquie came in. 'Sheila and I talked to his ex. Nice woman, glad to be rid of him.'

'Could the neighbours shed any light?' Hall wanted to know.

'Didn't seem to be anyone long term,' Bronson checked his notes. 'But Ingleneuk is a big place, set back from the road and mostly surrounded by a high wall. It's not likely anyone would be seen if Lemon didn't want them to be.'

'No complaints?' Hall asked. 'From outraged girlfriends? Hookers? Anybody expecting a night of torrid romance that turned into something else?'

'Nothing reported, guv,' someone called from the inner recesses among the VDUs at the back of the room.

'So he's either behaving himself or he's found someone like-minded or he's not getting any,' Hall mused. 'Dead end.'

'What about the lizard, guv?' Jacquie asked. 'The one the boys found at the Point? Any link with Lemon?'

'In case any of you missed this on the bulletin board or at briefings,' Hall thought it best to fill everybody in. 'A lizard pendant was found by two lads near the body of David Taylor. The lab have confirmed that it did not belong to the dead man – or at least, did not form part of his own jewellery collection. Of course, there's nothing definite to tell us it was linked to the crime at all. It could have been dropped by anyone at about the same time. Not, in itself, helpful.'

'But Benji Lemon traded in goods like that,' Jacquie persisted.

'Not precisely,' the ever smart-arsed George Bronson corrected her. 'If you check out zest1967's list of items, they're exclusively British. The lizard was foreign. German silver, to be precise.'

'So, what are we saying, Inspector?' Jacquie asked. 'That Benji Lemon only sold British gear so that made him some sort of target?'

'He could have been a member of the bloody KKK as far as I'm concerned, darling,' Bronson snapped back. 'It doesn't get us any nearer his killer, does it?'

'All right, all right.' Time for Henry Hall to wade in. When his own Number Two started locking horns with his sergeants, it was time to call it a day. 'Thank you, boys and girl. Let's wind it up for now. George, you on the graveyard shift?'

''Fraid so, guv,' Bronson shrugged. He had a wife and kids somewhere.

'All right, then. Tomorrow, I want you and Hare to revisit this gangland thing. Get back to Brighton.'

'You want us to pick up Jimmy the Snail again?'

'No, he'll only have an army of legals with him. Go one down. Find out when he was in Brighton, what Wide Boy Taylor did for laughs. We're all missing one thing about our three wise men; they were all relatively loaded, but nothing was taken from them as far as we know, as a motive for murder. Let's find out how they spent it, shall we?'

Little Nolan was fast asleep in his buggy that evening as his mum and dad wandered along the sands.

'And what, now that you're King and Prime Minister all rolled into one, Nolan Maxwell, what is your earliest memory?' Jacquie was playing a chat-show host of the future. 'Well,' her voice deepened to become her son in the years ahead. 'My fondest memory is my parents wheeling me round murder sites,' she growled. 'Made me the man I am today.'

Maxwell looked over the buggy's handlebars. 'He's sparkers,' he said. 'Anyway, whose idea was this?'

And they both chorused 'Yours' as a tired, happy family clumped past them, bound for the hotel and supper. It was cool down here on the beach after the searing heat of the day and the shadows were beginning to lengthen over Dead Man's Point.

'OK,' Jacquie said. 'You've had a butchers from up top. Now, you've seen it from below. Any ideas, Sherlock?'

'Excuse me.' He stopped the buggy as it ran into wet sand for the first time. 'But you've already done this.'

'That's what they pay me for, Max,' she said. 'It goes with the territory. Only usually there are canvas tents and blokes in white suits and Jim Bloody Astley with his wisecracks.'

None of that was here now. The tents, the SOCO men,

even the fluttering 'Do Not Cross' tape had gone. And since Mayor Ledbetter had not yet had time to put up his 'This Way To The Corpse' sign, complete with entry fee, no one would ever know that a man had hurtled out of the sky to land in a bloody pulp more or less where Nolan's buggy stood now.

'Max, what's going to happen?' Jacquie asked. When she'd come home, exhausted, clammy with the humidity and heartily pissed off with all her colleagues, but George Bronson in particular, she'd held her man like she'd never let go. She hadn't wanted to let go. But Maxwell had been to collect Nolan from Pam's and the smaller of her men had held out his arms to her, gurgling with that sweet impish grin of his. Part of her wanted to say 'Not now, darling. Now your daddy needs me.' But she was a mother too. And so she held them both.

'You're going to solve the case,' he said. 'Oh, you may need a little help from Henry Hall, but you're getting there.'

'I'm not talking about that,' she said. 'All right, it's a horrible thing to say, I know, but that's somebody else's problem; somebody else's tragedy. This is us. You. What's going to happen about these complaints?'

He looked at her. He could hold her, smooth her hair, pat her cheek, kiss away her fears. But she was a detective sergeant, for God's sake, used to facts and hard evidence. She'd prefer the rational.

'For a start,' he said, wheeling the buggy around and making his way back along the lapping water's edge, 'it's a complaint, singular. The next thing I want to find out is who sent the letter.'

'You can't possibly think it was Dierdre Lessing,' Jacquie was walking with him.

'No, of course not,' he said. 'She hates my guts but she doesn't have the imagination for this. Anyway, it'll be all right. Only part of it is true.'

'Which part?' Jacquie asked.

He looked at her in mock horror. 'Oh, ye of little faith,' he scolded. 'The part about my hands in the girls' knickers, of course. Everything else is made up.'

'Max,' she stopped him. 'Don't joke about this. You remember Oscar Wilde?'

'Not personally,' Maxwell smiled. 'But if you mean his flippant, smart-arsed arrogance in court at his libel trial, yes, I do.'

'"I am a lover of youth,"' Jacquie quoted. 'And that landed him in a helluva lot of trouble.'

'Poor Oscar,' Maxwell was looking out to sea where the ocean liners passed each other, lit by the gold of the evening sun like a Maxfield Parrish painting. 'He was his own worst enemy.'

'And so are you, Max.' She was standing there shivering slightly, for all it was still July and Leighford still in the middle of a heatwave. 'I don't know what you said to that tribunal this morning, but I'll lay you any odds you like you got right up their collective noses. You just can't help yourself. Oh, darling,' she suddenly hugged him. '*Please* be careful.'

'Let's teach it to them before they teach it to us,' he growled in his best *Hill Street Blues* take off. 'Yes, I know.'

'You went to The Dam with those girls,' Jacquie said. 'Why?'

'Are you being a prosecuting counsel now?' he asked her.

She shook her head, walking on with him. 'I'm just trying to find out what happened.'

'All right. No, technically I didn't go with the girls. I met them there. I didn't even acknowledge that much for the tribunal, by the way.'

'OK,' she said. 'Who were they?'

'Steph Courtney and Emma Austen.'

'Do you teach either of them?'

'Not now,' he told her. 'I used to in Year Nine. Emma does History, I think, in Paul Moss's set. Steph doesn't. Media, I believe, after the school of one Michael Mouse Esquire. Technically, of course, no one teaches them. They've left.'

Jacquie nodded. 'That might work in your favour,' she said. 'You can't be charged with interfering with your students if they're not your students.'

'Jacquie.' Maxwell stopped the buggy again, Nolan turning over in his sleep. 'I didn't interfere with anybody. Except you, of course,' he smiled, 'and I seem to remember that was your idea.'

But Jacquie wasn't laughing and Maxwell's attempt to lift the mood of the moment wasn't exactly a success.

'How old are they?' she asked. 'Exactly.'

'I don't know, exactly,' he said. 'Steph may be sixteen. Emma, I don't think so. I'd have to look up their files.'

'Great. So at least one of them is under age. Why did you meet them on The Dam?'

'You know why,' Maxwell said. 'Steph saw a murder. Or what she took to be a murder. I wanted to know the precise place.'

'But you'd been there before.'

'Yes, I had, but I couldn't be sure if I was in the right position. Turns out I was a couple of hundred yards out.'

'Does it make a difference?'

'Probably not,' Maxwell pondered. 'It all depends on exactly what Steph actually saw.'

'Max, you're rambling.' Jacquie was at her wits' end.

'No, I'm not. Look, you've been to police college, forensics lectures. Tell me about rigor.'

'Rigor mortis?' she frowned.

'With that spelling, is there any other kind?'

'All right,' she sighed. 'Someone once poetically put it as "a sure indication of the hopelessness of any attempts at resuscitation". Technically, it's the contraction of voluntary and involuntary muscles that stiffen the limbs. It's all caused by coagulation of protein in muscles.'

'Talk me through it,' Maxwell said, checking that Nolan was still happily in the land of nod. It may all be 'zicker zicker' to him, but one of the first words Maxwell senior had learned to say was 'bugger, bugger, bugger' as he chased up the road in exasperation after a cousin who was older and faster than he was. You couldn't be too careful.

'It starts with the lower jaw and eyelids,' she told him. 'About five hours after death.'

'Five hours?'

'Give or take. It's not an exact science, Max. It depends on room temperature, body being inside or outside, time of year.'

'Car,' Maxwell said. 'June.'

'*This* June?' she asked.

He nodded.

'The stiffening spreads to the neck, shoulders, arms, trunk and legs. In "normal" conditions I'd expect the deceased to be as stiff as a board from head to foot after twelve hours.'

'Twelve hours,' he repeated.

'Max, what *is* this about?'

'Humour me,' he said. 'Go on.'

'The body usually stays stiff for another twelve hours,' she said. 'Then the whole process goes into a kind of reverse, except the head loosens first and so on down to the feet.'

'David Taylor was killed by strangulation.'

'That's right,' she nodded. 'What point are you making?'

'There'd have been a struggle?'

'Almost certainly. The marks on the neck and fingernails proved that. There were no drugs found in the body, so he'd have been fit enough to put up a fight, certainly.'

'And does that have any effect on rigor mortis?' he asked.

'Yes. Exertion speeds up the process. You'd have to ask Jim Astley by how much.'

'Hmm,' Maxwell murmured. 'I think I'll leave that stone unturned, thank you very much. So it's not possible, then.'

'What isn't?'

'Hold your arm out.'

'What?' Jacquie was chuckling now.

'Your right arm. Hold it out.'

She did, oblivious to the knots of holiday-makers plodding back across the pebbles.

He tapped her arm lightly with his hand. It wavered. 'Ow!' she said.

'I'm going to pick you up.'

'You dirty old man!' she scolded. 'I'm virtually a married

woman.' And she shrieked as he lifted her bodily off the ground. 'No, no,' he shouted. 'Keep your right arm up, rigid.'

'Max, for God's sake. This is ludicrous.'

There was a sharp cry from Nolan, disturbed by the mock violence around him. 'It's all right, little one,' his father said. 'Just Mummy and Daddy playing silly...beggars. Did you notice, though, how Mummy's legs were dangling down, all floppy, as was Mummy's left arm? That's because she's alive. Hey ho!'

Jacquie swept the startled infant out of the buggy, throwing him in the air and catching him expertly. 'It's all right, darling. Your father's mad.'

'Quite possibly,' Maxwell said. 'But we've established one thing that's quite important. Whatever Steph Courtney witnessed at The Dam the other week, it wasn't a m-u-r-d-e-r.'

CHAPTER FIFTEEN

It rained in the night. In Quetta and all points south they'd have been singing like Gene Kelly, splashing in the puddles and thanking whichever God they worshipped. In Leighford, it was all very quiet and all very British. Mrs Troubridge put all her cutlery away and draped towels over the mirrors – lightning was so unpredictable, wasn't it?

The youngest member of the Geography department at Leighford High went out along the Front as the wind rose and bounced the coloured lights roped between the street lamps. He spent an hour or two standing like Ben Franklin, trying to capture sheet lightning on his digital camera. There had been a time when Peter Maxwell had done mad things for the sake of his kids – though never, it was true, quite as mad as that. But he'd been a young man, then, at a different school in a different place. And now he had no job at all.

Jacquie unplugged the modem and sat with Maxwell under the skylight, listening to the rumbles of thunder as they died away to the west and watching the world suddenly illuminated by the flash. Nolan, of course, slept through the lot. As did Metternich, the seasoned hunter. When he was awake, the flashes were quite useful, in fact, lighting up as they did the trajectory of some hapless creature hoping to make it home tolerably dry and tolerably alive. Uh uh; wrong on both counts.

So no one saw the gaunt young man with straw-coloured hair under his hoodie standing along Columbine in the rain. He was staring hard at Maxwell's house, committing it to memory, getting his bearings from the road. Then, as silently as Metternich, he crossed into the darkness of Maxwell's side gate and was inside before the next flash of lightning hit. He wasn't in Maxwell's garden for long; just long enough.

It was still wet, warm and like treacle when Peter Maxwell on Surrey purred into the car park at Leighford's B&Q. The rain had all but stopped now, but the humidity was frightening. Even so, this was an English summer and Maxwell never ceased to be amazed at the astonishing number of people who seemed to have time off. He wanted to shout at them 'I know why I'm here. I've been suspended from my job on suspicion of gross indecency with minors and I'm following up a murder enquiry, like you do. What's your excuse?'

But somehow, he felt, as his eyes lighted on an old girl who appeared to be Methuselah's elder sister, he wasn't likely to get much of a response. Jacquie was clearly worried about him, had dropped Nolan off at Pam's herself and told the silly old bugger to stay home. True, Maxwell had another white, plastic, unmade-up soldier kit in 54 millimetre waiting for him when he'd finished Landriani. Why didn't he indulge himself, Jacquie has suggested, and start work on the next? But Peter Maxwell was no fool; he recognised therapy when it was suggested to him. Busy, busy, busy. But there were other things on Maxwell's mind today. He had a murderer to catch and he couldn't help thinking this little misunderstanding at Leighford High was something or other to do with it.

'Got any seven eighths Whitworths?' he asked the lad in the overalls halfway up a ladder. They were the screws Noah had used to build the Ark.

'I'm sorry, sir, I...oh, Mr Maxwell. It's you.'

It certainly was when Maxwell looked last; now, he wasn't so sure. 'Have you got a minute, John?' he asked.

'Sure.' The lad clattered down.

'Look,' Maxwell looked into the boy's face, earnest as always, eager to please. 'Have you got a coffee break due or something? It's rather personal; I don't want to talk about it in...' he looked about him, 'Plumbing.'

John Mason smiled. He'd always liked Maxwell. Never found him mad at all. That was only stupid idiots who didn't know him, couldn't see the decent man under the scarf and the cycle clips and the outer shell of bravado. He'd actually noticed once, when Maxwell had left his wallet open in his office at school, a battered photo of a woman and a baby. And he'd always wondered who they were. 'Out back,' he said. 'Smokers' Corner. Don't worry, it's too wet for them today.'

Actually, John Mason was wrong. A scrawny employee with designer acne lurked there, his fingers curling around his roll-up.

'Oh, sorry, Alf. Give us a minute, can you, mate?'

Alf was a reasonable sort of bloke. The old bastard with the silly hat and the barbed-wire hair was probably the kid's dad. He had a dad like that. Well, not like that, exactly, 'cos his dad had no hat. And, come to think of it, no hair. But he kept turning up at inopportune moments too. Alf winked and sloped off, to Smokers' Corner Two, round the back of the Creosote store.

'Can't offer you a seat, I'm afraid, Mr Maxwell.' University had done wonders for John Mason. He'd always been bright, clever, quick on the uptake. But now he was what headteachers the world over liked to call 'a rounded individual', whatever that meant. In the case of John Mason, it meant he was a bloody nice fella.

'John, I spoke to Louise a few days ago…'

'I know,' Mason nodded, his face suddenly serious. 'She told me.'

'I think I upset her.'

He nodded again. 'I think you did,' he said. 'But I'm sure you didn't mean it. You had your reasons.'

'Yes,' said Maxwell. 'Yes, I did. You see, Louise wasn't quite honest with me, was she?'

'I don't know what you mean,' the lad said.

'Yes, you do, John. Let me tell you something about teaching. Oh, it's nothing you learn on PGCE courses, although you might just come across it in some of the more down-to-earth Child Psychology books. Kids lie. Yup! An unpalatable truth, but a truth nonetheless. They don't at first, of course. It's not an original sin. But like everything else, they learn it from their elders, if not betters. They realise that by telling porkies, they get away with things, don't get told off. If they're *really* good at it, they can get somebody else into trouble. But often, little things give them away. Like looking to the left when they're telling those lies. Like Louise did when I spoke to her in the café – like you're doing now, John.'

'No, I…'

'John!' The old Maxwell bark still had the power to make the lad jump. For all he was Mr Sophisticate these days, the rounded individual, right now he was back in Year Seven again with a big scary man trying to teach him some history. 'Three men are dead, son,' his old Head of Sixth Form was talking more softly now. 'I think your Louise knows something about that.'

'No, Mr Maxwell.' The lad was horrified. 'No, you don't understand.'

'Well, then,' Maxwell said. 'Suppose you enlighten me.'

'On the game?' Jacquie sounded incredulous at the other end of the phone.

'No, not actually.' Maxwell had just kicked off his soaking wet hush-puppies. The rain may have stopped, but the spray over the Flyover was something else and he was wringing wet. He grabbed a towel and began attacking his hair while juggling the cordless. Metternich wasn't in to see this meaningless ritual; he'd seen it before and it had embarrassed the hell out of him. He was in a hayloft somewhere, listening to his next meal rustling away to his left, gnaw gnaw west. 'But someone made her an offer she felt bound to refuse.'

'Say on,' Jacquie told him. 'If I see any more cross references on this bloody computer, I'm going to throw it out of the window. And what were you doing in B&Q, by the by?'

'Oh ye of no faith at all!' Maxwell sighed, stumbling out of his trousers and landing gratefully on the bed. 'I needed more gravure for my pyro if you must get all the dirt. We modellers never sleep, you know.'

'Bollocks, Max,' she grunted. 'Cut to the chase.'

'All right. The Gardens were a favourite trysting place of Louise Bedford and John Mason.'

'Yes, we know that.'

'But what you don't know, because neither of them told you, is that in going back there on the night they found Gerald Henderson, they were actually exorcising a ghost of sorts.'

'How do you mean?'

'They'd had a bad experience there the previous week.'

'Oh? What?'

Maxwell was trying to disentangle himself from the damp wrinkles of his shirt. And that wasn't easy with one hand. There was, of course, a speaker button on the cordless, but such niceties had never occurred to the dodo who was Peter Maxwell. 'A gentleman of certain years had been watching them from the bushes. The bushes were shaking. Are you getting the point, or shall I start breathing heavily?'

'All too clearly, thanks,' Jacquie told him. 'By the way, this call is being recorded for training purposes. Your liberty is at risk if you look at us funny. Catch my drift?'

Maxwell did. 'The gentleman emerged from the bushes brandishing a huge...wallet. And he offered both of them, but Louise especially, a rather sizable amount of spondulicks if she'd care to go to a party with him.'

'A party, eh?' Jacquie had been around. She'd heard this sort of offer before. In fact, unknown to Maxwell, she'd once been on the receiving end of one. 'Where?'

'Littlehampton.'

'Littlehampton?' Jacquie repeated.

'Said gentleman was prepared to drive the pair of them, but Louise especially, to said party the very next night.'

'They didn't go for it?'

'No,' Maxwell was wrestling with his left sock. 'Louise just grabbed her bra and they did a runner.'

'Did they recognise the man?' Jacquie asked.

'Oh, yes,' Maxwell said. 'He's in the *Advertiser* most weeks. It was Chester Harris, Leighford's answer to Percy Thrower – if you remember him? By the way,' he grunted hoarsely, having collapsed backwards on the bed, 'want to know what I'm wearing?' His voice returned to normal again. 'A rather soggy pair of Y-fronts.' But Jacquie had already gone.

Juanita Reyes was a rather tricky one as international police protocol went. Rodrigo Mendoza had gone to see somebody – it turned out to be Sheila Kindling – to the effect that the girl was light-fingered and was to be found at her parents' home in Sant Lluis on the island of Menorca. It was all highly embarrassing and could everyone please tread as softly as possible?

The Menorcan police had emailed back, in a translation that left something to be desired, that the girl was indeed there. They found no sign of stolen goods, nothing from England except a photograph of a baby with a bloke with mad barbed wire hair and no evidence that the girl had fenced anything. Juanita's people were honest, upright types, pillars of the local community and good Catholics. The good people of Sant Lluis were lining up to act as character witnesses for them and the local priest was so fulsome in his praise for the family that Leighford Nick was left wondering why there wasn't a shrine outside the Reyes' home and the odour of sanctity emanating from their outside loo.

So all the girl had done, as far as actual facts were concerned, was do a runner back home, cause unknown. Yes, she'd abandoned the baby, which was hardly in keeping with the girl that Jacquie and Maxwell – and indeed the Hendersons – knew. But was it an indictable offence? No, the Menorcan police decided. It was a civil matter and up to the Maxwells to take whatever action against the girl they deemed appropriate. As for dumping the Hyundai, well, that was just common sense, really – the thing was a death trap, anyway. Goodbye, that's all she wrote.

Jacquie Carpenter was clicking on the tape recorder that morning in Interview Room Number One at Leighford Nick. Three miles away at Leighford High, the whole place was limbering up for its Sports Day, in other words, the annual skive. Who would do the running commentary over the tannoy now that Maxwell wasn't available? Rumours of course abounded. He'd broken his leg, finally flipped and run along the seafront stripping off and shouting 'Beecham's Powders' at the top of his voice. Nobody, but nobody, believed that concocted nonsense about the girls at The Dam.

'DS Carpenter and DC Palister interviewing Mr Chester Harris and Mr Paul Barsdale, solicitor,' she said.

Harris could not have been more transformed from his usual appearance. The open shirt, bandana and fringed shorts had gone and in their place, he wore a dark suit and sombre tie. The brief looked like a hippy alongside that.

'I must emphasise, Mr Harris, that this is merely a chat. When I asked you to come in this afternoon, I didn't expect you to have representation.'

'My client believes he has been maligned,' Barsdale said. Jacquie had come across this man before. He was scrawny and off-hand, one of the all-coppers-are-Fascists school who'd come up the hard way via legal clerk. 'And not for the first time.'

'We'd just like you to tell us about your links with the Wilbraham Golf Club at Littlehampton, if you would.'

Harris blinked. He looked at the brief. 'Wilbraham?' he repeated.

'Yes,' Jacquie said. 'Are you a member?'

'I am,' Harris conceded. 'What of it?'

'When were you there last?' Jacquie asked.

'God, I don't know. Three, four weeks ago. Why?'

'Did you go to a party?'

'I may have done,' Harris shrugged. 'I really don't remember.'

'Say, week last Thursday,' Jacquie persisted.

'My client has already answered that question,' Barsdale countered.

'Switch the tape off for a minute,' Jacquie told Palister.

'I don't think so,' the brief snarled as the lad's hand moved towards it. 'I don't know what game you're playing here, detective sergeant, but there *are* rules, you know.'

Jacquie laughed. 'Well, that's just it,' she said. 'It's just one of those silly things about golf, talking of games. It's got nothing to do with the interview. Something I thought Mr Harris could explain to me. What, in God's name, is a single Stableton? I've often heard the expression and here you are, a golfer. I just thought that...'

'I have some Botanic Gardens to run.' Harris snapped. 'Will you please get to the point.'

'Why did you invite Louise Bedford and John Mason to a party at a golf club in Littlehampton?' Jacquie wasn't smiling now. Her grey eyes were cold and hard as she watched the veins throbbing in Chester Harris's temple.

'Er...'

'My client knows no one with those names,' the brief sensed Harris's difficulty.

'All right,' Jacquie said. 'Let me make it easy for you. The young couple you spoke to in the Gardens a week last Wednesday – that would make it July 2nd. Why did you invite them to a party?'

'I am not in the habit of inviting strangers to parties,' Harris insisted.

'Are you in the habit of spying on strangers from bushes while masturbating?' Jacquie asked, as if she was asking the price of a bus fare to the town centre.

Both men exploded, the needle on the tape dial rocketing into the red. In the event it was the brief who was coherent first. 'Are you actually accusing my client of committing an act of indecency?' he asked.

'Is he admitting to one?' Palister countered.

Then Harris was on his feet. 'That's it. That's enough. I'm out of here.'

The brief spun back to the police persons. 'You *will* be hearing from me,' he said.

Jacquie nodded to Palister who spoke into the machine. 'Interview terminated at the request of Mr Harris's solicitor at...three-eighteen.'

'Can't wait,' muttered Jacquie.

* * *

'London, Max? Why?' Jacquie was back in the Incident Room, reading for the umpteenth time depositions from witnesses at all three murder sites, yards apart though they were.

'I can hear the bloody tannoy,' Maxwell told her from his end of the phone. 'Oh, it's coming and going, of course, but a) I don't want to know who's won the one hundred metres and b) it's that joke Cole making the announcements. It's all a bit raw at the moment, petal. I need a change of air. Somewhere where I won't hear the name Leighford High School.'

'All right, sweetheart,' Jacquie said. 'But *London*? Doesn't it seem a bit extreme?'

'Humour me. Can you pick up Nole?'

'I'll sort that,' she said. And he was gone.

The great thing about travelling by train in term time is that there aren't many kids. There are some, of course, whose parents haven't realised it's been compulsory to send kids to school since 1886, or whose parents are too stupid to realise they're being lied to, by said kids who could bunk for England. Of course, if you time it badly you end up in the same carriage as hordes of them, on their way home from said school.

As it happened, Maxwell struck lucky. There was only one, very well-behaved nine-year-old (clearly the product of a private school) who added to the levity of the day by looking out at the Westminster skyline as the train rattled into Waterloo and shouting, 'Look, Mummy. Big Dong!' Maxwell had checked his clothing, just in case.

He had forgotten just how hot London was in July. The sun

burned off the pavements and reflected off the plate glass. You could probably have fried an egg on the MI5 building on the Embankment, and the old Scotland Yard, where the ghosts of Greeno and Cherill and Fabian and Charlie Artful still wandered, positively wilted in its red-brick heat. Happy holiday makers chattered and laughed on the bright pleasure boats slicing through the sparkling brown of the river and the queue for the Eye seemed to stretch forever into the hinterland that was Southwark.

By the time he'd got to the Strand, Maxwell just wanted to lie down with the winos on the Embankment, drinking whatever they were drinking. His bow tie had gone. He'd left his jacket at home and cycle clips seemed odd on a train, so they hung with Surrey in his conservatory. As a concession to the demonic afternoon sun, he'd even left his famous hat behind. So no one at all would have recognised the glowing figure shambling into the Levington Agency, just off Villiers Street. Damn, was his first thought – no air conditioning.

'Can I help you?' A rather elegant, brassy woman sat poised at a computer. There was something of old-world charm about these offices, Maxwell thought – all wall-to-wall oak and leather and marble. He'd have preferred that the computer was an upright Remington or at a pinch an Olivetti, but he couldn't afford to be choosy.

'I hope you can,' he beamed. 'I'm in need of a girl.'

The brassy blonde smiled. 'Could you be a little more specific?'

'Well, I had one from you before – Spanish girl, Juanita Reyes.'

'Could I have your name, please?' the secretary asked.

'Maxwell,' he told her. 'Peter Maxwell.'

Her fingers flew over the keyboard and a series of reflections flashed across her face as the screen jumped with images. She frowned. 'I'm afraid I don't have that name on our books, sir. Good afternoon.'

'Oh, how stupid of me,' Maxwell said. 'Henderson. Try Gerald Henderson.'

The secretary's eyes narrowed. Didn't this man know his own name? Or was he just wandering through the phone book trying to strike lucky? She pressed an intercom button near her left knee. There was a click. 'Mrs Pedersen, could you come out here, please?'

Mrs Pedersen was probably the wrong side of fifty, but she carried it well. A tall brunette with a statuesque figure, she filled the doorway at the end of the marbled hall. 'Can I help?' she asked. Her accent was unplaceable – Uppsala meets Roedean, possibly – but Maxwell couldn't be sure.

'Peter Maxwell,' he crossed to her and extended his hand. 'I'm sorry. I should have rung ahead for an appointment.'

'Yes,' Mrs Pedersen agreed. 'Yes, you should. But since you're here, Mr Maxwell, why not pop into my office? Can Ingrid get you anything? Iced tea? Perrier?'

'Thank you, no,' Maxwell smiled.

Mrs Pedersen and Ingrid were alone for the briefest of moments while Maxwell settled himself into a huge leather sofa; but it was long enough.

'Ingrid tells me there is some complication, Mr Maxwell,' the boss-lady said, 'in that you do not appear to be on our books.'

'No, indeed,' he said, 'and I apologise for that. I think I'm guilty of an irregularity.'

'Oh?' She sat down behind her desk and, like Ingrid, went to work on her computer's keyboard.

'You see, I had one of your girls, Juanita Reyes.'

'Really?'

'Yes. The reason I am not on your books is that I found her via your actual client, Gerald Henderson.'

There was a flurry of keyboard activity. 'Could you give me Mr Henderson's address, Mr Maxwell?' she asked.

'Tottingleigh,' he said. 'Near Leighford.'

'And Mr Henderson's occupation?'

'Construction.'

'And the girl's name again?'

'Juanita. Juanita Reyes. Lovely girl, from Menorca.'

'I don't understand, Mr Maxwell.' Mrs Pedersen leaned back from her machine. 'The girls of the Levington Agency are hand-picked and of top quality. It is understood that if contracts are terminated, either by the client or by the girl, we are to be informed immediately.'

'Quite.' Maxwell's feigned embarrassment was legendary. 'Hence my little irregularity. Innocent, I assure you, but Gerald was looking to downsize. I needed a girl. He advertised in the local paper...'

'The local paper?' Mrs Pedersen was aghast. 'More than a little irregular, if I may say so, Mr Maxwell. Where is Juanita now?'

'As I understand it, back home with her parents, in Menorca.'

'I see.' Mrs Pedersen looked less than pleased. 'Well, I can appreciate that your involvement may have been innocent, as you say, Mr Maxwell. But the same cannot be said, I'm afraid, of Mr Henderson. He knew exactly what the rules were. He signed papers. He shall be hearing from us.'

'Of course,' Maxwell frowned, shaking his head. 'I wouldn't expect anything less. Now...er...'

'You require a replacement. Quite. Could I have a few preliminary details, please? You may have enjoyed the services of one of our girls, but, I fear, by default. As far as we are concerned, you are a new client. Very welcome, of course, but new, nevertheless. Name and address, please.'

'Peter Maxwell, 38 Columbine Avenue, Leighford, West Sussex. Postcode...'

'Niceties like that we can leave 'til later. Telephone?'

'01903 618555.'

'May I ask your age?'

'Fifty-something,' Maxwell smiled.

Mrs Pedersen laughed and leaned forward conspiratorially. 'Join the club,' she said. 'Mother's maiden name?'

'Hemmings.'

'Now. To more pertinent questions. Is there a Mrs Maxwell?'

'I have a partner,' Maxwell admitted.

'Disabled in some way?' Mrs Pedersen was still poised at the keyboard.

'Not noticeably,' Maxwell told her.

'Doesn't understand you, though?'

'Sometimes not,' Maxwell chuckled.

'Broad-minded, though.'

'In her profession, she has to be,' Maxwell conceded.

'Oh, what is that?'

'Um…teacher. Even in infant schools, the playground language these days…'

'Shocking. Yes, I know. And your profession, Mr Maxwell?'

'Chartered Accountant.'

A warm smile spread across Mrs Pedersen's face. 'And your *raison d'être*?'

'I'm sorry?'

Mrs Pedersen looked closely at the man. Perhaps his French wasn't up to much. 'Your reason…for wanting a girl. On paper, of course.'

'Au pair.'

'Huh, uh.' The keyboard was in action again. 'It hardly matters, but do you have children?'

'One,' Maxwell said proudly. 'A boy.'

'Oh, really? How old?'

'Nearly a year.'

'Well,' Mrs Pedersen's eyebrows appeared above the rim of her spectacles. 'Congratulations. Now, what sort of girl had you in mind?'

'Well,' Maxwell chuckled. 'It sounds corny, but I'd like Juanita back. We were very fond.'

'We?'

'My partner and I.'

'Ah, I see.' Another knowing smile broke over Mrs Pedersen's lips. 'You *both* liked her. Well, I think we can accommodate. Obviously, all joking apart, Juanita is out of the question. I don't know what made her leave the country, but, like Mr Henderson, I fear she'll have some explaining to do. Do you particularly go for Hispanics? Eastern Europeans are cheaper, of course, but there's often a language barrier – not that that presents an immediate problem, if you know what I mean. I could show you some photographs.'

'Lovely,' Maxwell said. 'Tell me, are these girls available at once?'

'Some are already in England,' she told him. 'Others will need to be sent for.'

'So, immigration? Visas? Work permits? I don't know much about it, really.'

'Don't worry,' Mrs Pedersen said. 'We do. Now, Mr Maxwell, I hate to raise it and I don't know what sort of arrangement you and Mr Henderson came to, but…well, not to put too fine a point on it – money. Would a deposit of, say, £5000 be in order? We take Visa, American Express,' she wrinkled her nose. 'Whatever you find most convenient.'

CHAPTER SIXTEEN

'So you don't want to know about the Levington Agency, then?'

'I told you, Max, we're not speaking.'

'Not even the merest hintette?'

'If I can't trust you,' she turned to him, all nobler than thou and hackles raised, 'when you tell me you're going somewhere and then you go somewhere else entirely, then I can't see any future in our relationship. We've got a son now, for God's sake.'

'It's a knocking shop.'

'No!' Jacquie was suddenly all ears, squeezing in next to Maxwell on the sofa. 'You are having a laugh!'

'Not at five grand a pop I'm not.'

'What?'

'That's what the late Gerald Henderson shelled out for Juanita.'

'You mean he bought her?' Jacquie checked. 'That's positively Dickensian.'

'Well, W T Steadian, certainly. Dickens wasn't allowed to write about such things. William Stead bought a girl for a fiver just to prove he could and that such things went on in Mr Gladstone's England. 'Course, he did time for it.'

'Nobody believed him?'

'No,' Maxwell said, ruefully. 'They believed the girl's mother – she who'd taken the fiver gleefully in the first place. As soon as Stead, who was a journalist, went to press with the story, the mother screamed Merry Hamlet, claiming she'd been duped.'

'But she hadn't?'

'Did Disraeli have bad breath?'

Jacquie didn't know, but around Maxwell you didn't challenge that sort of thing.

'So, let's get this straight. Juanita Reyes, the girl who was living with Mrs Troubridge, Puritan of this parish, that sweet, charming Catholic girl to whom we entrusted our son, is a whore.'

'It's an old-fashioned name for it,' Maxwell said, getting outside his double Southern Comfort, 'but yes.'

'Max, we must have been blind,' Jacquie was shaking her head.

'Ah, no,' so did he. 'You have to hand it to the Levington Agency, they've got a pretty smooth operation going. It was only because I had the buzz words of Juanita Reyes and Gerald Henderson that I got across the threshold. As it was, I had to give my inside leg...'

'And five grand!' Jacquie went cold. 'Max, you didn't give them five grand?'

'The kids think I'm mad, dear heart, but it's only a cover for being the most boring man in the universe. No, I asked for a cooling off period. Marashkova starts week Thursday.'

'You...You lying bastard!' and she hit him with a cushion.

'Actually,' he chuckled, defending himself as best he could,

'Poles, Czechs, and Russians are on special offer this week. They'll be in touch.'

'So...let me see if I understand this. Gerald Henderson lashed out five thousand pounds for his own personal hooker.'

'Fronting as an au pair for his daughter.'

'And when little...whatserface...Katie...goes to boarding school, the cover won't work any more.'

'Something like that,' Maxwell said. 'Although a little drive out to Tottingleigh wouldn't come amiss to confront the widow Henderson with what we know.'

'Indeed,' Jacquie's mind was racing. 'So Henderson gets rid of her.'

'Yes, but not via the usual channels. He was supposed to contact the Agency to terminate the transaction, as it were, but instead he chose to advertise locally.'

'Why?'

'We can ask Mrs Henderson that when we visit.'

'What's this "we", white man?' Jacquie came out with the old Lone Ranger joke, though it was long before her time. 'Henderson could hardly put an ad in the *Advertiser* "Slapper for Sale, One Careful Owner. Goes Like a Train".'

'Exactly,' Maxwell agreed. 'Her alias was as an au pair, so that's how he advertised her.'

'But he couldn't have gained anything...Do you think it was Juanita's idea? To hang up her fol-de-rols for good? Turn over a new leaf? Had she seen the light?'

'Whoa, whoa, Dobbin,' Maxwell laughed. 'I've no idea. Why don't we – oops, there I go again – ask her?'

'Hmm,' Jacquie was deep in thought. 'She's a nice kid, Max. Used her real name, notice. No doubt her parents thought she was going away to *be* an au pair; they'll be devastated.'

'So will Rodrigo Mendoza.'

'Who?'

'The boyfriend – if that's what he is.'

'But he thinks she's a tea leaf.'

'Ah, but does he?' Maxwell extricated himself from his live-in policewoman, and reached for the bottle of liquid gold posing as Southern Comfort. 'What if he found out that Juanita was on the game and, with an attack of the goody two-shoes, helped her get away? What's more shaming to a good Catholic family – that their daughter's a thief or that their daughter's a prostitute?'

'Could go either way,' Jacquie shrugged.

'Bearing in mind Juanita's parents presumably weren't given either option. She'll have a perfectly good story for them. Katie Henderson went to boarding school. Nolan Maxwell…I don't know; she'll have thought of something.'

Jacquie looked at him in the twilit lamplight of their lounge. 'I'm still not speaking to you, Peter Maxwell. You're still a lying shit. By the way,' she leapt at him, pinning him to the sofa again, stealing a snifter of his drink, 'what do you know about golf?'

Jacquie was right. The revelations about the Levington agency did shed a new light on the Henderson murder. And new light was something DCI Henry Hall could do with about now. Astley and the lab had run out of forensic information. House-to-house was picking up tiddly squat on Benji Lemon's movements. Gangland Brighton was being, as usual, tight-lipped about the elimination of Wide Boy Taylor. And, as always, the Press were buzzing around the enquiry like the irritating flies of summer. No news was bad news for a paper, be it national or local, so most of them went for the 'Are Our Policemen Really So Wonderful?' line, commenting on the lack of progress, the blandness of press releases, digging up old cases of corruption from Meiklejohn and Druscovitch back in 1877 up to the Stephen Lawrence debacle.

It was all guaranteed to get right up Henry Hall's nose and he drove out to Tottingleigh that bright, burning morning with Sheila Kindling at his side. It didn't help, of course, that Jacquie Carpenter had come upon the Levington information by that eternally annoying source Peter Maxwell. Every time Henry Hall called on Maxwell for help – and he had to admit, he'd done it a few times now – there was always Hell to pay. And every time, Hall promised himself he wouldn't do it again; until the next time. On the other hand, Peter Maxwell was a member of the public. He had every right to go up to London whenever he liked, visit any outwardly respectable institution he chose. He comforted himself with that thought, with the thinly held belief that the interfering old bastard wasn't really running his own, but parallel, murder enquiry.

'Mrs Henderson,' Hall stood in the woman's doorway, warrant card at the ready. 'DCI Hall, Leighford CID. This is DC Kindling.'

'Is there any news?' Fiona Henderson had been a widow now for fourteen days. She was attending counselling sessions at the Elms in Leighford, but it all seemed pretty pointless, really. Others sitting around in their sad circle had lost husbands, wives, children, but most through illness or old age. One woman's son had died in a car crash. But no one's nearest and dearest had been murdered, except hers. Only Fiona Henderson's husband had had a kitchen knife rammed repeatedly into his chest and had his body dumped unceremoniously under a rhododendron bush. Fiona Henderson was having difficulty coming to terms with that.

'Pretty girl.' Hall was handling a photograph of a kid covered in ice cream in the spacious living room. 'Katie?'

'Yes,' Fiona said. 'Taken with her father some time ago.'

'How is she coping with all this?' Sheila Kindling asked.

'Well.' Fiona was straightening cushions, busying herself, finding things to do. Sitting face to face with anyone she found difficult; like the sound of silence, it was hard to bear. 'She was away at school when...it happened. She's broken up now, of course, staying in the Midlands with my sister. They've got a farm, lots of ground, horses. Katie's happy there.'

'Was she happy here?' Sheila asked her.

Fiona looked at her, frowning, puzzled. 'Of course,' she said. 'Why shouldn't she be?'

'But you weren't, Mrs Henderson, were you?' Hall was looking straight at her. He slowly and carefully took the cushion out of her hand. 'Why did you send Katie away? To boarding school, I mean?'

'We...Gerald and I...we thought she was ready.'

'Did you go, when you were a girl? To boarding school?'

'Me?' Fiona's laugh was brittle. 'No, no, my parents couldn't afford it.'

'Gerald?' Hall persisted. 'Was he a boarder?'

'No,' she flickered. 'No. It sounds snobby now, but Gerald's family were working class and proud of it. No snobby school for him.'

'But you sent your daughter to one?' Hall checked.

'I told you,' Fiona was being as patient as she knew how. 'We thought it was best.'

'No, Fiona.' Hall's voice was soft, seductive even. And who told him he could call her by her Christian name? 'No, *you* thought it was best. And it had nothing to do with Katie's education, did it? You did it because of Juanita Reyes.'

The widow broke away from his stare, those difficult-to-see eyes behind the blank lenses that she *knew* must be burning into her soul. She hadn't met this man before. In all the days of the enquiry, Henry Hall had not come her way once. She'd read his bland words in the papers, seen him giving nothing away in the press conference on the telly. And now he was here, in her house, like some sort of avenging angel. Wasn't he supposed to be on her side? Just who was the victim here?

'All right.' She was looking out of the window across the carefully manicured lawns that stretched to the little orchard. 'All right. I had to let Juanita go because she…wasn't very good.'

'Did she steal anything from you, Mrs Henderson?' Sheila Kindling asked.

'Yes…yes, she did. I didn't want to make a fuss. I know I should have called the police. It's silly, I know, but I didn't want any sort of international incident…'

'What did she steal?' Hall asked.

'What? Er…money. She stole money.'

'How much?'

'Um…I don't know exactly. A thousand, I think. It wasn't the amount. It was the principle.'

There it was again; the sound of silence that she hated. Hall let it last. He was a connoisseur of the guarded moment, the pregnant pause.

'Juanita didn't steal any money, Fiona, did she? She stole your husband.'

'What are you talking about?' the woman blurted. 'I don't understand.'

'Yes, you do, Fiona,' Hall said.

Sheila Kindling looked at her boss. He could be a heartless bastard at times. Even when it was in a good cause. She knew then she'd never make DCI, glass ceiling or not, because she couldn't be that heartless.

'All right,' Fiona said quietly. 'I thought perhaps Gerald and Juanita were having a bit of a fling.'

Hall looked at the widow and then at his DC. 'You found out they were,' he said. 'And it didn't just happen, with two people thrown together by circumstance. She, a lonely kid in a strange land; he, drawn irresistibly by some ill-thought-out middle-aged fling. She was a bought woman, Fiona, and you knew it. Gerald bought her from the London agency, pretending she was an au pair when all the time she was a prostitute.'

'No!' Tears were streaming down Fiona Henderson's cheeks, dripping off her chin.

'Face it!' Hall snapped.

'No.' Her voice was barely audible now and she sank to the sofa, burying her face in her hands. Instinctively, Sheila Kindling moved forward. She was a woman too and she couldn't imagine what Fiona Henderson was going through. She'd been kicked around by men for long enough – first her husband, now the DCI. But Hall's hand snaked out, palm down to signal her to stop. She looked at his face and he was shaking his head. In the years of her career that lay ahead, she would reflect that Henry Hall was right; this precise moment would never come again.

'When did you find out, Fiona?' he asked softly. 'About Juanita, I mean?'

There was a long pause when no one moved. Then Fiona was sitting up, sniffing defiantly. There was no point any more. The man *knew*. The details were irrelevant. 'Three months,' she said. 'I caught them in bed together. In his den. Through there…' She jerked her head towards it in contempt. 'He laughed. I think…I think Juanita was terribly embarrassed. She kept apologising and said she would go away. Gerald was…Gerald was appalling, saying how useless I was in bed and that was why he had hired Juanita. I…just ran. I had to get out of that room. I could hear his mocking voice all the way down the corridor. "Come and join us," he said. "Come and watch. She's very good."'

'So you decided to kill him,' Hall said. It was a simple statement. And the silence that followed was so loud it hurt. Sheila Kindling hadn't even, in the raw emotion of the interview, got her notebook out, still less slipped the biro behind her ear. She just stood there, transfixed.

'I wanted to,' the widow said. 'It hurt like hell. I wanted to kill them both. Except for two things, I would have. I didn't know how and I didn't have the bottle.'

'So what did you do?' Hall asked her.

Fiona sniffed again. She was calmer now, with that sense of aching relief you get when a pain suddenly stops. 'I took Katie and went to my sister's for a few days. She knew, of course, something was wrong and I told her. We worked out what had to be done. If there was anything Gerald loved more than himself, it was money. I knew that if I blew the whistle in the right quarters, told certain people about the Juanita thing, he could kiss vital contracts goodbye. His so-called friends would leave him in droves. Leighford is a small place, Chief Inspector, you know that. Oh, most people would stomach his having an affair with a girl young enough to be his daughter. But this was something altogether more sordid. He'd be bankrupt inside a year.'

'You confronted him?'

'Yes. I told him we were sending Katie away to boarding school. I hated doing it, but I knew that without her, he'd have no reason to keep Juanita on. Tongues would wag. And Gerald valued his precious reputation as much as I thought he did. He placed an ad on Juanita's behalf in the local paper.'

'But he should have gone back to the Levington Agency,' Hall said.

'I wouldn't allow it. I wanted no truck with that revolting place.' She looked up at him suddenly. 'You know about them, obviously. Can't you close them down?'

Hall looked at his watch. 'I suspect my colleagues in the Met are doing more or less that now, Mrs Henderson.' He was all formality and correctness again. 'I think their books should provide some interesting reading.'

'I insisted that Gerald went through with removing Juanita. Poor kid. I felt sorry for her that night I caught them together.

I felt even sorrier for her afterwards. But the couple who answered the ad, the Maxwells, they seemed very nice.'

'Oh, I'm sure they are,' Hall said. He was smiling inside.

'One thing is certain, Chief Inspector,' Fiona Henderson said, more at peace with herself than she'd been for months. 'Whoever killed Gerald, it had nothing to do with Juanita Reyes.'

'Right,' Maxwell had finished the washing up, put the baby to bed, read him a story of crushing banality and was just rounding off on the hundred and one things that house-husbands like him do, day after day, without prompting, without complaint. 'You were asking me about golf.'

Jacquie frowned at him. 'Was I? Good God, Max, that was nearly twenty-four hours ago. Try to keep up, there's a good chap.'

'I must confess,' he said pompously, hauling off his pink rubber gloves and untying his pinnie, 'it is not, as you know, my natural game. I'm more of a rugger man. But I'll give it my best shot.' He cleared his throat. 'It probably originated in Holland, although the first records seem to show a game played with a curved stick and a ball in Flanders (that's more or less Belgium to you) in 1353. Of course, in Gloucester cathedral…'

'Single Stableton,' she interrupted, cradling her coffee with both hands.

'Sorry?'

'You told me you didn't know how to use the Net,' she bridled. 'I leave you alone for one day and you're out there on the Information Superhighway.'

'Bollocks, darling heart,' he bridled right back at her. 'I have a book on golf I didn't know I had stashed away in the attic, along with *A Thousand and One Things to Do With a Split Condom* and an early venture by Enoch Powell, *Send the Black B—s Home*. Neither of them made the bestseller list.'

'So your little book didn't tell you about a Single Stableton, then?'

'Must have been in a later volume,' Maxwell bluffed. 'What is it?'

'Well, that's just the point; it doesn't exist. I made it up. The actual term is a Single Stable*ford*; a golfer would know that.'

'As opposed to…' Maxwell had to admit he'd lost track of the conversation.

'As opposed to Leighford's answer to *Gardener's World*. Chester Harris, as well as being a flasher, pervert and general purpose weirdo, is not a golfer.'

'Well,' Maxwell tutted, finding stirring his own coffee quite a trick after the day he'd had. 'In a busy life…we can't all be good at everything.'

'Yet, he's a member of a golf club,' she told him.

'Well,' Maxwell said. 'Perhaps he just goes for the…social life.'

She was nodding smugly.

'Woman Policeman, you are nothing short of a genius. Chester Harris spies on courting couples and suggests they join him at a party at the golf club. So this golf club…'

'Wilbraham,' she filled in the details, 'Rather like the Levington Agency…'

'…is not a golf club at all. Or if it is, it's a front for something else.' He kissed her on the nose. 'Brilliant. And it gets even better.'

'It does?'

'It does,' Maxwell sipped his coffee. 'Think back. Our little visit to the Hampton School, to see Rodrigo Mendoza.'

'Hm,' Jacquie smiled, curling her toes.

'Stop it!' he growled. 'You're dribbling.'

'Sorry.'

'Mendoza said he took Juanita to a party, not at school because English schools are not places you want to have parties. They went to a party at a local golf club. And what's the betting that's the Wilbraham?'

'My God.'

'And who did Mendoza say got them in because he was a member?'

'Oh God, Max,' Jacquie whined. 'I don't know.' She flapped her hands uselessly. She'd been doing so well. 'I can't remember.'

'Exactly,' he beamed, and that's why I'm a Detective Sergeant and you're a mere Head of Sixth Form at a bog-standard comprehensive. Oh, no, wait a minute...'

'Who is it, you shit?'

'My old sparring partner, Aaron Felton, that's who.'

In the olden times, Peter Maxwell would have thrown caution to the winds and cycled out to Littlehampton. It was twelve miles from Leighford as the crow flies, but as the A259 went, considerably further. But there was no use deluding himself; he was not a young man any more and Surrey's saddle seemed to be evolving into some sort of Inquisition torture implement. So, he chickened out and took the train.

There was a lethargy about the Hampton School on this,

the last day of term that he knew would be happening over at Leighford High by now too. Just how many times could Seven Gee be shown that episode of the Simpsons where Ned Flanders has a fling with Marge? And how many more Personal Statements could Year 12 write in preparation for their university applications?

Maxwell caught a cab from the station and found himself reporting to Reception like the upstanding citizen he was, rather than skulking in the shrubbery ready to pounce on some unsuspecting girl blossoming into Year Ten. Last time he'd snuck in the back way, but last time he'd had the law with him. Now, he was on his own.

'Mr Mendoza.' He saw his quarry emerging from the Modern Languages Block, a young man in a hurry. '*Buenos dias.*'

'*Señor* Maxwell,' the man smiled. 'What is the cliché you English have? "What are you doing here?"'

'That's right,' Maxwell shook the man's hand. 'That's the line we usually say in thrillers just before the victim gets his.'

'Gets his?' Mendoza frowned.

'Is killed by the villain,' Maxwell clarified.

'Oh, yes,' he laughed. 'Yes, it is very similar in Spain.'

'Rodrigo,' Maxwell became confidential. 'Look, I'm sorry to appear like this, out of the…unannounced. You'll be going home, soon, I suppose. Back to Spain?'

'Yes,' Mendoza told him. 'I have booked my flight one week today.'

'Well, I wanted to clear something up before you went. About Juanita, I mean. And I didn't want to do it over the phone.'

Instinctively, the two men wandered away from the buildings, towards the perimeter hedge. Lessons of a sort were still going on and the sun was relentless on the iron-brown of the playing fields.

'I know why she left,' Maxwell said.

Mendoza stopped walking, looking at the older man. 'Yes,' he said. 'We talked before. She stole. It was embarrassing.'

'No, Rodrigo.' Maxwell shook his head. 'Juanita didn't steal anything.'

'Yes,' he insisted. 'She did. Did not Carolina tell you this? Carolina Vasquez at your school?'

'Yes, she did,' Maxwell conceded.

'Well, then…'

'That was just the story you gave her,' Maxwell said. 'The story you and Juanita put about. When did you find out she was a prostitute?'

The Spaniard's head came up and he stared hard at his man. He muttered something in Spanish that Maxwell couldn't understand and he guessed it was as well he couldn't.

'How did you find out?' Mendoza asked.

'It's a long story,' Maxwell said. 'When she worked for me, I assumed she was an au pair. When she worked for Gerald Henderson, she was something else.'

Mendoza nodded. 'She did not like the life particularly,' he said. 'But she needed the money for back home.'

'The Levington Agency were presumably taking a cut?' Maxwell asked.

'A percentage of her income, yes. We talked about it and she said she had to go home. We…er…concocted? Concocted the story about her stealing and she drove to some place and left her car. Then she flew home. She feels very bad, Max, about leaving your baby. In fact, it was because of him that she left.'

'Because of Nolan?'

'Yes. You and your partner and the little boy. She has a little brother back home. It reminded her of the life she once knew, before she sold herself. She was disgusted. But her parents are good people. They would never understand. She wanted to go away. Away from Menorca, perhaps elsewhere in Spain. She said she could not face them. I persuaded her that everything would be all right.'

'But it wasn't all right, was it, Rodrigo?' Maxwell said. 'Because somebody killed Gerald Henderson.'

Mendoza shook his head. 'I know,' he said. 'But it could not have been Juanita.'

'Why not?' Maxwell asked.

'Because she had gone home by then,' he told him. 'By the time Henderson's body was found, Juanita was back in Sant Lluis. We had prepared another story for her parents. We have both been to confession about this, Max. I don't know how much it helps. It was the way we were brought up. Are you a religious person, Max?'

'Me?' Maxwell smiled. There was a time perhaps, when he had been. Before his wife and little girl were killed, for no reason, for no point. But he had a new family now, a new wife in all but name and a little boy. They weren't replacements for those he'd lost. But he'd lost too much to believe in a God who wasn't there. 'No,' he shook his head. 'I'm not.'

'That,' said Mendoza, 'is a pity.' He patted the man's

shoulder. 'I will tell Juanita,' he said, 'that you know. It will make her feel that little bit better about herself. And she will light a candle for you.'

A candle for Maxwell? That would be a first.

CHAPTER SEVENTEEN

It wasn't until nightfall that it hit him. Peter Maxwell, the Head of Sixth Form at Leighford High School was under suspension. Oh, the charges were nonsense, of course, but mud had a tendency to stick. He was staring retirement in the face anyway, but he hadn't planned to go like this.

He sat late that night in his Inner Sanctum, the War Office at the top of the house with his curmudgeonly cat and his plastic miniature Light Brigade and he brooded. He'd missed the end of term bash, which wasn't much of a bash, really, but it was a chance to say goodbye to a few people who were moving on, moving up, moving out; people, in fact, you'd probably never see again. There was a bloke on the staff, a reasonable cartoonist, who did farewell cards for those he reckoned; Peter Maxwell would have secretly liked one of those.

He looked at the plastic *Chasseur à Cheval* still in its wrapping on the table in front of him. He would make this one into…well, a Hussar, obviously, by virtue of the braided jacket. Douglas's 11th or Shewell's 8th? And if so, who? He was about to consult the oracle, Canon Lummis's list of those who rode the Charge of the Light Brigade, when he suddenly thought, 'Bugger and poo!' and threw the book across the room.

Metternich didn't even flinch. It was just the old git in a bad mood again. In the floor below, Nolan turned in his sleep, dreaming whatever nearly one-year-olds dream of. Jacquie was fully awake, sitting up in bed, reading. She heard the book. She knew the signs. It wasn't something she could help with. Maxwell just had to ride it out, like the 54 millimetre soldiers he was creating. She'd wait for him to come down, in a lifetime or so.

The people who work at County Hall, like those of the Abyss, don't work on Saturdays and Sundays. On both blistering days, as the youth of Leighford ran amok through the town screaming 'Yippee, the hols are here!' Maxwell took Nolan out on a hike. He'd normally have strapped the wee lad onto that contraption behind Surrey's saddle, but the heat seemed to have warped one of the uprights, so it was the bus and Shanks's pony.

The boys were out on the uplands skirting the golf course and they picnicked in the shade of the Leigh's oaks. Maxwell had a ploughman's, Nolan something gooey and indescribable concocted by his mother. Even so, he found his dad's lunch infinitely more engrossing, especially the bottle of Bud which seemed to have his name written all over it. One sip, however, and his face told the whole story.

'Well, there you go,' Maxwell said. 'You wouldn't be told, would you? Oh, dearie me, no, not you as would. I said you wouldn't like it. Mind you, I can remember my first snorter like it was yesterday. I didn't care for it either and now I'm proud to say I'm a full-blown alcoholic. Bottoms up! No, no, not literally!' The wee lad had flopped sideways, what with the exhaustion of the carry, the excitement of the bus ride and the rather acute angle of the hillock he was sitting on and rolled quietly away. His father reached out with an expert hand and just saved them both from a fate worse than death – Nolan Maxwell rolling through a cowpat.

The next day that County Hall didn't work was Sunday, but Maxwell knew that the library did. He'd been baulked of his prey here once before, but the old dragon Edna Roxbury was deep in conversation about the merits of Harry Potter, so he snuck past her. He knew, of course, that by definition the conversation wouldn't last long, so he had to work fast. He dodged behind the Mills and Boon, out beyond Occult and was through the door into the secret garden before you could say Frances Hodgson Burnett.

'Can I help you?' a doddery voice made him turn. 'Members of the public aren't allowed in here.'

'I'm terribly sorry.' Maxwell was on his best public school form. 'Edna's tied up at the moment and said it would be all right, since it was me.'

'Did she?' a startling set of teeth appeared over a pile of books with an elderly woman attached to them. 'That's not like her.'

'Ah, but this is an emergency, you see,' Maxwell gushed. 'I understand that many of the books on local history have been transferred to Public Records?'

'That's right,' the teeth told him. 'All of them, in fact.'

'That is a pity,' Maxwell said. 'In that case, do you have any older books on the Balearic Islands? Menorca in particular?'

'Well, most of that category will be out on the open shelves. Numbers 910 onwards.'

'Sadly,' Maxwell shook his head, 'not what I'm looking for. Anything else – in here, I mean?'

'Well, let me see.' Maxwell was delighted that the old girl didn't rush to a computer to check, but wrinkled up her nose and turned east. Ah, a true librarian. Once upon a time, they were all trained to track down a book by sense of smell. He followed her through a rabbit warren of metal shelving where dusty volumes were on their way to the library books' graveyard. 'Here we are,' she said. '*Rambles though Minorca*. Oh, is that the place you mean?'

'It is indeed,' Maxwell smiled, noting the author. 'And if it was good enough for Sir Compton Mackenzie, it's good enough for me.'

'I'm afraid you can't borrow it,' the old teeth told him.

'No, that's fine,' Maxwell said. 'May I crouch here, in the corner, and dip? I promise you won't know I'm here.'

'Well, I'm not sure...'

'Edna will be so grateful to you for helping me.'

'Oh,' the teeth preened her iron-grey hair. 'Do you think so?'

'I know it,' Maxwell beamed, ready to vomit at his own nauseatingness. Still, all in a good cause.

It must have been all of ten minutes later that the door crashed back and a stentorian voice bellowed, 'There's a man in here.'

Maxwell looked up and placed a solemn finger to his lips. 'Ssh. Please, Ms Roxbury, this used to be a library.' He was already on his feet and sliding past the speechless old besom.

He tapped the Mackenzie book and placed it carefully in Edna Roxbury's hand. 'Your colleague over there has been an absolute brick. If only all librarians were like her, eh?' and he tipped his hat. 'Good morning, ladies. Don't trouble – I'll see myself out.'

He didn't sleep that night. For all he tried to make light of it to Jacquie, Monday was weighing heavily on his mind. Jacquie knew of course and she made light of it too. But she held him tight as the dawn came up like thunder over Leighford gasworks and another week creaked and groaned into life.

'I'll take you,' she said, supervising as Nolan smeared his egg yolk over most of his face.

'No, no, I'll take Surrey.'

'I thought you said he was playing up.'

'Bit of a rattle, that's all. Like the rest of us, he's getting on.'

'I'd rather take you,' she said.

He looked at her and smiled. The honest, trusting face, the caring eyes. He reached out and stroked her cheek. 'I know you would,' he said, 'and I know why. But you know why I'd rather go this one alone. Besides,' he reached for his toast, 'you've got a killer to catch.'

'I meant to ask you about that,' she said, glad for the moment that he'd changed the subject. 'The library visit. Any luck?'

'Yes and no,' he said. 'It was always going to be a long shot. Oh damn – oops,' he covered the boy's ears – 'I'm late, family. Got to pedal!' and he kissed the one small bit of Nolan not yellow with egg and grabbed his bow tie. Jacquie stopped him at the door and kissed him long and hard before holding him close. 'Knock 'em dead, Max,' she said.

He smiled at her. 'That *is* my intention, dearest.' And he was gone.

The spire of the Norman cathedral was visible long before Maxwell's train rattled into Chichester station. He got off, got his bearings and walked through the city to find County Hall. The Romans had laid this place out with their usual uncompromising grid mentality and the Normans had built a church there, clattering along the Pallant in their mail with their harsh Viking-French voices and their dreadful haircuts. Assorted louts loafed on the steps of the market cross, chewing gum and swilling lager, though the Sussex sun was scarcely yet over the yard arm. Maxwell sighed; he just hoped they were up to date with their coursework, that was all. Pan pipes incongruously assailed his ears as a little Peruvian band entertained or annoyed passers-by, depending on their musical persuasion.

The clock was striking eleven over the Sixties monstrosity that was West Sussex's County Hall as Maxwell sprinted up the steps. In the curious twilight world that was local education, it might have been striking thirteen. He followed signs to the Education Department, up two flights past fierce-looking paintings of fierce-looking Council Chairmen of yesteryear, whose names were, even today, still carved with civic pride into the foundation blocks of public conveniences throughout the city.

'Are you Peter Maxwell?' a square, solid-looking man in a suit met him at the top of the stairs.

Was this a trick question, Maxwell wondered. Best not be *too* paranoid. 'That's me,' he said.

'Bob Wentworth, regional NUT.'

'Ah, the Seventh Cavalry.' Maxwell was genuinely glad to see the man. He didn't know Wentworth personally, but the man was legend in West Sussex. He was Clarence Darrow, George Carman and Michael Mansfield all rolled into one. He hated Headteachers with a passion as people who had sold out to the enemy. And as for the top brass at County Hall, Wentworth took a personal delight in scraping them off his shoe.

'Were you expecting me?'

Come to think of it, Bob Wentworth *did* have the look of the Spanish Inquisition from the old Monty Python joke of the same name, but Maxwell didn't want to go there. 'Not exactly,' he said. 'You *are* on my side, I assume?'

'On the side of the angels, Mr Maxwell,' Wentworth winked. 'Have you met Alex Morrow?'

'The CEO? Yes; bit of a shit, I thought.'

'That goes double for their lawyer, James Timmins. The dealings I've had with your Chair of Governors – Inkester, isn't it? Complete tosser. As for Diamond, well, the least said.'

'This is going to be a piece of cake, then.' Maxwell was walking with the man, matching him stride for stride down the darkened corridors of power.

'All in a day's work,' Wentworth chuckled. 'How much do you want to keep your job?'

'Bugger the job,' Maxwell told him. 'I'd like my reputation back.'

'Oh, you're going for the innocent ploy?'

Maxwell stared at him. 'What?' he asked, straightfaced.

'Just joking,' Wentworth winked. 'I think we can promise you that. It's whether or not I can get Diamond on malicious intent – that's always a tricky one. All Heads lie like sleeping dogs, it goes with the territory; it's *proving* they do, that's the problem. Here we are.'

Wentworth led Maxwell into a panelled room. There was a desk on a raised dais at the far end and if Maxwell recognised the feel and smell of his first tribunal, the small-fry, hole-in-corner version in Diamond's office at Leighford High, he recognised this as something altogether grander, more intimidating. He could just hear the ranting of yesteryear echoing over the microphones – 'Are you now, or have you ever been, a member of the Communist Party?'

Wentworth checked his watch against the clock above the dais where a coat of gilded royal arms shone bright in the late morning sun. 'We've got a couple of minutes before Judge Dredd turns up. Evidence.' He sat down and started rummaging around in his briefcase.

'Have I gone through some sort of time warp or is this Number One Court at the Old Bailey?' Maxwell asked. He could almost catch the distant clang of St Sepulchre's bell tolling for him.

'What's the evidence against you?' Wentworth asked.

'Um…I don't know,' Maxwell was trying to focus. 'Tittle tattle. A letter.'

'This one?'

Maxwell looked at the paper the man passed to him. 'Yes, I…Holy Mother of God.'

'Have you seen this before?' Wentworth asked. 'It's a photocopy, of course.'

'I have,' Maxwell nodded, still a little non-plussed by what he'd just read. 'All except the signature.'

'Ah, yes,' Wentworth smiled. 'Don't like to let you know who your accusers are, do they? Why?' He suddenly caught the look on Maxwell's face. 'Do you know the name?'

'The Christian name not at all,' Maxwell said. 'But the surname is definitely ringing bells.'

The door clicked open to one side of the dais and four suits walked in. The Four Just Men. Nods were exchanged all round and the Chief Education officer took his seat on the dais. He appeared to have forgotten to pack his wig, though no doubt he had a black cap somewhere. Were this a court martial, Maxwell knew, his sword would be lying sheathed on the desk in front of him.

'This is a preliminary hearing,' the Chief Education officer began, 'to decide whether Mr Peter Maxwell, Head of Sixth Form at Leighford High School in this Education District, has a case to answer concerning an accusation of gross indecency with a minor and a student of sixteen years. Neither of the students' names may be used in the course of this hearing. We need to decide whether this is a matter for the police.'

'Alex,' Wentworth was on his feet when everyone else was sitting down. 'I don't want to take up the tribunal's time unnecessarily. For the record...' he glanced at one of the suits who was busy taking all this down in shorthand, 'my client denies any wrong-doing and has substantiated evidence in support of his claim.'

The NUT man pulled out a sizeable sheaf of paper from his briefcase and separated out smaller batches, placing them in front of each man in the room. 'I apologise that I have not had time to get this documentation to you all before,' he said, 'but the hearing *was* convened rather hastily and of course, County Hall doesn't work weekends, does it?' He smiled broadly.

'What is this, Mr Wentworth?' the CEO was formality itself. 'Can you give us the gist?'

'Certainly.' Wentworth could patronise for England, or at least West Sussex. Made Maxwell glad he was on his side. 'What you have before you, gentlemen, are four documents. The first is written by Child A who did indeed consent to meet my client at the area of common land known as The Dam at Leighford on Saturday last. As you see, she makes no comment on any impropriety whatsoever. Indeed, she thanks Mr Maxwell for protecting her from what I believe she refers to as 'an old pervert' by whom she felt threatened. The second is written by Child B who was also at the place, time and date in question and her testimony matches that of Child A in every particular. The third and fourth documents are from the parents of Children A and B confirming as far as they are able the gist of events in their children's testimony. Neither child was in a distressed state when they came home from The Dam nor subsequently, and they express their total support of my client who they believe – I think they actually use the word "know" – to be of upright and utterly reliable character.'

'Collusion, Mr Wentworth.' The note-taker looked up for the first time.

'Would you care to repeat that, Mr Timmins? I assume you are familiar with the laws of slander in this fair land of ours?'

'How do we know we can trust the hearsay evidence of those parents?' the County's brief asked. 'That is, after all, all it is – hearsay.'

'As opposed to the complainant's letter,' Morrow chimed in, 'which is prima faciae.'

'May I ask,' Maxwell interrupted, 'who my accuser is?'

Papers were ruffled, glances exchanged. 'I believe you have the name in front of you,' the CEO answered.

'I can read,' Maxwell reminded him. 'Would I be right in assuming that this gentleman describes himself as an ornithologist?' he asked. 'A watcher?'

Murmurs from the dais.

'Have any of you actually talked to this man?' Maxwell asked.

'I have,' Timmins told him. 'He stands by every word of what he saw.'

'Of course he does,' Maxwell smiled.

'Max...' Wentworth whispered, but the Head of Sixth Form was on a roll and he waved him aside.

'Tell me, then,' he said. 'Does this...watcher...have a scrawny beard? Glasses? Thinning, lank silver hair? Eight, nine stone, perhaps five foot seven?'

Timmins was frowning. 'That's essentially correct.'

It was Maxwell's turn to confer with his aide, leaving the dais rattled, perplexed.

Wentworth straightened, triumphantly. 'It is clear from Mr Timmins' acceptance of my client's description of this man, that the complainant, the writer of this letter is precisely the – and I quote – the "old pervert" alluded to in the letters of Child A and Child B.'

'He can't just throw mud back like that,' Inkester bellowed.

'Headmaster,' Maxwell cut in. 'I may still refer to you as that, I suppose?'

'Yes, Max,' Diamond said. If he felt uncomfortable when he suspended Maxwell in the first place, he was positively cringing now. Mostly because he knew what was coming.

'Could I ask you to read out for us, please, the name at the bottom of the complainant's letter?'

'Oh, really!' Inkester threw his hands in the air.

'Max...'

'You'd better humour him, James,' the CEO said. 'I've no idea where this is going.'

'To Hell in a handcart,' Maxwell said. 'Headmaster?'

Diamond looked at them all, then cleared his throat. 'Yours sincerely, Oliver Lessing,' he said.

Maxwell slid his chair back slowly so that it grated on the floor. 'Would you like a few minutes to confer, Headmaster?' he said. 'Mr Wentworth and I will wait outside. I believe you have something to discuss.' And he led the NUT man out.

'Max,' Wentworth said when the door had closed. 'What are you doing here? I'm with Morrow, I don't know where this is going either. Look, there's no case to answer. If the kids and their parents don't bring charges, there's no alternative but to reinstate you. I don't...'

The door clicked open and a rather peeved County solicitor stood there. He had 'don't shoot the messenger' written all over him. 'Gentlemen,' he said. 'Could you come this way?'

The look on Legs Diamond's face was one that would stay with Peter Maxwell for ever.

'I'm so pleased this has been resolved, Max,' he'd said, while shaking the man's hand.

'Resolved, Headmaster?' Maxwell was not in the forgiving vein today. 'Hardly.'

Martin Inkester was all beams and light, muttering gushingly about misunderstandings, knew there was nothing in it, glad to have you still on board, fine teacher, inestimable contribution blah, blah, blah. The CEO, who always needed time to prepare a U-turn speech, merely nodded and said 'Excellent' a few times. Only Timmins, the County Doberman, said nothing. He was too busy collecting up his papers and making yet another wax model of Bob Wentworth to drive pins into later; clearly these two went way back.

The NUT gun-for-hire held out his hand. 'We must do this again, sometime, Mr Maxwell.'

Maxwell shook it. 'I'm sure you can understand when I say I sincerely hope not,' he said.

As he walked back through Chichester, the day was even more glorious. The louts had wandered away from the Cross, probably to enrol in the Open University, the Peruvians had gone for lunch, a quick condor and chips at the local eatery. Even the bells of the cathedral were pealing out Maxwell's victory. He toyed with trying to find a phone that hadn't been vandalised, and succeeded, outside the station. He checked his watch. Twelve-thirty. Jacquie would be either on her lunch break now in the bowels of the nick, tucking into a pastrami on rye, or she'd be glued to her computer screen, elbow deep in dead men. Either way, he'd have to get past that miserable bastard Den Morissey on the switchboard and that was one victory Maxwell knew he wasn't going to be able to celebrate. He just hoped that when the time came and he appeared, cycle clips in hand, before the pearly gates, it wasn't on Den Morissey's watch, or he'd never get in.

He caught the twelve-forty-three to Leighford, watching the Sussex countryside flash by, gilded by the sun, the horse chestnuts throwing deep lunchtime shadows on the fields. He was a free man again. And yet...and yet.

Surrey was still waiting patiently in the station car park as the Master arrived. At moments like these, Maxwell swore he saw the front wheel turn, the handlebars come up and a low whinny of recognition escape from the derailleurs. And he hadn't touched a drop all day. What *was* it with this bloody combination lock? In the end, brute strength rather than the patient, skilled teasing of a cracksman won the day and he was in the saddle, pedalling north-west.

Traffic was a nightmare that Monday, the Flyover sluggish from the moment Maxwell got on it. Then he was taking the shortcut down Latimer Road and around the Asda, heading for home. He'd grab a bite to eat there, twist Norman Westbury's baby seat back into shape somehow and collect Nolan from Pam's. Then, they'd go together to see Mummy and Den Morissey could go to...

'What the Hell?' Maxwell was easing the brakes and they weren't working as he soared down the incline past the new shopping centre. They still weren't working as the traffic lights at the bottom of the hill turned to red. What was he doing? Twenty, twenty-two miles an hour, hurtling downwards with the wind and gravity behind him? 'Look out!' he had time to shout before Surrey bucked violently to the left. His front wheel hit a bollard and the High Street turned upside down in his vision. He heard the shattering of glass and a scream. He hoped, as a dullness swept over him, that that hadn't come from him.

'Rhododendron bushes.' Henry Hall was lolling back in his swivel chair. 'Jacquie – tell me about rhododendron bushes.'

The DS looked at her DCI. Had it come to this? They were sitting in Hall's office, away from the Incident Room where they'd spent all morning. They both needed a break.

'Guv?'

'You've been to the Hendersons,' he said. 'Their garden's full of them. And that's where they found Gerald Henderson – under a rhododendron bush at the Botanical Gardens. Do you believe in coincidences?'

'No,' she told him. 'Not to that extent.'

'Neither do I,' he said, his fingers together near his lips. 'Not to that extent, as you say. There's a sort of...symmetry about this, Jacquie, that I can't quite...Let's look at the MO again.'

Jacquie had lost count of the times she and the team and she and Henry and she and Maxwell had looked at the MO. But the DCI was right to keep worrying it, teasing it. They were all missing something.

'The big one, guv,' she said, 'is: are we looking at one killer or two, or even three here?'

'We're back to coincidences again,' Hall said. 'Let's go with copycat for the moment. What are the options?'

'Not feasible,' she'd decided.

'Why?'

She let him have it. 'What are copycat killings all about? Some saddo who craves the limelight like you and I crave oxygen. He reads about the murder of Wide Boy Taylor and thinks "I want some of that, I want the limelight, the attention." So he finds Gerald Henderson and does him in. Then what?'

'Then, so that we think he's our boy for the Taylor killing too – enhancing the demented bastard's ego – he drags Henderson to the Gardens. It's as close as he can get, for whatever reasons, to the Point.'

'And, not content with that,' Jacquie went on, 'he latches onto Benji Lemon and shoves him over the edge, again near the Point, just to make the point, so to speak.'

Hall looked at her. 'Got more holes than a sieve, hasn't it?' he said.

She nodded. 'Where's the contact?'

'Exactly,' he took up Jacquie's idea. 'Where's the confessional letter, the taunting tape, the offer to assist us with our enquiries? Copycats don't lie low, smugly congratulating themselves on a job well done. They want to be out there, front and centre.'

'And we've heard nothing.'

'Nothing,' Hall agreed. 'Except...'

'Except?'

'Oh, it's probably nothing,' Hall shrugged. 'You start to get a bit paranoid about now in a murder, don't you? Start looking at the furniture funny.'

'You've got somebody in mind?'

'I don't know why I remember him but there was a lad at the Press Conference – I may have to call another of those soon, by the way. He looked so…out of place. Not Press, I'm sure of that. He seemed to be staring straight at me. Well, there you go – as I said, paranoia.'

'Out of place,' Jacquie murmured. 'A whale on a beach that shouldn't be there.'

'Sorry?'

'Nothing, guv,' she said.

There was a knock on the door and it burst open before Hall could give the usual 'Come'.

An ashen-faced Benny Palister stood there. 'Sorry, guv,' he said. 'Jacquie. There's been an accident. It's Maxwell.'

CHAPTER EIGHTEEN

She sat alone in the darkened room, listening to the sounds of the ward around her. Machines bleeped and pinged in electronic regularity. In the corridor outside, nurses and auxiliaries came and went in the plethora of colours they wore these days, chatting away in the snatches of conversation, lending her, for seconds at a time, a glimpse of their lives.

Jacquie Carpenter had been here before. She'd sat at bedsides without number, talking to victims, trying to make sense of their ramblings, attempting to piece together some coherence that the police could take to court. And she'd been here, too, when that dreadful beeping had stopped and the flat line on the screen had told its own story – there'd be no rambling, no evidence, because there was no life. And only Dr Astley's medical mumbo-jumbo to carry the flag of truth. Police person or not, she'd been manhandled out of the room while screens were erected, machinery wheeled in, staff dashing this way and that in what looked like chaos but was actually a well-ordered and well-rehearsed routine.

'Clear!' and the dull thump as they applied electrodes to the torso on the bed and the body jumped as the volts shot through it. But still the whine of the machine and the flat, dead line.

Jacquie wasn't actually alone. She was holding the hand of the man she loved. Peter Maxwell lay in the bed in the separate room they'd set up for him. There were tubes into his nose and mouth and his head and face were bandaged. As calmly as she could, Jacquie had taken in the news from Benny Palister. A cyclist appeared to have lost control at the traffic lights in the town centre. Brake failure almost certainly. He'd gone over the handlebars in an attempt to avoid shoppers on the pavement and hit a plate-glass window – Boots, ironically enough.

Jacquie shook her head as she squeezed his hand. 'You public schoolboy,' she murmured. 'There *are* times when it's not women and children first, you know.'

He wasn't listening. He couldn't hear. There was no movement in his whole body. He was in a coma, the doctors said, and there was no knowing when, or if, he'd ever come out of it. Some people lasted for years, kept alive by machines. Others came round, but their lives were never the same. Paralysis. Paraplegia. Life at waist height in a wheelchair and people who meant well asking if he took sugar.

She felt the tears starting again. Henry Hall had gone with her to Leighford General and stayed with her while Maxwell was stabilised. Apart from the unknown damage to his head, he'd got off lightly. Cuts and bruises, a pair of shiners and a broken nose. They had reset his dislocated shoulder. That would hurt like buggery for a long time, but all would be well, if... The scans looked good. But you could never tell as early as this. The DCI had had to get back to work. He had three murders on his hands. He sent Sheila Kindling to sort out Nolan with Pam and the woman had come hot-footing round to the hospital where her daughter and Jacquie's son had been born, full of concern and full of love.

While people had been there, Jacquie had been fine. The old professionalism had kicked in and she could be a policewoman first, a wife second. But now, at the witching hour, it was different. Hospital staff went about their business. The kind auxiliary with the dreadlocks looked in once or twice. She took Maxwell's temperature and talked to him as if he was a vegetable. No doubt she meant well. Jacquie found herself smiling in spite of it all at the thought of what Maxwell's response would be when he woke up...if he woke up. And the tears started again.

'It's pissing down out there now,' Tim Wallace shook his cape all over the floor as if to prove it.

'Yeah, well,' Geoff Hare took the opportunity to rub his eyes after what seemed like days of staring at his VDU screen. 'We've had a pretty good summer, all things considered.'

'How's it hanging, sarge?' Wallace asked him. 'The Point murders, I mean?'

Tim Wallace was one of the ever-growing band of foot soldiers on this one, the knockers on doors and ringers of doorbells. The kind of bloke the *Daily Mail* wants to see more of – a uniformed copper out on the streets, making us all feel safe.

'Don't bloody ask, mate,' Hare yawned. 'What time is it?'

It was worse than Wallace feared. There was a clock not three yards to the detective's left and no doubt the time was on the bloke's computer screen too. No wonder CID weren't getting anywhere.

'Half twelve, sarge,' he told him. 'Missing your beauty sleep?'

'You'd better believe it,' Hare yawned.

It was infectious, as these things are, and Wallace followed suit. 'I know you blokes are busy, but Den Morissey thought I ought to have a word – with CID, I mean.'

'Oh, did he?' Hare reached for his coffee. Stone cold. He looked across to the window with the rain trickling the length of the pane. 'Well, there's a bloke with not enough to do. What about?'

'What do you make of this?' The PC held up a length of metal tubing, or, to be exact, two lengths; the centre seemed to have snapped. 'Shall I give it to forensic, or what?'

'I'd be able to answer that better if I knew what the bloody hell it was,' Hare said.

'That accident down the town this afternoon. Cyclist went through a plate glass window. Feeblest case of ram-raiding I ever saw.'

Hare wasn't laughing. 'You know who that was, don't you? Peter Maxwell, Jacquie Carpenter's other half.'

'Never!' Wallace grunted. 'Well, that makes even more sense now.'

'What does?' Hare was tired, but he wasn't *that* tired. The man was talking in circles.

'Well, isn't he the bloke who keeps helping us with our enquiries?' Wallace asked. 'Whether we want him to or not?'

'Something like that,' Hare said.

'Well, that's it, then. He's obviously been pissing somebody off big time, 'cos these are his brake cables. Or they were. Look at that.' Hare did. 'Filed through. They've been going for days. Only a matter of time before they snapped completely.'

'Not your natural wear and tear then?' Bikes weren't really Hare's thing.

'Wear and tear my arse,' Wallace grunted. 'That's deliberate sabotage. All I want to know is which one of you blokes did it!'

Jacquie watched the dawn come up over the Leighford Gasworks. It had rained about midnight; she'd heard the drops bouncing on the window pane. After so long in the hot dry summer, it seemed like another little miracle, like the one they'd experienced a few nights ago. But, then as now, day brought the sun again and the promise of another scorcher.

She'd slept on and off and the chair had taken its toll. She ached everywhere, she realised, and stood up and stretched, hearing and feeling her spine click back into place. It was as she turned that she heard the voice.

'What's a man got to do around here to get a corned beef sandwich?'

'Daddy's fine.' Jacquie was rubbing noses with her little boy, kissing him over and over again.

Now, Nolan Maxwell didn't like to call his mother a liar, but that…thing in the bed didn't even *look* like Daddy and he sure as hell wasn't fine. He was sitting up, certainly, but he had this white thing where his hair should have been and his eyes were all puffy and purple. There was an angry red line across the bridge of his nose and what made it *certain* that it wasn't Daddy is that Mummy wouldn't let Nolan touch him.

That was because, she said, Daddy was sore all over. Daddy had come off his bike. And for Nolan, that settled it. He'd been riding around on this bloke's saddle for weeks, putting his young life, literally, in his hands. Well, no more. He'd learn to walk now if it killed him.

'Max, you cannot be serious.' It wasn't a very good John McEnroe as they went. 'A party?'

'Why not?' He was already dialling the number. 'Just what I need after what I've been through.'

'You've been through a plate glass window,' she reminded him.

'Oh, that little thing.'

Actually, Peter Maxwell couldn't remember what he'd been through. He remembered hurtling downhill towards some traffic lights and that his brakes weren't responding. After that, nothing. Until he'd come to and seen his Jacquie, silhouetted against the dawn light like a Jack Ventriano painting.

'Hello, Aaron? Now how did I know you'd be at your desk at the chalkface when all the rest of us are enjoying a well-earned break?'

'Max!' said Hampton's Deputy Head. 'How the Hell are you? I heard there was spot of bother.'

'Did you?' Maxwell tried to frown, but thought better of it. 'Bad news travels fast.'

'Look, I'm sure there's nothing to it. You and I go back a few years, don't we?'

'We do,' Maxwell conceded. 'Ever since you were a wet-behind-the-ears NQT not quite knowing which way was up.'

MAXWELL'S POINT   323

He heard Felton chuckle, 'I wasn't *that* bad, was I?'

'No,' Maxwell attempted the same, but ended up wheezing like an old pair of bellows. 'You were a bloody good teacher. That's why I was particularly appalled when you opted out of the profession by becoming Senior Management.'

'Oh, ha,' Felton said, 'Well, I just want you to know that if there's anything I can do…'

'Well, actually, there is.'

'Character witness?' Felton cut in. 'Certainly. I mean, obviously, I have no actual knowledge of the case itself…'

'What are you talking about, Aaron?' Maxwell asked. 'You didn't see the accident, did you?'

'Accident?' Felton repeated. 'Well, that's a *slightly* odd way of putting it, but…'

'Whoa up, Aaron,' Maxwell reined in the conversation. 'Can we back-track a little? What do you think I'm talking about?'

'Well, the incident, surely?' the Deputy Head explained. 'The way I heard it you'd been touching up a couple of students. I knew that was bollocks, Max. If you'd wanted to do that, you'd have got some Roman orgy re-enactment going, involving the whole class. Ofsted likes that sort of thing.'

'Thanks for the show of support.' Maxwell was determined to manage a frown from now on, pain or not. No other facial movement did the trick.

'Nothing elitist about you, Max. A couple of students, indeed! Who's making the allegations?'

'Who indeed?' Maxwell was trying a smile now. When he'd attempted it earlier at dawn, when Jacquie was crying all over him and when Nolan insisted on biffing him on the nose, he'd found it difficult. But it just got easier every time. 'But all that was so twenty-four hours ago, Aaron. I am speaking to you from my hospital bed.'

'Hospital? For God's sake, Max. You don't believe in doing things by halves, do you? What happened?'

'Came off my bike,' Maxwell told him.

'I knew it!' Felton thundered. 'I don't want to sound ageist about this, Max, but for Christ's sake! This is God's way of saying stop riding the bloody thing. That bike of yours has been a death trap for years.'

'I won't hear a word against Surrey,' Maxwell insisted with as much vehemence as he could with a swollen lip. 'And to make up the slur, you can bloody well invite me to a party.'

'A party, Max?' There was a pause. 'Look, old man, how badly are you hurt?'

'I'll let you know at the party,' Maxwell grunted. 'Look, Aaron, all joking apart; I'd like you to do me a little favour...'

They kept Peter Maxwell in overnight for the usual tests and how's-your-father. Nolan's father was bloody lucky, in fact. He was back on solids by Tuesday night, complaining about the hospital cabbage. He was back on form by Wednesday morning complaining that there was no full English option on the menu for breakfast.

'What's this?' he asked the auxiliary with dreadlocks.

'Breakfast,' she told him, wondering if the expected brain damage might not be a factor after all.

'Yes,' Maxwell sighed. 'But specifically.'

'It's a croissant.' She gave it her best French accent.

'When we took in the Free French government during the war and were incredibly nice to the repellent Charles de Gaulle and got his country back for him from those nasty Nazis, little did we know he'd repay us in the years ahead with curved bits of cardboard at our breakfast tables and endless televisual ramblings about va-va-voom. Take it away and bring me a kipper.'

The dreadlocked auxiliary thought that was a tie her dad used to wear, but she took the croissant away anyway.

The entire hospital staff were delighted when Peter Maxwell was able to hobble out with the minimum of aid that Wednesday lunchtime (before he had a chance to complain about the lunch), not merely because head injuries like his could make or break a life and his results were extraordinarily good, but because Peter Maxwell well was appreciably more of a handful that Peter Maxwell poorly. He was, in fact, a pain in the arse, even if other parts of his anatomy were giving him the greater gyp. A young houseman shook his good hand and asked if he might write a paper on him; he'd never seen so spectacular a recovery. Maxwell agreed, but only as long as he could proofread the thing for spelling mistakes and have full casting rights for the movie; perhaps Brad Pitt would be available for the Maxwell character.

Exactly how Peter Maxwell got up to the War Office under the eaves remained one of those little mysteries that niggle at the doorways of logic, along with who built Stonehenge, how do they get toothpaste into the tubes and why, when sweeties taste of all sorts of flavours, worms only taste of worm? That last conundrum was one that Nolan Maxwell was still trying to work out. He was lying doggo on another sweltering night on the floor below. Jacquie had been with him until he'd dozed off – her turn for the night-night story. Then she'd been with Maxwell until she dozed off and he'd let her head fall back softly on the pillow. She was worn out, what with the worry and the lack of sleep. Henry Hall permitting, he'd let her lie in in the morning.

'She who is to have a lie-in doesn't approve, Count,' Maxwell said. 'But then, what's new, pussycat?'

Metternich had heard that one before. He didn't understand it then and he didn't understand it now. But what did he care? It was another hour or so before the next rat-raid behind the abattoir, so he could get in a bit more zizz. Maxwell couldn't get the pillbox cap on over his dressing, although Nolan had been pleased to see that his daddy still had hair when he'd staggered home earlier in the day. 'No alcohol,' the cheeky young houseman had told him. 'Not for another forty-eight hours at least.' To a hardened modeller like Maxwell, this was torture. 'How's a man supposed to model, Count, when he's stone cold sober?'

He'd decided, at least, on his next challenge. And the houseman had said, with the consultant's blessing, that *limited* close work might be good. Maxwell was a teacher, wasn't he? Didn't he have any books to mark? That sort of thing? Maxwell was aghast. Ruin the holiday with the intrusion of the day job? Never.

So Lieutenant Daniel Hugh Clutterbuck of the 8th Royal Irish Hussars lay in dismembered pieces of white plastic on the desk in front of him. 'Hit in the right foot during the Charge, Count, by a shell fragment. He pulled through, of course, like we all do, and the Queen, God Bless Her, presented him in person with his Crimea medal on Horse Guards Parade the following spring. We know what he looked like, as an old boy at least. Kindly eyes, smiley mouth, set of Piccadilly Weepers to die for...' he glanced up at the Great Beast. 'Yes, I know,' Maxwell said. 'He'll have to go some in the whiskers department to outdo yours.'

He placed the right arm against the torso. 'Bit of pyrogravure on that, I should think,' he said. 'Just give it a *little* bend in the other direction. No,' he changed the subject, 'what the Mem doesn't approve of is the whole party vibe. What a killjoy, eh?'

'I'm not being a killjoy, Max,' she said. 'But from what you've told me—'

'All I've told you is speculation, darling heart,' he said. 'It's about as far from hard evidence and actual proof as Black Bishop to White Knight.'

'But this is so risky, darling.' She held his purple and black face between her hands, very gently.

'Tish, tosh,' he took them away just as gently. 'Now, remember; midnight. If you're a minute after that, I'll have turned into a pumpkin or whatever and there'll be Hell to pay. You,' he turned awkwardly to the boy strapped in the back seat, 'shortarse, look after your mother. Don't let her worry. And don't let her talk you into a game of Snap – she cheats.'

He kissed them both and did his best to stride out across the lawns. Jacquie watched him go with something akin to dread. She knew what each step cost him and she knew why he was doing this. Conventional police enquiries could still take weeks. And they didn't have weeks. Even so, it could all go horribly wrong. It could either achieve nothing. Or Peter Maxwell's life could be in danger. Worst-case scenarios wherever you turned. She drove off into the night.

Maxwell cut quite a figure tottering through the bar in the Club House that Thursday night. He was swinging one leg that was catching him just behind where his knee used to be and his left arm was stiff at his side, braced as it was to prevent his shoulder from pinging out again. At close quarters, people could see his face was a rather prismatic melange, purple turning yellow with a scattering of red-brown where the glass splinters had had to be tweezered out.

'Jesus!' Aaron Felton was the first to hail him. 'It's worse than I thought. Max, are you up to this?'

'Just pour me a drink, mine host, and I'll be as right as rain.'

To the Deputy Head of Hampton School, Maxwell appeared to be three sheets in the wind already. 'This one's on me, Jock,' Felton said and a Southern Comfort miraculously materialised on the bar's mahogany surface.

'Your very good health, Mr Felton,' Maxwell said and raised his glass to him. Many others followed.

The Wilbraham Golf Club wasn't all that old. The décor in the Club House was mock Twenties, though the exterior screamed 1984. Golfing memorabilia filled glass cases and shelf tops and there were framed, signed photographs of the great and the good of the golfing world – Henry Cotton, Jack Nicklaus, Severino Ballesteros, Nick Faldo – none of whom had ever played here. The place was full of men in blazers and old school ties despite the warmth of the evening and the sun sank like a golden orb behind the terrace.

'Good God,' one of them said. 'You can't be a member. I'd have recognised...all that.'

'No, no,' Maxwell slurred. 'Here by personal invite.' He tapped the side of his nose. 'I've heard all about these parties.'

'Have you?' The member blinked. 'Good for you. Er...look, I've got to ask – have some trouble in the bunker, did you?'

'No,' Maxwell discovered he was able to chuckle tolerably well. 'But I like a bit of rough. Know what I mean?'

The member clearly didn't and wandered away.

For what seemed like months, Maxwell got himself involved in a conversation with two other members on the finer points of casual water. Even when Maxwell staggered off to pass some of his own, there they were on his return, still engrossed in the topic.

But Peter Maxwell had not come here to talk golf. Although no one knew it apart from Aaron Felton, this was his party and he'd pry if he wanted to. And on the other end of the bar, as July seemed to melt into August, was a face he knew.

'Rodrigo,' he extended his good hand. 'How good to see you again.'

'Max,' the Spaniard shook his hand. 'I keep saying this to you "What are you doing here?" And more to the point, what happened to you?'

'Oh, this,' Maxwell waved vaguely in the direction he took his head to be. 'I had a little misunderstanding with an irate husband.'

'An irate husband?' Mendoza frowned. 'I don't understand.'

Maxwell closed to him. 'Come off it, Rodrigo,' he muttered. 'We're both men of the world. Don't you have flings in Spain?'

'Flings?' Mendoza repeated. 'Oh, I see.'

'You see, my partner, Jacquie,' Maxwell was leaning on the bar, seeing triple about now. 'It's a bit of a cliché, I know, but she just doesn't understand me. You see,' he was leaning as close to the man as he could, 'I like 'em a bit younger. Now, Juanita. There was a little cracker...'

'A cracker?' Mendoza looked even more confused.

'Went like a train,' Maxwell assured him. 'But I don't have to tell you... Oh God, no. Rodrigo – whatever happens in the next few minutes, play along, yes?'

'Please?' The Spaniard was even further out of his depth now and was quite glad to step back to allow a newcomer to muscle in on the conversation.

'Mr Harris?' Maxwell raised a glass. 'A pleasure indeed.'

'Mr Manton.' Chester Harris couldn't believe it.

'Maxwell,' Maxwell groaned. 'Remember?' He tried to make various movements with his eyebrows, but only succeeded in looking as though he was having a fit.

'Er...of course, yes. Maxwell. How silly of me. At the risk of asking the obvious, what the Hell happened...?'

Maxwell closed to him. 'My little weakness,' he said.

'What?'

'A drink!' Maxwell did his best to shout above the hubbub. 'A drink for my very good friends Mr Harris and Señor Mendoza.'

'Thank you, no,' Mendoza smiled. 'I have to drive, Max.'

'I'll join you,' Harris beamed, then closed to his man while the barman was fixing his usual. 'What little weakness?'

Maxwell looked around furtively, trying to focus, trying to see who was in earshot. 'S and M,' he whispered.

'Really?' Harris's eyes widened. 'But you're a policeman.'

Mendoza had lost the plot of all this completely, but Maxwell had warned him – play along, whatever happens. So he did.

Maxwell's laugh sounded like a donkey with asthma. 'What's that got to do with the price of baby oil? No, no, Mr Harris, I'm strictly off duty tonight. Checking this place out.'

'The Wilbraham?' Harris asked. 'Why?'

'Why?' Maxwell's eyes bulged in his head. 'The tottie, dear boy, the tottie.' He edged his stool closer as their drinks arrived. 'Look at that piece over there – the brunette in the red dress. Is she wearing any underwear, would you say?'

'Probably not.' Harris licked his lips. 'That's Sadie. Quite a corker, isn't she? Specialises in oral, I understand.'

'Really?' Maxwell nodded.

'But for your sort of interests,' Harris went on, 'you might try…ah, there she is. Redhead. White top. Look at the biceps on that. She swings any way you like. Pony Girl, whatever.'

'I didn't realise you were a regular here.'

'Oh, yes.' Harris almost drooled. 'And the best part of it all is, it's a perfectly respectable golf club as far as the management is concerned. Take that tosser Felton over there, for instance. Actually comes here to play golf. Er…who are you, by the way?'

'I am Rodrigo Mendoza,' the Spaniard said, straight-faced. 'That…tosser…is a colleague of mine.'

'Is he? Oops,' and Harris downed his pink gin. 'Well, all's fair in love and golf. My shout!'

'You aren't into all this, are you, Rodrigo?' Maxwell asked.

'I just got my invitation from Aaron,' Mendoza said. 'A sort of farewell party. But apart from him, oh, and you, there is no one here that I know.'

'Soon put that right,' Maxwell clapped the man as best he could on the shoulder, 'Drinks are on me, everybody!' There were whoops of delight all round and he was all but crushed against the bar.

'Hello,' Sadie's pert breasts were within nodding distance of Maxwell's nose. 'You look like you could use some tlc.'

Maxwell peered downwards. 'Now where have I met you two before?' he asked.

'Max, you look like shit,' Jacquie's comment was cruel, but fair.

'I'm sorry, Jacquie.' Aaron Felton's face loomed though the passenger window. 'I didn't realise he'd had so many.'

'Neither did I,' Maxwell straightened up now he was out of sight of the Club. 'Thanks for that, dear boy.'

'Max?' Felton took half a step back. 'You're sober as a judge.'

'Even more so,' Maxwell drew the line at trying to wink; that was a bridge too far. He shook the man's hand. 'You have a good holiday, Aaron,' he said. 'And thank you for arranging tonight at such short notice.'

'Not at all,' the Deputy Head said. 'I still haven't the first clue why you wanted me to do it. You don't even play, do you?'

'The kind of game I'm talking about,' Maxwell said, 'Nobody plays for long. Do me a favour, will you? As someone who's been at the chalkface a tad longer than you – actually *have* a holiday, OK?'

Neither Aaron Felton nor Jacquie Carpenter had ever heard Peter Maxwell use the OK word before. It must have been that bump on the head.

'So what's the upshot?' Jacquie was helping Maxwell into his jimmies. The night was still, as they eventually said in *Throw Momma From The Train*, sultry, but he'd rather have *some* padding between his cuts and bruises and the bed. And, adore Jacquie though he did, he wasn't sorry to be sleeping in the spare room.

'We'll just have to wait and see,' he said; shrugging was totally beyond him.

Jacquie would settle for that. Her man was still in one piece, just about. And if the gamble hadn't come off, well, so be it. Maxwell had been wrong. And she knew all too well, it was better to be wrong and alive than right and dead.

'I had a call while you were partying the night away,' she said. 'From my place of work.'

'Oooh,' he did his best to raise an eyebrow. 'Call out?'

'No,' she said, easing him down on the pillows. 'Just confirmation from the lab. Somebody had half-sawn through Surrey's cables using a file. Bog-standard, the lab thinks. B&Q.'

'Give me a month or two,' he said, 'and I'll finish the list of who might have done that.'

'Don't make light of this, Max,' she said, sitting on the edge of the bed. 'We're talking about attempted murder.'

He nodded, pushing her on the chin with a gentle, slow

motion swipe. 'I know,' he said. 'But all this is going to be over soon.'

'Is it, Max?' she asked. She held his face softly and kissed him on the tip of the nose, the only bit of him she reckoned didn't hurt and she couldn't even be sure of that. 'You get some sleep now,' she said.

Maxwell had half drifted off. Drunken old farts with cherry faces came and went in his vision. He heard the sound of glasses. People talking about casual water and bunkers and single Staplefords. Sadie and the Pony Girl were writhing together in a lascivious embrace, Chester Harris between them, coming up for air every so often. The Point loomed there too, in his half-waking, half-dreaming, a dead man with a silver crucifix round his neck, his chest saturated with blood and a messy pulp where his head used to be.

'Max.' Was that Jacquie's voice in the middle of it all? 'Max, darling?'

He woke up, jarring his shoulder as he did so, to find Jacquie looking down at him. 'I'm sorry to wake you, my love,' she said, 'but I thought you ought to see this. We've had an email from Juanita. She wants to meet you at the Point.'

CHAPTER NINETEEN

'No, Jacquie.' Hall was shaking his head. 'It's not going to be possible.'

Jacquie Carpenter looked at her DCI. In an unguarded moment, Sheila Kindling had confided to her what a bastard she thought he was. It wasn't her place to say so, of course, but she hoped the Detective Sergeant understood, woman to woman. She, Sheila, just had to tell somebody.

The Detective Sergeant understood all right. Here was living proof, right here in front of her, across the desk in his office at Leighford Nick.

'Guv,' she began. 'I've put myself on the line, here. So has Max.'

Hall's hand was already in the air. 'Let me stop you right there,' he said. 'You and I have had these conversations, Jacquie, without number. Peter Maxwell has no legal right whatsoever to go poking his nose around in other people's business. *We* are the professionals, you and I. This is *our* job. It's what they pay us for.'

'Is that what all this is about?' she asked. 'Ego? The plain truth is that Peter Maxwell is bloody good at what he does. The fact that he's my partner and the father of my child doesn't mean jack shit in this context. If I didn't know the bloke from Adam, I'd have to concede he gets results.'

'He gets in the way,' Hall insisted.

'The Red House case,' she rounded on him, giving him the chapter and verse he always insisted on. 'My first murder. Who solved it?'

'The jury's still out,' Hall shrugged.

'The Ofsted murders?'

'Maxwell *may* have been influential,' Hall conceded.

'The re-enacters? That film company down on Willow Bay.'

'I thought that was you,' Hall told her.

She had one trump card left and she used it now, closing to her boss with a bravado and a steel she didn't know she had. 'When the theatre caught fire last year,' she said levelly, 'who pulled you out of the burning building?'

He paused, then nodded. 'That would be Peter Maxwell,' he said.

'Too bloody right it would,' she said.

And he growled right back. 'The answer is still "No".'

So Maxwell, back at Columbine, now that the hols were really here, weighed his options. What did dear old Clint Eastwood do in *Dirty Harry*? He carried a .44 Magnum in his shoulder holster and sellotaped a switchblade to his ankle. That must have hurt like buggery to take off and anyway, Maxwell didn't own one. He had a comb that looked like one; they'd used it in *Grease* at Leighford High some time back, but it wouldn't fool anybody. And it sure as Hell wouldn't slide with a sickening thud into anybody's flesh; he'd have to do the sound effects himself.

And what did poor old Richard Widmark do as Billy

Gannon in *Warlock*? His own brother, the no-good, low-down stinkin' rat, had stabbed him in his gun hand, but even so he went after Henry Fonda in Main Street the next day, unwrapping his bandages, hoping to get the sympathy vote.

Maxwell weighed his options more deeply. Come to think of it, Clint Eastwood had a partner with a radio link-up only yards away from him the whole time when he went to meet young psycho Andy Robinson. And even so, Robinson crippled the partner, beat Eastwood half to death and got away with a sizeable bag of cash, if memory served. And as for Richard Widmark, he was lucky Henry Fonda was about to retire that day anyway. Fonda, with his gold-handled Colts, outdrew the crippled Widmark not once, but twice, threw his guns into the sand of Main Street and quietly rode away, probably into the sunset.

Now Maxwell knew what it felt like to be crippled. And he knew the Point. Exposed. Open. Uneven ground. If he had to run, he'd had it. And who would he be facing? Cool, noble, essentially good Henry Fonda? Or vicious, unstable, unpredictable Andy Robinson? He shook himself free of it. All that was celluloid fiction. He was either going to meet Juanita Reyes or...and he could narrow it down, by his own logic, to one of three. Of course, if it was little Juanita Reyes, all red-eyed and remorseful, come to beg his forgiveness for abandoning little Nolan, how would he feel with a Colt .45 heavy on his hip, and a .44 Magnum under his armpit and a flick knife taped to his leg?

It didn't help that he'd had a screaming row with Jacquie that morning and that she'd driven Nolan away without so much as a backward glance. She hadn't wanted him to go to the party last night. And now that it was just possible that someone was nibbling at the bait, she certainly didn't want him to go to the Point. But he was going anyway; she saw it in his eyes. So she'd screamed and ranted and Nolan had done the same. He didn't know why, but he knew that Mummy was cross and scared and that made him cross and scared too. It seemed to have something to do with Daddy or whoever this bloke was in the horror make-up. All good practice for his first proper Halloween.

And, of course, what Maxwell didn't know, was that all day, Jacquie had been hammering on to Henry Hall to provide just the back up that Clint Eastwood had. And it wasn't going to work for him either.

He caught a cab from Columbine, waved to Mrs Troubridge endlessly battling with her privet. Mercifully, the old girl hadn't noticed the bandages and the limp before he got into the car, otherwise he'd have been there all day explaining what had happened. She merely gawped at him in astonishment and Maxwell had to explain it all to the taxi driver instead.

The Point car park was thinning out now as the evening drew on. The shadows were sharp from the three parked cars and Luigi was about to draw down his blinds at the end of another long, hot Leighford day.

'Bloody 'ell, mate,' he bellowed. 'What in God's name happened to you?'

'Slipped on an ice cream, Luigi,' Maxwell told him.

'Not one of mine, I hope,' the ice cream man guffawed. 'I ain't picking up the insurance tab.'

'No, no,' Maxwell smiled slowly. Even the saunter from the cab had taken it out of him. 'Have you got the time?'

'Half six, near as dammit,' he said. 'Fancy a Ninety Nine? That's your tipple, ain't it?'

'It is indeed, Luigi,' Maxwell said. 'Well remembered. But no thanks; I'm meeting someone.'

'A doctor I hope,' Luigi laughed.

'No. A girl. Early twenties. Short. Dark hair. Pretty. Seen anyone like that around in the last few minutes?'

'Nah.' Luigi shook his head. 'I tell you who I have seen, though. That old pervert.'

Maxwell's face straightened. 'The old bloke?' he checked. 'Shorts, vest, knapsack?'

'That's him. He was heading for the Point not five minutes ago. Makes my flesh crawl that bloke. I don't know why the police haven't given him a bloody good hiding.'

'It's early days,' Maxwell nodded. 'Thanks, Luigi. You have a good night, now.'

'Yeah, mate. You too. And don't go slipping on no more ice creams.'

And he slid down the grille with a terrible finality of metal. Maxwell moved towards the path. This was worse than he thought. Every step was a nightmare. All right, he hadn't been off his face last night, despite letting the good folk at the Wilbraham Club believe he had been, but the Southern Comforts he had downed had helped him cope with the pangs and twinges. That was then and the painkillers the hospital had given him weren't even touching the sides today.

He leaned heavily on the wooden rail by the steps, grateful that there were only four of them. The wood felt smooth and warm under his hand. Now he was in the deep shadows of the oaks, cool in the canopy that rustled overhead. He could see the light at the end of the tunnel now, the sun bright on the short, cropped grass below the cloudless blue. Another long, hot Leighford day.

The breeze was stiffer than he'd expected up here on the Point. He was standing on the dunes where the rabbits dug, the wind lifting tiny eddies of sand at his feet. Here was where the tape had fluttered that Jacquie's people had tied there, where Jim Astley's make-shift tent had stood and where Patches had half dug up the body of Wide Boy Taylor. The Downers had come this way too, intrigued to discover what their dog had unearthed, then horrified in their turn. And before any of that, those toerags Pearson and Thomas from Leighford High had helped themselves to the most crucial clue of all – the clue that in a few minutes, perhaps, might catch a killer.

Maxwell swung to his left, trying to cope with the rising ground. Ahead of him stretched the path, snaking inland to his left, through the upright ears of corn, more than ready for the harvest. To his right, the cliffs fell away sheer and the gulls slid silently on the air currents, unperturbed by the faster, darting swallows, flitting in and out of their sandstone nest holes.

Here was where Benji Lemon had gone over, noiselessly, without a struggle. Others had gone that way, too; sad, lonely people unable to face the world any more, unable to cope. Were they marks of erosion on the cliff's edge or were they the last ghastly scrabblings of Lemon's boots on the rim of the world, to which he clung so desperately and so hopelessly?

Maxwell felt the old pull again, as he always did, of the downward surge. Just to peer over the edge, just a little further...

'Well, well,' a voice made him stop. 'You're a little bit off the beaten path, aren't you? Not your usual haunts at all, this.'

Maxwell turned to see a scrawny man with silver hair and a white, wispy beard. His glasses were glinting in the evening sun. Maxwell had only ever seen him in dappled shade before, like the creature of the night he was.

'Mr Lessing,' he said. 'I didn't see you at the party last night?'

'Party?' The old man's usual sneer had vanished. 'What party? I don't know what you're talking about. And how do you know my name?'

'More or less for the same reason you know mine.' Maxwell hobbled towards him. He had to admit, the old pervert *was* one of his three wise men who had cottages by the sea, one of his unholy trio of suspects, but he was also the least likely. Well, you couldn't win them all. And he was really quite relieved, because of all three, this was the one who could do him the least physical harm. Just as long as he kept his wits about him. Just as long as he didn't stand too close to the edge.

'I'm afraid you've lost me,' Lessing said, the crooked smile having returned. 'I'm just on the lookout for herring gulls.'

'You're on the lookout for anything that moves,' Maxwell corrected him. 'Female, preferably. Under age all the better. But couples fornicating would do just as nicely.' With a speed that surprised him, given his delicate condition, he snatched the haversack from the old boy.

'Give me that,' Lessing hissed, but even in his crocked state, Maxwell was stronger. He whipped out an expensive pair of binoculars.

'Handy for bird-watching,' he nodded, flinging them carelessly on the grass with a thud. Then the camera, equally pricey. 'Of course, what more natural than to record the fledglings in their nests? Zoom lens, too. Oops, there, I've gone and dropped it. Ah, now then,' his hand reached the bottom of the bag. 'Now I wonder what function these serve in the world of ornithology?' He held up a tiny pair of briefs and a bra, reading the label out loud. '"To fit ages ten to fourteen". That would be in bird years, would it, Mr Lessing?'

'Now look,' the old man's eyes were blinking uncontrollably, watering in the still powerful sun. 'You've no right. They're my property.'

'Well, I'm sure the binocs and camera are,' Maxwell said. 'One to observe teenage girls in their...what? Gardens? Bathrooms? Bedrooms? Courting couples canoodling in cars. It must have been a great day for you when dogging became an official pastime of the younger generation. Handed it to you on a plate, didn't they? I'm surprised you bother with all this skulking around and ornithology front. Why not just knock on a car door and say "Hello. I'm a weirdo. Mind if I join in?" I'm sure if the couple are blind and not too choosy about wrinkly old flesh, you'd be all right.'

Lessing was stumbling backwards, Maxwell in full flow now. 'The camera, of course, is to record such sightings on digital. Now, I take my hat off to you here, Mr Lessing,' and he did, a sweeping, mocking gesture that hurt like hell, but which he felt was worth it. 'Because you're rather older than

I am and I just bet you're more than familiar with the murkier sites on the Cybernet Highway. Downloading, uploading, freeloading – I haven't the first idea what it all means, but you do and you do it with the best of them, don't do, sharing your nasty little fantasies with like-minded filth across the world. So, yes, you own the binoculars. You own the camera. But you don't own the undie set.' Maxwell was shaking his head. 'These,' he pointed to the little wisps of cotton still in his hand. 'These you stole. Otherwise, what would be the point? Items of underwear from Matalan or Tesco or whatever; big deal. But items of underwear from little Doo-dah's mother's washing line – that's the real McCoy, isn't it? Because you know who little Doo-dah is and you can picture her wearing said items.' He tossed them in the old man's face.

Lessing screamed as he lost his balance and scrabbled on his back on the ground. 'No, don't hurt me, please.'

'Hurt you?' Maxwell growled, bending over the wreck as far as he could. 'If it weren't for the fact that the police would try to pin the Point murders on me, I'd push you over the edge myself, you repellent old bastard.'

He straightened up, calming himself down, fighting down the urge to kick the whimpering, gibbering pervert all the way back to the car park. He'd proved one thing to himself, however. However much he'd like it to be, this was not the man who'd garrotted Wide Boy Taylor and buried him near the oaks. Not the man who'd driven a kitchen knife into Gerald Henderson's chest and dropped him under the bushes at the Botanical Gardens. And if he was the man who pushed Benji Lemon over the cliff face behind him, then Benji Lemon must have been fast asleep at the time.

'Now, get out of my sight while you can still walk,' Maxwell grunted. His head throbbed like Hell and the horizon was beginning to wobble in his vision. Lessing scrambled to his feet, leaving behind all the impedimenta of his perversion. 'Unless of course you'd care to write another letter to my headmaster complaining that I *am* the Point murderer.'

And he was gone.

Chester Harris only heard snatches of this bizarre conversation as he made his way from the Botanic Gardens. Partly because he was some distance away and the wind did weird things with the sound up here. And partly because he was trying to have his own bizarre conversation on his mobile.

'I still don't know how you got my mobile number,' he was saying, striding out along the path where the corn was waist high. The sun was blazing off his blond hair and beard and he couldn't see very far ahead because the bloody thing was dazzling.

'It doesn't matter,' the voice said. 'Can you see anything, ahead on the coastal path? Where are you?'

'Look, I don't know why the hell I'm doing this. First you people let murders take place in my Gardens, then you accuse me of indecency. Why the hell should I help you?'

The voice on the other end of the phone was trying to stay as calm as possible. 'Because if you don't, Mr Harris,' she said, 'A man is going to die. There'll be another murder at the Point. And the man is my husband.'

'Your husband?' Harris stopped and looked at the phone, then put it back to his ear. 'Who is this?' he asked.

'I told you,' the exasperated voice exploded. 'I'm DS Jacquie Carpenter. My husband is'…but she'd gone.

'Shit!' Jacquie had lost contact. She threw the mobile onto the driving seat and hauled the Ka's wheel over. All afternoon, she'd been trying to find a way to be with Maxwell on that insane bloody rendezvous with death. She'd known, even if he hadn't, that he wasn't going to the Point to meet sweet, innocent Juanita Reyes. He was going to meet a killer face to face. And that unutterable shit Henry Hall was letting him do it.

And that same shit had given her some pointless dead end lead to follow up in Brighton. She couldn't even find Annie Taylor as was, never mind talk to her, and the traffic on the A259 had been impossible. She'd refused to go at first, but Henry had come the heavy and threatened her with suspension if she didn't. 'Go on, then,' she'd screamed at him. 'Suspend me.' If it was good enough for Peter Maxwell, it was good enough for her. But a little voice in her head told her to stop being so silly and to do as you're told. When she realised the little voice was Peter Maxwell's, she went quietly.

She went quietly because she thought she'd be back before this. Thought she'd be up at the Point with her love. What was he thinking? He wasn't well, had just gone through a plate-glass window and he was a bloody amateur, for God's sake. *She* was the professional. *She* had the bloody badge. 'Get out of the fucking way!' she screeched at a pensioner risking his life on a pedestrian crossing.

'Women drivers!' He shook his stick at her.

Her brain wave of contacting Harris had disintegrated on the rock of bad reception. He was a shaky hope, certainly. The

Leighford police were in the process of compiling a dossier on the man that might put him in the slammer and of course there was an outside chance that he was the Point killer himself. But Jacquie was desperate. And outside chances were all she had. Now, thanks to what Maxwell had always railed against, the uselessness of technology, she had no chance at all. Her foot was to the floor as she snarled over the Flyover, bouncing on her horn like a thing possessed. And the Point was still ten minutes away.

Chester Harris flicked the phone back into his pocket. For a moment he hesitated, unsure what to do. The cheek of it! Leighford police phoning him – and on his mobile – asking for help. They who had rousted him only days before. And come to think of it, that woman's voice sounded familiar. Hadn't she been the very one who had accused him of... Yes, he was sure it was. Then she'd come out with some guff about her husband. What sort of crank call was this?

By this time, however, Chester Harris was well along the path. A sensible man would have turned back, but Chester Harris was anything but a sensible man. He enjoyed the limelight, the adulation, the cut and thrust of defending his particular ecological stance. And as for his little sideline, well, that offered a certain frisson too. He suddenly stopped short and instinctively crouched in the corn. His little sideline had taught him to be swift and silent. Peeping Toms did time.

But the pair before him were nothing like the usual couples he spied on. He couldn't see them terribly clearly because they were silhouetted against the sun, but they were obviously two men and that had never been Chester Harris's thing. Then, as his eyes became acclimatised, he realised who they were, and he stood up, turning slowly and edging his way back towards his Gardens. One of them was that man after his own heart, DI Manton from West Sussex CID. Harris found himself chuckling at the fool the man had made of himself last night. Anybody too pissed to get it off with Sadie really was a no-hoper. He glanced back, just once. That other bloke had been at the party too. Spaniard, wasn't he?

'Rodrigo,' Maxwell had only just recovered his balance after dealing with Lessing. 'I hoped it wouldn't be you. Thank you for your email.'

The Spaniard bowed.

'I assume Juanita *is* all right? I mean, you haven't buried her out here somewhere?'

'She is fine, Max,' he said. 'I told you, she is back home in Sant Lluis. When that silly goose Carolina thought I had gone missing, I had to invent the stomach bug so that my colleagues would not suspect. In fact, I went to visit Juanita, just to make sure all was well.'

'Yes, you told me she was back home. You also told me she was a thief and that she had nothing to do with these killings.'

'I lied,' Mendoza shrugged. 'But as I told you, I have been to confession about that.'

'And have you been to confession about the murders?' Maxwell asked.

'Not yet,' Mendoza told him. 'I will.'

'That will put your priest in an impossible position.'

The Spaniard nodded. 'It goes, as you say, with the territory.'

'What now?' Maxwell asked. Rodrigo Mendoza was thirty years his junior and he hadn't just gone through a plate glass window. He didn't really have to ask the question.

'Now I have to add one more confession for the priest,' he told him. 'But first, how did you know it was me?'

'I didn't,' Maxwell said. 'Not at first. It was your excellent English that gave you away.'

'My English?' Mendoza laughed.

'It was a conversation we had,' Maxwell told him. 'You, with your careful use of tenses. You said Juanita need*ed* help. Not needs. Past tense.'

'So?' the Spaniard shrugged.

'So you gave her help, didn't you? You found out she was a whore and you were horrified. You see, I am a historian, Rodrigo. And the name of Mendoza is an old and proud one in Spain, is it not? You are descended from one of the oldest families in Castile y Leon. Captain Juan de Lopez Mendoza went down with his ship, didn't he...' Maxwell pointed, 'somewhere out there in the Armada, under the storms of the Channel or the guns of Howard of Effingham, I don't suppose it matters which.'

'It matters,' Rodrigo grunted. 'Juan de Lopez Mendoza was the finest gunner in King Philip's navy. But even he could not defeat the winds of God.'

'You see, that's what I missed,' Maxwell admitted. 'And I should be drummed out of the Historians' Union for it. The Point has special meaning for you, doesn't it?'

Mendoza nodded. 'There was a beacon up here, at the time of the Armada. When Juanita came to me with her problem, crying so desperately because she was being abused by these men, I knew there was only one solution. They had to die. And what better place than here, where you arrogant English have let the world believe you beat the great Armada. You did not. Only God!'

'Well,' Maxwell smiled. 'That's all right, then. We all know that God is an Englishman.'

Mendoza spat on the coarse grass. 'The most despicable thing is that you, too, soiled Juanita. All of you – Taylor, Henderson, Lemon and Maxwell – passing her round like a cigarette or a pint.'

'Not me, Rodrigo,' Maxwell said.

'There is no point in denying it now,' Mendoza hissed. He was undoing his Cordovan leather belt. 'It will not save you.'

'That was what the party was all about. The one last night. I needed to join that happy band of perverts to find out how it all worked. Juanita was there, wasn't she, at just such a party, with you? You probably didn't know it at the time, but Taylor, Henderson, Lemon, they were all there too. That was how it worked, am I right? Henderson bought Juanita in the first place from the Levington Agency, then passed her round, for a suitable fee, to his *amigos*? Our friends in the police knew there was a link between Henderson and Taylor, but they couldn't match Lemon up. That's because none of them was actually a member of the Wilbraham Club, only casual visitors.'

'You are very clever, Max,' Rodrigo said. 'Juanita said you were.'

'Ah, yes,' Maxwell realised that the Spaniard was making him turn and moving backwards, especially to his left at the moment, was not a good idea. 'Now, help me out here, will you? You and Juanita planned Taylor's murder together? Am I right?'

Mendoza checked the path. Still all clear. Still no one in sight. This was the optimum time, he knew. The time he had brought Henderson to the Gardens, the time he had pushed Lemon over. No one walked the path at this hour and he still had the daylight to see what he was doing. 'That is right,' he said.

Maxwell wanted to keep his man talking, playing for time, trying to decide what to do. His left arm was all but useless and his head throbbed like buggery. 'You practised,' he was saying, 'with a mannequin. A shop dummy. At The Dam.'

Mendoza nodded. 'How did you know that?' he asked.

'Let's just say a little bird told me,' Maxwell said. 'A bird being watched but she didn't know it. That would have been what, a week before the Taylor murder?'

'Ten days,' Mendoza corrected him.

'Then Juanita got cold feet.'

'Got…'

'Became frightened.'

Mendoza nodded. 'I could not blame her,' he said. 'And to be honest, it was better with her out of the way. This Taylor, he never locked his car. So I waited for my moment and hid in the back passenger seat.'

'Strangling him from behind?'

'It was easier than I thought it would be. But I had to pay the whore he was with to get out and lose herself.'

'That was a risk,' Maxwell said.

'A risk worth taking,' Mendoza spread his arms. 'To this day, she has said nothing.'

'Henderson?'

'He was the biggest pig of all. A whore-monger. He would violate Juanita in the rhododendron bushes when his wife was out. I paid him a visit one day pretending I wanted some building work done. I killed him in my own house with my own bread knife. Placing him near rhododendron bushes in the Botanic Gardens had a certain...poetry, don't you think.'

Maxwell did.

'And Lemon?'

'He was a fool. Obsessed with this...eBay thing. I met him in a pub and said I had lots of Spanish silver if he was interested. Sixteenth century coins. He was so stupid that he agreed to meet me up here. The rest was easy. I told him they were hidden in the sandstone, just behind you. Now, enough talk. You tell me, did you defile Juanita?'

Maxwell shook his head. 'I told you, Rodrigo,' he said softly. 'No. I merely said that to get you here. To flush you out as we say.'

'So honour is not a thing confined to Spain?' Mendoza asked.

'No, *Señor*,' Maxwell said. 'It is not.'

'Because of that,' Mendoza suddenly threw up his hand, 'I give you a choice, *Don Quixote de la Mancha de Inglaterra*. Slowly, by strangulation with the belt? Or quickly, like *Señor* Lemon, over the cliff?'

'Hold it there, you bastard.'

Mendoza stopped in his tracks. Maxwell spun round to the voice behind him and instantly regretted it.

'Who are you?' the Spaniard asked.

A pale young man stood there, in the embers of the dying

sun, his pale blue hood thrown back, his fierce grey eyes burning out of his pallid face. He was standing with his legs planted firmly apart and his arms outstretched in front of him, firmly holding a gun.

'I'm Jack Taylor, you mad bastard,' the boy hissed, 'and you killed my dad.'

There was a crash as the gun went off and Mendoza hurtled backwards, his head exploding and a spray of blood spattering over Maxwell's face. The Spaniard staggered back one more pace, two and disappeared over the edge of Dead Man's Point.

Suddenly, there were men everywhere. Dark in SWAT flak jackets, they swarmed out of the bushes and broke cover from the oaks. Two of them stood upright in the corn; weapons gleaming like the Guards at Waterloo. Only Maxwell, the Historian, heard the echoing cry of the Duke of Wellington, 'Now, Maitland, now's your time'.

'Drop it, son.' It was Henry Hall's voice, calmer than Wellington's and very much of the here and now. Taylor stood there, the semi-automatic still smoking in his hand, but the stare had gone and he slowly lowered his arms, two men snatching the gun from him and pinning him to the ground.

'You all right, Mr Maxwell?' Hall asked.

Maxwell was swaying a little, bearing in mind how close he'd come to death, but in essence, yes; he was fine.

'That little trinket, Chief Inspector,' he said. 'The silver lizard.'

'What of it?' Hall asked as his team led Taylor away and others began to detach themselves to recover Mendoza's body.

'It wasn't Wide Boy Taylor's. It must have been dropped by Mendoza.'

'Why do you assume that?'

'Look it up for yourself,' Maxwell told him. 'In a little old travel guide by Compton Mackenzie you'll find in the back room of Leighford Library. The lizard is a motif of the Island of Menorca.'

He hobbled towards the cliff's edge, Hall nearby, and he leaned over. He could see Mendoza's body lying at the water's rim, being buffeted by the ceaseless surge of the tide. And as he heard a scream from an hysterical woman rushing from the car park, he hummed to himself a snatch of a tune he'd been hearing at home on the radio all day – 'A whale on the beach that shouldn't be there.'

'Max!'

And he groaned in agony as Jacquie threw herself at him.

CHAPTER TWENTY

'Thanks, guv,' Jacquie Carpenter held out her right hand, her arm straight, her head high. 'I owe you one.'

'What's this?' Hall asked.

The pair of them were standing in Hall's office the next morning as the sun filtered in through the slats of the blinds, the particles of dust swirling in the atmosphere.

'It was either going to be a handshake or a smack in the mouth,' she said. 'I must confess I was ready to give you the latter last night. You sent me on that wild goose chase to Brighton to get me out of the way, didn't you?'

'Tsk, tsk,' the DCI shook his head. 'Know what you can get for striking a police officer? And yes, of course I did.'

She smiled at him. 'For striking a police officer, I can get a lot of satisfaction, guv,' she said.

He *almost* smiled back. But then, he was Henry Hall, so that wasn't going to happen this side of Hell freezing over.

'If it's any consolation to you and Max,' he said. 'Jack Taylor's been singing like a canary all night. He's not the brightest apple in the barrel is our Jack, and for some reason he got fixated on the fact that Maxwell was involved in his dad's murder. Got a little confused at the offices of the *Advertiser* apparently – well, which of us hasn't? He overheard a couple of journalists talking about the Taylor case and, as you'd expect, they happened to mention Peter Maxwell as somebody who might know something. Jack jumped to the wrong conclusions and so he fixed Maxwell's bike – but not in a good way.'

'Well, thanks for that,' Jacquie said. 'I think he had somebody else in the frame for that one. What's going to happen to Juanita, guv?'

'According to what we heard from Mendoza,' Hall said, 'she's an accessory before the fact. We'll have to inform the Spanish authorities and then it's over to them.'

'Rather ironic, really,' Jacquie said. 'Rodrigo Mendoza goes to all those lengths to hush the whole thing up, and it's all going to hit the fan anyway.'

Hall nodded. 'That's Africa,' he said. But he probably meant Spain.

Surrey was on the mend. He would forever be rather like the very axe that took off the head of Charles I, with a replacement blade and a replacement haft, in that his frame was new and his wheels had been resoldered and the tyres were hot off the press. At least Maxwell took some comfort from the fact that the agonising old saddle was still the same; that and the fact that it would be a while before he was in it again.

So it was on that Saturday morning, with Nolan ensconced with Pam and talking once more to little Zoë – zicker, zicker – and Jacquie getting back into harness after the scare of her life the night before, Peter Maxwell embarked on a journey he never thought he'd make.

'Well, well, Dierdre,' he could actually beam by this time,

'what a lovely house. And to think, all these years we've been colleagues, I've never once been invited over the threshold.'

'Max,' the Medusa's face appeared to have turned to stone. 'What...'

'...time is it?' Maxwell finished the sentence for her. 'Day is it? Are you doing here? The fuck? Which of those questions would you like me to answer first, Senior Mistress?'

Dierdre Lessing hadn't been called that in a long time. It was no longer her role, but little things like educational exactitude never fazed Mad Max for long. 'I was going to ask what happened to you?' she said.

'May I come in, Dierdre? I have a few things to say that I am prepared to bet your neighbours won't want to hear. Or perhaps they will, depending on the precise nature of your relationship.'

'Oh, please,' she said, gushing more than a little. 'Max, be my guest.'

'Joy,' growled Maxwell and entered her portals. He didn't stumble over too many corpses in the hallway, though he was in the Lair of the White Worm.

'I didn't know you knew where I lived,' she said. 'What—?'

'Questions, questions,' Maxwell cut her short. 'Let me ask you one, Dierdre. One I put to you, in fact, only days ago when I was still marginally employed by Leighford High School. How did the concerned member of the public who wrote that charming letter that maligned my character and libelled me know that Stephanie Courtney was in Year 11? I have added a few words there, because, as I'm sure you know by now, Dierdre, the little plan has been blown out of the water.'

She was staring at him open-mouthed.

'Let me add a few more words for you, just for clarity – how did Oliver Lessing, who wrote that charming letter etcetera, etcetera...' again, the immaculate Yul Brynner from *The King and I*; again, as so often in the past, wasted on Dierdre Lessing. 'Now, talk me through this one, Senior Mistress mine, because, you see, it's the similarity of the surname that has me fooled.'

She still hadn't spoken.

'Cough, Dierdre!' he barked and immediately wished he hadn't because he saw stars.

'All right!' she shrieked back. 'Oliver Lessing is my uncle. I swear I didn't know he was as...odd as he is. We were just talking the other day and he happened to mention that he'd seen you in the woods at The Dam with the girls.'

'How did he know me?' Maxwell wanted to be certain.

'He'd seen you in the *Advertiser*, apparently.'

'How did you know who the girls were?'

'He described them,' she muttered.

'What?' he asked.

'He described them. In minute detail; what they were wearing, what they looked like. It couldn't be anyone else.'

'So you and he concocted the letter?'

'No, no,' she was adamant. 'I merely said that I didn't think it appropriate for a male member of staff to be alone with students like that.'

'So the hands up the skirt and me exposing myself...?'

'Max,' she said, and there were tears in her eyes. 'As God is my judge, I didn't know he was going to write a letter at all. Obviously, it was to divert suspicion from himself...but, I had no idea. All that was just in his sordid imagination. I am so, so sorry.'

Maxwell looked at her. 'Has Diamond been in touch?'

'Yes,' she said. 'He's delighted, genuinely delighted, Max, that it's all been cleared up. You've misunderstood him all these years.'

'Have I?' Maxwell sneered, giving her his best Eddie Izzard. 'Have I really?'

She turned into the kitchen and handed him a letter lying on the surface there. 'You might like a copy of this,' she said. 'It's my resignation from Leighford High. Uncle Oliver has done a bunk. I don't exactly know why and I don't want to know. Mother always tried to warn me about him, but…well, I didn't listen. My part in this whole wretched business was stupid and irresponsible, but I swear, it was not intentional. I hope you'll believe that, Max.'

He took the letter and read it. It was from the heart and the last line read 'Peter Maxwell and I have rarely seen eye to eye on anything in the years we have worked together, but that has largely been my fault. He is, as you must know, one of the finest teachers and most caring men I have ever had the pleasure of knowing.'

Maxwell looked at the woman. The serpents seemed to have vanished from her head and her eyes, no longer hollows of horror, still had tears in them. He tore up the letter and let the pieces fall to the floor. He tipped his hat.

'You have a good holiday, Dierdre Lessing,' he said. 'And I'll see you in September.'

He was surprised to see Jacquie and Nolan waiting in the Ka outside Dierdre's house.

'Thought I'd pick you up,' she smiled. 'Bet no one's done that in a long time.'

'Bitch,' he hissed, so that Nolan couldn't hear.

She handed him a couple of tickets.

'What's this?' he asked.

'Danny Goodburn and the Denvers; they're playing at the Town Hall tonight. I thought we'd go.'

'"Whale on a beach"?' mused Maxwell. 'Yes, I think we shall.'

a&b

If you enjoyed this book, you
may like to read the other books in
the Peter 'Mad Max' Maxwell series.

Turn the page to find out more…

M. J. TROW

'Trow has the reader chuckling while tussling over the intricacies of his dexterous plotting. Tragic and humorous by turns, the Maxwell novels are packed with dry wit and keep the readers guessing to the last page'
Good Book Guide

'Trow's skill at spinning mysteries a twist further than expected keeps him at the top of the form'
Sunday Telegraph

'No one, no one at all, writes quite like Trow... It's almost impossible to second guess Trow, so top marks for the scholarly sleuth'
Yorkshire Post

Maxwell's Inspection

0 7490 8371 9 · 978-0-7490-8371-7 · £6.99 · Paperback

There comes a time in every teacher's life when he must face his Nemesis – the four-yearly Ofsted Inspection. The investigation begins at Leighford High and Sally Meninger, the dangerously attractive chief inspector, is gunning for Peter Maxwell, Head of Sixth Form, from the start. But the tables are turned when Maxwell finds her in an intimate situation with her fellow inspector, Alan Whiting. Soon after, Whiting is found stabbed to death in the Inspection team's office, and Maxwell can't help but notice that Sally is not as upset as you might expect. In fact, her calm demeanour has more than a hint of the *femme fatale* about it. But it's when Leighford High's head teacher James Diamond becomes embroiled in the affair that things really start to turn nasty. It's up to the embattled Head of Sixth Form to prove his friend's innocence; the time has come to inspect the inspectors.

Maxwell's Match

0 7490 0621 8 · 978-0-7490-0621-1 · £6.99 · Paperback

As part of a two-week staff exchange scheme, Peter 'Mad Max' Maxwell is swapping the delights of Leighford High for the altogether more sophisticated charms of local private school Grimmonds. This is a school where the teachers wear gowns, a school with inter-house rugby, debating societies and fencing lessons. It's a far cry from his familiar comprehensive – Grimmonds is steeped in tradition and dripping with money. But within a day of stepping through the imposing school gates, Maxwell has yet again stumbled upon an unnatural death.

One of the Housemasters has fallen from the school roof – but did he jump or was he pushed? Two days later another teacher is found floating in the lake and this time it's definitely murder. As the pack of journalists at the gates grows and parents start removing their children from the school, the headmaster has his work cut out to protect Grimmonds' reputation. And when DS Jacquie Carpenter, Maxwell's girlfriend, gets assigned to the case, Mad Max finds himself caught up in a complex police investigation and a tangled web of secrets.

Maxwell's Grave

0 7490 8271 2 · 978-0-7490-8271-0 · £6.99 · Paperback

When Peter 'Mad Max' Maxwell took his kids from Leighford High on an archaeological dig, all should have been about learning and fun. The professionals were very excited – was the grave they had found that of Alfred the Great? No, because the corpse was not Saxon and it wasn't a king, but an altogether more recent murder.

No sooner has the first body been unearthed than another is discovered: a policeman on the case is found dead at the wheel of his car. What knowledge did he possess that led to his death? And does his colleague, Maxwell's partner Jacquie Carpenter, unwittingly have the same information?

Maxwell locks horns with the great and not so good in a vicious world of skulduggery, academic back-biting and religious mania which can only end in murder.

Maxwell's Mask

0 7490 8145 7 · 978-0-7490-8145-4 · £6.99 · Paperback

Deena Harrison was one of Leighford High School's 'characters' – and we all know what *that* means – but she had the voice of an angel and could act the skin off a rice pudding.

Now an Oxford graduate, Deena returns to her old school to help out the drama department – their production of the *Little Shop of Horrors* is in danger of closing down. So Deena's back on the scene. And people start dying. Oh, just tragic accidents of course – loose cables, carelessly placed ladders. Just minor health and safety issues, really. But somebody is killing the company, and it isn't Audrey II, the man-eating plant.

With murder treading the boards, DCI Henry Hall has his hands full. Especially when Peter Maxwell, Deena's old Head of Sixth Form, stumbles into the spotlight. You see, Mr Maxwell has a habit of solving murders... Mad Max is once again on his bike.